The
LAST
SUMMER
of the
WORLD

The

LAST
SUMMER

of the

WORLD

Emily Mitchell

W. W. NORTON & COMPANY
New York London

For information about permission to reproduce selections from this book,
write to permissions, W. W. Norton & Company, Inc., 500 Fifth Avenue,
New York, NY 10110

Manufacturing by Courier Westford
Book design by Anna Oler

Library of Congress Cataloging-in-Publication Data

Mitchell, Emily.
The last summer of the world / Emily Mitchell.—1st ed.
p. cm.
ISBN 978-0-393-06487-2
1. Steichen, Edward, 1879–1973—Fiction. 2. Photographers—Fiction.
3. France—History—1914–1940—Fiction. I. Title.
PS3613.I854L37 2007
813'.6—dc22
2007005200

W. W. Norton & Company. Inc.
500 Fifth Avenue, New York, N.Y. 10110
www.wwnorton.com

W. W. Norton & Company Ltd.,
Castle House, 75/76 Wells Street, London W1T 3QT

1 2 3 4 5 6 7 8 9 0

For Joshua

The

LAST
SUMMER
of the
WORLD

ONE

June 1918

ON THE DAY before he was due to leave for Paris, Edward woke early. He hadn't slept well since arriving in St-Omer, his natural tendency to restlessness exacerbated by the cold, the damp, the discomfort of the straw mattress under him. He was never sure when he crossed the boundary between uneasy sleep and wakefulness. He came up into darkness, blinking, and for a minute or two, didn't understand where he was. Still tangled in the frayed ends of a dream. He lay motionless, staring at the place where the walls must be, until his eyes adjusted and he saw the outlines of his room: the thin window showing sky still black, the high ceiling rimmed with crumbling moldings, the wooden crucifix mounted on the wall above his bed. These rooms had been part of a seminary before the war, and the Englishmen who slept in them now liked to tip their hats to the displayed figures of Jesus and ask Him whether He wouldn't like a cup of tea, or whether His arms were getting tired. They seemed to find this joke endlessly amusing.

He felt on the floor for his lamp and some matches, lit it, dimmed the surge of flame. He pulled his legs out from under the blanket, flinched at his bare feet on the cold floor. He rose and made his way across the room, the circle of brightness bobbing with his steps.

Some days it seemed that, as long as he could remember, he'd risen before first light, unfolded sore limbs, washed and shaved at the corner basin, cold water by unsteady lamplight; other times, he felt he'd only just arrived. Standing before the sink, he saw his face emerge into the dusty square of mirror, pale, suspended in darkness. In truth, he had been here a little more than a month. His ship had docked at Brest on the same day the Germans hit the Place de la République with a long-range shell. He'd boarded a train and come here, to St-Omer, where the British trained their observers and pilots to do aerial reconnaissance. It had not been very long since then. But the repetitive nature of army life simultaneously stretched and condensed time, so he lost track of how many days, how many nights, how many weeks had passed. It did not seem so important after a while.

He was learning to take photographs: this was what mattered. It was a skill he'd thought he already possessed, but these were not the kind of photographs he was accustomed to. Their purpose was wholly different; they were not made to be beautiful, but to be clear. The pilots and observers went out each day, taking pictures of this sector of the lines, which were then developed, printed and assessed. Had the observer managed to bring the ground into focus from 10,000 feet above it? Had he compensated for the movement of the airplane, for the angles of flight? When they were ready, the prints were put together into a mosaic, showing an area miles long and wide, the work that used to take cartographers painstaking years reduced by the new technology to a matter of hours. Then the interpreters would examine the pictures, decipher them, and this Edward was learning, too: how to see what these pictures had to reveal, to interpret their language of shape and line. A columnar darkness, the sign of smoke and therefore fire; this cluster of buildings, appeared since yesterday and therefore not really buildings at all, but tents, a sign of soldiers on the move. He'd worked with the British observers, trying to absorb as much of their knowledge as he could, all the while waiting for the orders that would send him out along the front to do the same work for his own army under his own command. Now he had his orders; they had arrived by courier two days ago. He would make one more flight at St-Omer and then he would be gone.

He soaped his neck and face and drew the razor carefully over his skin. An image from a half-lost dream, a darkness, rose up in his mind, like a flock of birds startled out of a field, but when he tried to lay hold of it, it slipped from his grasp and vanished. He stood still and waited for it to return. It didn't come, but it left an uneasy hollow in his chest. He finished shaving, and got dressed, pulling on the quilted flying suit over his shirt and trousers. It was heavy canvas padded with down, and it made him sweat even in the cold air of the dormitory. There was a knock at his door, and his batman, Jones, opened it and looked in.

"'Morning, sir," he said, and tugged his cap at Edward, then, discreetly, at Jesus.

"Good morning," Edward replied. He finished doing up the buttons on the front of his suit.

"Tender's leaving in five minutes," Jones reported. "You're to fly with Knightly for your last trip. Is there anything you need?"

"No. I'm ready." He went to get his gloves and jacket.

"A letter came for you by the first post this morning. I had it sent over to your office."

"Well, I'll read it when I'm back. There's no time now."

"As you like, sir."

When he arrived downstairs, the other men were already waiting outside on the front steps for the driver to collect them and take them to the airfield. They greeted each other with nods, exchanged looks, and he thought that this was the last time he would see them like this, waiting expectantly in the half-dark of early morning. He scanned the circle of faces; he liked them all, but among them he felt out of place. They were men in their early twenties; he was thirty-nine, and as a captain he outranked them all—noncoms, sergeants and corporals, a few lieutenants who had worked their way up through the ranks. He was older; he was supposed to know more of life, and in some ways he did. But in men who had served at the front as infantry or gunners, the war upset the normal course of aging. This group preferred silence and were terse when they did speak; their shoulders sagged as though they carried something heavy and invisible on their backs. More than Edward himself, they seemed to resemble his father after he left the mines for the last time, when he was no longer strong enough to work and instead gardened and growled at his children to pass the time. They were wary, irritable when disturbed, always tired. They did not ask him much about his life before the war. They seemed to have lost the knack of curiosity, and Edward found that he was grateful for this; it saved him the wearying effort of trying to explain the past or trying, one more time, to understand it himself. But when he was with them for a while, he saw the wild blankness that sometimes stole into their eyes; he knew that he had somehow become years younger than the men who'd been at the Somme. What had he been doing at their age? He'd been at art school in Paris. He'd been courting Clara. He could see their unlined faces and buried eyes in light spilled from the dormitory windows.

The squadron leader called the roll of pilots and observers slated to go out that day, and after each name came a single-syllable reply. A couple of other stragglers came noisily downstairs, saying, "We're here, we're here. Don't leave without us."

"How are you this morning, Yank?" someone asked.

"Oh, fine," Edward replied. "Room service at this place could be better . . ." The men chuckled, the sound moving through them like wind in grass. A darkness inside his head turned over. It was the same one that had come to him before while he was shaving, leftover from his dream but now it was a little clearer. It was the black mass of a woman's hair, shifting, catching light among its tangles. Clara's hair. He must have been dreaming about his wife. In bed some mornings she used to open her eyes and ask him this same question: how are you this morning? When she asked him that, he knew it would be one of her good days, that there would be no fights or shouting, that they would get along, and he would always say, Yes, yes, I'm well, even if it was a lie.

The truck came and the men loaded up their equipment and huddled together in back. The driver passed around canteens of coffee that tasted like charcoal. They drank it anyway, heads bowed forward, elbows propped on knees. They listened to the engine whine and judder over the stone-filled road until they reached the airfield. The CO passed out route maps. Edward and the other observers picked up cases of plates and heavy K-2 cameras in their metal carapaces.

Then they went out to the planes.

In the blue light of predawn the airfield seemed full of quietly grazing animals, noiseless and peaceful. When he looked at the still machines, it struck him as impossible that they could ever get off the ground, these cradles of string and wood and canvas. The men moved among their silhouettes in pairs. Edward found Knightly and they shook hands. Together they walked among the shadows to Knightly's RE-8.

Knightly went to say something to the mechanics, while Edward hoisted himself up the stepladder into the second cockpit. He heard the first cough of an engine from somewhere across the field, the first propeller whirr. One by one, the planes were towed to the foot of the runway, gathered speed, rose, and shrank to dark dots against the lightening sky.

The mechanic flung the propeller and the engine stuttered, then burst into life. Edward's heart punched the inside of his chest as they started to move, and he fought an urge that came to him at the start of every flight to undo the seat belts linked across his chest and jump over the side, back onto solid ground. Instead, he clamped his fingers around the rim of the cockpit, gritted his teeth, and tried to remember the words to "Delilah," all of them, in the right order. Someone had put that record on the Victrola in the officer's lounge a few days before and then annoyed everyone by singing along out of tune. Edward would recite things during takeoff, songs or poems, or sometimes, if nothing else came to mind, just multiplication tables until the rhythm met his pulse and he felt calmer. Now he mumbled the first verse under his breath, words falling rapidly out of his mouth. He got to the chorus where they danced all night (*Holding one another tight*) as he heard the motor run higher, the cylinders drumming their steel casings. The plane began to gather speed, and he kept reciting, verse, chorus, next verse, until he felt the machine around him gather its force and lift, carried up by air that speed made solid, flung into the waiting sky. At the moment the wheels left the ground, he exploded into song, his voice swallowed by the roaring all around them: *Oh, oh, lovely Delilah, she left him standing, standing in the rain,* and very faintly he heard his words joined and echoed in Knightly's gruff baritone: *Standing, standing in the rain,* they sang, and they arched up into the sky.

They climbed among the invisible tides of air until they reached 18,000 feet. Around them, the day was clear, just a few lost low clouds. Dawn shot over the horizon, its bright blades sliding into the sky. Knightly said something over his shoulder that was instantly snatched away, and Edward disentangled himself from his seat belts, shaking the worst of the kinks from his arms. He unclipped the lens cover from the snout of his camera and checked to make sure the first plate was ready. Then he leaned out into the wind.

At last, he thought, at last, the earth made some kind of crooked sense. Looking over the airplane's side, he could see design, function in the cuneiform inscription of trenches, embankments, derelict towns. There was the front-line trench, S-curved, a set of jagged teeth grinning upward. There was the sap pushing forward at a zigzag until it stopped abruptly out in No Man's Land.

There were men down there, too, though from this height he couldn't see them. Right then, he guessed, two or three of them would be crouched against sandbags in the sap's dead end, wrapped in rubber ground sheets against the early morning cold, sharing a cigarette. They'd pass it between them, watching the orange bud move gently in the gloom, imagining the taste of the tobacco until their turn came; the dream of smoke, powerful as the real thing. Perhaps they were silent. Or perhaps they talked about someone they knew who got shrapnel in his arm and had to be taken out of the line, who was lying in hospital waiting to be sent home. Old so-and-so, he'll be just fine, they'd say.

Surrounded by pretty nurses. Some fellows, one of them might have joked, have all the luck, and over their words would come the sound of the day's first barrage, a high whine growing louder like the sound of a train in the distance.

Edward, from his plane, could see the guns begin, the simultaneous flash and boom far across the lines on the German side. Then nothing, the shells' invisible flight. Spasms of fire, the blast of smoke and flying debris, momentary silence, followed by more firings in quick succession, illuminating the fields. He always thought (he couldn't help himself) how beautiful it looked. The barrage started at dawn, earlier and heavier if an attack was planned, but otherwise regular as clockwork, anticipating day by a few hours. Then the British guns answered in kind. Day began.

Through the sights of his camera, he had watched this system taking shape day by day, an infection spreading through the soil, repeating itself. Down there, they were preparing for another round of offensives. This year will be the year, they'd say as they dug into the already blighted ground, this year will be the year— without really believing it, bone-weary hands white from cold around the rough handles of their shovels. They worked at night because it was safer, seeing no more by their lanterns than the ditch they were digging and their own pale faces mirrored in the other men. Occasionally, a flare called the world back into existence, or the red flutter of shell fire. They fell asleep for a few hours when they reached an exhaustion that even artillery couldn't tear. Then they were kicked awake, given a shot of whisky to pour into their shivering skeletons, and told to prepare for an enemy attack by standing on the firing step, peering into the dawn.

Each morning he looked down and saw the results of the work parties' nighttime labors, how the system had embedded itself deeper in the world's skin. After months in these positions the men were well dug in. Behind the front line, connection trenches wormed back to the support trench and then again to the reserve trench. Out in front, spools of wire and then No Man's Land, boiling with craters.

What he could also see, unlike those on the ground, was that the pattern repeated, identical in every detail, on the other side. The Germans had their front-line trench, support, reserve, their supply lines, gun emplacements, saps and wire, to match the British. But only from the air could you know it. The hours he'd spent above the lines had given him time to think of how to describe this new map: characters from a lost language; the root system for the shell craters that bloom between the wire; the plans for a city drawn by a lunatic.

Gazing down, he felt weightless, wordless, without history. He'd escaped, and all the things he'd loved and hated and struggled for were confined to that flat print of the ground: houses huddled together in corners of spring fields, and slender lines of roads that ambled through the green, then disintegrated as they neared the front. There, he could see them vanish into ruins that had once been towns, or sink into nightmares that had once been fields. Above it all, the blue hung imperturbable.

THERE WAS A story that the British pilots told about how the war in the air began.

In the early days, back when the fighting was going to be over by Christmas, the aviators on both sides went out unarmed. They considered themselves gentlemen, and even though war made them officially enemies, they viewed this as unfortunate and ignored it as best they could. They waved greetings when they caught sight of each other's planes.

Then one day in the sky over Ypres, or Soissons or Reims, a pilot saw his counterpart bank to take a second pass over a section of the front. Instead of waving, he drew a long-barreled rifle from his cockpit and fired. He missed the pilot but punctured the fuselage, hitting a fuel tank. Gasoline poured out, a glinting translucent thread, fanning across the air currents in the plane's wake. The man who had fired just had time to see fuel spinning through shafts of sunlight, before a spark from the combustion chamber caught and the engine burst into flames. He watched the pilot struggle for control as the plane began to lose altitude, tilting sharply. He watched as black smoke swallowed the man inside it, as the plane became a cruciform darkness falling back to earth.

After that all the pilots carried guns. When Edward asked which country the first man to shoot came from, the British pilots laughed and said that the French insisted he was German; but that in the German story, he was a Frenchman.

By now, 1918, all observers doubled as gunners, and the planes had machine guns mounted behind the second cockpit. In training in the States, Edward had practiced swinging the gun through its long arc, firing rounds of blanks at an imaginary target. The gun was heavier than it looked; once he got it moving, it was difficult to stop or change direction until it slammed into the limit of its radius, sending a shock back up his arms. Eventually, he got so that he could control where the bullets went, throwing his whole body as a counterweight against the inertia of the gun as it moved on its steel ball-and-socket. His aim was good enough to hit a plane at close range, he thought, though to date he'd never had to test it out.

The pilot had a machine gun, too, forward-facing, pointed ominously toward the propeller's long arms. When he first saw it, Edward had asked how the pilot avoided damaging his own plane when he fired. The man training him laughed, and then explained that the plane was equipped with a synchronizer. Its mechanism allowed the bullets from the pilot's machine gun to pass between the whirling blades of the propeller by timing their release. It regulated them to within a fraction of a second. At least, he was told, and again the instructor laughed, that is how we all hope it works.

EDWARD SLID THE last plate from the camera into its paper envelope and locked it back into the case. In the east, light was climbing up the day, shifting away from golden. He leaned forward and tapped Knightly once on top of his head, to signal that he was finished. The pilot looked back at him, grinned, then banked the plane and began to descend. At 8,000 feet, with the airfield in sight, he cut the engine. This was the most fantastical part of the flight, the time that it felt most unreal. Nothing around them but the air cradling them back to earth. They glided smoothly home, the wheels touching gently onto the runway. As the brakes hauled them to a stop, Edward thought, The next time I fly, I'll be over the Marne, seeing my old home from far above. He felt again the bittersweet excitement he'd experienced when his orders arrived. He was going home! Although what that meant, he was no longer completely sure.

He climbed from the plane and made his way across the field to turn in his plates and camera. He trod slowly, almost gingerly. Always, after they landed, the wind and drone of the engine still rushed through his head, drowning the sounds of ordinary life below a hissing tide of ghost-noise; the pilots and the other observers had developed a crude sign language of pointing and shrugs to substitute for speech while they waited for their hearing to return. His limbs were numb from the cold and enforced stillness, and his feet became masses of quarreling nerves that fizzed with each step back on solid ground. He had stumbled and nearly dropped his equipment when he first began flying; now he took care to watch what his legs were doing.

At the edge of the airfield a group of observers and pilots were clustered, waiting for the tender that would take them back to their billets. They stood together, quietly, the sound of flight beginning to fade from their heads. When Edward reached them, they shifted their circle to let him in. Knightly was there; he clapped Edward on the back and said, "So that's it then. Off tomorrow."

Knightly came from Wales, and his rounded voice seemed to drop words like stones into water. He had blunt features and pale, bright eyes. In the time Edward had been at St-Omer, they had become friendly. Knightly mimed a piece of paper and a pen.

"You must write a letter when you arrive, tell us how it is there. Where is it they are sending you?"

"To the Marne sector."

"What you wanted, wasn't it?"

Edward nodded. "I asked for this assignment back in Washington. I'm going for briefing in Paris, and then to an airfield near Épernay." He felt sudden vertigo as he said this. You wait for something for so long, he thought. Then when you get it, you find you're afraid.

There were murmured congratulations. A couple of the pilots came over and shook his hand.

"Lovely country that, near the Marne," one of them said. His name was Sanders; he had just finished school and come from England the week before. "Beautiful in the summers."

"Yes. I know," Edward replied. "The French call it 'smiling country' after the way the valley is shaped," and he drew a semicircle in the air in front of him to show them what he meant. "I used to . . ."

He stopped. He was going to say, I used to live there, for six years before the war. We had an apartment in Montparnasse, but my wife grew tired of the city and wanted more light and air, so I found a house for us in the Marne, on a rise above the river. My wife, Clara, loved that name for it: the smiling country. But she'd get it wrong—her French is, well, not bad exactly, but absent-minded. She used to tell people that we lived in the laughing country. Of course, all this was some time ago. I don't know what the hell she calls it now.

His throat tightened, and his eyes went hot; it must, he thought to himself, be some delayed effect of the flight.

So he said nothing more to Sanders. Instead, he just nodded. He turned away and walked toward the road, his limbs full of restless energy. Damn it, the tender was late, as usual. Damn it all. He felt like kicking something, like dancing. He was going to Paris, at last, after four years away. And then after that he was going back to the Marne. My house, he thought. My garden, my paintings and my photographs. So many of the things that I had to leave behind. He stared down the road looking for the truck to arrive. When he looked back at the faces of the other men, it seemed as though he were seeing them in a photograph from a long time ago. And he remembered that he had a letter waiting.

ON HIS DESK lay an envelope. He did not recognize the hand in which the address was written, but he noticed the postmark was some weeks old. It must have been sent to him in Washington and redirected here. He opened it and glanced down at the signature at the bottom of the page.

To his surprise he saw it was from Marion Beckett. It had been four years since he had seen her. An image came to him: her arm raised to hide her face in the crook of her elbow; it was from the last summer before the war began. It shocked him with its vividness after all this time. He looked down and began to read. *Steichen*, the letter began bluntly:

> *I am sorry to break the silence that we agreed upon. You know that I would only write to you in extreme need. I will be brief, therefore, and come to the point. You may be aware of this already. Clara has filed suit against me in New York. She charges me with alienation of affection. The action has been postponed because I am abroad serving in France with the Red Cross; it will resume when I return to America. My parents have offered her a significant sum to settle out of court, but she will not accept it and seems determined to go ahead. If the suit does come to trial, I will need your help to counter the accusations against me. They are accusations against you, too.*
>
> *I need not tell you how much pain this brings me. I'm sure that you feel something like it. Please discuss this matter with as few people as possible. I'm sure that everyone will know about it soon enough.*

His head went light and his body felt drained of energy. He sat down leadenly at the desk and reread the letter, trying to absorb the grotesque news that it brought. He willed himself to comprehend, but he could not quite bring himself to believe it. It seemed too outlandish, too unlikely, even for someone with Clara's penchant for dramatics. Anger flared inside him: How could she do this to him, to their daughters, to Marion? How could she even do this to herself? And based (the most ludicrous thing of all) on a mistake. God damn her! He slammed his fist down on the desk hard, so that it hurt enough that he knew this was not a dream.

The door to his office opened. Jones came in. He stopped when he saw Edward sitting at the desk.

"I'm sorry, sir," he said. "I didn't know that you were back yet." He began to retreat toward the door, and then he paused again and looked across the room—at Edward, holding his sore right hand cupped in his left one, at the letter lying opened on the desk—taking these things in fully for the first time.

"Sir," he said, "is everything quite all right?"

"Yes," Edward said, then changed his mind and decided not to lie. "No. I've had some bad news."

"I'm sorry to hear it. I don't want to pry, sir, but if you need to confide, I don't mind listening."

Edward considered this. He felt that he wanted very badly to tell someone else what he had learned, so he wouldn't be carrying this horrible thing around alone. He would be going against the letter's admonition to tell no one, but Jones did not know the people concerned, and he, Edward, was leaving tomorrow anyway. What harm could it do?

"My wife is suing a woman who was her dearest friend," he said. "She accuses her of having had a liaison with me before the war. I have just been told of it today."

Jones frowned and nodded. He seemed to be uncertain how to react, and Edward thought he understood this. His own emotions had been sickeningly whirled around so he was not sure which he felt most strongly: sadness or anger, guilt or fear, or something else entirely. Jones was opening and closing his mouth like he wanted to ask something but didn't dare.

"Sir . . ." he managed.

"Yes?"

"Did you? I mean, have a, well, liaison, as you put it, sir. I wouldn't judge you if you had. Gentlemen do sometimes."

"No, I didn't. That is the best thing about it. The accusation is completely wrong. The woman in question was a friend, that was all."

Again, Jones looked confused.

"Well, why does your wife believe you did?"

It was a good question, and one to which he really had no answer. How had they arrived here? When he tried to understand, he thought, first, of that final summer before the war, when everything had seemed to come undone at once. He thought of the fights and accusations; the terrible business with Marion; their flight from the war to America. All these had opened a gap in understanding between Clara and himself that afterward neither of them seemed able to bridge.

But he also knew that it had not started then. The events of that year were only the last part of something that had begun long before; perhaps before they'd even known each other, as though this end was already marked on them, indelible but unseen, like a latent image on a glass plate before the developer makes it visible to the eye.

Where had it begun?

Self Portrait. Milwaukee, 1898. Platinum print.

HE'S STANDING AT the right edge of the photograph. He looks as though he's about to enter through a doorway in its frame, crossing the threshold, eager but a little nervous. This is the angle of his stride—inclined slightly forward, up on his toes with each step, his energy carrying him too far too fast. He looks like a question mark when he walks, his sister Lilian says, racing to get to the next thing, whatever it is. He talks excitedly with his hands as he goes, always in the throes of some new enthusiasm that won't last the month. Last year it was chemical experiments, and the stench from the mixture of sulfur and manganese that he brewed during that phase can still be detected in certain corners of the basement. At least, it could until a spate of oil painting and then this current passion for photography made him bring home even fouler-smelling things.

His dark hair falls over his face, obscuring one eye while the other peers at the camera mischievously, a half-smile on his lips that you can't be sure is really there. He has some grand plan afoot, and he won't tell you what it is until you are already too deeply involved in it to say no. This is the expression that he must have had on his face when he convinced the man in the camera store on Vine Street to sell him that secondhand box Kodak for cheap. For weeks he'd been hovering over the display cases, plaguing the storekeeper with endless questions: What happens if you move the lens out like this, away from the plate? What's the difference between this camera and that one? What happens to the plate when you make the exposure? Which chemicals? How long? If there were no other customers in the store, the old man—Schwarz is his name—would answer his questions patiently, his labored English embroidered with German. He would wipe the chemicals from his hands on his apron before lifting the cameras gently to the counter. He didn't mind this. The boy seemed intelligent, and he certainly was curious. Besides, he knew the mother, Mary Steichen, who kept a millinery shop; everyone did. Every woman in Milwaukee wore her hats these days. Better to cultivate good relations with your influential neighbors, he thought. He let the boy handle the less expensive cameras for himself, the Kodaks, the Scovill Waterburys.

Then one day that mischievous glint appeared in his eyes, and the boy started asking a lot of questions about one particular Kodak and, before anyone knew what had happened, he'd convinced old Schwarz to sell it to him at a huge discount. His father, Jean-Patrick, rolled his eyes as Edward related the story, his hands working, estimating the dimensions of the camera, pointing out this feature or that one to his sister on an invisible model that both of them seemed perfectly able to see.

"How much does he want for it?" his father asked.

"Oh, five dollars or so," said Edward airily.

"Too much," said Jean-Patrick, and went back to reading his newspaper.

Edward earned $2 a week at the American Fine Arts Company of Milwaukee working as an apprentice to the lithographers. He saved his pay and bought the camera. It was square and heavy and took the new roll film. Schwarz loaded it for him in the dark room behind the store. At home he took pictures of everything: his mother as she fixed roses to the crown of a hat, her mouth full of pins, her lap covered in the red spirals of silk flowers; his father, smoking his pipe in the front room, who scowled and waved him away. He photographed his sister Lilian dancing in the garden that their father labored over in his spare time. She raised her arms above her head as the teacher had told her to do in her ballet class, her elbows round and her hands almost touching, and drew her foot up to her knee. "This is fifth position," she said matter-of-factly, and smiled at him, embarrassed, but pleased at getting so much attention from her older brother. It was sunny that day, and the light fell mottled over the lawn. Edward felt that he didn't want to lose this moment, that he'd like to stay like this forever, watching her dance and feeling the warmth of the sun on his neck. He took the picture.

Then he photographed the flowers in the side beds, the view down the street from their front porch, the old lady next door and her cats. He photographed the piano, the bookshelves, the potted geraniums on the windowsill. He finished fifty pictures in three days and took the roll back to be developed at the store.

When the prints came back, the envelope felt light and mysteriously empty. He opened it in the store and found only one print—the picture of Lilian in the garden.

"What happened?" he asked Schwarz. "Why is there only one in here?"

"Not clear enough to bother. They look like, how do you say? *Schneesturm.*"

"Why?"

"Focus. You must focus before you make your exposure."

Edward stared disconsolately into the envelope. Lilian stood frozen in the fifth position, the shadow from her arms stretching across the grass beside her.

"More care, less haste next time. Here, a present." Schwarz handed him a fresh roll of film. "Let me show you how to load it."

On the second try, things went better and almost half the prints came out. Gradually, he learned how to set the aperture to the level of light, the focal length to different depths of field. He started to go out looking for subjects, rode the streetcars out of town as far as they would take him and then set off on foot. Lilian came with him sometimes, and they'd wander through fields and woods, clambering over fences and jumping across the irrigation ditches. Sometimes they'd be chased off by an angry farmer who didn't know what two town kids were doing traipsing through his pastures, disturbing his horses, pointing that contraption at his cows, that dark box with its single ominous glass eye. Lilian would bring a book and read to Edward aloud when they got tired of walking. She read him Maeterlinck and Mark Twain. She was always reading.

One time, Lilian lost a shoe as they scrambled through a fence to get back to the road. They'd been trying to reach a wood where Edward had seen a white birch tree he wanted to photograph. As she pulled herself under a broken section of the fence, her right shoe stuck in a patch of mud just out of reach, then sunk, filling with water and disappearing under the turgid surface. She had to walk all the way back to town in one sock, which was brown and torn by the time they reached home.

"I'm going to get punished," she said.

"Don't worry, I'll tell them it was me."

"Don't be stupid. How can it have been you? It's my shoe that's missing." She was calm and dry-eyed, accepting the consequences as inevitable. "If you tell them it was you, you'll just get in trouble too."

"But it was my fault . . ."

Lilian shrugged. "Say that if you like," she said.

When they reached home, Edward told his mother that it was his fault that Lilian's shoe was missing. He explained about the woods, the birch tree, the photograph. She looked at him as if he were mad.

"Why do you make up these ridiculous stories?" she shouted, in German, which is what she speaks at home, especially when she's angry (she speaks French to her customers). "Go down to the basement right now and don't come back until you've thought about what you've done. Both of you." Lilian and Edward trooped downstairs to the basement. Lilian sat down cross-legged on the floor in the square of light that fell through the one small window and pulled her book out of her satchel.

"Want me to read to you?" she asked.

"Yes, if you like . . ." he replied, looking around him. The basement was cold and unfinished. It was almost empty, apart from a set of shelves in one corner where his mother kept pickles and jellies. Except for the light from that single window, high up near the ceiling, it was dark. It would be easy, he thought, to cover the window and keep all the light out . . .

"What?" said Lilian, peering at him in the dimness. "What are you smiling at?"

"I just realized," he said slowly, "what a great darkroom this would make . . ."

HIS MOTHER THREATENED to turn him out of the house if he didn't move the pickles into the larder. Lilian helped him ferry them up the stairs while his mother watched them from the kitchen counter, where she stood chopping vegetables for a stew and muttering about how he was going to blow them all to kingdom come and then would he be happy? But she didn't stop him. He covered the window with red felt and at night he put a candle on the sill behind it—just enough light.

For his first attempt at developing, he chose a picture of the

Chamber of Commerce Building in downtown Milwaukee. A skyscraper—fifteen stories tall—and the pride of the city. He loved the repeating geometry of its windows, how it dwarfed the people on the sidewalk next to it. He'd traded in his old camera for a better one that took proper glass plates, and so he made two exposures, brought them home and went straight down to the room in the basement, where he'd got his chemicals ready. He immersed the plate in a tray of ferrous sulphate and rocked it back and forth—"with vigour," as the manual instructed—until the whole thing was covered and the latent image began to show up on the glass. He squinted at it through the darkness. Had he developed it well enough? Should he rinse it yet? He rocked it back and forth some more, peered at it again. It was beginning to turn black. He removed it from the tray gingerly, rinsed it in salt water to fix it and took it around to the faucet at the side of the house to get rid of the excess iron salts. They ran down the drain, ribbons of black marbling the water. The manual said, "Rinse for one hour." He ran his plate under the faucet for two.

"Ach, I doubt you can make a print from this thing," Schwarz told him when he saw the negative. He held it close to his face and looked at it intently, tracing the lines with his fingers. He put it up to the light. "It's too dark. What is this supposed to be again?"

After a few more attempts, Edward began to get negatives that he could print from. He made prints on the new silver chloride paper, which gave a gray finish, nearly blue, cold and precise, or when he could afford it, on platinum paper that made the pictures warmer, illuminated and full of movement.

"It's like the difference between what you see when you walk out of your door, and what you see when you are dreaming," he told Lilian, showing her two prints of a farmhouse seen across a field of long grass. "All the best photographers in America use platinum paper now. They call themselves Pictorialists." He had found books on photography at the public library, copies of a magazine called *Camera Notes*, edited by Alfred Steiglitz for the Camera Club of New York. "They believe that photography is art," he told Lilian solemnly. "That's what I believe."

It was from *Camera Notes* that he learned about the Second Philadelphia Photographic Salon. A panel of judges would be considering entries over the next few months. All photographers, amateurs as well as professionals, were invited to enter their work. He decided to try. When he asked Schwarz about it, the old man shrugged and said, "Yes, send some of your pictures. What harm can it do?"

"I CAN'T COMPETE with the other photographers for technique," he says to Lilian as he sets up the camera in the long hallway that leads back to the kitchen. "So I'll have to do something unusual. That's the only way I'll get into the show." He's peering into the viewfinder on top of the camera, which he's set up on a tripod borrowed from Schwarz for the day last Tuesday. It's now Saturday, but Edward is sure the old man doesn't need it. After all, he has other tripods besides this one, right? He smiles as he adjusts the aperture and focuses in on the dark square that he's put dead center in the frame.

"I'm going to make it a study in contrasts," he says. "The use of space. There. Perfect. Come and have a look through this and tell me whether it's OK."

Lilian is sitting on the staircase a little above him, watching through the banisters. She's been kicking at a place where the carpet had come away from the wood beneath, worrying the frayed edge with the toe of her boot. She stands up wearily and stomps down the stairs. She looks into the viewfinder for maybe half a second and says, "Sure. It's fine."

"You didn't even look," he says.

"Yeah, I did."

"No, you couldn't have." He looks at her. Her face is sullen and she seems, he suddenly notices, like she might be about to cry. "What on earth is the matter?" he asks.

"Nothing. Mama says that I can't apply to the state college next year. I have to get a job, like you did. I have to help her in the store."

"Oh, Lil." He puts ·an arm around her. "Can't you talk her into it?"

"I already tried—too many times. She told me if I bring it up again, she'll be mad. You don't know. You can talk her into things a lot more easily than I can."

"Getting a job isn't so bad."

"You didn't want to go to college," she says, and sits down heavily at the foot of the stairs. She puts her face in her hands.

"Oh, come on, Lil. Don't be sad. Come here." He takes her by the hand and stands her behind the camera. "This is the dial for the aperture. This is the f-stop. It tells you how deep your focus will be. This is the button that makes the exposure." He goes and stands around in front of the camera. "I've got it all set up. Just check that it's focused and then go ahead."

She looks into the camera and sees him standing to one side of the framed box of light. He is looking at her through the glass lenses of the camera, his blue eyes filled with that brightness, that delight of his that seems completely waterproof—sadness runs off him and pools at his feet. It is a quality she loves and hates in equal measure.

"Ready?" she asks. He nods gently.

"Ready."

TWO

June 10, 1918

HE HAD NOT felt like celebrating, but the St-Omer men insisted on throwing him a farewell party anyway. At least, his departure was the nominal excuse for the gathering; it did not take much, admittedly, for the British pilots to decide on a long night of drinking. They'd gotten hold of some bottles of gin and drunk it straight, insisting that he keep up with them until they were all silly from it.

Around midnight they ran out of liquor. This dampened their mood until one of the pilots remembered that he had hidden some whisky under his mattress, and those still awake went off to find the bottle and, as Sanders said, "liberate it." Edward took the opportunity to stagger off to bed, feeling old and knowing that he would pay for all of it in the morning.

Now, waiting for the Paris-bound train, he felt like someone had screwed his skull on too tight. When the train came, he boarded and sat next to the window of his compartment, pressing his forehead to the cool of the glass, letting his breath mist the pane.

He had put Marion's letter in the bottom of his suitcase and piled his other belongings on top of it, as though this would somehow smother it and help him to forget that it was there; but the out-of-sight, out-of-mind principle wasn't working very well today. Eventually, he gave up trying to ignore it and instead decided to focus on thinking clearly about how to respond to it.

The easiest thing would be to do nothing at all. The letter had not requested any specific action, except to help when the time came, and perhaps the best course was to just continue as he would have had he not received it. He was not at liberty in any case to go where he liked. He was under orders from the Air Service. Clara could sue the pope if she liked, he would still have to go and take up his command. He could simply write to Marion and tell her he would do whatever she wished; he would wait to hear what she needed and then go on with his work as well as he could.

But this felt insufficient. The letter's brevity, its lack of demands (so like Marion, that restraint) only served to make it more upsetting. He had never been someone who could just sit quietly while things happened around him. He wanted to do something more than just wait anxiously. But what could it be?

He could write to Clara and plead with her to withdraw the suit. He could tell her, again, that her accusations were wrong; that she had misunderstood what she had seen that day, four years ago in Voulangis. He could beg her to stop before she inflicted any more pain on the people who had loved her. But so far, all his pleading for her to come to her senses had not succeeded in swaying her. It seemed unlikely that any protestation from him would change her mind now.

His most powerful impulse told him to go and find Marion. The letter had revealed to him that she was in France now. The return address was a hospital near Arras to the north—a day's journey. But on second thoughts, seeking her out began to seem like the worst and most fruitless course of action. The perverse result of Clara's suit was that his presence near her now would be incriminating. He should not be seen with her because it could add credibility to Clara's absurd charges. Besides, what help could he offer her in person that he could not offer in writing? No, he thought regretfully, he should stay away.

There was one other person that he could try to contact, someone who might still have a chance of convincing Clara to pull back from her present disastrous course. This was Mildred Aldrich. She was an old friend to both of them, almost a second mother to Clara, and had been their neighbor in the Marne. She had remained in France after the war began, when so many foreigners were fleeing to their own countries; she had written about living near the war zone, books that had been widely read in America. *I cannot fight,* she had told him. *This is what I can give.* She had stayed in her house in the village of Huiry until this year, when the new German advances had put that part of the country in danger as it had not been since 1914.

When Clara had left him in the spring of 1915 and, taking their younger daughter, Kate, with her, came back to live in their old house in Voulangis, Mildred, who was then living just a few miles away, had been one of her only companions. Clara trusted Mildred. She was one of the few people of whom this was true.

Maybe Mildred could prevail with his wife where he had not, where Marion and countless other friends had failed. Mildred lived in Paris now, in Montparnasse. He did not know if he would be able to see her while he was there. But he would try.

The flat expanse of northern countryside spun by under a low sky, and he watched the city begin to gather itself. From the train, the streets were a series of still lifes: square, suburban houses arrayed along tree-lined avenues, sturdy and ordinary. He peered at their windows, trying to see something of the lives that were lived in them. He saw a woman hanging laundry across her garden, and, in a third-floor study, a man sat at a desk writing, glancing out distracted by the Paris train rolling past his window. And in a downstairs room he thought he saw a woman playing the piano, leaning forward to peer at the music on her stand. What was she playing? Clara had always played Mozart in the daytime, and Chopin at night. Once, very early in their marriage, he had asked her why. She said she'd never really thought about it. She just played whatever came to mind, whatever seemed right, though now that he mentioned it, she did think that Chopin wrote nighttime music; it was music for autumn and spring, the uncertain times of the year; and it sounded far better in Paris than it ever could in America. Had she laughed then? He tried to remember—it was strange to recall such ordinary details now—and the movement of the train snatched away the woman in the window, so that soon he couldn't see her house among the others built to look just like it.

Brown brick gave way to the pale sandstone façades of the central arrondissements, the little parks among them green as emeralds. The railway cut through the gentle rises and falls of the 18th Arrondissement, and on his right he could see Montmartre, with its white crown of Le Sacré-Coeur. He felt an involuntary pleasure at how familiar it all was, his Paris, still so beautiful in spite of everything.

And yet he knew this was not right; it was not the same as it had been. Of the Americans he had known here, Mildred Aldrich and Gertrude and Leo Stein had stayed; but many more had left:

Arthur Carles and Mercedes de Cordoba had married at last and were in Philadelphia. Alfred Steiglitz was in New York. Of the French and British, many had gone to the war; some had not come back.

His oldest friend in Paris, Auguste Rodin, had died early that year. Edward had been on board ship when it happened, and so he'd received the news standing on the quay at Brest, among the unloaded crates of supplies and ammunition, the shouts and confusion of disembarking soldiers. He read the telegram three times: PNEUMONIA. FUNERAL WEDNESDAY. What day is it today? he'd asked the courier. Friday, said the boy. Today is Friday. Thank you, Edward said quietly, and the boy saluted and ran off, weaving his way down the crowded dock until he disappeared.

Of course, some of Americans had come back to France to help with the war effort, and Marion Beckett, it now turned out, was among them. He had not known she was here until he received her letter. When they had parted in 1914, she to catch a ferry for England, he on his way to Marseilles to get passage for himself, Clara, Kate, and Mary to New York, she had said that, after the incidents of the summer, they should not stay in touch. As she spoke, she had folded and refolded her hands as though to contain something inside them that kept trying to escape. He had disagreed and told her so. They were innocent of any misconduct; why shouldn't they write to each other if they wanted to? She had looked at him as though he were speaking a foreign language. Honestly, she said, you are like a child sometimes, Edward.

The train pulled into the Gare du Nord, easing to a stop with a sound like a sigh. The guard called the station, the end of the line, and up and down the carriages doors creaked open, shoes and baggage clattered on the platform. Passengers crowded past his compartment, moving toward the exit and the street. He pulled his bags from the rack above his seat, pushed the door open and was about to climb down the carriage steps when something happening on the platform below made him stop.

A man in the blue-gray uniform of a *poilu* was standing and waving at a small boy running toward him. The boy struggled against the tide of people walking the other way, wriggling through spaces left by big adult bodies, crawling between legs and over luggage. The waving man dropped his kit bag and stooped down, his arms open. After the boy came a woman, walking, slow and determined, as though wading upstream. She stopped a few feet from them.

She was dressed in a red overcoat and a hat with dried flowers around the brim. She was short, and under the coat her body was thick, pendulous, as though it had been tugged slowly downward piece by piece. Her face was pale and tired, her dark eyes marooned among features too clumsy to be pretty. But her stillness—she could have been alone except for the kneeling man and the child in his arms. She did nothing, merely watched, her eyes dry as though tears would have been disruptive.

Other passengers pushed past them; they were almost all soldiers, dressed in the drab uniforms of this war, the French in gray, the British in khaki, a few Americans in the same muddy brown but wearing their overseas caps jauntily to one side, as though to say they were not yet completely a part of all this grimness. He had watched through his window as the train collected them along its route, but it was not until this moment, seeing them pass under the station arches, that he understood how many there were. Among them, the small woman in her red coat drew the eye like a lone poppy in a field.

Edward pulled his kit bag to his shoulder, remembering all at once that his head ached, and allowed himself to be swept down the platform with the crowd. He lost sight of the woman in the red coat. All around him reunions were taking place; people embraced and kissed. To his left a man hoisted a small girl onto his shoulders, and she laughed out loud with delight, the sound magnified in the cavern of the station.

Some people glanced at his uniform, curious and approving; American officers were still a rarity in Paris. But mostly they ignored him, too caught up in their own homecomings to pay attention to anything else. He walked quickly to the end of the platform and through the ticket barrier. He tried not to look at the faces around him too intently, or to allow himself to hope for one that was familiar. No one would be waiting to meet him on the station concourse, and so there was no point, he thought, in lingering there.

MAJOR JAMES BARNES, waiting outside the station, drew his watch from his breast pocket and checked it for the fifth time in as many minutes, opening its case with a snap.

"Thirty," he said to his driver. The driver nodded.

"It's always thirty minutes late, sir."

Barnes snorted and put his watch away. Yes, of course the train was late, he thought. The St-Omer train, late again today, was only one example of the way that things worked, or didn't work, in this country.

"If this war were run any worse, the Germans would be in Gibraltar by now," he said. He paced around the outside of the car, his hands in his pockets, and peered into the stream of men issuing from the station gates, looking for an American uniform among them.

Barnes had worked with Steichen in Washington before they

had both been sent abroad. He remembered the first time they met, at Steichen's interview: a tall man walked jauntily into the room and shook hands with everyone present, including the junior staff assistant who was only there to serve the coffee and take minutes. The kind of man who couldn't help making jokes even under the most serious circumstances. When they gave him the standard army test for color blindness, a bundle of multicolored threads in which he was asked, simply enough, to find the red ones, he'd insisted that there were no red threads in the batch he'd been handed. None at all. He'd looked around at the blank faces of the interview panel with a curious expression: one couldn't say for certain if he was smiling or not. No, he'd repeated. No red threads. Only cherry, vermilion, carmine and scarlet ones. The junior assistant had snorted with laughter, and very nearly spilled the cup of coffee he was carrying onto Major Barnes's lap. Not an auspicious beginning.

But it turned out that the man knew about cameras. He knew about printing and developing, how fast it could be done, which companies made the equipment they would need. He said he wanted to photograph the front the way Mathew Brady had in the Civil War. He already had opinions about which cameras would be most suitable for use there based on their weight, sturdiness, dimensions.

"I've been looking," he said, "at the English reconnaissance pictures in the newspapers. They are good, useful, but you can see that they have no standard for linking the focal length to the altitude, so some of them are out of focus. If we drew up tables for this, even someone with no experience could take these pictures and get them perfect every time."

"What is your current occupation?" Barnes asked.

"I am an artist. A painter and photographer."

"Where do you reside?"

"I live in New York. But until three years ago, I lived in France."

That had clinched it. They offered Steichen a commission as a lieutenant in the Signal Corps and, with another round of handshakes, he accepted. It was only subsequently that Barnes learned that the man had quite a reputation. He'd taken portraits of a number of famous men: J. P. Morgan, Auguste Rodin. He was well known in certain circles, well thought of by people who cared about such things.

Also, it turned out that he worked hard enough for two men. He arrived early each morning at the Photography Division offices off Pennsylvania Avenue and sometimes left well after dark. Barnes never made it to work before him. When he left for the day, the light on Steichen's desk would still be burning. Steichen was efficient too; by the end of his first month he'd set up a supply chain for all the components they needed to send the first photographers to the front.

Barnes was inclined to think of artists as a slovenly lot, shirkers, malingerers, people prone to a certain degree of moral laxity, so this surprised him. Then there was the man's apparent demeanor outside the office. Steichen, despite being commonly acknowledged as a good-looking man (Barnes, of course, couldn't really tell such things about other men), wasn't seen out with girls. When he had leave, he traveled to New York to see his daughter Mary, who was at school there. Otherwise, he didn't go out much in the evenings. He kept to himself, and so naturally this gave rise to rumors. There was whispering about the peculiar situation of his marriage. People said that he was estranged from his wife. That there was a mistress involved. Others said that Steichen's wife was unwell, and then they would tap their temple with their forefingers and nod to make sure they were understood. They said that she had taken one of their children with her when she left, that she was living in France near the war zone.

In all the time they'd worked together, they had never spoken of these matters directly. Steichen had never volunteered the information, and Barnes had always felt that it would be impertinent to ask. They spoke about photographic equipment; appropriation of funds; the war; not about themselves.

There he was. Coming out of the arched entryway of the station, Barnes recognized that same tall form, slightly stooped under the weight of the bag he had hoisted onto his right shoulder. He looked like a sleepwalker, moving against a current of air that his dream made heavy as water. He began to cross the street as the driver ran to take his kit bag. Barnes watched Steichen wave the other man away, shaking his head. Instead, he handed him a much smaller case, square, suspended from a leather strap; a camera case.

"Pleased to see you again, Captain," Barnes said.

Steichen was looking around him at the station building, the people coming and going through the entrance, the cars pulling in and driving away. "How long is it since you've been in Paris?"

"Four years," Steichen said. His voice faltered as his spoke. He cleared his throat. "It seems like not much has changed. I somehow thought the damage from the shelling would be worse." His voice fought its way steady through the words.

"Yes," said Barnes. "This part of town has been all right, so far."

The driver lifted Steichen's pack into the car, then opened the door for them to climb in. They slid into the backseat, and the car pulled out into traffic. Barnes watched Steichen staring out the window at the huge façade of the Hotel Terminus Nord crouched on the corner of the Boulevard Sebastopol, its hive of windows and front entrance buzzing with cars and people. He seemed transfixed by what he saw.

"It turns out that you'll have some time to decide how much things have changed. More than we thought," Barnes said. "The sections you were supposed to meet tomorrow are going to be late. Held up at Dover. Problem with the railway schedules. You'll stay in Paris until they arrive, and you'll have a little time to yourself."

"When do you think they will get here?" Steichen asked.

"I'd estimate two days from now. That's if we are lucky. Don't worry. You'll get used to it. Nothing in this war ever happens on time."

THE PUCKERED SKIN around a scar—in photographs, that is what trenches at the front resembled. They were jagged, instantly distinguishable from the other features of the landscape seen from above. Rivers meandered, black cut by the white blades of bridges. Roads sliced through the country, near-straight lines in different shades of gray. Hedges and stone walls softly bisected fields into wheat, woods, pasture. These had been written carefully over many years, the works of slow, steady force. They had balance to them; they made sense in the eye.

The structures of the war, however, had a different character. The trenches bit back and forth into the ground, incisions trembling maniacally across the fields, the wire between the lines, two parallel tracks, strands of blindness. Around them the earth had been blasted into a chaotic new topography. Designed by a god with the shakes, one of the photo interpreters at St-Omer had muttered as he peered at a mosaic of prints, and this description came into Edward's head whenever he saw a picture of the front. There was an abruptness to this map that the guns had drawn; a frenzy. Hypnotized and repelled, he felt he was seeing something that human beings were never supposed know about themselves.

Barnes pointed to the diagonal transverse of a road across the left side of the photograph. He followed it with his forefinger.

"What do you make of that?"

Edward picked up the print and held it to the light.

They were in the Photography Division offices. This large back room was taken up by a central table on which were arrayed pictures of the front near Paris. Besides this there were two offices, desks piled with papers and barely enough room to walk between them. A boy with red curly hair sat behind one talking on the telephone in French and scribbling notes. An office off to one side belonged to Barnes, though he spent most of his time at headquarters in Chaumont, to the southeast of the city. The main staff of the American Expeditionary Force had moved there some months before.

Edward squinted closely at the photograph.

At St. Omer he'd learned that when a road was used, it wore away. The boots of marching infantry, the wheels of the field guns and supply wagons, the horses' hooves—all these stripped away the dry surface, revealing rock and soil beneath. From the airplanes, this appeared as a darkening. Compare two prints of the front taken on different days. If a road had turned in the second from pale gray to near black, an army had moved along it.

"This," he said, pointing to the road Barnes had indicated, "was recently traveled by a large number of men. They were moving away from the front. They were cutting east, deeper into their own territory. They camped for the night in this field here." He pointed to the upper right-hand corner: churned soil, the discoloration where campfires and stoves had scorched the grass.

"This was taken three days ago by British reconnaissance in the Somme," Barnes said. "They have been seeing men leaving that part of the front for weeks. Emptying ammunition dumps, taking supply wagons, triage tents and machine guns and . . . disappearing. Pack up quickly. Depart at night. The British have no idea where these units are going. Lose track when they get further back behind the lines."

Barnes fished in his breast pocket. He drew out a cigarette case and offered it to Edward, who shook his head no.

"The French think that they are going north, to Flanders, to try for an advance there. Follow up their successes earlier in the year. Separate the French forces from the British south of Ypres and come down through Normandy. That would be the strategically sensible thing to do."

"Do people do sensible things anymore? I thought we had all given that up . . ."

Barnes cleared his throat. "General Pershing thinks the French are mistaken," he continued. "He thinks the push will come further south, out of the Aisne salient. You see, their other option is to follow up Operation Michael, make another push over the Marne, try to take Reims and the road to Paris. Threaten the capital and hope that the Allies will sue for peace."

Barnes lit his cigarette and pulled on it, and Edward watched the smoke curl from the burning tip into its strangely intelligent patterns in the air.

Out of the Aisne River valley and over the slow fields of the Marne, toward Paris, toward this room where he was sitting, looking at photographs of their traces. Edward imagined German soldiers walking through the country near his house, the sound of their heavy boots on the road. The few families who had not fled the shelling watching from doorways, hearing their blunt language, calling their children inside, bolting their front doors. It had happened, in 1914 during the first advances of the war. The Germans had reached his house in Voulangis and advanced past it.

Then they had been pushed back eastward by the French in late autumn. His house had escaped unscathed that time.

"I agree with Pershing," he said. "Just a feeling. They're going to make a push for Paris."

"Well, this is your assignment: go and find us some evidence to back up your hunch," said Barnes. "There are marines, 42nd Division, in the line in that sector, so Pershing wants American reconnaissance there. You'll have seventy-five men and three officers. They're bringing cameras and some other photographic supplies with them. It'll be designated special equipment for the Photography Division. When they arrive, you will meet them at Épernay and then go on by road from there to the airfield near the town. The French were using it for reconnaissance until this year, so you should find some of the equipment you need already there. The CO is a man named van Horn; he's a West Pointer, believes in discipline above all else. Volunteers are not his favorite people, but he's a good officer, efficient. He was with the Lafayette Squadron before we came into the war."

"Impressive," Edward said.

"Indeed. Once you arrive, get your operation up and running as quickly as you can. We need to have pictures of that area, as many as possible, by next week.

"In the meantime, I've got the French intelligence reports from the region for you to read. I'll get Gilles to find them when he has a minute. And when you're done with the work, let me stand you a drink, eh? To mark your return to Paris."

THE BOY IN the front office had been born near Meaux. He'd grown up in a village three miles from the city. His father had been a tailor. He did typing and translation for Major Barnes. He did not like Paris much. It was noisy and smelled bad. His name was Gilles Marchand.

Why, Edward asked, was he in Paris if he disliked it so? Gilles shrugged.

"To work," he said. Couldn't he help his father in the tailoring business?

"My father went to war with the Territorials from our commune. He is dead now." He went on sorting and clipping papers, his hands moving in a strange precise way, the minimum motion necessary to accomplish the task, as though movement was a scarce resource that must be used sparingly. Edward thought he was finished speaking, but then he continued, unprompted: His brothers, too, had been called up to the Territorials. They had been killed at the great fortress of Verdun. In February of '16. All four together, all in one week.

"My mother and one sister are left. So, I must work."

"Why weren't you called up?" Edward asked.

"Because my legs are no good," Gilles said. The telephone on his desk rang, and he reached to answer it, ending their conversation. Edward opened the first file of reports and began to read.

A little later the doorbell rang for the second post, and Gilles bent down and pulled a pair of crutches from the floor beside him. As he came out from behind his desk, Edward could see his body clearly for the first time. One of his legs was almost normal, the foot pointing forward, the knee moving in counterpoint to the swing of his crutches, but the other dragged behind him, useless and buckled. This was why he hadn't gone into the Territorials with his father and his brothers. This was why he was still alive, and they were not. He moved to the door with an uneven lope, and as he made his way along the corridor outside, Edward could hear the swaying sound of his progress. A sharp clack and then a slow dragging sound, as though the bad second foot was hushing the good one.

About half an hour later, Gilles came to give Edward his letters. He put the bundle of small envelopes down on the desk.

"Thank you," Edward said. He smiled briefly and went back to the report he was reading. But the boy remained where he was, standing just to one side, waiting.

"Yes?" Edward said, looking up.

"What is it like to fly?"

THE PLACE THAT Barnes took him after work was full of soldiers. They took seats at the bar, and Barnes signaled for the bartender. In the far corner, a group of Englishmen had taken over the piano and were howling out songs. One of them started with the first couple of lines, then the rest joined in when they recognized the words, lurching along until they couldn't remember any more and the song fell apart. Then they would begin another.

At the next table, some French infantrymen were talking, their voices loud, so they could hear each other over the singing.

"Over seventy miles away, and still they can reach us."

"At the Tuilleries, six buildings are gone all of a sudden, like that." The man talking snapped his fingers.

"Like the Zeppelins in '14."

"Worse than the Zeppelins. Those you could see coming. Those you could shoot down."

"Nothing left on one side but rubble. Children climbing on it . . ."

"This is how it will go from now on. You are standing there and then, bang, gone."

". . . climbing and chasing each other. Laughing, until the police chased them away. They didn't understand there were people trapped underneath."

"This is the new kind of war. A modern war."

"What happened in the Tuilleries?" Edward asked Barnes. He pointed to the men at the next table.

"Oh, they're talking about Bertha. The German long-range gun. What'll you have to drink?"

"Whisky, please."

When they had been served their drinks, Barnes said, "You used to live near Épernay, didn't you?"

"Not far from there. I have a house near the Marne, in a town called Voulangis. A nice place, with beautiful views of the river. That's why I asked to be sent to that part of the front." He took a long swallow from his drink. He felt it right away, sinking into him, warm and heavy.

Barnes took a cigarette from his case. "How long did you live there?"

"Six years, right up until the war."

"And your house has been standing empty since the war started?"

"No. First the Germans used it as a billet for their officers in '14, and then the French and the British. And my wife . . ." he stopped. "Could I have a cigarette? I came out without mine." Barnes handed him one. Edward took his time lighting it, and drawing in the smoke. "Thank you," he said. He swirled the remains of the drink in the bottom of his glass and downed it. He looked for the bartender, but the man was nowhere to be seen.

"Go ahead, Steichen."

"Yes, right . . ." Edward wondered which would be more awkward now: to change the subject or to go on. Barnes sat beside him, waiting for him to finish his sentence, perhaps a little more eager than was polite, because a man who began a sentence about his wife and then didn't finish it must have an air of scandal about him. This was how it had been since Clara left. There was always the trapdoor waiting inside even the most innocuous conversation about the past, dropping him through into things that were difficult to describe and more difficult still to understand. He took a deep, resigned breath.

"My wife, you know, came back during the war."

"Came back?"

"To France, and lived in our old house."

"By herself?"

"No. With my younger daughter, Kate."

Some combination of exhaustion, drink, the shock of being in Paris, was conspiring to loosen his tongue. He hadn't spoken about this to anyone in Washington or St-Omer. He wasn't sure he wanted to tell it now, but he went on anyway.

"She lived in our house in the Marne for nearly two years," he continued. "Now she lives in Tennessee and has a job working for the Liberty Loan effort."

"I see," said Barnes. "No . . . I don't see."

"We left France when the war started and went back to America. But then Clara came back here. In 1915. And then last year, quite abruptly, she picked up and went back to the States again."

"That is a lot of ocean voyages back and forth," Barnes said.

"Yes, it's almost comical. She left America for France shortly after the *Lusitania* was sunk. Then she left France for America not long after America came into the war." He laughed mirthlessly. "As if she'd just waited for the crossing to become even more dangerous than it was before."

"And why did she . . ." Now it was Barnes's turn to stop in mid-sentence and look down at his glass, embarrassed.

"Leave me?" Edward asked, forcing the question to its conclusion.

"Yes." Along the bar, Edward spotted the bartender at last and raised his arm to call him over.

"Because of a misunderstanding," he said. "Would you like another drink?"

They ordered and then sat for some minutes in silence. The English at the piano started a new song: *O my darling, oh my darling, oh my darling Clementine. You are lost and gone forever . . .*

Edward spoke first without looking at Barnes. "Yes," he said. "Wife gone; house still there. When the war is finished, I'll go back to it. Replant the garden. Repair the studio I had. The house looks down on the whole valley. It has a grange and a walled garden behind, and a field where I used to grow vegetables. My photographs are still there, actually, and my paintings. Whatever else is left of my worldly possessions."

"Well, in that case," Barnes said, "I hope that you are wrong in your intuition about where the next big push will come. I hope the Germans will attack in Flanders after all. If it happens in the Marne, as you think, your house could be badly damaged by the shelling." Barnes took a long drink. *Where are our uniforms?* one of the Englishmen roared, his voice hoarse, and the others joined in: *Far, far away. When will our rifles come? Perhaps some day.*

"Have you been to the front yet?" Barnes asked. "Up to the actual lines? On the ground, I mean, not from the air. There are some things you can't tell from an airplane, even when you fly low. The smell, for one. You don't get that up there. It smells like . . . well, nothing I've ever been near before."

"I went in March to the trenches near St-Omer."

"Then you know. I drove down to the front near Chaumont after GHQ moved there. Not much left standing, just broken trees, mud, ruined buildings."

He trailed off, his eyes far away. Then suddenly, he turned toward Edward and raised his glass. "To the next German offensive. May it take place in Flanders," he said. "To your house in the Marne still standing," he said. "To whatever is left."

"Whatever is left," Edward echoed. He liked this new toast; it seemed apt. "Although," he went on, "that seems to be less and less. Even in Paris. You know, my oldest friend, in years of age and in years of acquaintance, died just before I arrived in France."

"I'm sorry to hear it," Barnes said.

"I wanted him to see that I had come back to fight for this country, but I never had the chance. I'm hoping to stop by his old house, where he's buried, while I'm here."

"Where did he live?"

"Just out to the west of the city," Edward said, "in Meudon."

Rodin in His Studio. Meudon, 1901. Pigment print.

THE AMERICAN BOY in the jacket with patched elbows is coming toward the house. He's pedaled up the hill with great determination, a camera case slung across his back and a portfolio balanced precariously on the handlebars in front of him. He is out of breath by the time Rose sees him. He dismounts and wheels his bicycle up the last rise toward the wrought-iron gates at the end of the drive. He stops when he reaches them, taking deep breaths and gazing back at the long street behind him. He raises a hand to shade his eyes. Rose watches him through the curtains of the upstairs bedroom where she has been dusting. She shakes her head and sighs.

Standing at the front entrance, Edward doesn't sense the woman looking at him from the dim interior of the house. He puts his head back and swallows gulps of the cool air, and he thinks he can taste the river in it. Below him Meudon and then Paris stretch away to where the Seine wanders gleaming across the distance. He is telling himself that the fluttering sensation in his stomach is just the exertion of the ride; that he isn't really nervous. Why should he be? All the way up here, in his head, he has rehearsed what he will say. He's gone over the exact words he can't count how many times. And if it doesn't work, well, then he'll just go back and tell everyone that Rodin said no to his request. What would be so difficult about that?

But before the imposing black gates he feels his confidence draining away. In Montparnasse, he'd announced brazenly to a roomful of people that he was going to cycle up to Meudon and just ask the mighty Rodin to let him take his photograph. The whole Dôme crowd, Gertrude and Leo Stein, everyone heard him say it. It was late, and they were all somewhere between awfully and exceedingly drunk. It seemed simple at the time. He leans his bicycle up against the railings. He straightens his tie. He buttons, then unbuttons, his jacket. He clears his throat. He pulls the bell chord.

A dull metallic clanging sounds. He hears it echo, and die away, and for several minutes nothing happens. He begins to feel relief. There is nothing he can do if no one is at home to receive him. He'll just have to come back another day. But then the front door opens, and a woman comes out. He recognizes her—she was present when Fritz Thaulow brought him here last Saturday for supper, but she wasn't introduced. He guesses she is probably the housekeeper. She is dressed in a plain dark shirtwaist, a skirt that falls past her ankles, and an old-fashioned mop cap. As she approaches, he sees that she is perhaps fifty, perhaps a little younger, her skin just beginning to take on the softness of age. She is not beautiful and he thinks that probably she never was. But in her dark eyes there is something sharp and certain.

"Yes?" she asks. Under her gaze, he has already forgotten his prepared speech.

"Excuse me," he begins, then thinks it isn't auspicious to start by apologizing. "Good day," he tries, hopefully. She doesn't return the greeting. "I wondered if it might be possible, that is, if there was any way that I could . . . My name is Edward Steichen." She is watching him patiently, her arms folded across her chest, her mouth unsmiling. She shows no sign of recalling him. "Fritz Thaulow, the painter, I came to dinner here with him just a week ago." She is nodding, still waiting. "May I come in?" he tries, at last.

"Monsieur Rodin is in his studio working," she says. "He cannot be disturbed."

"Oh, well, that's OK. I could come back. Or I could come in and wait until he's free. You see, I'd very much like . . ."

"You can come in," she says. "But I don't know if he'll see you today."

"Yes, please, if that's all right, thank you," he says, and she slowly begins to swing the gate open.

He walks ahead of her down the drive. She watches him striding eagerly toward the house. There is something pleasant and guileless about the way he carries himself. He is good-looking, and he has the enthusiasm, the utter lack of self-consciousness, of the very young. She guesses he must be about nineteen or twenty. She does remember him a little, though she did not sit with the guests at dinner the night he came. Monsieur does not always like her to be around when he is entertaining, especially if the guests are Americans; her lack of English makes things awkward, as does her lack of education. But she recalls that this boy is a photographer, and that his friends, at least, believe he shows much promise.

He is not the first person to think that they can show up out of the blue and ask to see the studio. For many years no one came to see Monsieur. Meudon was too far away from the fashionable parts of town—that was one of the reasons he'd chosen this villa. But recently there have been many unexpected visitors. Monsieur's reputation as an artist is growing, and people have started to take more of an interest in him. Most of the unexpected arrivals are art students; some are just members of the public who like sculpture. They appear at the gate at all hours of the day, and sometimes at night, expecting to be admitted. Monsieur himself does not help matters by issuing thoughtless invitations to anyone who, after a glass of port, he takes a liking to—especially women. To counteract this tendency, he has left it to her discretion whether to invite them in or not. He says he trusts her instincts about people.

She isn't sure yet why she's let this boy in. Something about the way he tucks his dark hair behind his ears as he stoops down to look at the sculptures that Monsieur placed beside the path. Something about his smile as he looks back over his shoulder at her and says, "Even his smallest pieces are . . . are . . ." He looks for the right word. "Promethean," he pronounces, obviously pleased with his choice. She grunts in terse acknowledgment and goes to open the front door.

As far as Edward can tell, everything about the house is ugly. It's square like a saltbox, and its façade is brick painted a garish red and topped with a steeply slanted gabled roof. Its windows are too small and thin. Its proportions are awkward to look at. Edward thinks, It isn't the sort of place where you'd expect a great artist to live, a heavy suburban villa, cheaply made. But then where would you expect him to live? Maybe in a cave. He suppresses laughter at this thought as the woman pushes open the front door.

She shows him into a drawing room.

"You can wait here," she says.

"Thank you . . ." Edward responds, but she is already gone. He looks around him. The room is high-ceilinged and drafty. It has been kept very clean, but the impression of neglect goes beyond its surfaces. There is no fire in the grate. The furniture is old, the patterns on its upholstery faded. Everything seems to be in some phase of a slow collapse, and he is almost afraid to sit on the chairs for fear that they will disintegrate beneath him. He paces restlessly, fighting down his disappointment, looking for some sign that this is the house of a genius. Through those gaunt windows, the light moves unevenly over the walls. Trees toss webs of branches against the pale sky.

The woman comes back with a pot of tea on a tray.

"Wonderful light you get up here," he says. She sets the tray down on a wobbly table beside the settee. "And you have such an amazing view of the city. You can see all the way to the river."

"He likes it," she says without looking up. She pours tea into a cup. "Sugar?"

"Do you like it?" he asks. She peers at him, questioningly. "It must get quite isolated," he continues. "I mean, you must wish to be nearer to the city, to . . ."

"God, no," she says. "I wouldn't want to be down in all that nonsense. Who is wearing what this week, who is having secret affairs with whom, though the whole town knows of it. Paris can be unbearable."

"Oh, I think Paris is terribly exciting," Edward says. "It's so full of life, in all its different . . . permutations." He tries on the word like a new hat.

"Where are you from?" she asks.

"Milwaukee," he says.

"Ahh," she says, as if that were all the explanation necessary. "You are young, too. The city is for the young. I am glad to be away from it. Besides, we get plenty of visitors. More all the time, coming up here, inconsiderate, unannounced, disturbing him . . ." She glances up, puts a hand over her mouth, realizing her mistake. "I'm sorry," she says, "I didn't mean . . ."

"It's all right," he says, and sits tentatively down on the couch near her. "I would like some sugar, please." She spoons white crystals into the warm orange liquid, stirs slowly, then offers him the cup.

"My name is Rose Beuret," she says. Though they are seated already, she gives him her hand, and it is so small it feels like a little girl's when he takes it. "I'll go and see if Monsieur would perhaps like to come in for some lunch soon. When you've finished your tea, you can look around the garden if you like. It's more pleasant." She smiles and leaves him, pulling the door quietly shut as she goes out.

In the garden, sculptures in bronze and marble sit out among the trees; stone steps link different levels of paths, flower beds and lawns. It's a day of ragged clouds, and the leaves blow a tattered brightness over everything. This, Edward thinks with some relief, is more what he expected. Behind the house an extension with tall windows juts over the grass, and he guesses this must be the studio. In there, right now, *he's* at work. What is he doing? He contemplates climbing up onto a windowsill and peering in but decides against it. He is here on sufferance, he reminds himself, and spying doesn't strike him as a way to make a good impression. Still, it is tempting: to get to see the man at work without him knowing you were there, even if it were just for a few minutes.

Years earlier Edward had come across a picture of Rodin's statue of Balzac in a Milwaukee newspaper. He'd encountered it quite unexpectedly one day, flipping through the pages, looking for the baseball scores, and, suddenly, there it was. He remembers how even in that grainy, imperfect photograph, it held him. He'd never seen anything like it before. He thought, This is the artist I want to learn from. He squinted at the caption beneath the picture: Auguste Rodin, Paris, 1894. He traces his desire to come and study in France to that day.

And so, on his very first day in Paris, as soon as he had installed his few belongings in the small guesthouse room he rented for himself off the Boulevard St-Germain, he went to the World's Fair and, once there, made a beeline for the Exposition Rodin in the Pavillon d'Alma. He saw it, to one side of the entrance, surrounded by a crowd of onlookers, a dark monolith surging off its plinth, the man rising out of the solid sweep of his cloak, just barely distinguishable from it. It advanced on the crowd like a wave about to break over them. He stood in front of it for what must have been ten minutes without moving, staring up, until some passing wag told him he'd get flies in his mouth if he let it hang open that way. He shut his mouth and went on staring.

Now, waiting in Rodin's garden at last, he is nervous and elated. In a sunken patio, he sits down on a bench. Then he stands again and begins to pace the length of the stone enclosure. Around the edges there are willow trees, and he puts his head back to gaze directly up through the branches. The long fronds fall straight down toward his face, and he thinks, in a photograph, it would seem as if the branches were growing right out of the sky. He puts his hands up, his thumbs and forefingers as right angles to each other, making a frame for the picture. And then behind him he hears footsteps. He turns around and there is Rodin.

He comes down the stairs from the direction of his studio, wiping his hands on a cloth. He's dressed in work clothes, a coarse cotton shirt and dark trousers, and an apron covered with fingerprints in hardening clay. There is clay caught in his long spade-shaped beard and in his hair. He moves deliberately, as though contemplating the possibilities presented by each step: forward or not? The left foot, I think, now—he seems to intend every gesture to be just as it is.

"I'm modeling today," he says, indicating the clay in his beard and on his clothes. He encloses Edward's palm in both of his hands, and Edward can feel their immense, careful strength, the articulation of each finger. The skin is dry and rough in places. He feels like he's being scrutinized by these hands, appraised.

"What's your name?" Rodin asks.

"Edward. Steichen."

"You came here with Fritz Thaulow, last week."

"Yes. I study painting at . . ."

"Well, of course you do. Only a student would have the time or the nerve to come calling at this hour." Edward feels himself color. "Where are you from?"

"Milwaukee."

"An American. Your French is not so bad."

"My parents are from Luxembourg. My mother spoke French when she was in a good mood, and German when she wasn't." Rodin nods at this but doesn't smile.

"Well, Edward Steichen from Milwaukee," he says, "you seem to have made friends with Madame. It isn't often she'll interrupt me in the middle of a Wednesday afternoon for a stranger who shows up uninvited."

"I . . . I'm sorry." He needs to explain himself, give some reason why he is here at all. "I saw a statue of yours, in Milwaukee, in a newspaper," he blurts. "Two years ago. I've wanted to see your studio ever since."

"Hmmmph." Rodin continues to wipe his hands methodically, turning the cloth around each finger in succession. "Well, in that case, you'd better come and have a look at it," he says. He turns and leads the way back up the stairs toward the house.

At the Exposition Rodin, Edward had decided he must try to get a photograph of the statue he'd seen. But he was told that only photographers from the press were allowed to bring cameras into the exhibition halls. He argued with the man at the ticket counter hoping to win him over, but he got the same reply: no press card, no camera. He wandered disconsolately through the exhibition, trying to figure out what to do. He thought about trying to sneak the camera in under his shirt, but gave this idea up as ridiculous. He wouldn't even be able get his coat buttoned up over it, much less make it inconspicuous enough to pass by the ticket collectors. He thought about lying, telling them that he was from the press but had left his card on the train. But he didn't even know what kind of identification men from the newspapers carried. He sat down on the steps outside, feeling fed up and discouraged. Two men in dark, new-looking suits and bowler hats were coming up toward him. One of them was carrying a Kodak 4. He had a card in his hat with ST. LOUIS POST-DISPATCH written on it in black letters.

"Hey," Edward called out to the men in English. "Are you from the newspaper?"

"Yeah, kid," said the one holding the camera. He smiled broadly, but didn't slow down. The two men hurried past. When they reached the top of the stairs, the ticket collector tipped his hat and waved them through. That was all. Edward stood up. He walked back to the tiny guesthouse where he was staying and took one of the pieces of writing paper from the desk in the dingy downstairs lounge. On the back he wrote, MILWAUKEE DAILY COURIER. He looked at his own uneven letters, unconvinced of the efficacy of his plan, but inserted the paper as best he could into the band around his hat. Then he picked up his camera and went back to the exhibition. He chose the opposite entrance from the one he'd used before. He walked quickly and purposefully toward the gate, as though he was in a terrible hurry to get the story and get back to the offices. He expected any moment to feel a hand on his shoulder, a voice demanding to know just what he thought he was doing. I should turn back, he thought; I'm sure to get caught. But instead, he waved to the man at the ticket gate and the man waved back. He smiled, an imitation of that broad, bland smile he'd seen the reporters use before him, and strode to the gate. No one stopped him. He went straight to the Pavillon d'Alma.

After this he thinks he's discovered a secret, which is this:

most people follow the rules because they are afraid not to. All you have to do to successfully break them, then, is act like you deserve to. It is this idea, which has stayed with him ever since, that makes him think he can come to Meudon and ask Rodin if he can take his portrait.

THE AIR IN the studio is cool, and when Rodin opens the door, a cloud of pale dust swirls up into the shafts of sunlight that come through the long windows. Edward follows him inside. A million things flash through his mind to say, but none of them seem important enough for this moment. Rodin himself says nothing and seems in no particular hurry. There is only that steady, deliberate motion of his to show that he is more alive than his statues. Edward can't tell if he's being welcomed or merely tolerated.

To one side of the room are workbenches covered in small clay models—some torsos, some limbs alone. At the far end of the room are larger forms covered in cloth. Rodin beckons him toward these and begins to remove the sacking from the biggest.

"These will be shipped to an exhibition next week," he says. Edward leans his portfolio up against one of the workbenches and moves forward to help him. Together they lift the material off the statue. Underneath is a form in bronze: the figures of six men, arranged in a rough circle, walking or standing still. Each one has a different expression on his face—fear, anger, contrition, resignation . . .

"What is it called?" Edward asks.

"*The Burghers of Calais.* Do you know the story?" Edward shakes his head. "They were town officials who sacrificed themselves to save the city. In exchange for their lives, the English king agreed to lift the siege he'd laid. So they volunteered to be executed."

Edward walks slowly around the statue, looking at each figure in turn. A man with a lined and weary face is raising his hands in prayer. A young man holds an old man in his arms to prevent him from falling to the ground in exhaustion. All the faces are convulsed with terrible understanding. All the eyes are blanks.

"They have just made their final decision to go," Edward says. "This is the moment when they know they are going to die."

Rodin nods slowly. "That's quite correct. Here—have a look at a piece I just had cast." He moves across to a second covered form, this one much smaller, and begins to unknot the slim ropes that bind the cloth around it. When they remove the covering, the torso and legs of a man are revealed. The figure is at the midpoint of a stride, its feet apart and its chest slanted so the tilt of the shoulders balances the angle of the hips. It is maybe three feet high and the back leg is curiously elongated out of proportion with the rest of the body.

"Why is the back leg like that?" Edward asks.

"Like what?"

"So long. It is much longer than the front one."

"I wanted to show movement, two consecutive moments, two consecutive steps. Because a body in this position, walking, is never frozen." He demonstrates, posing as though in the middle of taking a step, one arm swung out in front and one behind him. "This looks ridiculous because it is artificial, right? We are always in motion, so I tried to show this. Do you see?"

"Yes. The back leg is still caught in the previous instant."

"That is one way to put it. Now, you take photographs, I remember Fritz told us. Is that right?"

Edward nods nervously.

"Photography claims to capture the world as it really is. But in fact it does not do this; because time doesn't stop, the world cannot be captured, only evoked. So it is the artist, not the photographer, who tells the truth."

Rodin stands back from the statue and folds his arms across his chest. He is watching Edward with an air of expectation. Edward realizes that he is being offered a challenge, that the glib condemnation of photography is a gauntlet that the older man has thrown down between them. He scrambles to come up with a rejoinder that will impress, but won't offend, and of course his mind chooses this moment to go completely blank.

"I don't know," he manages. "I suppose so." Whatever the right answer might be, that obviously isn't it.

Rodin says, "Hmmph," and then wanders away to another part of the studio. His eyes dart back to the bench where his clay models are lined up waiting for his attention. In this sudden detachment, Edward can see his hopes begin to fade. Rodin replaces the cover on the walking man and goes to take the sheeting off one more statue with a weary perfunctory gesture. This will be the last one. Then he will be politely shown out of the studio, possibly thanked for coming, or possibly not, and then promptly forgotten before he has even cycled all the way down the hill into town. His heart sinks. He has missed his chance.

The statue is in the form of a seated man. He leans onto his hand, his fingers forming a ledge under his chin, his whole body hunched forward balancing the burden of his head. Rodin paces slowly around the statue. He stands face-to-face with his creation. He is gazing up at it intently, almost smiling for the first time since Edward arrived. And Edward suddenly sees his photograph. Standing slightly in the foreground, the man appears to be built on the same scale as the statue; it looks like a meeting of likes, of equals; they might both be flesh or they might both be stone. He puts his hands up to his face, framing the scene between the right angles of his thumb and forefinger. Yes. There it is. That is what he wants.

Rodin looks over at him, breaking the communion.

"What are you doing?" he asks. Edward thinks, well, now or never.

"I wanted to ask you, that is, I came here to see . . . I'd like to photograph you. I'd like to take your portrait." Rodin doesn't reply. "Suppose," Edward continues, "that photographs didn't try to show reality in a scientific way, but instead they were more like a painting or a sculpture, and gave an impression, a feeling. What I mean is, suppose it were possible to photograph more than just surfaces? Maybe a photographer can be an artist who . . . who tells the truth."

"Well, I have heard arguments to that effect," Rodin says, "but I have never yet found them convincing." His voice is skeptical, but he is listening now, he is paying attention, Edward can tell. So he plunges on: "I took pictures of your statue, when it was on exhibit in Paris. I've got them with me." He puts his portfolio down on the table and opens it. I may rue this day forever, he thinks, but it is too late to worry about that now. He pulls out the pictures of *Balzac* that he took using his fake press pass. He places them down on the workbench for Rodin to look at. "I tried to take it in as many kinds of light as possible. I hung around all day, until I could capture it in shadow. I think the evening pictures work best, don't you?" He is babbling now and he knows it, his nerves making him talk too fast. Rodin picks up the photographs and studies them, his brow furrowed. He leafs through the first few prints, raising them to his face to study them closer. He begins to nod slowly.

"These are not bad," he says. "Not bad at all. Not without interest."

Edward says, "I'd like to take your portrait here, in your studio. I could come whenever you wanted, whenever was convenient. It would be part of a series of photographic portraits I'm working on. Of the great men of our time."

"Great men," says Rodin, and he looks at Edward with an amused gleam in his eyes. "That's interesting. A series. What other great men have you photographed for it?"

Edward shifts his weight uneasily from one foot to the other.

"Well, none yet," he admits. "You'd be the first."

Rodin regards him for a minute, confused. Then, slowly, he begins to laugh, a huge round orchestra of a noise. Edward looks at his shoes, thinking, I've blown it. He thinks it's the most ridiculous thing he's ever heard. I should just go now before I embarrass myself any further.

And then Rodin strides around the bench and puts an arm around his shoulders and says, "Wonderful. Wonderful. What gumption you have," and then laughs again. "Rose!" he bellows. "Rose! You were right."

Rose comes in through the door that leads inside to the house, and Rodin goes over to her and takes her hand.

"Rose, dear," he says. "You were right as usual. This one is very much alive." He kisses her on the cheek. Edward feels momentarily foolish: how could he have ever imagined that she was the housekeeper? She is smiling now, her face open and unguarded.

Rodin turns to Edward.

"You will stay and have some lunch with me and Madame?"

"I wouldn't want to impose," Edward says, but Rodin fixes him with an intent gaze, and he says quickly, "Of course. I'd be delighted."

"Good," says Rodin. "And after lunch you'll show me the rest of your portfolio. You know, we should have some wine. I'll bring some up from the cellar. Go ahead with Madame and I'll meet you in the dining room. How marvelous," he says as he leaves. "Enthusiasm is not dead yet!"

THREE

June 11, 1918

EDWARD SPENT HIS second day in Paris reading the intelligence reports that Barnes had given him. In the late afternoon, Barnes handed him a memo that had just come in: *Company arriving this evening in Calais. 75 men, carrying equipment ordered. Please be ready to take the 8:00 A.M. train for Épernay tomorrow.*

He had determined to go to see Mildred Aldrich and talk to her about Clara's lawsuit that evening after he was done with work. He would not now have time to go to Meudon and visit Rodin's grave before he left for the front; he could not make both visits in a single night. It struck him forcefully that he had no idea when he would be back in Paris. He had not even had time to accustom himself to the place, and already he was being pulled away from it again. He tried to swallow his disappointment, but it wouldn't entirely go away. He finished the report he was reading, then left the office and returned to his hotel room to wash and change his shirt.

Edward had with him only two bags, though officers out of the line were permitted more, and one of these was his camera case. Circumstances had taught him the difference between what he actually needed and what he had merely grown accustomed to through the years of comfortable life before the war. His needs, it turned out, were fairly few.

He had his uniforms, some changes of shirts and trousers, a spare pair of boots. Underwear. His flying suit, scrolled up as small as it would go in the corner of his suitcase. His shaving kit. The only substantial item he still carried that he wasn't sure he needed was his camera. He'd brought his favorite from France in 1914 to New York and then from New York to Washington, each time debating whether to leave it behind. He'd hardly used it since he left France four years before. In Washington he stopped taking pictures altogether. He was so busy with his war work, so drained by it, that he lacked the store of curiosity necessary to find subjects for his own photographs. When he finally sailed for France, he thought of leaving it behind, but somehow couldn't bear to. It was the only thing that connected him back to the abundance of his old life. Again, leaving St-Omer, he had looked at the worn leather case, the bulk of it, and thought he should leave it for someone who might actually use it. But instead, he'd put it beside his single other bag to bring with him to Paris, unable, in the end, to let it go.

He had, in addition, only a few personal items, but these he guarded with great care. A bundle of letters brought with him from Washington, some from his mother, some from Lilian—Lilian disagreeing with him about the war, trying to dissuade him from going: *It is terrible, wasteful, not our fight. My dearest brother, I cannot bear to think of you in danger for this empty cause. You say this is for liberty, but who is made free by it?* As socialists, Lilian and her husband, Carl, had opposed American involvement in the war, and they had tried to persuade him not to volunteer. Edward and Carl had been good friends for many years, but this put a rift between them, and between him and his sister. Since he'd arrived in France, Lilian's letters had been full of news but conspicuously empty of politics.

He also had letters from Mary telling of her life in New York, her classes at school. She loved chemistry and biology. Drawing was all right, too. She missed him, but she was proud of him, she said in the last letter he'd received before he left for France. *I know that I will see you soon.*

His recent letters to Kate had been returned unopened, turned away, he imagined, by her mother. He continued to write to her anyway, hoping that one of them might reach her, but so far it had been to no avail. The envelopes came back, still sealed, and she had not written anything to him in many months. He kept her letters from earlier in the war, when her mother had first taken her away from him. She used to write to him often in those days. Sometimes she sent poems too: *Beautiful world, beautiful world / How can you bear the war?* That letter he had wrapped up inside the other papers, carefully, for safekeeping, as though it were a child he was tucking into bed.

Books: *The Winding Stair* by Yeats; Maeterlinck's play *The Blue Bird*, and, slipped inside its pages to keep them flat, some photographs. His parents outside their house in Milwaukee. Lilian and Carl. Kate and Mary, in the walled garden of the house in Voulangis.

This picture of his daughters was one of the last photographs he'd taken before the war began. It was from late in the summer of 1914, on one of those perfect days that seemed so abundant that year; he'd looked out of the window at breakfast and seen that the delphiniums had bloomed. When he told them he was going to take their picture beside the flowers, Mary had bounced happily out of the house; but Kate—Catkin, he'd always called her, little Catkin—had lingered on the kitchen step, not wanting to come forward into the sunlight. She had grown, that year, into a new self-consciousness, a shyness he didn't remember seeing in her before. She was six years old; she approached the world with an intense wonder that he loved—and recognized as his. Mary was the beauty, like her mother, aware of how the world related to herself, and warmly, sociably intelligent. But Kate got lost in her fascination, vanished into what she was seeing. Sometimes she was so overcome that she forgot how to speak. She could only point and gape at a new discovery, the bird's egg in her palm or the glowworm in the grass at her feet, her eyes wide and astounded. In the end, he promised to buy her some licorice when he drove into town later, if she'd only go and stand next to her sister.

In the photograph Mary stood looking into the camera, her head held up. Kate stood beside her and a little behind, her fingers laced in front of her pinafore, her brown hair coming loose from its braids. They both wore white dresses. Behind them the delphiniums climbed up their stakes and flung out extravagant trumpet-shaped blossoms from their towers of leaves.

In each of the many new rooms he'd slept in over the past few years, he'd kept this picture by his bed, the two little girls, the flowers, the bright day. Looking at it he felt, as he always did, the abrupt opening of sadness like a door inside him; and he would have kept it hidden from sight had this feeling not been preferable to the numbness it replaced. With Clara his memories were adulterated by anger. But for his children he felt only the simple shock of loss.

Edward set the picture gently on the nightstand. Then he put on his jacket, went out into the street and hailed a taxi headed toward the river and Montparnasse.

WHEN SHE OPENED the front door, Mildred Aldrich looked at him like she didn't quite believe what she was seeing.

"My God, Steichen! Let me pinch you to make sure I'm not dreaming," she said, putting a hand on his shoulder and patting him to be certain he was solid.

"I think traditionally you're supposed to pinch yourself," he said. "Not me."

"Well, why on earth would I do a silly thing like that? Come in, dear boy. Come in. Alfred wrote and told me you were in France now, but I had no idea that you would be darkening the doorsteps of Montparnasse."

She stood back so he could step inside, and he saw that she had a cane clasped in the hand that was not holding the door. He had never seen her use one before.

She led him down the hallway and up a small staircase.

"My old studio is just a few blocks away from here," Edward said.

"I remember that place. Where you and Clara lived when you were first in France. I remember, mainly, that it was painfully small."

"Yes; it was all we could afford at the time, though. You know I should still have the keys to that place somewhere in Voulangis. That is, if Clara hasn't thrown them down a well in a fit of rage."

Mildred looked over her shoulder at him, disapprovingly he thought. She opened a door into a tidy front parlor and ushered him through. Two armchairs were arranged either side of a small unlit fireplace. A desk stood by the window, and in the typewriter a half-typed sheet of paper lay furled over the barrel. Mildred saw him look at it.

"I was just in the middle of writing a letter. My sister in Boston wants to know whether everything here is all right for the umpteenth time. I'm so tired of reassuring people at home that I'm thinking of giving up letter writing altogether. Honestly, you'd think they'd be able to figure out for themselves that things are very much not all right just by opening a newspaper. There, sit, sit." She gestured him to one of the two chairs.

He sat down where she pointed. His heart was flooded with a mixture of gladness and melancholy: his old friend! She was her same cantankerous, talkative self. But then there was the cane, and when he looked at her, he saw she had grown noticeably thinner and more stooped. She sat down opposite him.

"Well, tell me. How long have you been here?" she asked.

"I just arrived yesterday. I was stationed up north until now, in the British sector. I'm doing reconnaissance work."

"Yes, Alfred mentioned that."

"Aerial photography."

"You're flying?"

"Well, no," he said. "I don't fly. I just sit in the backseat and hang on for dear life. I leave the flying to someone younger and more foolhardy."

"But not much more foolhardy."

"No, I suppose not."

A stout, dark-haired woman opened the parlor door and looked in. Edward recognized her. Amélie, who was nominally Mildred's *femme-de-ménage*, and who in truth was a great deal more than that. He remembered when he had first realized that the two women were lovers; what gave it away was nothing spectacular—after supper one night, a particular look that they had given each other, a look of fire that excluded everyone else in the room. On the way home, he asked Clara, *Is it true?* And she laughed that it had taken him so long to understand.

Now Amélie crossed to where Mildred sat and put a hand gently on her shoulder.

"Madame," she said affectionately. Mildred reached up and patted her hand.

"Amélie, do we have any coffee left?"

"I don't think so."

"Tea?" Amélie shook her head.

"Well, bring us something to drink, even if it's just cordial." Amélie nodded and went out. Mildred sighed. "These days in France," she said, "we sit around at dinner and talk about the food we aren't eating. It's the new small talk. To praise oranges and chocolate while eating string beef."

"Has it been very hard here?" Edward asked.

"Well, there have been shortages since the war began. Every year something different. Coal, then lamp oil, then salt. At least in the countryside we could grow our own food—I would have rather stayed there but the war is too close now even for me to ignore. The Germans may be back at your house in Voulangis before the year is out, just like they were in '14."

"Well, we are here to prevent that," Edward said.

"Yes. It is good to see Americans in uniform in Paris." Amélie reentered and set a tray with two glasses and a jug of blackcurrant cordial on it.

"Thank you," Mildred said to her. "Will you sit with us?

"Later, I will come back," Amélie said. She smiled at Mildred and went out.

"I am only sorry," Edward said, when the door closed behind

her, "that I didn't arrive in time to see Rodin. I wanted to show him that I came back to fight. I wish I had at least made it to his funeral."

"In a way, you were lucky you missed it. It was a disgusting affair," Mildred said. "All government men, talking about defending Alsace-Lorraine, fighting to the bitter end. Half of them never even knew him when he was alive, and the other half did, but never cared about his work until after he was famous. So many vultures."

"I still wish I had been there."

"Yes. I understand that. It is hard not to be able to pay your respects, especially to someone who was so dear to you," she said.

"And Rose gone too. So close together."

"A lot of people were sick this winter, including me . . ."

"I didn't know. What did you have?" he asked. "Are you recovered?"

"I caught a bronchitis and yes, officially, I am well again. In truth"—and here she lifted the cane to illustrate—"it turned me into an old woman, and I have not turned back. I'm not nearly as steady as I used to be. I haven't my former strength. Don't get old, Steichen, if you can help it: it has very little to recommend it."

"I'll try to remember that," Edward said.

"Anyway, the fuel shortages were the worst since '14. Rose used to let the fires go out all over the house, except the one in the studio. Then she'd sit in the cold until he was ready to come in for his supper. Did you know that she and Rodin were finally married a few weeks before she died?" She shook her head. "Clara always used to admire the way Rose sacrificed for Auguste. But I don't know. There is such a thing as sacrificing too much."

Edward shifted in his seat uneasily. The mention of Clara's name recalled to him the purpose of this visit. He didn't want to poison the conversation by bringing up the difficult past. For a moment he considered saying nothing about the lawsuit to Mildred, and just enjoying the short time they had together. What good could she do anyway?

She was looking at him, her sharp eyes seeing into his silence.

"I have not had a letter from her in some weeks," she said. "But the last I heard from Clara, she was doing fine. She is good at her job for Liberty Loan. She leads the choir. You can ask about her if you want to. You needn't stand on ceremony with me."

"Actually, I do want to talk to you about Clara," Edward said slowly.

"Go ahead."

"I got a letter from Marion Beckett before I left St-Omer. It was the first I'd heard from her in four years." Mildred looked noticeably surprised. She only let the expression stay on her face for a moment, but he caught it and understood. She thinks that we were lovers, he thought. She's heard Clara's version of events and believes it.

"What did she have to say?" Mildred asked. So he told her. About the letter, and the lawsuit it described. He saw Mildred's face grow grim as he spoke. She looked away from him, her eyes cast down.

"She will not win it," she said when he was finished. "She will only bring herself to grief. Poor child."

"Poor child?" Edward said, incredulous at where her sympathy lay.

"Yes. That is what I said. She is a poor child, for all that it's her own wild temper that causes her to suffer most. Some women are never very good at being wives; I claim to be among them. Clara got worse at it the harder she tried. But you were no help to her."

"I didn't do the things that she accused me of before the war.

She was mistaken, and then she wouldn't listen to me when I told her she was wrong."

Mildred snorted in frustration. "Oh, God. I don't know which of you to believe. I care for you both, and it is hard enough to see you causing each other pain without having to decide who is right." She stood up and paced to the window, then turned to look at him, her back to the glass. "Don't ask me to choose," she said. "I will choose Clara if I have to because she does not have the friends and chances you do. But I will hate to do it."

"You don't have to decide who is right," Edward said. "Even if you don't believe me, please, if you can, persuade her not to drag this matter into court. It wouldn't do her any good, even if she could win. It will hurt Kate and Mary as much as it hurts me. You know that. Just write to her; that is all I ask. She may listen to you."

Mildred's lips were a tense line. Slowly, she began to nod.

"All right," she said. "Of course. I'll see what I can do."

"Thank you," Edward said. He felt exhausted.

They remained silent for a few minutes. Mildred returned to her seat by the fireplace, her cane clicking on the floor with her steps.

"You know, I used to see Clara often when I lived in Huiry," she said at last. "She would ride over the fields between there and Voulangis, whenever she had tea or coffee, or chocolate. Her sister, Lottie, would send her those things from America. It was strange and sad to see her and Kate without you and Mary. Kate seemed to be coping with all the changes she'd been through. At first she was afraid of the soldiers—even ours. She'd hide when they came into town on their way to the front. But she had friends among the children in the village. She read a lot. I used to lend her books whenever I visited, and she'd finish them before I could even choose which ones to give her next.

"Clara, too, seemed to manage quite well by herself at first. She was sad and sometimes angry. But the work of the household seemed to solace her, and she played music everyday.

"Then they passed the law in '16 that banned foreigners from traveling outside our communes. They made us register at the *mairie* and get papers from the *garde champêtre* to travel. And Voulangis is on the other side of our commune line, so going to see each other became much more difficult. It was ridiculous. I had to submit an application just to go four miles down the road. And you know how long it takes papers to get processed in those local offices.

"When America entered the war, they finally relaxed the travel restrictions. I went up to Voulangis soon after. Clara told me then that she was planning to leave. She'd had enough of living with the shortages and the isolation. She wanted to go home. She talked about going back to her father's house in Missouri, staying there until she could find a job. Something in her aspect had changed and . . . I don't know . . ."

"What?" Edward asked.

"Hardened. Yes, that is the right word. Three weeks later they went back to America. I am glad that they left when they did. It was no life there for a child or for a young woman alone.

"I didn't see them again . . . Wait, no, that isn't quite right." Mildred put her hand to her forehead, as though trying to draw out the memory. "I saw Kate once more, briefly, just before they left. She drove over one morning in the dogcart. She brought a suitcase, which she said contained a few valuables. She didn't want to leave it in an empty house for the soldiers to damage, she said. She asked me if I would take care of it until someone could return to collect it. Actually, just before she drove away, she said, 'If Papa comes back here, please give this to him.'"

"She said that?"

"Yes, I remember it quite clearly. It seemed important to her."

Edward put his face in his hands.

"It is just hard for me to believe," he said, "that Kate is old enough now to make the drive from Voulangis to Huiry on her own. The last time I saw her she was six years old. Now she's ten."

Mildred said: "Living as they did made her act old for her age. But even so, with children, four years is a long time."

In the darkness behind his closed fingers, Edward tried to picture the girl who was grown-up enough to drive, to say the self-possessed things that Mildred had related, but was still also the shy, melancholy child he remembered. The beautiful life they had in that house—he could almost reach through the glass of the present and touch it. And yet here he was getting news of his daughter, secondhand and two years late, trying to put together the pieces of her life like sections of a puzzle. It was only by chance that he had even learned this much—if his men had arrived on time, he would have missed this too.

"The case she left," he asked, uncovering his eyes and looking up, "do you still have it? Can I get it from you?"

"I left it stored in my house in Huiry when I left and came up to Paris. I haven't done a very good job of looking after it, I guess."

Edward shook his head. "I'm sure you had enough to worry about when you moved here." They lapsed into separate silences again.

"My God!" Mildred said suddenly. "To think I introduced you and Clara." She started to shake, and for a moment Edward thought she was crying; but she wasn't. She was laughing. He looked at her, shocked.

"I know," she said, "I know, I shouldn't laugh, it's not the time for it, but if I ever, *ever* say I'm going to try matchmaking again, you absolutely have to stop me."

At the Piano. Paris, 1902. Platinum print.

ALL EVENING PEOPLE have been asking Clara to play, and it is really becoming most tiresome. Just a couple of pieces, they say, just the Chopin that you played for us last time, please. We won't even ask you to sing.

But she tells them, no, she is resting her voice, and anyway she isn't inclined to play this evening, because she practiced all day. It is Lottie and Mildred who are the most insistent, and their hostess, a woman called Judith, whom Clara doesn't really like much, but who is rich and might buy some of Mildred's photographs, so they have to be nice to her. She tells them they must stop pestering her at once and let her enjoy the party in peace. Then she laughs to show that she doesn't really mean it, and that she is just pretending to be annoyed.

This is her very first summer in Paris. She and her sister Charlotte are traveling with Mildred Aldrich, the noted photographer and writer. She likes the way this sounds: *noted photographer.* Far better than saying *famous photographer.* That is really much more vulgar. When her own career gets started, she decides, she wants to be known as the noted concert pianist and coloratura soprano Clara Smith.

She and Lottie met Mildred in New York this past spring, quite by accident. To earn money, they had been giving music lessons and, ever so occasionally, taking in sewing work to add a little to their income. Mildred had come to their small apartment to drop off a dress to be altered, and while she was there, she heard Clara practicing in the other room. As Lottie told it later, she stopped dead in the middle of discussing a hemline and listened silently until Clara finished playing. Then she applauded slowly.

"Who is that?" she'd asked Lottie. "And where can I hear a concert?"

"Only in this apartment," Lottie replied. "It is my sister and she has no professional engagements yet."

"Well, I had better find another dress that needs hemming," Mildred said, and stayed for supper.

Soon they all became fantastic friends, and when Mildred decided to go to Paris that summer, she invited Lottie and Clara along. She would be their chaperone, she said, rolling her eyes and pronouncing the word "chaperone" as though no one could imagine such a ridiculous, old-fashioned notion. The appropriate letters were nevertheless sent to their father, who gladly gave his permission, so long as they were to be looked after by such a pleasant and obviously respectable lady. They bought their tickets for the packet the same afternoon they got his reply.

To Clara, everything about Paris is delightful. All the women are elegant and their clothes are so beautiful, even more than in New York. She and Lottie have met so many people since they arrived she can hardly remember all their names, and they have gone to more parties than she can count. Mildred knows everyone here, everyone who matters, that is, everyone who cares about music and art and things like that. In Paris people drink red wine and have the most marvelous conversations about ideas, important and sophisticated conversations, not like people at home in Missouri, who never seem to talk about anything except each other. Or like father, who just worries about his patients all the time, whether they can afford to pay him, whether he will make ends meet himself. On the boat on their way over here, she had imagined telling people in France that they were from New York or New England or else that they were descended from Elizabethan courtiers or exiled Russian aristocrats. Something a little more urbane, at least, than being daughters of a country doctor from the Ozarks. But when she mentioned this idea, Lottie had frowned and said that *she* wasn't ashamed of where she came from and Clara shouldn't be either. Besides, Mildred already knew where they'd grown up, so in addition to being wrong, Clara's suggestion wasn't even practical. Clara pointed out to her that she hadn't been saying they should do it, only thinking that it would be fun if they could transform themselves into new people for the summer. Really, Lottie could be such an old stick-in-the-mud, never wanting to try anything new or daring. She should have expected her to say something like that.

Mildred has taken them to Notre-Dame and St-Chapelle and to the Louvre. On Monday they will go to see the palace at Versailles. She has read about it in their Baedecker, about the hall of mirrors and the secret passage where Marie Antoinette escaped from the angry crowds during the Revolution. She is looking forward to it immensely.

Tonight, they have come to an apartment in the Latin Quarter, which belongs to this woman Judith Cladel, for a party in honor of Mildred's visit. The rooms are full of people, and some of Mildred's recent photographs have been hung on the walls of the parlor. Some of the guests are people Clara and Lottie have met before. There is a couple who have recently arrived from New York, a man called Alfred, who is a photographer, too, even more famous than Mildred and whose mustache droops down and covers his entire mouth. He is awfully serious and impatient with people, especially with his wife, Emmeline, who couldn't be more different from him if she tried. Emmy is so gentle, moves and speaks so slowly; her attention wanders. She is forever apologizing and asking people to repeat themselves because she got distracted halfway through what they were saying. Clara thinks secretly that she is not especially clever. But she is very nice.

There are younger people, too, although here even the old people act like they are young. This man Arthur Carles, who is a painter. And a Spanish girl, Mercedes de Cordoba, who sings, like Clara, although she is a mezzo, not a real soprano. Arthur is always following Mercedes around, looking mournful and love-struck while simultaneously trying to pretend that he is *not* following her around and that he just happens to turn up by accident wherever she is. Then there is another American girl, Marion Beckett, who Lottie discovers from Mildred is only sixteen, though she seems much older. She has, Mildred says, remarkably enlightened parents who have sent her to Paris to study painting and to live with her unmarried aunt for the summer. Both Clara and Lottie like Marion best of all the people they have met. She is so sensible in her opinions and intelligent that sometimes, Lottie says, she seems older than they are, not younger. Clara agrees. Marion is a delightful girl, pleasant and thoughtful, though it is a pity she should be so plain. She's all orange hair and freckles, and much too skinny, no figure to speak of. They like Mercedes, too, though they don't think so much of Arthur, who is well-meaning but clumsy, always knocking things over, or saying the wrong thing at the wrong time, or raising his voice much too loud so that everyone can hear him and not each other.

For example, right now, just as Lottie and Mildred promise they won't ask Clara to play the piano for them ever again, at least not *this* evening, Arthur's voice sounds from the front hallway so loud that you'd think he was a carnival barker, not a party guest.

"Here he is!" he shouts. "Finally. We thought you'd never get here."

"My God, the world must be ending right in this apartment," murmurs Mildred, making both Lottie and Clara stifle giggles behind their hands. From the direction of the entrance hall come sounds of less raucous greetings, the shuffle of coats being removed. Judith bustles over, and they hear a high-pitched cry of delight, "*Chéri,* so beautiful," and then Mildred, smiling, stands up, as though she's figured out who's just arrived.

Judith comes around the corner first, carrying an enormous bunch of yellow roses, which Clara does not think go very well with her pale skin. In fact, they make her look rather sallow. Then Arthur comes in with his arm around the shoulders of another young man, who is slender and tall, with dark hair and wide-set blue eyes.

"Here he is!" Arthur repeats. "I told you he'd make it. Didn't I tell you?"

Mildred goes over to this new arrival and takes both his hands: "Naturally, my dear, you are late for my big night. And naturally, I forgive you." She kisses him on both cheeks.

"I'm sorry," the young man says, "I only just got back from London this afternoon. The show went marvelously. Two of Alfred's pictures sold right away. Is he here? He'll want to know what happened."

"He is here, and I'm sure he'll be through in a second. But before you two start being unsociable and talking shop, you must let me introduce you to everyone." She puts her arm through his, and, wresting him bodily from Arthur's grasp, brings him over to where Lottie and Clara are standing on the far side of the room.

"Steichen," she says, "this is Charlotte and Clara Smith. They are my traveling companions this summer."

He bows to them each in turn, Charlotte first, then Clara. Now that she has a chance to look at him up close, she sees that he really is quite handsome. He is simply dressed, but his clothes hang easily on him, as though they were aware of the good looks of their owner. She feels a flutter cross through her. She straightens up, and pushes her lips out into their most fetching pout. She looks at him, his hair falling over his face as he bows to Lottie, and she wonders, idly of course, whether she could make him fall in love with her. It would certainly be amusing to try.

Back in Missouri, she could make almost any boy fall in love with her just by smiling at him, or by looking his way for a minute. So many boys came calling on weekends, only to sit awkwardly on the porch, sipping lemonade and saying nothing. Once she received three marriage proposals in one month, none of them from boys that she liked even the least little bit. Two were farmers' sons, slow-spoken and heavy-limbed, who told her they would take care of her, provide a good home and a steady income, as if this was the most enticing thing that they could imagine in the world. In private, she and Lottie imitated them, lumbering across the floor and saying "errrrrr" and "uummmmm" between every other word, until they fell about laughing, or until Lottie said it was too mean-spirited and they must stop. The third suitor was a boy from town at least, the son of a department-store owner, who was known locally as something of a dandy, which meant his clothes were too flashy and he had a reputation for getting girls into trouble. But she didn't want him any more than she wanted the other two. In the end, they were all the same to her: they were just dead weights pulling her down, down, into the ground of this awful small town where she knew perfectly well that she didn't belong. Clara's music teachers had been telling her for some years that she must go to the city and study with someone who could develop her talents fully. She was leaving, moving to New York, and she had already talked Lottie into coming with her, and nothing so dull and usual as marriage would spoil their plans. She told her suitors that she wouldn't have them. But she kept the rings they'd given her. Those, after all, were gifts, and what would they do with them if she did return them? Give them to other girls?

Mr. Steichen bows to her next, and as he takes her hand, she feels again that brief flutter, like a bird stretching its wings out inside her. He presses her knuckles to his lips, which are dry and soft, the skin around them a little rough from traces of beard. A sweet shock travels up her arm from the place where they are touching, and she is surprised, almost frightened by it. She has only just time to compose her face before he looks up at her. His eyes are implacably blue. She puts on the expression she has practiced for meetings like this, the one where her eyes say that she could be just as happy anywhere, really, in the company of anyone. A slight indifference is what men find most alluring. She wouldn't want to seem too enthusiastic: it would betray a lack of sophistication. Yes, she decides, it would be great fun to try to charm him. But then she sees a fleeting look of amusement cross his face, and for a second she's convinced that he is thinking the same thing about her.

"Miss Smith is a pianist and a singer of immense talent," says Mildred. "We are all expecting great things from her."

"Is that so?" Mr. Steichen hasn't looked away from her, and she finds herself smiling under his gaze in spite of herself. Somehow she cannot seem to rid her face of this ridiculous grin.

"It would be wonderful to hear you play something," he says.

"No, I'm afraid not tonight," says Mildred. "Clara has made us promise not even to ask her . . ."

"Well, I was only teasing, really," Clara says quickly. "I'd be delighted to play something a little later." And Mr. Steichen smiles, but before he has a chance to reply, Alfred bursts in from the back drawing room, looking more animated than he has all evening. He strides across the floor toward them, his eyes dancing.

"The prodigal returns!" he cries.

"He's hardly prodigal," says Mildred. "Just tardy."

"Well, I have not seen him for months," Alfred replies. "You must tell me about the show." He draws Edward away into a corner of the room, and in a minute the two of them are deep in conversation. Mildred stares after them, her arms folded across her chest.

"That's our Stieglitz," she says, looking toward Alfred's stooped back and gesticulating arms. "Brilliant, but no manners whatsoever. Honestly, we all owe him such a debt. He is our champion. The only reason we have art photography in America to speak of. But he really doesn't seem to have any sense of when he is stepping on people's toes."

"I suppose that is part of what allows him to stand up for what he believes in so well." Marion has come up beside them, quietly, and now stands watching the two men conversing in the opposite corner.

"Yes," Mildred says, "it helps him to be so stubborn and a little blind to social niceties. Well, my dears," she turns back to them, "before he got swept away, that young man was Edward Steichen. A very promising photographer and painter. Alfred discovered some of his work among the entries to the Philadelphia Salon three years ago. He is studying now, here in Paris."

"I should like to talk to him about where he studies painting," says Marion. "Do you think I could?"

"Oh, certainly, if you can pry him away from Alfred. Which I'm warning you is no easy task." Marion nods. She goes over to where Alfred and Edward are still standing and talking, ignoring everyone else, and waits patiently for an opening.

Lottie leans over and tugs Clara's sleeve. "Let's get another glass of wine." And so they go into the next room where the glasses are all lined up being served by waiters in dark ties and long white aprons, and they run into Judith, who wants to talk to them about all the sights they simply must see while they are in Paris, as if Mildred hadn't been here before and knew perfectly well where to take them, and it is all very dull. Clara's mind keeps wandering back to the strange way that Edward had looked at her, laughing but not laughing exactly, curious, self-assured.

"What do you think of that Mr. Steichen?" she asks Lottie, when Judith finally lets them go.

"He seems nice," says Lottie. "He's a friend of Mildred's, so he's probably clever."

"He seems a bit conceited to me," Clara says.

"Why? Clara, he hardly said anything at all."

"I don't know. Just an air he gives off. He is used to getting his own way."

They pass back into the front salon and see that Edward and Alfred are still in the same place that they were twenty minutes before, but that now Marion and Mildred have joined them and they are all four talking animatedly together. Edward turns to Marion and asks her something, then cranes his neck down to hear her answer. Marion is smiling as she replies.

"I think that if I am going to play," Clara says, "I better do it now before I am far too tired."

"Really? Now? Oh, how terrific," says Lottie. "Judith will be so pleased. I'll just go and let her know."

They all arrange the chairs in the front parlor around the piano. Judith comes to her and squeezes her hand. "I'm so glad you have decided to entertain us. You seemed so set against it. Whatever was it that changed your mind?"

"Oh, just a mood that took me," Clara says. "I can never tell when I'll feel like playing. The inspiration is rather mysterious even to me, you know." She settles herself on the bench and looks around the room to see who is there.

At last she finds him. He is sitting near Alfred and Emmy, but a little pulled away by himself, with his legs crossed and his chin in his hands. He is watching her with that same curious, amused expression, and when she catches his eye, he smiles and doesn't look away. She chooses a sonata by Beethoven and a Chopin nocturne. Then she will sing, something short, perhaps a song by Haydn, though Haydn might be too sensible for this evening, when she feels so dark and dizzily excited though she cannot understand quite why. She turns to face the piano, but she is still aware of him watching her from across the room.

When she plays, her arms join the instrument and become wings. She described this to Lottie once, how the keys are feathers along an arch of bone, how the world vanishes once she begins. Lottie, who was honestly never much more than a competent pianist, said that she knew just what Clara meant when obviously she didn't understand at all. Clara doesn't mean that she actually grows feathers or anything ridiculous like that. But all the snagged colors and thoughts that have been in her head that day, words people have said, what she has felt and seen, even the things she's half-forgotten already—all of this stuff inside her flows down her arms and out of her hands into the keys. When she is playing, even the faces of strangers she passed on the street are in it. She is borne up on this, her hands pulling the notes out of the keys so the sound blooms around her into something bigger than she could ever be, and she feels terribly bright and clear. The music goes out and fills up the room and drowns everything in it. And she loves this sensation more than anything in the world.

Tonight, then, she begins from the curious dizzy feeling of being looked at by this boy, who hadn't been content to just see her face, but wanted to look inside it, too, and as she plunges down into the first notes of the sonata and then calls up the swollen broken chords with her left hand, she remembers how she had wanted to draw back from him but instead, she had stared right back into his face as though she was not afraid. The music complicates, brings in more and more fragments of the day: there is Judith's scratching voice in the high notes; there is Emmy Stieglitz's slow meandering in the adagio. Mildred and Lottie are there, too, and she feels how she has bound them all together in this. They will be part of each other, and of her, whenever this piece of music is played. They will not be able to undo it, even if they want to.

When she is finished, she is quiet inside, and, as she stands and bows, she can hear them applauding but from far away, as if they're in another room. She looks over to where Edward is sitting. He shakes his head as he claps slowly. "Beautiful," she sees him mouth to Alfred on his right. And then he does a curious thing. He raises his hands with the thumbs and forefingers at right angles to each other, so he is looking at her through a rectangular frame. What is he doing? How odd he looks with his hands up in front of his face that way. She smiles, and decides that she will sing Mozart, Susanna's song "Deh vieni, non tardar" from *The Marriage of Figaro*.

When she finishes the song, there is more applause. As it fades, Edward stands up and comes slowly over to her.

"What did you think?" she asks. She feels bold at that moment, aware of her own loveliness. For a minute he is actually at a loss for words. Later on, she will remember this as one of the few times when he really did not know what to say. She will recall exactly the way his voice cracks when he finally speaks.

"I would like to photograph you. While you are playing," he says. "Do you think that I could?"

"Well," she says, slowly, drawing out the moment, "let me consider it."

FROM HER CHAIR near the back of the room, Marion sees Steichen go over to the piano while the applause and shouts of bravo from the assembled company are still dying away. He touches Clara gently on the elbow, and she turns her flushed, bright face toward him and, my goodness, how beautiful they are together! It is really quite astonishing. One wants just to look and look at them. She has to tell herself forcefully that it isn't polite to stare just to get herself to tear her eyes away.

She gets to her feet but doesn't know what to do with herself after that. She does not want to go over and interrupt whatever conversation is passing between her friend and the man beside her. She looks around for someone to talk to but sees no one she knows nearby. So she sits awkwardly down again and folds her hands in her lap, and as she does so, a familiar feeling of disappointment wells up inside her. She has been here before. All of the light has gone over to the other side of the room and left her here among the middle-aged ladies and gentlemen who are beginning to talk of taxis home, the wretched weather, how the food did not agree with them. She feels the ordinariness of it all very keenly in contrast to the wonderful expanse of the music just minutes before. She feels it, too, in contrast to the mysterious energy moving between the couple by the piano.

It is not that she envies Clara her beauty or the ease of her talent; she sees already that these things bring with them their own kinds of trouble. Besides, she likes Clara, likes the way she has of making everything she does seem special, illuminated, demanding of particular attention like a theatrical performance. To be around Clara is to feel like one is at the center of things.

And she certainly isn't, she assures herself, jealous of the attention of that particular young man, Mr. Steichen. True, they had been having an interesting conversation before Clara said she would play. He is pleasant and he listens to what is being said to him, something which young men, especially those in the midst of their first success, cannot always be relied upon to do. But it would be silly to be jealous on account of someone one had only just met and about whom one knew almost nothing.

No; really, it is only this: for her somehow that world of mysterious flight, the kinds of emotions so powerful they are visible, tangible, seems to be something she can have only at one remove. She can observe but not participate—that is her role. It is why she is a painter, someone who spends her time looking at things outside herself, while remaining invisible. She is not, she senses, intended for any grand drama or passion. That she is not a beauty may have contributed to this, and perhaps her nature is too sensible in any case for such things.

Still, she cannot help but feel lonely for that brightness she does not possess, as she watches part of someone else's story unfolding across the room.

She shouldn't stare, she reminds herself once more. She stands up again, and this time determinedly goes to find Mildred, who is in the dining room talking to Lottie Smith.

"Wasn't that terrific?" Mildred says.

"Oh yes," Marion agrees. "She is extraordinary."

"We won't be able to keep her to ourselves for long, I fear. Look—here she is. Brava!"

Clara is smiling as she enters.

"Oh, you are spoiling me," she says. "It was really only just serviceable. I wobbled terribly on the high notes."

When there is a break in the conversation, Clara pulls Marion off into a corner where they won't be overheard.

"I am going to model for Mr. Steichen," she confides. "He wants to take photographs of me playing the piano. What do you think of that?"

Marion takes her hand. "That is exciting. I'm sure the photographs will be very good indeed. You can tell that Mildred and Alfred think the world of him."

"So you think it is a good idea?"

"Ye-es."

"You don't sound very certain."

It is true, but when she thinks about it, Marion isn't sure why she has hesitated to give her blessing. Why should Clara not model for Steichen's camera? What could be bad about it?

"Oh no. It's only that I don't like to have my photograph taken," she says. "But you will look beautiful in his pictures, I am certain."

FOUR

June 12, 1918

THESE MEN HAD never been to war. Edward could tell from the way they were disembarking, the way they filled up the small station at Épernay with excited chaos that belied their small numbers. They climbed out of the train, passed bags and cases through open carriage windows, collected in small groups, smoked, talked in loud voices to hear one another over the din. One of the men dropped his pack as he handed it down, making the soldier below him jump backward out of the way, the abrupt movement of a startled animal. The men around them laughed. The sound was warm.

"Hey, careful with that," said the man whose bag it was, leaning out of the window. "Clumsy idiot!"

"Why? What's in there that's so damn special? Your mother's best china?" The jumper folded his arms and stuck his chin out defiantly.

"No. Your wife's wooden leg," said the man at the window. Again laughter, and this time the man on the platform rushed to the window and swung upward with his fists at the face that vanished, grinning, into the interior.

"Kelsey, hurry it up over there!" called one of the sergeants, a broad-shouldered man with a dark mustache. The noncoms were circling the confusion like sheepdogs. "Save your fight for the Huns, for God's sake."

Three men wearing lieutenant's high collars and insignia on their shoulder straps came over to where Edward was standing at the end of the platform.

"Captain Steichen?" asked the first of them. Edward nodded. They saluted smartly.

"At ease," Edward said, feeling foolish as he always did with formal military gestures. He looked down at the mimeographed list of names he'd received from Barnes. "Which one of you is Eric Lutz?"

"I am, sir," said the man who had spoken previously. He was tall and heavy-set, and his square, ruddy face was a mask of earnest enthusiasm.

"And you are . . . ?"

"John Dawson."

"Lewis Deveraux, sir."

Dawson was dark-haired, with a sleepy, handsome face; Deveraux was short, wiry, with a nervous restlessness about him. He shifted his weight from foot to foot as he stood. They all looked, to Edward, excruciatingly young.

"OK. When your men have disembarked, take roll and make sure everyone in your section is present. It's four miles to the airfield. Have them form up for the march. Extra baggage can be put in the tender that is waiting outside the station. Make sure you pack the cameras so that they won't move around too much during the ride and don't pile any heavy baggage on top of them . . ." The three lieutenants were exchanging anxious looks. "What is it?"

"Well, sir," Lutz spoke up. "Which cameras would you be referring to?"

"The cameras that you brought with you. You are supposed to have a consignment of equipment for the Photo Division, which you brought with you from the States. Do you?"

"Oh yes, sir," Deveraux put in. "Each man in these sections brought a sealed case with him. Special equipment."

"Well, that's OK then . . ."

"But I don't think that they are cameras."

"Why not?"

"Sir," Lutz said, "perhaps you should take a look at the cases."

Edward looked at the three perplexed faces before him.

"OK," he said. "Deveraux, will you bring one over here?"

"Yes, sir." He ran off down the platform and disappeared into the crowd.

Edward turned to the two lieutenants still beside him.

"Tell me about the men. They've all had training with cameras, I suppose," he said. Dawson looked at his feet, then away down the platform.

"Well . . ." he said.

"Perhaps I had better not suppose anything. What kind of training have they had?"

"They've all had basic training. Army wouldn't send them abroad otherwise."

"What about flight training? Have they flown before?"

"I have. So have Deveraux and Lutz here, and the noncoms, Sergeant Daniels, a few more. Some of the others have some experience with taking pictures."

"About how many of them know how to use a camera?"

"I really couldn't say for certain. Perhaps ten or so."

"In each section?" But he knew the answer before Dawson spoke:

"No, sir. Ten in all."

Edward shook his head in amazement. "OK," he said. "OK. It isn't your fault. You'd better go and help the rest of the men get ready to move out."

"Yes, sir." The two men saluted energetically, as if to say at least they could do that right, and walked rapidly away. Edward raised his hand after them in a half-effort, but he was too overwhelmed to hide his disappointment. Only ten of them with training in photography. It was a disaster.

A few minutes later Lutz came back down the platform toward him, with one of the sergeants following close behind. They both wore worried expressions.

"What's the problem?" Edward asked.

"There's a man with our unit who isn't on any of the rosters. None of the others have ever seen him before. He insists he's meant to be here. Says he knows you, sir."

"Knows me?"

"Yes, sir."

"Well, send him down here. Tell him to hurry. I don't want him to hold us up."

"I don't know if he can do that . . . hurry, that is . . ."

"What do you mean?" asked Edward.

"Well, his legs are kind of a mess."

A moment later he recognized the slow, uneven gate and unblinking eyes as Gilles Marchand pulled himself down the platform until he stood in front of them. Gilles saluted, his face expressionless as ever.

"What is he doing here?" Edward asked. The men looked at him blankly. He turned to the sergeant.

"What's your name?"

"Reece, sir." He was a tall man with colorless skin and hair, as though he had been bleached slowly by the sun. His chin sloped into his neck until it vanished.

"What is he doing here?" Edward repeated.

"I don't know, sir."

"What did you think a kid with one good leg was doing headed for the front?"

"I didn't notice his legs."

"Well, I'm glad we've hired you as an observer. So far you're doing an excellent job."

He turned to Marchand.

"What are you doing here?"

"They are closing up the office in Paris in a few weeks and moving everyone to Chaumont. They won't need me. I know as much about cameras as the others. I want to work as an observer." He met Edward's gaze and stared straight back at him, his eyes unwavering.

"But you aren't American."

"Lots of Americans fought for France before America came into the war."

"What about your foot?"

"I don't need to walk around inside the airplane, sir," said Marchand as if nothing could have been more obvious. "Please. I want to fly."

Edward hesitated.

"Come in the car with me up to the airfield. We'll talk to Colonel van Horn when we get there."

Deveraux appeared carrying two identical wooden cases, one in each arm. When Edward saw them, his stomach sank. There was no possibility that they contained cameras. They were oblong and nearly flat. They looked like cases for woodwind instruments.

"Are they all like that?" Edward asked.

"Yes, sir," Deveraux said.

"And those are the only things they have?" Deveraux nodded.

"Well, we'd better have a look inside them and see what we've got here." They laid the cases on the ground. Deveraux knelt down beside one. He broke the seal and sprung the two catches at either end, then began to pry open the lid. Lutz, Reece, and Edward all bent over him, peering down, like people crowding around a man who has fallen in the street. Edward thought, What a comic spectacle we would be to anyone with the time to notice.

Lutz eased the lid up on the first case. Inside lay a long, wooden handle with a flat steel trowel at one end that finished in a point.

"An entrenching tool," said Reece, nodding, pleased with his own perspicacity. Edward stared at it in disbelief.

"My God," he said. "They sent you men all the way from America with seventy-five top-secret shovels." He turned away. "Special equipment . . ."

Edward walked up the platform to clear his head. He looked back at where the lieutenants were gathered in a small group near the case open on the ground. The men stood around awkwardly, shifting in place, unsure of what to do next, of how to respond to this new turn of events. They kept looking down at the entrenching tool, as though they were checking to make sure it was still a spade and hadn't turned into a camera while they weren't paying attention.

Through his irritation he suddenly felt a wave of sympathy for them. They were well meaning and certainly not stupid. They had just arrived and they clearly wanted to do their best. But they looked to Edward like a flock of confused birds, all alarmed by the same noise but not knowing whether to fly off or stay where they were . . . and all at once he began to laugh. He tried to stop so the men wouldn't notice, but he couldn't, and the infection spread. Lutz looked up and saw Edward with his hand over his mouth. He snorted once and immediately tried to suppress it but instead let out a sound that could have come from a donkey. That set the rest of them off.

"Entrenching tools . . ." Edward mouthed between spasms of giggles. "Entrenching tools . . . unbelievable . . ."

Eventually, he caught his breath and wiped his eyes. He turned to Lutz and Deveraux. "Get the men formed up into companies," he said, trying to sound stern and commanding. "We have several miles to walk to the airfield before supper."

From the station steps he watched them getting ready to march, the lieutenants counting heads and calling roll. How, he wondered, are we ever going to begin work? Barnes had said they wanted photographs of the front by the middle of the week. But with no cameras, what could they do?

"We're ready to go, sir," Dawson reported to him.

"OK. Move out, Lieutenant," Edward said. And they filed down the road, the sound of their footsteps keeping clumsy time.

COLONEL ROBERT VAN HORN was a short man with big, solid shoulders and a face that fell naturally into an attitude of barely contained irritation. He spoke in short, explosive bursts and paced while he talked, a combination that made him seem threatening even when he was pleased.

"Have a seat, gentlemen," he said when Edward and the three lieutenants entered his office. He flung his arm toward a circle of chairs opposite his desk. "Find your rooms comfortable? Good. Pleased to hear it." He had not waited for a reply. "We've had a new advance out of the Aisne salient in the past two days, at the western side, toward the railway junction in Compiègne. Not the huge show we are expecting soon, but some fireworks. They crossed about ten miles on a front south of Noyon and then halted without reaching the junction." Van Horn himself stopped pacing when he said this, as if to illustrate. Then he began again in the other direction.

"We still can't say for sure whether this is preparation for a big push, or a decoy," he continued. "If this is the real thing, they will want to make good on these advances soon. The longer they wait, the more Yanks will be added to the line. So we are expecting another large-scale offensive soon. I'm sure I don't have to say that this makes the work you are doing even more urgent."

Van Horn pointed to a map that covered one wall. It was thick with different-colored pins "These are French units," he said, pointing to the green markers, "these," indicating the black ones, "are German. And these," he pointed to a couple of isolated red pins near them, "are American."

"We've got boys from the 42nd Marines in the line, and 2nd and 3rd divisions up between Château Thierry and Lucy-le-Bocage." Above them the semicircle of black pins swelled forward menacingly. "We need to know where the Germans will come from next. We have a squadron of DH-4s that can start taking observers on reconnaissance flights as soon as you can process their photographs. When will you be ready?"

Edward cleared his throat. "There's a problem," he said. "The equipment that was supposed to come for these men has not arrived. We have no cameras for them, and none of the other photographic materials we'll need. No paper, no developer—"

"I didn't ask you about problems," van Horn said, catching him up short. "I asked for an estimate of when you can have your operation up and running."

"Three days." Edward was almost surprised to hear himself

speak with such certainty, but there it was: he'd said it and he sensed that it was the right answer. He felt the other men in the room exhale collectively, relieved. Across the desk, van Horn waited for him to continue. "Where are the other American installations in this section of the front?" He stood up and walked to the map, so he was standing beside the colonel.

"Here," van Horn pointed, "at Châlons-sur-Marne. There is a supply depot and an American Red Cross hospital. There's also a French airfield."

"Give me a telephone and a car," Edward said. "We'll have our men ready in three days to start shooting."

"Very good, Captain," said van Horn. He turned to the lieutenants. "The tasks will be divided up as follows: Dawson, you will be responsible for the observers and the flight schedules and routes; for the moment, you'll want to send them out on high-altitude runs keeping close to our side of the lines.

"Deveraux, you'll oversee developing and printing; and Lutz, you're in charge of the photo interpreters. You'll also be Captain Steichen's assistant. Any questions?"

"Sir . . ."

"Yes, Lutz?"

"If I'm to work with the interpreters, will I be flying?"

"Everyone will be expected to fly when they are needed. As the ones with the most experience, officers will go up everyday."

"Excuse me, sir," asked Deveraux. "But did you say we'll be flying in de Havilland 4s?"

"That is correct, Lieutenant. Is there a problem with that?"

"No, sir. Just . . ."

"The pilots at Tours," Lutz said, "thought DH-4s were . . ."

"What is it Lieutenant?" Van Horn drummed his fingers on the desk impatiently.

"They called them 'flaming coffins,' sir. They said they were badly designed and dangerous. That they crash during landing."

"All airplanes are dangerous," van Horn said. He looked fixedly at Deveraux. He seemed to be daring the lieutenants to continue this line of questioning. Lutz sat looking unhappily at his folded hands.

"Yes, sir, of course, but . . ."

"The DH-4 is nose-heavy," Edward cut in. "But the pilots here have been trained to fly them and they'll know how to compensate for it. I went up in them with British pilots at St-Omer many times. They are fine planes."

While he was speaking, he'd avoided looking at van Horn, but now he glanced over and the colonel looked, not pleased exactly, but less annoyed than Edward had yet seen him.

"Oh, well, of course, sir, we didn't mean to imply . . ."

"No, of course you didn't," Edward said.

"Well, if there are no other questions, you three are dismissed." The lieutenants stood, saluted and filed out, obviously grateful to be going. Van Horn watched them leave, then turned to Edward.

"That was not badly handled, Steichen," he said. "You restored their confidence."

"Thank you, sir."

Van Horn sat down in the chair behind his desk. He seemed about to say something, but instead he looked Edward over with narrowed, appraising eyes. At last he said: "I'm curious. What were the St-Omer pilots doing with the DH-4's? I've seen those damn things fall on their noses like rocks, back when I was flying. Not pretty."

"They sandbagged the tails," Edward said. "Made them murder to steer, but at least they could land."

"Sandbags?"

"The height of modern technology, sir."

Van Horn frowned. "Well, I don't know what these kids are complaining about. They come out here expecting it to be some kind of cakewalk, and then they are surprised when it is hard work." He looked across, again with his eyes narrowed. Edward wasn't sure if he was looking for agreement or disagreement; he sat, saying nothing.

Abruptly, van Horn stood up and rang the bell to call his secretary.

"Well, Captain, unless there are any other matters we need to discuss . . ."

"Actually, sir, there is one more thing." Van Horn folded his arms across his chest and waited for Edward to continue. "We have a boy who would like to join our section who is not officially enlisted." And he explained about Gilles Marchand, how he had followed them east, how he wanted to fly.

"It shows spirit," van Horn said, "following you out here. It shows initiative. You say he can work a camera?"

"He claims to be able to. And if he can't, he's no worse off than most of the others."

"Well, I'll consider it." There was a knock at the door and van Horn's secretary came in. Van Horn said: "My assistant will show you to an office you can use. My driver is at your disposal," and he presented the door to Edward as though it were a work of art. The interview was over.

Two Women. Île de La Cité, 1903. Pigment print.

SHE HAS NEVER seen him act like this before. He is restless and uneasy. Several times during dinner he jumps up from the table and paces the room for no reason. He's not really listening to a word anyone says; he just nods and looks away toward the dark squares of the windows.

She doesn't know what to make of it. Usually, he is so attentive to the people around him, to her. When Marion Beckett asks him about the exhibition in London, he changes the subject right away. Usually, he likes nothing more than to discuss his work, especially with Marion, who generally has insightful, useful things to say. Clara wonders if perhaps he is tired from his journey—he arrived home just this morning—but that would explain only the dark circles under his eyes, the fatigued way he leans his elbows on the table, not the agitation, this energy that seems to have no specific purpose. Even Arthur notices.

"What is wrong, Ed? All night you've been wriggling around like a fish on a hook."

"Nothing's wrong."

"I don't believe you. Miss Smith, what have you been doing to him? Or is this how all young men act when they're six months engaged?"

"I haven't been doing anything to him," Clara says. Typical of Arthur to be so appallingly crass. "You must remember, Mr. Carles, I've not seen him in a week. There must be some other girl who is driving him to distraction."

"Don't be ridiculous, darling," Edward says. He fishes in his jacket pocket for his cigarette case, then goes over to the open window and leans out of it. He lights a cigarette, flinging the match into the darkness below.

"I know," he announces so the whole room can hear. "Let's all walk down to the river and look at the cathedral. This is too nice of an evening to be cooped up indoors. Who's coming?"

"I'm in." Arthur stands up. Never short of enthusiasm, at least.

"Marvelous idea," says Leo Stein. "It's a sight worth seeing, on a clear night."

"Isn't it very spooky?" asks Clara.

"Not at all. It's magnificent."

There are murmured affirmatives from the rest of the group—Mildred, Marion, Lottie and a boy called Billy Paddock who is courting her.

"Good," says Edward. "Let's go."

Then there's a scramble for hats and jackets as they make their way into the hallway, down the stairs and out into the evening street. Edward comes last, a quietly triumphant grin on his face. He loves things like this, loves to be the one who directs the next scene, who decides where the players will stand. He's good at it—people follow his lead naturally. He takes Clara's arm, and she feels that flush of excitement that comes over her when he is around. They have known each other now for more than a year, and she still experiences that same dizzying sweetness when he touches her.

"Oh," he says, suddenly, "let me just run home and get my camera."

"Must you?" Clara asks. "Won't you walk with the rest of us?"

"It will only take me three minutes. I've wanted to shoot that place at night for ages."

"Well, I'll come with you, then. For the walk."

"Oh no, darling, there's no need. You go ahead. I'll meet you on the bridge." He is already several paces down the street, waving them to go on without him.

"What he means is that he really wants to take more pictures of his lovely fiancée," says Arthur.

"Well, in that case," she says, "I give him my blessing."

"Go on, Ed. I'll escort the lady." And he puts his arm through Clara's before she can say anything to object.

Edward nods and blows her a kiss, then runs off down the street without another word. She stares after him. He has never made that gesture before, and at the moment it seems to her like the combination of a cough and the motion one makes when swatting at a troublesome insect. She cannot shake the sense that there has been something evasive about his actions this evening. Something is wrong. And she is going to find out what it is.

She turns to Arthur with her sweetest and most engaging smile. "Shall we go?" she asks.

EDWARD WALKS TOWARD the river feeling buoyant, swinging his arms. His camera case hangs on a strap across his shoulders. It feels good to be outside at last, to be walking, to lose himself a little in the motion of his own limbs. The evening streets are crowded with people and noisy with the sounds of their talk and laughter. He makes his way along the Boulevard St-Michel, past the red awnings and open doors of restaurants that spill sharp electric light onto the pavement, through the dull orange flicker of the streetlamps where the shadows of strangers turn like clock hands and vanish. He is thinking about Kathleen.

He knows he should not be thinking about her, but he has told himself to stop a hundred times and none of his attempts have worked. So he has given up censuring his brain and instead he is floating quietly along on the memory of her hands, her soft mouth, the way she has of opening her eyes very wide when she wants to say something serious. She really does have wonderful hands: long articulate fingers, each knuckle a little rough and dry where the clay she uses for modeling has sucked out all the moisture. He inhales deeply and feels a precarious exhilaration. The street around him resonates in sympathy. This city, he thinks, is like magic, a trick of the light. You can drink it through your skin.

Does Clara suspect something? He dismisses this thought: Of course she doesn't. What is there for her to suspect? Almost nothing. He has hardly done anything wrong.

He met Kathleen Bruce last year when he was in London for an exhibition. She introduced herself and complimented him on some prints of the Brooklyn Bridge that he'd taken. It turned out she was an artist herself, a sculptress. They liked each other right away. Since then they have written letters back and forth, mostly about their work, a little about their lives outside it. When she came to visit Paris earlier in the summer, he showed her some of the sights. They dined together and attended the theater. She met Clara, and the two of them got along famously. After that they had continued to correspond, and when he learned he would be in London to exhibit again this year, he wrote and told her. She made arrangements to come down by train from Edinburgh, to stay with an aunt who owned a house in Kensington. This time, she wrote, I can be your guide.

But then there was that afternoon, just two days before he was due to return to Paris. They were walking in Hyde Park together, Kathleen's idea, intending to stroll over to Kensington Palace. They were alone. Edward was in a bad mood: his prints had sold badly and he believed it was because of where they had been hung—a rear corner of the exhibition hall, in bad light. Kathleen had sympathized, but she seemed distracted, sad for some reason she didn't explain, and the conversation had slowed, then stopped altogether. What's wrong? he asked her eventually. She didn't reply right away, just kept walking, looking away from him so he couldn't see the expression on her face. He took her wrist and pulled her around toward him. Her face was contorted, her mouth held in the rigid effort of a smile. You must be stupid to ask that, she said. Then: I'm sorry. Please excuse me. I don't know what I'm saying. She cleared her throat. Why don't you walk me home? I don't feel like seeing the palace today after all.

No, he said. He held on to her wrist. I don't want you to go home yet.

Oh, don't, she replied. She sounded tired. Playing the overwrought romantic doesn't suit you, Edward. I'm sure your fiancée would agree. Will you take me home, or do I have to go by myself?

Irritated he let go of her hand and they walked out of the park. They hailed a cab to take them the rest of the way. They sat in silence as the streets rolled by the open windows, and at the end of her aunt's road, Kathleen reached up and knocked on the ceiling. When the cab stopped, she held out her hand to him. Well, goodbye, she said, her voice wooden. He took her hand and instead of the perfunctory shake that she'd intended for it, he drew it up and kissed it slowly, one small knuckle after another. She pulled it away, a sharp, angry motion, and for a minute he thought she might smack him, but then she was kissing him and he forgot about everything else.

It is this kiss which pulls him into its whirlpool, drawing him down, so he tastes her mouth again, and feels her body rise against him in the shaded interior of the cab. He tries not to remember it. It was only once, after all, and afterward they had fallen away from each other, guilty, unable to speak. Kathleen had wiped her mouth with the back of her hand, slowly, still watching him as she did it, her eyes slitted narrow like a cat's.

"Edward!" Clara calls from the other side of the street. The sound of her voice breaks in on him, and he starts as though he has been discovered doing something illicit. There is the whole party waiting for him on the riverward side of the Quai Montebello. He waves and calls out: "Hello, darling!" then wonders if he sounds too falsely hearty. He crosses toward them. Clara comes and slides her arm though his, and they move off across the bridge. In the middle she stops to look down at the black water slipping away beneath them. "How I love rivers," she says, and cranes her neck down to peer into this one. "It's so dark, you can't see anything in its surface. Not even us."

Through the sleeve of his shirt he can feel her body pressed against his arm, and when he leans down to see what she sees, he smells the dark scent of her hair. He looks into the water where she is pointing, and she is right: there is nothing below them to show that they exist at all. But for the fact they can sense each other's life and warmth and solidity, they might easily be ghosts. He has an overwhelming feeling of tenderness, of wanting to protect her from the world, from the worst parts of himself. Surely this feeling is love, he thinks. This is what separates love from all those other transient desires that we lazily call by that name. And then, suddenly, he is terribly sorry for what he has done.

THE CATHEDRAL RISES into the darkness until it disappears, and at night the great rose window looks like an empty eye, the arched doors like open mouths. Gas lamps send a dim, wavering glow over the hunched figures of the patriarchs and saints that crowd the western face.

"Like bees," Marion says, and Clara thinks this is a good way to describe them.

"For years," Leo says, "there was no stained glass in the nave. Since the revolution, in fact. It's only recently that they've restored the windows to their original state."

"I don't care what you say," Clara says, "it is spooky."

They walk around to the side of the building. When they are a little way from the others, Clara says to Marion, "Edward seems out of sorts this evening, doesn't he?"

"Perhaps he is tired."

"Oh, no. I don't think it is only that. He seems so, well, absent. Like his head is somewhere else entirely. I don't know what's gotten into him."

Marion sighs. "I think I know what it might be," she says. "Something to do with his trip to London. I don't know whether or not I should tell you."

"Oh, you must!" says Clara.

"Are you sure? I could be wrong about this, you know. Wouldn't it be better to simply ask him yourself if there is anything the matter?"

"Men don't tell you things just because you ask them."

"Well, I would hope if you were marrying them, they might."

"Just tell me what you heard."

"All right." Marion draws her away along the side of the cathedral. They find one of the wooden park benches and sit down on it. They are almost fully immersed in shadow so they can hardly see each other's faces.

"Something unexpected happened while he was in England. Mildred told me this. At the exhibition."

"Well?"

"The photographs that he took to the show. They didn't sell—or not very many of them. Mildred said it was a great disappointment for him, all told. He thinks they were put away in a corner where people couldn't see them. He was quite angry—apparently he argued with Fred Holland Day about it; I don't think that they parted on good terms."

"Oh, the poor thing!" Clara cries. "Why didn't he tell me?"

"Well, perhaps he didn't want to burden you with it. Think about it. He is getting married to you next year. He wants to be certain he can provide for his wife. He doesn't have family wealth to fall back on like some of us, so he must earn money. He doesn't want you to start to doubt him now."

"But if I'm going to be his wife, he needs to tell me things like this. I have to help him through difficulties, support him—that is what wives are for!"

"Listen, I'm not certain about any of this," Marion says. "It is all hearsay. I'm not sure that is what is really troubling him, or that he didn't intend to tell you eventually."

"No, I'm quite sure you are right," Clara says. "It is the only reasonable explanation."

"Please, don't be hasty, Clara. Think before you say anything to him."

"Of course. I must draw him out on it. He must learn to trust me." She jumps to her feet and grabs Marion's hand. Almost at a run, she pulls her back toward the western end of the building where the others are, pausing only to kiss her on the cheek and whisper, "Thank you. You are such a good, wise friend."

That must be it, Clara thinks. He is disappointed. His work was received badly, and he doesn't want to admit it. He is a man who has had a great deal of acclaim almost from the very beginning of his career, and he is not accustomed to dealing with failure. He isn't even used to being disappointed. But she can help him learn to do this—every artist will have good and bad times, and surely it is the love and support of their wives that gets them through the difficulties. Look at Rodin and Rose Beuret. Look at Amélie and Henri Matisse. Yes, helping him to accept this setback in London and move on from it will bring them closer than mere romance. It will be her first real act as his wife. As she walks toward where he is setting up his photographic equipment, she feels as though an entirely new chapter of her life is beginning.

HE SETS HIS tripod across from the western façade while the others wander around the immense perimeter of the cathedral. He can see them as vague shadows in couples and threes, their individual figures nearly indistinguishable. If he peers closer, he can see Leo's pointed beard and spectacles, and Mildred's slightly stooped form beside him. He can see Arthur pointing up at the flying buttresses and gremlins on one corner. He isn't sure if there will be enough light to capture this scene, but he will try with a flashbulb. He puts his eye to the viewfinder, and through it he sees one of the figures separate from the darkness at the side of the building, no, two figures, walking quickly and close together, one pulling the other along by the hand. Marion and Clara, though in this darkness and distance he cannot tell which is which. One woman stops near the main door to the nave, and the other continues to come toward him. As she gets closer, he sees that it is Clara.

"Stop right there," he calls. "I wonder if I can get you and the cathedral together. Will you look out toward the river for me?"

She obliges by turning away from him. "Is this right?"

"Yes," he says. "Perfect. Just let me get the flashbulb set up. Don't move."

He loves night photography because it can suggest forms without having to show them in stark detail. At night the world softens, its distinctions blend, its objects bleed into each other. Their imperfections are hidden; they can tell a larger story than they could if they were photographed straight; they can keep their mystery. It is a process that he can enhance later with his brushes when he prints the exposures, altering them to make the forms less individuated and distinct. In this way photography can ascend toward the level of painting as a means of creating beauty; it can become more fully an art.

He will open up the camera and let as much light in as possible. The cathedral will not go anywhere, so he can afford to extend the exposure time. If Clara will just stay right where she is . . . there. He can just fit Marion's silhouette into the frame, where she stands some twenty feet further away, gazing up at the balustrades. Two women, and the moon just risen in the black face of the river.

"Hold still," he says to Clara. The flash goes off and he takes the picture, but with night photography it's hard to be certain it will come out. He wants to make sure he captures this scene. "Just one more," he says.

"Darling . . ." Clara says quietly.

"Yes, my dear?"

"I don't mean to bother you, but is everything quite all right? I mean did everything go well in England this time?"

He stops adjusting the camera and stands up straight so he can see her with his own eyes.

"Yes. Fine," he says. "Why?" His heart jumps in his chest. His palms feel suddenly damp. She knows. She must know. Otherwise, why these questions? But she doesn't seem angry or upset. In fact, if he looks at her, she seems almost to be glowing, her eyes shining and calm.

"You seem a little out of temper. That's all. I just wanted you to know that if anything happened, that was, well, *unexpected* or even *bad*, that you can tell me about it. I won't be upset or doubt you—if I'm going to be your wife, my purpose is to help you. Through whatever happens. No matter what it is."

He stares at her. He is speechless.

"I'm sorry," she says. "You seemed upset so I asked people about it. I know you had an *incident* with a certain acquaintance there. Forgive me for going behind your back about it."

Does he know this woman, standing not ten feet from him, whom he has courted and loved for nearly a year now? Did he have any idea of the depth of her generosity, her greatness of spirit? He would never have predicted this from her. If anything, though he loves her, desires her, he has felt, at times, a certain parochial rigidity to her opinions and ideas; he has suspected her of not really being very freethinking after all. How has he misjudged her so thoroughly? This is more extraordinary than he could even have supposed. She does know about Kathleen, and she has chosen to rise above it, to recognize it for the folly that it was. In his surprise he forgets to wonder who knew and who has told her. He goes to her and kneels down and puts his arms around her hips, and buries his head in her skirt.

"My love . . ." he says. "Do you really mean it?"

"Of course I do," she says serenely. "Every word."

"I wanted to tell you. As soon as I saw you, I wanted to tell you about her, but I was afraid of what you would say."

He looks up in time to see the smile freeze on her face as she takes in his words. Something, he realizes, has gone terribly wrong.

"Her?" she asks.

—

THEY LEAVE AS quickly as they can.

"Miss Smith is feeling fatigued," Edward tells the others. "I'm going to see her back to her rooms."

"Yes, it just came over me all of a sudden," Clara puts in, the recklessly strained attempt at a smile stretched across her face. "Thank you for a lovely evening, Mr. Stein." Her voice comes out in squeaky bursts. Not noticing this, Leo waves easily to them, and goes back to discussing the architecture with Arthur.

"Clara, are you sure you are quite all right?" Marion comes running toward them.

"Yes, yes. I'm fine." Clara backs away from her, trying to conceal that she is on the verge of tears.

"Well, if you are sure you'll be fine . . ." Marion says.

"Quite fine," Clara says. "Good night!"

They walk quickly, in silence across the bridge. When they reach the other side Clara says, "I'm perfectly able to see myself home from here."

"Clara, I'm not going to leave you in the middle of the city at night on your own. Let me get a cab."

"Thank you, but I can get one for myself." She begins to walk away down the street.

"Stop!" He strides after her, reaches out and grabs her by the shoulder. He holds her there, his hand fastened around her upper arm. She pulls against him, but he doesn't let go. He is surprised by his own reaction. He had not intended to reach out for her when he did, or to prevent her going by force. He does not know where the fierce energy comes from that now flows through his arms and says that she must not, cannot, leave him.

"Please, Clara," he says. "Stay here. Just let me find a taxi." She nods, slowly, assenting, and he charges off down the street hailing every wheeled vehicle in sight.

Eventually, he finds one and helps her inside, then climbs up himself. He gives the driver the address of the hotel where she is staying and sinks back into the seat. She sits at the other end of the bench, as far away from him as she can get, looking out of the window with her face turned away. He feels he must say something. He must say it now. But he cannot think of what it should be.

"Clara, it was a mistake," he says. She doesn't even acknowledge that he is speaking. All he can see are her contours, cheekbones and neck in amber relief. Too soon they are at the hotel where she and Charlotte have taken rooms for the summer. The cab halts in front. She stands up and he climbs down to help her from the carriage, but she pushes his hand away. He stands aside and lets her past, then pays the driver and waves him on. They stand facing each other at the foot of the front steps of the hotel.

"I'd think it only courteous if you take steps to avoid our meeting socially, while I make arrangements to return to New York," Clara says.

"What? You can't be serious."

"It is the least you can do."

"Don't you think you are overreacting to this just a little?" Clara doesn't reply. "I mean," he goes on, "can't we at least discuss . . ."

"Discuss what?" she asks. "I don't feel inclined to discuss anything at all with you, Mr. Steichen. Unless you would care to manhandle me again as you did before," and she holds out her arm to him, crooked, elbow foremost. Her eyes on him are sharp, illuminated. "No?" she asks. "Well, then." She searches in her pocketbook and withdraws her key, then abruptly turns away, hurries up the stone steps and disappears inside the building.

He stands looking after her. The street is quiet. He can't imagine trying to sleep right now. His body and brain are still alight, so that the events of the past half hour don't seem completely real. He can't stop picturing the way she looked at him as she held out her arm, goading him, daring him to lay hold of it and reveal how far his anger would go. How could he sleep after that? Perhaps he can just wander through the city until he is so tired that he can slip into unconsciousness untroubled. Perhaps he should find a place to get a drink.

As he begins to walk down the street, he sees something on the pavement almost directly under his feet. He stoops down to look at it more closely. It is a single woman's glove. When he picks it up and holds it to the light, he recognizes it. It is Clara's. She must have dropped it as she searched for her keys, though how she couldn't have noticed it falling—something that big—is beyond him.

He thinks that he had better take it back to her. If she was indeed serious and intends to depart for New York and, he supposes, to break off their engagement, she will miss this when she is packing. And if her words were only a threat . . . well, she'll still miss it. He should still return it to her. Shouldn't he? He decides to walk around the block, calm down and then go after her. Holding the empty fingers of the glove in his hand, he sets off down the street.

THE LADY CONCIERGE is insistent, however.

"No gentlemen visitors in the hotel. What time of night do you call this anyway?" she says.

"But the young lady dropped her glove. I am only returning it. Can someone go up and knock on her door and tell her that I have it?"

"At this hour?"

"Please, madame." He has run out of arguments. "Please."

"Well," she says, her voice like a door creaking open, "I suppose gloves are an important item in a lady's reticule."

"Yes," he agrees.

"Especially in high summer."

"Definitely."

"I'll send the maid up to see if . . ."

"Miss Smith."

"To see if Miss Smith is still awake. Wait here please."

She rings and a girl comes from beneath stairs and is given Clara's room number. He waits, while the concierge eyes him from behind the desk, amused. Running a ladies' hotel, it must be one of the consolations of her job to see young men in his distraught state on a fairly regular basis. Fortunately, it is only a few minutes before Clara comes downstairs, taking each step one at a time, watching him as she descends. From her eyes, he can see that she has been crying, but otherwise she is still dressed as she was when she left him. He is struck with the conviction that she dropped the glove on purpose, intending for him to find it. She has been waiting up for him to come and return it to her. Her reaction was, at least in part, an elaborate performance, her idea of how a wronged woman ought to behave. It seems absurd, but he is nonetheless convinced that this is the case. When she reaches the foot of the staircase, she holds out her hand to him solemnly. He takes it and feels again energy, anger, desire for her inextricably entangled.

"May we sit in the front parlor?" Clara asks the concierge.

"He said he wanted to return your glove."

"Only for a few minutes." The woman nods resentfully and ushers them through into a small sitting room.

"I'll be just out here should you need anything," she says, looking meaningfully at Edward. Then she goes out, drawing the door closed behind her.

—

WHILE WAITING FOR him to come, she has been making rules in her head. She can accept it, as long as it was only a single occurrence, not an ongoing affair. And as long as no one else knows about it. And as long as he is genuinely contrite. As long as he agrees not to see this other woman, whoever she is, ever again.

When the door closes behind that fussy, officious concierge woman and they are alone together, he takes both of her hands in his.

"Please," he says. "Let me explain. Hear me out."

As long as he never does anything like this again. People, men especially, make mistakes like this out of momentary fancy and make amends for them. And women put up with a lot worse than a man who strays a little once. Rose Beuret, for example; everybody knows the infidelities she suffers; and with women who she must then see when she goes into society. That would be unbearable, Clara thinks, and though she admires Rose for her steadfastness, it is not what any woman would wish for herself.

As long as she is never brought to their house as a guest or as a friend. As long as whatever he did is hidden, far away, separate from their life together. As long as this is not an omen for the future, she can take him back with her dignity intact. Here he is, standing before her, his face full of pain and concern, and she loves him so much that she is actually quite certain that taking her hand out of his right now and walking away would feel something like dying.

"All right," she says. "Tell me."

FIVE

June 12, 1918

AFTER HIS DISCUSSION with van Horn, Edward set to work right away, scavenging. The British could spare a few cameras and the French could give them developer, fixer, and plates. Next week, if nothing else went wrong, their equipment would arrive from the States. Until then they would have to make do. They could send up some planes, take some images. It was better than nothing.

Edward could collect the emergency supplies from the depot at Châlons in two days' time. His plan was to take a car there the following evening, stay overnight and return with the supplies when they arrived the next day. In the meantime, he set the men to work building the developing lab and setting up equipment for the interpreters.

The war took over objects, turned them to its own purposes.

Where before a hill was just a hill, now it became a problem, a weapon or a threat, depending on where you stood. A flat field became a landing place for airplanes. A wood became cover during a retreat. The things of the world weren't innocent anymore.

This airfield, for example, had been improvised out of the farm that had stood on this spot before; first the officers' quarters, lounge and mess were installed in the old stone house, then the pavilion with the airfield offices and the barracks for the men was hastily constructed behind it. The huge canvas hangars that stood to the left side of the field when you faced the pavilion had followed. And now they were starting work on the lab in a building a short distance from the airfield that used to store grain and winter feed, a heavy, stone-walled barn with a corrugated tin roof. In the corners of its two large rooms, they found slippery traces of wheat stamped into the hard earth floor.

They cleaned, built dry walls for a darkroom on one side, hung lines where the prints could dry. They stationed a mobile acetylene generator outside to give them electricity and light. They carried lumber in from the storerooms, and built long wooden workbenches and a tilted central table to display a photo mosaic of the surrounding region. On the benches they set up the machines that the French had left behind when they ceded this airstrip to the Americans: stereoscopic *explorateurs*, which Deveraux said looked like the viewers at dime museums; they would show two images laid one on top of the other so they appeared three-dimensional. Then stereoscopic printers, which printed two images onto the same sheet of paper.

"Why do we use stereoscopic images for reconnaissance?" Edward asked the interpreters, trying to compensate a little for the training they should already have had. "If you lay two images on top of each other, you get depth. Look at this print." They all gathered around where he laid it out on the table for them. "See the shadow in the side of this trench here? In a single image, all we'd see would be a slight discoloration in the ground, but if we use double images, we can see that it has height, bulk. It's artillery, camouflaged so we can't detect it from the air. How big is it? If we know that, we can guess what kind of gun it is, its range, how many men it takes to fire it. If you know the altitude from which a picture was taken, you can judge the scale of what it shows you.

"You have to learn to see the meaning in these lines," he told them. "You have to use the distances you know to measure the ones you don't."

WHEN THEY FINISHED work for the day, Edward went to sit in the officers' lounge and read the day's papers. He was just about to turn in for the evening when he heard someone begin playing the piano and then, singing, a rich, pleasant baritone voice. When he looked, he was surprised to see Lutz standing behind the pianist reading lyrics over his shoulder. He didn't know the song: it was a fox-trot, something popular and romantic.

After the song was finished, he went over to them.

"You have quite a voice," he said. Lutz bowed, his square head bobbing shyly. "Wherever did you learn how to sing like that?"

"In Iowa, sir," Lutz replied.

"Care to be a little more specific?"

"Des Moines, Iowa." Lutz looked at him, his face earnestly innocent. "Actually, you know, I was thinking to myself just the other day how much Paris resembles Des Moines. I feel like I've hardly left home."

"Really?" Edward said, incredulous. He saw Lutz's face crinkle into a grin. "Lieutenant, I think there is a rule on the books someplace against humor at the expense of a superior officer. Now, seriously, tell me: have you ever sung Mozart?"

"I know *The Magic Flute.*"

"What about *The Marriage of Figaro?*"

"Some of the parts."

"I like Mozart's operas, and I haven't heard any of them sung since . . . well, in several years. Anyway, if you can remember any of it, another night, it would be good to hear *Figaro.* And then maybe I won't book you for disrespect. Good night, Lutz. Get some rest: we'll be at work again early tomorrow."

"I will. Good night, sir."

THE OFFICERS' MESS at lunchtime the next day was full of pilots eating, drinking coffee and smoking, back from their morning flights. Edward got himself coffee and a plate of food and sat down at one of the long tables with Lutz and Dawson. They had been up early and had neglected breakfast, so none of them felt talkative. They concentrated on eating, no sound but their knives clicking on the tin plates.

"So what unit are you fellows in? Whatever it is, you should tell old van Horn to quit starving you. I've never seen anyone scrutinize their potatoes so intently." Edward looked up and saw that the speaker was a man in a pilot's leather coat, seated a little way down the table from them.

"Photo," said Lutz, his mouth still full. "Observation. You?"

"Well, well. Our squad's been assigned to fly with you starting from . . . when is it?"

"It was supposed to be today," said his companion.

"Yeah, there was some problem, wasn't there? And now we are kicking around with nothing to do."

"Sorry about that. We arrived without the equipment we were supposed to have," Edward said. "No cameras, ergo no photographs."

"Having no cameras is definitely a hitch." The first pilot to speak wiped his fingers on a handkerchief and offered his hand. "Tom Cundall," he said. Introductions were made. The other man, the quieter and older of the two, was called McIntyre. He was the captain of the squadron that would be doing the flying for the observers.

"Where were you stationed before this?" he asked Edward.

"At St-Omer, for training; this is my first command."

"I was at the St-Omer airfield for a while a couple of months back. Who did you fly with?"

"Man called Knightly."

"Yes, I knew him. A good pilot." He took a swallow of coffee. "So can you tell us when we are likely to start making reconnaissance flights?"

"Well," said Edward. "I'm driving up to Châlons-sur-Marne this afternoon to get some substitute equipment that I begged, borrowed and stole. We should be able to send some planes up in two days. At least that is what I told Colonel van Horn, and frankly I wouldn't want to have to revise that estimate back even an hour. He doesn't strike me as a man who'd take that very well."

"Yep. He breathes fire." McIntyre chuckled. "You better hope that you don't get held up on your way to Châlons. Roads can get difficult this close to the line. One day they are there and the next, boom, a big hole instead. Say, have you seen this part of the front from the air?"

"No, I haven't. Not yet."

"Want to go up this afternoon? I have to go out on an evening patrol, but Cundall here could take you up to have a look around, and land you over at Châlons later tonight. Couldn't you?"

Cundall nodded. "No low flying or anything like that. Just to give you the lay of the land."

"You wouldn't mind?" Edward asked.

"Not at all."

Edward thought about it for a minute, then said: "OK. Can I request a particular route? There is one town, quite near here, that I'd like to see from above. If I show you on a map, could you take me over?"

Cundall nodded. "If it isn't too out of the way, certainly. Let's finish our coffee and then we'll get moving."

THEY ASCENDED INTO a day filled with fat, ghostly cumulus clouds, a landscape of fantastic ridges and canyons. Cundall wove among them, climbing to skim their surfaces, or crashing through them so the soundless impact left the small plane and the two men inside it sailing through white, their own wings vanishing above them. Then he would dive down, and when they emerged, Edward could see the dense green world below, clear to the horizon.

In the distance lay the bright mirror of the Marne, and the rise beyond it, the Chemin des Dames Ridge, and beyond that German territory, the Ourcq River cutting through it, forded by wooden pontoon bridges in several places. Soon, Edward could see the whole line of the front, the bare earth and broken trees, receding layers of trenches, supply lines leading up to them, stopping dead.

Cundall turned west and flew parallel with the front for a while, from Épernay along past Crécy-en-Brie and on in the direction of Paris. From here the trenches looked nearly empty, and so did the roads. In the middle of the day the men stayed hidden. But there were signs that ammunition and troops had been gathering at the front: tenders and guns that hadn't yet been properly camouflaged. They were preparing for something over there.

They saw some British planes nearby, squadrons of Camels flying in formation, and occasionally another two-seater like Cundall's DH-4. Once, in the middle distance, an Albatros appeared. Cundall pointed to it, a dark X against the white of the clouds. It slipped into a cloud bank and for a few minutes Edward was sure that it would appear suddenly beside them, or under them like a shadow.

"Will it come after us?" he shouted to Cundall.

"Not likely. The Huns are outnumbered up here, so they don't attack if they're alone, even a big old slow two-seater like this one. Although on a day like this, he could sneak up. We should keep our eyes open. Listen for his engine."

Edward thought, Yes: among these clouds, airplanes could appear and vanish like spirits. It was a landscape with no fixed coordinates, with nothing permanent to steer by, nothing solid; to survive, it would be necessary to get good at disappearing.

Cundall swung the plane around and headed away from the front. They descended until at last they were only 1,000 feet above the ground, and the roads and fields and houses grew back toward their normal size. Now Edward could tell the features of the landscape apart from one another, and he began to recognize where he was. Here, below them, were the farms outside of Huiry, the village where Mildred had lived, and there was the little town itself, its small main square, the church and the *mairie* opposite. Then it was gone, and they were flying over farmland again. Pastures full of cattle ran from the noise as the plane passed above them; horses turned uncomprehending faces upward. A road, sand-colored, cut through the fields and wound along the edge of the valley. The shadow of the airplane slid across the ground, stretching and shrinking with its contours. At this height, the sense of speed that had been lost in the vastness of the clouds returned, and the earth slipped underneath them in a blur. They were flying parallel to the road as it mounted the hill, racing up the escarpment toward a small outcropping of trees, horse chestnuts and lindens and there, there, he could see it rushing toward them, there it was: his house, the house he had come up this same rise and seen, its gate hung with the sign Á LOUER so many years before.

There it was, below him now, and the garden behind it and the crab-apple trees he had planted that second summer, now so tall their upper boughs hung over the walls. He could see the tiny kitchen yard where the children played hide-and-seek, where Clara and their maid, Louisa, hung the laundry, where in autumn he stacked cords of wood. Once, when he was carrying the logs inside, a splinter had slipped into his hand, and he ran cursing into the kitchen until his wife had made him sit down as though he were a child and pulled it out of his forefinger, and then poured methylated spirits on the bloom of blood beneath the nail. He could see the window which had been his bedroom, the windowsill where Clara always put the blue and white vase for flowers, and above, on the third floor, the window of the room his daughters had shared.

On the side of the house that he couldn't see was his study, where he'd stored his photographs and negatives when the family had left in 1914. In there, all these small, insignificant, marvelous things from the past were preserved, his memories were made into objects, stacked one on another, filed, locked away to prevent the light from fading them. He wanted to shout to Cundall to land the plane, please, just for a minute or two, let him go down there and drink it in, remember it, because right now he could hardly believe that he used to have a life consisting of such wonderful, ordinary things.

But as he opened his mouth, the house slid under their wings and away behind them, and soon they were over the town and then out above the open country. And though he craned his neck around to see, he couldn't catch sight of it again.

WHEN THEY LANDED just outside Châlons, it was almost evening and Edward went straight to the depot to see if the supplies had come in yet. The cameras (thank God) were there. He examined them and they seemed to be in working order. The plates and paper were scheduled to arrive early the next morning; he could take a truck from the depot back to Épernay then, and he could have a bed—Cundall, too—for the night in Châlons.

"Will you go back then or stay?" Edward asked Cundall.

"I think I can stay until tomorrow; they don't need me. Right now it's a lot of hurry up and wait for you fellows. I'll fly back when you leave in the morning."

"Good; it will be nice to have the company."

"Yes; a change of scene is always welcome. And Châlons is just big enough to have one important advantage over Épernay."

"Which is?"

"Girls. Beautiful, young, French . . . and old Madame Breillat has a personal fondness for aviators."

"You seem pretty familiar with the institution in question."

"Let's get some supper. I know this lovely little restaurant in town. Then we'll have a drink and then . . ."

"Oh, I think I'll have to excuse myself from this one."

"What for?"

"Just . . ."

"Come now. Even married men can't be expected to endure for so long away from the comforts of home."

"No, really. I'm not being noble. It just doesn't appeal to me."

"You'll change your mind. I'll convince you."

They walked into town as the sun dropped toward the horizon, their boots clacking on the road, the quiet intermittently broken by the approach of a motorcar, or the far-off boom of the guns. Cundall talked about flying, about the adventures he'd had in his short time at the front. He swung his long arms at his sides as he walked; Edward liked him, his easy manner, his good spirits and carelessness. But he knew already that he would not be convinced to go with him to the girls. Perhaps he couldn't, especially at this point in his life, have explained what he wanted from women. He only knew that was not it.

So they dined, and then over a whisky Cundall put the case in favor of whores very convincingly and earnestly, and then they parted ways outside the café and Edward went back to the lodgings that the major in charge of the depot had arranged for them, and Cundall went off to Madame Breillat's, shouting to him as he went that he was a prude and puritan and that he was denying honest women a living, until he was out of earshot and then he waved and loped off down the street.

LATE THAT NIGHT, Edward was woken by the sound of footsteps and shouting outside his room. He climbed out of bed and felt his way to the door. Outside in the corridor, he saw men running, pulling on overshirts and jackets as they went.

"What happened?" he asked, his eyes still unfocused with sleep.

"The hospital's been shelled," someone called as they rushed past. He lit a lamp, struggled into his clothes, and made his way down the stairs as quickly as he could. From the supply depot a stream of men were moving down toward town, their progress lit by hovering lamps and the headlights of tenders and cars that roared by them on the road. He fell in with the others, following the road through the houses to the outskirts of Châlons, where the hospital had been set up in an abandoned school. As he approached the main building, he saw what looked like streamers or long white fingers hanging from the trees. He blinked and stared, but he couldn't make out what they really were; he was still half-asleep and they seemed like part of an unfinished dream. He shook his head to wake himself more fully and kept walking.

Outside the front doors one of the doctors was giving instructions. The shell had hit a storeroom at one end of the building, he said, causing a wall and part of the roof to collapse. The electricity had gone out, too. The patients were being moved from that end of the building to temporary shelters on the old sports field. Some of the men could help put up tents, some could carry patients out of the damaged wing, those that could be moved. Those who could not be moved would have to stay and take their chances.

Inside, the front entrance was dimly lit, and the air smelled of burning. Edward followed the doctor down the hallway to a ward where men were being taken from beds and put onto stretchers. One near him cried out in pain as he was lifted, two orderlies moving his body from the bed to the stretcher waiting on the floor. The long high-ceilinged room magnified his shouting. The orderlies set him down gently, and a nurse who'd been standing beside them knelt and passed a hand quickly across the man's forehead. She beckoned Edward toward her.

"Take his head," she said. "Be as gentle as you can, but move him quickly." Another volunteer took the man's feet. They counted three and lifted the stretcher to their waists. Then they set off down the ward out of the doors and around the building to where the tents were being set up.

"Over here," one of the nurses shouted, and pointed them toward an empty space on the ground. They lowered the man down and again he shouted in pain. In the darkness, they had no way to tell where he had been wounded, no way to even see his face clearly. They put him onto the ground and left him. They went back to the hospital.

For hours Edward ferried wounded men out of the building and up to the tents. The man who'd helped him move that first stretcher fell into a rhythm with him and they worked steadily, never speaking but lifting, carrying, placing down in tandem, then returning together for the next one. He lost count of how many times he made the journey. Some of the men cried out in pain, or asked for a loved one by name again and again. Some let themselves be lifted without stirring and then lay silently on the ground, their open eyes shining in the dim light. Others stayed dreaming through it all, their nerves hollowed out by morphine. Occasionally, these men shouted in answer to the cries of others, half-articulated words in an alien language; but they were calling back from the other side of a veil that saved them from their own flesh. They didn't understand what was happening to them; it must be better that way, he thought. He picked each one up as gently as he could, hypnotizing himself with the task so that he could ignore the dark blood on their clothing and sheets where the dressings came away, the bandages around their bodies and heads, the hoarse struggle of their breathing, the heavy, almost sweet smell of decay that hung over everything. At last, near dawn, they'd emptied nearly the entire wing.

Toward the collapsed end of the building were a couple of small rooms that hadn't yet been cleared. Edward made his way down the corridor toward them; the fire in the storeroom had been put out, but the smoke from it still simmered in the interior air. He looked in through the glass pane in a door to his left; the beds in the room were full. He pushed open the door and went in, scanning the room for a nurse or a doctor, someone to tell him what to do. All the beds had been pushed up to the opposite end of the room away from the damaged part of the building. A nurse sat by one of them, a lamp burning near her. She was holding the hand of the man who lay in it, his top half propped up on pillows, his mouth working in a ceaseless murmur. The words drooled away down his chin, whispers, too vague to be heard. Edward approached the woman by the bed.

"Do you need help to move these patients?"

"No," she said. "These ones should stay where they are." She turned around, quickly, and peered at him. He heard her draw a sharp breath, saw her raise a hand to cover her mouth: she had recognized him a moment before he knew who she was, because the darkness disguised her features. Then she stood up, and he could see her more clearly in the light from the bedside lamp.

"They won't make it if we move them," she said quietly so that none of the men sleeping fitfully around them could hear. It was Marion Beckett.

For a minute they stood looking at each other without speaking.

"What are you doing here?" he asked at last. "I thought you were in Arras."

"I was reassigned." She watched him steadily, her eyes pools of black, their pupils swollen in the dim light until the irises were blotted out. "I guess it must have been a few weeks after I sent that letter to you," she went on. "I asked to come here because I knew the region from before the war. What are *you* doing here?"

"I'm stationed at Épernay. I just arrived, a couple of days ago."

There was the sound of movement in the hall outside, and the door opened. Two men looked in.

"Do you need any help?" one of them asked.

"No," Marion said, looking past Edward to the face in the doorway. "But there may be some left in the ward across the hall. You had better go and see about them."

"Will do," said the man. He went out, and the door swung shut behind him. Marion opened her mouth to speak, but the man in the bed beside her groaned and she turned back to him. She began to clean his arm inside the elbow, to tie off above it with a thin band of rubber. Her movements were quick and businesslike. Edward stood at the end of the bed, watching her as she took an ampoule of clear brownish liquid from the tray beside the bed, rolled it between her palms and snapped the glass seal. She took a syringe, drew off the morphine ready to inject it.

"Look," Edward said. "Are you all right? I mean, have you heard any more about the court case?" His words sounded strange and out of place. They came from another world where people had time for frivolities like the law. Marion didn't turn around.

"I have to finish this." She spoke without pausing from what she was doing. Gently, she pushed the needle in and held it steady, pressing the drug into the man's veins, letting it slide away into his blood.

She glanced over at Edward, at the fact that he was still standing in the middle of the room. She said: "I haven't had any more news. The action is suspended until I finish my service here; it will go ahead when I go home. I've decided to stay until my tour of duty is done. Beyond that, I don't know." She finished the injection, withdrew the needle and swabbed the man's arm with cotton. She took a fresh piece, leaned across to wipe his chin.

"If Clara goes through with this," Edward went on. "I will do anything I can to help you defend yourself. I'll testify, if it comes to that." Marion hesitated for a moment before answering him.

"Thank you," she said. "I am very grateful." She looked up at him, just for a second, with an expression that was an apologetic half a smile, a quizzical tilt of her eyes toward him. It was instantly familiar, and it brought a flood of memories rushing to the surface of his mind. Their return was like blood coming back into frozen hands. He felt the sting. He felt that he had been waiting to see that very look on her face and experience the rush of warmth that it caused in him for four years. He couldn't believe that in this place and after all the time that had passed it could affect him so much.

She crossed to the next bed and laid her palm across the patient's forehead, her back to him again. She took a thermometer, put it into the man's mouth. Edward stood rooted to the spot, watching her, wanting to find some reason not to leave yet. It was too little, these few words, and he tried to think of something to say to make this moment seem less like a dream.

"I . . ." he began. "I would like to see you, somewhere else, not here. How can I reach you?"

"I think you shouldn't try. I'm sorry. If we are seen together, even if we write letters, that makes things more difficult for me."

"It's ridiculous."

"Yes. It is. Please," she said. "You'd better go. There isn't anything you can do here."

Edward went out silently, closing the door behind him. In the hallway, he was surprised to find that he could see without a lamp. A cold blue light fell through the windows, illuminating the length of the corridor. It was almost dawn. He could hear his footsteps echo down the nearly empty wards.

Outside he found Cundall and some of the other officers from the depot collapsed on the front steps: they were waiting for a spare tender to drive them back to their billets.

"I met someone in there. One of the nurses," Edward said. Cundall looked at him, his eyes rimmed red.

"Lucky you," he said. "Aways nice to meet nurses."

"No, I knew her already. She was . . . a friend of my wife."

But he saw that Cundall was not really listening to him; he was too tired. The men sat or lay down, draped across the stone steps, not speaking. Edward found a space among them and slid to the ground with his back propped up against a wall. Exhaustion made his vision waver and the sunlight seemed too bright; it hurt his eyes. He put his head back and stared up at the sky, thinking of Marion, how she had looked in the darkened ward, how she had turned her back on him as though she was trying to pretend he wasn't there.

Eventually, a truck came and they piled into the back. As they drove out of the grounds, Edward looked over and saw that he had been right the previous night: the trees next to the building were full of white streamers. He had not imagined it. There they were, flowing and rippling in the morning breeze.

"What are those?" he said to Cundall pointing.

"Bandages," Cundall said. "I asked the doc in charge here and he told me that the shell hit a storeroom—all the bandages for the whole hospital were in it. I guess the explosion hurled them all up into the trees. Looks kind of festive, doesn't it?"

Edward watched them until they were out of sight.

Rodin and Isadora Duncan at the Villa des Brillants.
Meudon, 1905. Platinum print.

THE GATE HAS been left open. When Edward arrives, he finds it ajar, swinging unevenly, black and skeletal. It is a gray day, and an unsteady wind sends clouds down toward the city in the distance. Inside the fence, the house and garden are quiet. He can hear the sound of the gate whining as the wind pushes it back and forth on its hinges. How odd, he thinks. Rose is usually so careful about keeping it locked. He pulls the cord and hears the doorbell clang inside the house, but there is no response. "Hello," he shouts. "Anybody there?" No one comes. He checks his watch. It is ten minutes before two—he's only a little early; they should be expecting him. He hesitates, then slips inside.

At the door of the house, he stops and knocks and calls again. Still no reply, and there is no sign of life from inside, no movement at any of the casements. Rodin, he thinks, must be in his studio where he can't hear the bell. But that is OK: he can go in by the back door and find his friend there. He knows the older man well enough now to be that familiar. He begins to make his way along the path that leads around toward the pale bulk of Rodin's studio looming up behind, nearly as big as the house itself.

He is passing the greenhouse that leans against the western wall when he hears a voice. He stops and listens. After a minute he hears it again, a little different this time, not words but still articulate and varied, a sound somewhere between laughter and growling. It comes in short, erratic bursts as though someone is trying to stop it escaping. He has never heard anyone make a sound like that before.

He pushes open the door to the greenhouse and there she is, sitting on an upturned stack of terra-cotta plant holders. She starts when she sees him and immediately begins searching around herself with her hands, looking by touch for something that she has lost. Her eyes are red, her face run with water.

"Rose, dear, what on earth is the matter?" He comes to kneel down beside her and offers her the handkerchief from his breast pocket. She pushes his hand away.

"Nothing," she says. "Nothing is wrong."

"Are you certain?"

"Yes, yes, really." She wipes her cheeks with her fingers rapidly. "I'm so sorry to worry you. I picked up this dreadful summer cold. It's making my eyes run terribly. I came in here to water these things, and I felt so light-headed I had to sit down for a second." She indicates the table beside her, which is covered in the wiry stalks of tomato plants, marjoram and basil. She continues to feel around her on the floor, and finally she finds what she was seeking: a watering can, set down a few feet away from her.

"I found the gate open," Edward says. He thinks how the noises he heard from the path outside did not sound like a summer cold.

"Oh, did I leave it like that? How silly of me. How forgetful. I don't know where my head is. Oh, dear, let me finish these last couple of rows and then I'll go and tell Monsieur that you are here." She smiles at him and picks up the watering can. When she tilts its spout, the water vanishes into the black soil at the throat of each plant.

"Is he in his studio?" Edward asks, watching her make her way down the table. She nods.

"He has a visitor, a young woman. She's a dancer, quite well known. Her name is Isadora."

"Duncan? Isadora Duncan? She's marvelous. I saw her perform in London last year. I'd love to meet her. Amazing, one really feels that she has liberated the body from the constrictions of convention . . ."

"Well, she's here to see Monsieur's studio," Rose says, continuing her watering.

"You know what? I can show myself in. I'm expected, and that way you won't have to bother. Especially if you are feeling unwell."

"Oh no," Rose says, "I don't think . . ."

"Really, don't worry about me. I'm sure I can find the door all on my own."

And he goes out before she can say anything else, pleased that he has saved her the trouble of acting as hostess just for a little while. She has too much to do with all these visitors coming and going and, honestly, Rodin should arrange for her to have more help around the place now that his fortunes have improved so much. Clara said this to him one evening when they were returning from dinner here, that Rodin could certainly afford a *femme-de-ménage* and a cook as well if he wanted, and at the time he'd said that Rodin liked to live simply without frills like servants. But later he had seen the sense in what she was saying. Neither Rose nor Rodin are young anymore. They could use an extra pair of hands around the place.

He goes to the back door of the studio and lets himself in. The large main room is quiet and empty. It is filled with the hooded shapes of statues, covered in white sheeting and tied, so they look like big clumsy ghosts, their outlines muted by the white billows enclosing them. He likes the way the room looks full of these strange, soft shapes. I must ask him if I can photograph these when they are covered, as well as in the flesh, Edward thinks. In the flesh. Would that be the correct expression for a figure made of marble or bronze?

Rodin and his guest must be in the smaller room at the other end where he keeps his models in rows of glass-fronted cabinets. Edward makes his way across the wooden floor that wheezes under his weight. At the door to the other room, he pauses for a moment. Then he pushes it open and steps inside.

On the floor between two of the cabinets, Rodin and a young woman are making love. They have taken some of the spare sheeting from the studio and laid it beneath them so that it forms a nest for their bodies. Their moving limbs have made circular ripples in the sheet's smooth surface; it furrows around them like the impression of a stone dropped in water. From where Edward is standing, he can see Rodin's great back, still clad in his customary linen work shirt, and his bare hindquarters. He can see the face of the woman framed in dark hair, her eyes dreamy, half-closed, and, just visible beneath Rodin's arm, one lovely white breast.

They are so absorbed in what they are doing that they don't notice that he has entered the room, and Edward remains where he is, rooted to the spot, afraid to move for fear of making the noise that will alert them to his presence. The woman stretches and pulls herself up, letting out a little gasp of pleasure. As she does so, her eyes click over toward the door and suddenly they are on him. He feels his insides turn over in a mixture of terror and embarrassment. He expects that she will scream, or try to hide, curl up under the massive barrel body of the man above her. And then, what? Rage, banishment, humiliation. He has no idea what will happen next.

But the woman neither flinches nor cries out. She watches him for a moment, with an expression that is curious but not upset, and maybe a little amused. Then she looks back to her lover, reaches up and slides her arms more tightly around his torso, and Edward feels himself vanish from her mind entirely. Freed as though from a spell, he steps backward and out of the room in a single pace, pulling the door closed behind him.

After that he doesn't know what to do with himself. Confusion alone carries him back across the studio and out into the garden. He starts to circle the house but then halts, changes his mind and heads instead out into the pathways of the flower garden. He doesn't want to see Rose right now; he doesn't want to see anyone. He sits down on the bench in the lowest level of the garden. It is the same one where he'd waited three years ago when he'd first come here, nervously hoping for an audience. He leans against its wooden back and closes his eyes.

Of course he has heard about Rodin's affairs. It would have been impossible to avoid the rumors that followed the sculptor around constantly, linking his name with this woman or that one, whispered at dinner parties and implied in the society pages of *Le Figaro*. Edward has never had any reason to believe or disbelieve them either way—he and Rodin have never in their years of acquaintance had any reason to speak of such things. So to suddenly have such, well, vivid proof is a little bewildering. Edward doesn't know if he should leave or go back into the house and make some excuse to Rose, say that he couldn't get into the studio after all, although that would sound patently ridiculous, he knows. And anyway, how could he bring himself to look her in the face? At this moment, he has no idea how he should act, what he should do. He is off the maps of behavior he has known all his life, and all the more so because the woman (who must of course be Isadora Duncan) did not react with shame or fright but merely with a calm sort of pleasure that reached toward him and took him in almost as though he were meant to see this . . .

"There you are!" The round gong of Rodin's voice comes from the path above and behind him. It makes him jump; he hadn't been expecting to be disturbed, nor to be greeted quite so jovially. "I have been looking for you." Rodin comes down the steps and shakes his hand. He is smiling broadly and there is no sign of awkwardness or suspicion in his manner.

"I let myself in . . ." Edward says, and then realizes that this is the wrong thing to say. "That is, the front gate. I found it open."

"Well, I am glad you are here. You must come and meet my charming visitor. Mademoiselle Duncan, the dancer. And then I have some new models in clay that I have to show you."

"I . . ." Edward tries to think of a way he can get out of this, but none comes to mind. He pulls back instinctively, his mind racing.

"Come along, dear boy." Rodin is insistent. "Mademoiselle Duncan is sitting inside with Madame. I'm sure you will take to each other."

"She's with Rose?"

"Yes, yes." And he sets off toward the house with those great solid strides of his, leaving Edward nothing to do but trail after him, shaking his head in bewilderment that everything should seem to be so entirely normal.

So this is how it unfolds. From this moment on, the visit occurs exactly as one might expect. When they reach the house, Rose and Isadora are sitting in the front parlor, and if there has been any strangeness between them, it is erased by Rose's courteous attentions to all of them, her readiness to converse or to smile consolingly when her English fails or when Isadora's French (which is poor) does the same. Edward watches her, talking and listening, as she rises to bring their lunch to the table, or to pour each of them some more wine. He can detect no sign of the blustery sadness that had so overwhelmed her when he found her in the greenhouse just a little while earlier. She seems to be in good spirits and calm, and perhaps it is only because he knows her well that he thinks she is being a little more friendly, a little more polite, than usual. If there is anything troubling her, no one could tell.

Rodin, too, talks enthusiastically with Edward about his new commissions—for a set of doors based on Dante's *Inferno*. He has just begun planning them. He will use certain of the figures he has already modeled for other works and, he has decided, he will include a self-portrait in the bottom left-hand corner—something he has never done before—just to see if anyone notices. He laughs at this, delighted by the idea. He tells stories and is solicitous and gentle to Rose. He calls her sweetheart, lays his hand on top of hers on the tablecloth in a quiet gesture of affection.

And Isadora: she is full of such an intense energy that when she asks him a question, even a simple one, he feels that his answer is tremendously important.

"What was the first photograph you ever took?" she asks him. "I mean the very, very first one."

"My sister," he says. "Dancing. In my parents' garden in Milwaukee."

"Oh, it must have been beautiful. I wish I could see it right now. I think the loveliest art is made by free instinct, when we aren't scared by too much thinking and tradition. Don't you agree, Mr. Steichen? You must agree."

She is absolutely uninhibited, he thinks; Clara would have said she was too loud; "vulgar," that's the word she would have used if she were here, but she isn't and he finds himself increasingly relieved about that. Clara would not have liked Isadora at all, he thinks. And heaven knows what she would have made of the scene in . . . he blushes thinking of it. But he likes Isadora. He likes her very much. There is a gravity and a grace to her, a physical beauty that is its own engine, entirely self-possessed.

Gradually, the upside-down feeling leaves him. Here he is having lunch with his friends and nothing seems out of the ordinary. What he saw in the studio feels like he must have dreamt it, because how can it be part of this world where they sit and eat and drink coffee and then go for a walk around the edge of the property to take the air after lunch? It seems to have been cut neatly out of the flow of reality. If he wanted to, he could forget it entirely.

Rose and Isadora go down to look at the view from the bottom of the garden, and Rodin stays with Edward, smoking his pipe and pacing slowly along the stone paths.

"She is a marvelous girl," he says meditatively.

"Yes," Edward says, "she is very charming." Rodin nods but doesn't say anything and so he goes on: "I saw her dance with her troop in London. It was unusual . . ."

"No, no," Rodin says. "I don't mean Isadora. I was referring to Madame, to Rose. I am so grateful to her, I don't know what I would do without her." Edward stares at him, not knowing how to reply. Rodin stops and turns to him.

"You were surprised, I think, this afternoon." It is the first time that he has given Edward any indication that he was aware of his presence in the studio earlier. "You were a little shocked." Edward looks at Rodin, expecting to see anger, opprobrium, in his face, a stern warning. But Rodin looks unfazed. He is pulling on his pipe slowly, and the sweet smell of burning tobacco hovers around them.

"I . . ." Edward starts, but finds he has nothing at all to say.

"It is all right, you know. I am not annoyed, though I wouldn't wish to make that a regular occurrence." He chuckles, takes another draw from his pipe. "Two in the room, that is plenty. Well, usually." He chuckles again. Then he turns to Edward, his face serious now. He puts a hand on his arm to make sure he is paying special attention.

"The body," he says, "is not a thing to be afraid of. It is not something to hide from, to hem in with rules and regulations. You have to listen to it, use the energy of its needs for your work. Yes? As an artist, your body is part of your work, not outside it." He tugs on Edward's sleeve to emphasize this. "Even," he continues, and there is the laughing glint in his eye, "if you are a photographer.

"If you try to stifle the body, ignore its urges, you will never find your full power. Your work will be diminished, because you will not be experiencing the world to the fullest extent that you are able. I say this to you because I feel you very often pulling yourself back into the conventional life, the bourgeois life. I see these restrictions you place on yourself; they show in your work. This is how it is with Americans—always there is that wonderful energy choked off by a concern for morality. But you must learn to ignore the old restrictions and move toward what is new, what your senses can discover. Do you understand?"

Edward is bowled over by this. He has never seen Rodin so insistent, so directly concerned with the way he lives his life. In general, they have discussed only the art that they produce and they have spoken of it as the product of their conscious intentions; not as the fruit of their whole lives. It is thrilling to have this man, his hero, speaking to him with the earnestness of a father imparting wisdom to his son. "I think I understand," he says, although he isn't sure this is true.

"Good," Rodin says. He is looking out now at where the hill

slopes away down toward Paris. The late afternoon light is beginning to turn to evening around them. The trees and the stone
walks subside into shadow. Below them, Rose and Isadora are
walking along the perimeter of the property. "That is why I praise
Madame to you. That is why I say she is so marvelous—because
she understands this perfectly."

Edward watches the women make their way across the grass.
They stop when they realize they are being watched. Isadora
waves, and Rose smiles and nods.

"She understands," Rodin repeats, "and in this, she is very
much unlike most other women." Edward is silent. "You are thinking of your own wife, yes?" Edward nods. "It isn't easy, you know,
I am not saying it is easy. But she must understand that you need
freedom more than anything else. Otherwise, your work will
suffer. Does she understand this need for absolute freedom? I am
not sure."

Now the women are walking back up toward them, picking
their way slowly across the lawn in the growing gloom, and their
conversation is cut short, but he cannot stop thinking about what
Rodin has said, even as Isadora takes his arm and asks him more
of her fiery questions. Does Clara understand his needs as an artist?
As a man? He isn't sure, for though she took him back after
what happened three years ago with Kathleen Bruce, it was only
amid his protestations of regret and penitence; it was only with
his promises that it would never, ever happen again. But perhaps
he has been thinking about this backward: perhaps he shouldn't
have to apologize for simply following the promptings of his
senses. Perhaps it was not the desire that was wrong; perhaps it was
the shame.

Isadora by his side seems to sense his distraction and looks up
at him, and he sees that same wide, gently amused expression that

he recognizes from when she saw him standing frozen in the studio door. He feels her communicating a sense of conspiratorial delight. He finds himself smiling despite himself, and then they are both giggling, their faces close to each other, suspending their secret between them.

"How stricken you looked!" she whispers, and this sets them off giggling again. This is how it can be, he thinks, love can be given and received freely without possessiveness or jealousy or the suffering that we place on it artificially. How different this is from what he has known before. How much he still has to learn.

When it is time for Edward to take the train back into the city, Rodin suggests that he accompany Miss Duncan to where she is staying. He walks with them to the gate. He kisses Isadora's hand. Then he embraces them both warmly.

"You will come back again soon, to see us," he states rather than asks.

"Make certain she gets home safely," Rodin says to Edward as he closes the gate. They set off toward the station, and Edward feels as though he is on the edge of something dark, exciting and mysterious. A universe where none of the tiresome, restrictive rules apply, where his actions will be as weightless as they are in dreams. He does not have to do very much to break the glass that separates him from this. All he has to do, in fact, is to reach up and gently run his fingers along the line of Isadora's cheekbone, like so.

SIX

June 16, 1918

NOW THE MORNINGS came over the horizon as clear and as terrifyingly empty as diamonds, with skies so uniformly blue that Edward felt blind if he stared up into them for too long. The men flew out to the front each day at dawn with their cameras and cases of plates. The planes would go one by one, moving into lateral formation in the air. They would fly toward the lines, tracing parallel routes, so that each piece of ground could be recorded twice for the stereoscope; they swept up as far as Montdidier in the west and down beyond Reims and Souain to the south and east. They shot from a high altitude, making a map of the war's crooked frontier. Edward was relieved to find that, once they began work, the men learned quickly how to take useful photographs, how to time their exposures, how to spot artillery from the air. He went up on the morning runs in Captain McIntyre's plane.

The pilots they flew with were pleasant, boisterous, in love with flight. They were new to the war; they had just come from the training school at Issoudun and before that from Kansas, Maine, Georgia; they believed in the cause, in Liberty. They cracked jokes as they strode out to their planes; they stunted for fun, turning illicit loops above the airfield; they buzzed official cars or army buildings or sometimes herds of terrified cattle if nothing else was available, then rode off into the sky with impunity.

Those first two weeks at Épernay were mostly uneventful. The reconnaissance planes were not attacked, except by antiaircraft fire. Allied control of the air kept them safe; the Germans, as Cundall had said, rarely engaged in a fight. Edward would see a Pfalz or an Albatros across the lines, sometimes groups of them, patrolling at a lower altitude. But they just turned and flew away.

Gilles Marchand was allowed to join Photo Section 4 under Lieutenant Dawson, and the men adopted him as a kind of mascot. They mispronounced his name so it sounded like "congeals," but if he minded, he didn't show it. They would ask him the French for obscene words and he would reply with a perfectly straight face while they fell about laughing. They tried to repeat what he said in their round, careless accents: *Mayored. Space de saloud. Fairmee yer booch*, he overheard Kelsey say, *or I'll fairmee it for you*. They called each other *coach ons*. They taught Marchand to play poker.

Edward saw him after his first morning flight.

"How do you like it, then?" he asked.

"Like what?"

"Flying."

Gilles paused, considering, his face grave.

"Flying," he said, "is the most marvelous thing I have ever done."

Edward's days became absorbed with flight; developing the morning's exposures; making prints, then sending them out along the lines; writing up intelligence reports for headquarters at Chaumont. They didn't seem able to find conclusive evidence of the direction of the coming German advance, and this began, as the days progressed, to worry him. Sometimes he would wake up early in the morning, moving from anxious sleep to lying awake, his mind tracing and retracing the intelligence from the previous day. When this happened, he got up, put on clothes and walked over to the laboratory. He let himself in and stood over the table where they'd laid out a photomosaic of the front. He stared at it, trying to drag some meaning from the scrawls of roads and rivers, the stands of trees like clustered bruises. He wrote notes: *Troop movements to section five, near Vaux. Rotation or reinforcements? Extra canteens; additional traffic to supply depot.*

During these sleepless hours, he thought often of Marion Beckett. She played in his head like a song heard too many times, at once compelling and maddening. To find her there, and to have that intense flash of familiarity, and then to be cut off from her, made him restlessly unhappy. He found that the physical facts of her came back to him suddenly and uninvited: her face, drawn with tiredness; her hair pulled up off the nape of her neck; the way her hands moved steadily as she administered morphine to the patient on the bed. He started to write to her several times. He always broke off, though, crumpled up the paper and threw it away, mindful of the prohibition she'd placed on correspondence and uncertain of exactly what he wanted to say.

He wondered if she thought about him.

COLONEL VAN HORN was growing impatient. Two weeks these observers had been flying. Morning and evening they went out. The photographs were piling up in his office, sorted and dated, and still they had found nothing.

It was nearly the end of June. There would be a push, and it would come soon, and they still didn't know where. Each day more deserters slipped over the lines, cut their way through the barbed wire and came crawling over the shell holes toward the enemy hoping to be captured rather than killed. Those who succeeded talked about a big advance being planned. Sometime in the next few weeks, they said. Some claimed to know when it would be, stabbing at this date or that one with nervous insistence. July 17, one said. July 9. Near Amiens. North from the St-Mihiel salient. None of the claims agreed.

Van Horn had driven up to interview some of them, behind the lines near Compiègne. They were being held in a disused warehouse, seven or eight men, scruffy and thin, their eyes wide with fear or hunger or both. Rations had been cut again in March, they said. When they reached the British trenches after the first advances of the spring and saw what the enemy left behind, discarding as refuse foods that they hadn't eaten for years, tobacco, lamp oil, leaving the boots on their dead . . . that was when I knew we would lose, one of them said. No matter how far we advanced. I didn't want to die for nothing, for some ground we would only have to retreat over in a few weeks' time. He looked down and spat into the dirt. The others were nodding in agreement.

Where will the advance come? This big show you are describing to me. The men were silent. Maybe near St-Quentin, one offered. Maybe near Arras, said another. Van Horn sighed. They didn't know. They were cowards who had left their posts. They revolted him. He left them and drove back to Épernay.

Now he stood at the window of his office and watched the evening reconnaissance flight land. The men climbed from their planes and moved with that odd wooden gait toward the hangars. He heard them call greetings to each other, the sound carrying on the still air. They were boys, the pilots and these new observers too, and they had the enthusiasm and callowness of boys. And these men who were in charge of them. Who were they? What had they been doing last year at this time? Painting portraits? Taking pictures? Writing newspaper articles? What did they know about fighting a war?

Van Horn had been at war for a long time. He had seen boys come to France before these ones. He had seen bad pilots grind their airplanes through mission after mission, making it home safe, while brilliantly skilled pilots were shot from the sky because they flew low, or went further afield, or just happened, one day, to have bad luck. In the end, whether you survived or not had more to do with chance than anything else.

These boys, like the others, wouldn't last: they would have to become something else, something harder, if they were going to survive. They would change to resemble, more and more, the prisoners he had met in Compiègne. He had wanted to give them time before they were transformed. He had sent them up to trace the front from a high altitude, knowing that this would allow them to get used to flying. He had hoped that they could get the information they needed without losing any men or any airplanes. But he couldn't afford to keep them safe any longer.

He rang for his secretary.

"I need to see Captain Steichen and Captain McIntyre," he said. "Send them up when they are done filling out their reports."

He sat down to wait and turned his chair to face the window. A group of pilots were walking toward the barracks from the hangars on the far side of the field. At this distance he couldn't tell them apart from each other and he thought that, in fact, it was better this way, not to see them as individuals. That way there would be no sense of loss to impede his thinking. He slid open the drawer of his desk, took out the bottle of bourbon he kept there, and poured himself a glass. He took a long drink. The men were almost at the building now, and one by one they disappeared from view as they climbed the front steps to the entrance below him. He wondered which of them would be the first to go.

"HENCEFORTH ALL RECONNAISSANCE flights will go a speci-fied minimum distance into enemy territory. Routes will be revised on a daily basis. Additionally, we will be expected to inves-tigate any suspicious activity firsthand."

"Meaning what, sir?" someone asked.

"Meaning," said McIntyre, "if you see a group of Jerries pulling something heavy between them, fly down and find out what it is."

There was a dry ripple of laughter. While McIntyre spoke, Edward surveyed the faces of the men. Most looked serious but resigned. Some looked anxious. One or two were grimacing, and Edward noted that among these was Kelsey, the pugilist he'd seen at the station that first day. Deveraux, standing near the back of the room, rubbed his hands together nervously. Sergeant Daniels sat with his brow furrowed staring at the floor fixedly.

Edward thought of Rodin's statue of the Burghers of Calais: This is the moment when they know. One of the pilots raised his hand: "What is it, Shapiro?" asked McIntyre.

"How long will this go on?"

"The situation will be reviewed every three days and if neces-sary the distance required on each flight will be extended depend-ing on the progress we make in intelligence gathering. If we find information that allows us to determine the place and direction of their next advance, then we will be able to return to more routine procedures."

There were grumbles from among the pilots. Another hand shot up: "Sir? Will we be getting an escort of scouts? Since we're flying such big, slow buses."

McIntyre shot Edward a look before replying.

"No, we will not be getting an escort. We asked about that, but the colonel informs us—" McIntyre's voice was drowned out by the men, all beginning to talk at once.

"What does he think we are flying?" someone shouted.

"Come on! What are we? Little girls? We don't need help to do our jobs." When Edward looked around, he saw that it was Tom Cundall who had spoken.

McIntyre let them go on for a minute, then he held up his hand for quiet and said: "The colonel has informed us that there are no scouts that can be spared from their regular duties at the moment, so we have to fly these missions on our own. But we will be revisiting the subject with him at the earliest possible juncture." He looked over at Edward again, who nodded in agreement.

"Yes," he said. "You can rest assured of that."

FROM 10,000 FEET he saw it, at the horizon, something gray and dispersed. The day was hazy, blurring the boundaries between earth and sky, making objects bleed into each other. It was the fourth day that they had flown routes that took them many miles across the lines.

At first Edward couldn't identify what he was seeing: not earth, not buildings, a darkness scattered across two adjoining fields. As he looked, it seemed to move inside itself, shifting and rearranging. It could be an illusion created by the heat rising from the earth as the first daylight moved across it, making the fields appear strangely alive. Or it could be something solid. He leaned forward, squinted to try to see more clearly.

In the front seat, McIntyre had spotted it too. He looked around and pointed. "Let's go down and have a look."

Edward sat back, bracing in his seat as McIntyre arched into a dive. The rest of the squadron swooped to follow them. The ground surged up, and McIntyre eased back on the throttle until they were flying level, the fields racing beneath them. When Edward peered forward again, his sight lines were blocked: the ruins of a town obscured his view.

Below them were the remains of buildings, brick and sandstone, the outlines of streets nearly buried by rubble. Disemboweled houses, their walls tumbled out into what had been kitchen gardens. In places he could see inside them, into rooms where people once ate and slept. Among the spewed stones were tatters of curtains, a mangled brass bed frame. On another house the roof was gone and he could see, standing like sentries along the walls of a drawing room, shelves still filled with books.

McIntyre was gesturing to him. Up ahead the town ended, and in a minute they would be flying over open country. Now when he peered over the side of the cockpit, Edward saw clearly what they had glimpsed from miles back. There was an army camped out in these fields.

Their bodies covered the ground like leaves. They had spread themselves on either side of the road, so that for half a mile in every direction a carpet of men lay scattered. They were out in the open, no dugouts, a few tents here and there: they must have intended to reach somewhere farther along the front by nightfall. Then when it was too dark to see, they had halted in the shadow of the ruined town. They had parked the artillery beside the road and tied up the horses. They climbed into the fields to sleep.

In the east, the sun had come up and some of the men on the ground were stirring awake, lighting canister stoves, huddling around to watch them burn; they were boiling water in cans; frying their breakfasts. Thin columns of smoke rose from fires here and there. A few men looked up as they passed over and waved, not seeing the insignia and assuming, this far in the rear, that the planes would be their own. But then some of them began to point and shout, and run toward the road where the guns were.

Edward began taking pictures as quickly as he could: the road, the expanse of the army, the number of guns and horses, canteens—things by which the numbers of men might be estimated. More men were running now, and in a minute they reached their objective and stopped, clustering around one of the Spandau guns. They swung its nozzle upward and Edward saw bursts of flames at its mouth, heard the metallic, choked sound of its firing. Then there were bullets in the air around them, and McIntyre began to climb, pulling them out of range. Looking over the side of the cockpit, Edward saw that they had been hit. The bullet holes in the fuselage began about a foot behind where he sat. He could have reached out and touched them. He felt suddenly colder, as if they had passed into a deep shadow, though around them the day was bright. McIntyre turned west and began to head toward home, with the rest of the flight following.

They made good speed at first, riding a tailwind for about ten minutes, when a new sound reached Edward's hearing. Above the growling of their own engine came a furious buzzing that resolved itself into the rising pitch of an airplane approaching from the east. He looked around, but he couldn't see it, only hear its threatening noise. Louder and louder it descended, and then there were tracer bullets coming down around them, plowing into the upper plane and the end of the fuselage but missing the rudder and the tail. He heard one whiz close to his head and ducked down into the cockpit; over its lip, he could see the slim white trails the bullets left. He scanned the air around them, but the plane that had been shooting remained hidden from view. Where was it? He could hear it still circling, still dangerously close.

And then he saw it dart out behind them: a Fokker Eindecker, skimming away and up on its single tier of wings, slipping out of sight again. He lurched toward the gun mounted behind him and swung it around, in time to fire uselessly into thin air. Behind him he saw one of the other pilots from the squadron fire at it with his forward guns, but he also missed it. McIntyre put the plane into a dive, and when he leveled out began to let it sideslip so it would be less easy to hit. He turned and yelled back to Edward: "Don't let go of that gun. He'll be back around for another try."

On the second pass it came from below. Edward saw the tiny plane loop and dive beneath them, and he followed it with the gun until it dipped out of range. It was coming up at their tail, into the blind spot, the place where they had no defense. McIntyre dived again, but some of the bullets caught them on the way down, striking the underside of the fuselage. McIntyre cursed. They could see the other planes taking shots at the Fokker and missing it, the DH-4s, too slow and clumsy, and the observers too untrained to hit a small, agile monoplane. It would sail out of reach and come around again, moving at twice the speed of the two-seaters. In the distance they could see the lines and safety; still so far away.

Suddenly, the Fokker rose and spun like a corkscrew, turning on its own axis. The light glanced off its wings and Edward was struck through his fear by its beauty. This war, he thought, it tears men to pieces, but its machines dance. For a moment it seemed suspended, then it righted itself and turned east, moving away from them as fast as it could. Edward didn't understand why it had retreated: had it grown bored of this game, lost interest? He realized he was imagining that the plane possessed its own intelligence.

But then McIntyre pointed, and Edward saw a group of five Sopwith Camels coming toward them. They pursued the German pilot a short way, then turned and followed the two-seaters back up to the lines. When they were over onto their own side, the leader waved at McIntyre, who saluted, grinning.

WHEN THEY REACHED the airfield, they discovered that one of the observers, a man in Dawson's section named Clark, was dead. A bullet had caught him just between his shoulder blade and his spine. He had slumped forward, still strapped into his seat, kept upright by the belts around his torso until they cut him loose. His camera was still around his neck, but most of the plates had been exposed.

"I hope we didn't lose anything important there," said van Horn, looking at the ruined glass squares. "Anything you can do with those?"

"I don't know," Edward said.

"Well, send them over to the lab. See if some images can be salvaged from them." Van Horn watched the stretcher-bearers tilt the body upright and gently press its eyes closed. "Lieutenant Dawson will have to write the letter to his people."

The observers who'd gathered around fell back as the stretcher men lifted the body from the plane and lowered it onto a waiting truss. They set off with it suspended between them. Dawson followed as they carried it to the edge of the field. He watched over Clark's body until the tender came to take him away.

LATER, LUTZ BROUGHT EDWARD the pictures they had taken of the army that morning. A gray accident of men. From above they could have been thousands of versions of the same man, the barrier of their uniforms turning them into repetitions, making each individual invisible. Perhaps this was the truth revealed by distance, Edward thought, revealed by speed. All of us sleep poorly now, all of us dream of home. If you take away enough from men, if you boil us down to our physical needs, if you take away the people we love, we will lose the things that made us unique. We'll become identical. Machine parts. Components of the war.

Mary and Her Mother. Montparnasse, 1908. Pigment print.

MARY HAS HER own language. Mary, with her demanding blue eyes, who has never in her life slept for more than a few hours at a time, who has learned to run before she can even really stand, her momentum carrying her forward at a speed she can't control, so she falls daily, bruising her hands and scraping her knees. Clara says that this little girl is entirely and completely *his* daughter, sprung fully formed from his head, like the goddess in the story. *I* had nothing to do with how she turned out, she tells people. I was merely the vessel. Mary is Edward through and through.

Mary's language is as varied and subtle as any spoken by adults, with a grammar that sometimes uses her entire small body for punctuation, and a vocabulary ranging from intricate whispers to shouts of utter joy or unmitigated despair. She talks all the time. She is endlessly articulate.

The only difficulty is that no one else speaks her language, and this causes her immense frustration. Try as she might, they are all slow learners. Even her parents can only manage a pidgin version at best. Sometimes they don't even get that right.

They do know the more obvious, straightforward constructions: the command form, for example. Even though Papa has let himself quietly into the apartment, hoping not to disturb them, Mama and Mary, if they are resting in the middle of the afternoon; even though he's put his bags down softly beside the front door, Mary has heard him. She nearly trips over the doorjamb as she comes charging out of the bedroom toward him and lunges for his legs to steady herself on his trouser cuff. She looks up at him with his own eyes.

"Dadadadada," she shouts, tugging at the cloth of his pant leg, and this at least, he understands: Up!

He reaches and lifts her over his head, swings her back down, cradling her against his chest. She squeals, a single formless word of delight, then begins to gurgle earnestly at him. She pulls on his shirt collar. She tries to put it into her mouth but can't twist it around the right way.

Clara has chased Mary from the bedroom and now she is leaning, looking at them, one arm against the doorframe for support. Smiling sleepily, she watches Edward as he carries his daughter around the room in a victory lap.

"She seems recovered," Edward says. "Her color is good."

"She's much better," Clara replies. "No sign of that cough for weeks now. Careful—don't let her chew on your shirt buttons. She might swallow one. She's been putting things in her mouth all month. She's got two new teeth on the bottom. Take a look." And indeed, when Mary smiles, he can glimpse two tiny white squares, perfectly formed, poking through the pink of her gums into her mouth. Edward feels that it is immensely clever of his daughter to grow teeth; it is obviously the sign of innate brilliance and he feels proud. Surely no other child had managed this business of teething quite so well before now. She is trying to eat his collar again. He gently pulls it out of her grip.

Clara comes into the room and puts her arms around him from behind so her head rests between his shoulder blades.

"How was your journey? You must be exhausted. Would you like some coffee?"

He twists around to face her. "Yes. But a kiss first, please." She stretches up to kiss him and then runs her fingers lightly down his cheek.

"It has been a terribly cold, terribly long January without you."
She goes through to the kitchen, and Edward sits down on the
sofa, with Mary on his knee. Now she has moved on from his collar to the strands of hair that fall over his face. She encloses them
in her round baby fist and tries to pull them out.

"Ouch, that hurts," Edward tells her.

"What's she doing?" says Clara's voice from the kitchen. The
apartment is so small—three rooms, one his studio—that they can
hear each other wherever they are inside it.

"Pulling my hair."

"Ahh. Yes. She likes hair. It's almost as delicious as copper coins,
though not quite as yummy as newspaper. I almost considered
having mine all cut off; but I thought you wouldn't be very happy
to come back to find your wife bald, and heaven knows it is dis-
mal enough for me to look at myself in the glass right now without getting rid of my one remaining good feature. Here." She
comes through from the kitchen. "I'll take her if you'd like."

He looks at her as she slides across the floor, reaching out to
take Mary from him. In the two months that he's been away,
she's begun to take on the extra weight of her pregnancy, her
body slowly transforming into something new. Her limbs have
softened; the fine angles of her face have disappeared under flesh.
Her belly protrudes now so he can see where she is carrying their
second child; the skin over it will be smooth and purposeful. He
finds that he is just as astonished by these changes as he was
the first time. When she was pregnant with Mary, he would run
his hands over that strange tight skin at her middle, so he could
feel the child underneath begin to move, to demand its own separate life.

"No, I'll hold on to her. You mustn't strain yourself too much,"
he says.

"Oh, it's OK. I've gotten quite used to coping alone. I can hold her in one arm and do any number of things with my free one. You should see me."

"Hasn't Mrs. Leffert been coming to help you?" he asks.

"Mrs. Who? No; she vanished around the middle of last month. I told you that paying her in advance was a bad idea."

"What else was I to do?"

"Well, anyway, Marion helped take care of Mary when she could. And Mildred has been here a lot. She has been my rod and staff. I don't know what I would have done without her . . ."

She sighs and he sees how tired she is. Her face, the drag under her eyes.

"I am sorry," he says. "I thought Madame Leffert would be more reliable than that. I wish we could have afforded more permanent help."

"Oh well, it was all right. We managed." There is an edge in her voice when she says this by which he understands that it was, in fact, not quite all right. "Let me get your coffee," she says, and disappears into the other room.

He feels put out by this, because he thought that the woman whom he had paid to help Clara would be honest enough to come until the end of the month. True, the arrangement had been rather ad hoc, and she was not a professional, didn't have the right references. But at that time money had been tight and they had been able to do no better. Still, he thinks, his discontent clearing slightly, that time is ended now; things will be easier; and Clara will be happy when she hears the news . . .

"Here you are." She carries the service in on a tray and places it in front of him. Mary wriggles around and begins to reach toward the shiny pewter pot. Clara comes and sits down beside Edward and snatches her away from it.

"Oh no you don't. That is very hot and you will be very

unhappy if you touch it." She mimes putting her hand close to the metal surface and drawing it away suddenly. "Ouch," she says. "Hot. Don't touch." Mary looks at her, looks at the coffee pot and begins to cry.

"Oh dear," Edward says. Clara picks up the little girl and walks back and forth across the room, making hushing noises to her. Mary's crying becomes more desperate. Her whole body turns red with the effort, her face a scarlet knot of muscles squeezing out screams.

"Is she all right?" Edward asks.

"She'll be fine," Clara says. "This is just what happens if she doesn't get her afternoon nap." Mary calms for a minute then surges up again, her crying coming and going like gusts of wind. "Oh, you are too much for me," Clara says softly to the squalling bundle in her arms. "Much too much too much." She continues to pace and sway. "We'll have to talk around her. So tell me about the show. Tell me what happened."

"Well . . ." He pauses. He likes this feeling of having good news to impart. He almost doesn't want to tell her quite yet because the anticipation is so sweet in and of itself.

So he tells her first about his journey and his time in New York. He helped to hang the show, which took place at Alfred Steiglitz's Little Galleries at 291 Fifth Avenue. They got wonderful reviews, he tells her. Rodin's drawings, which he had brought from France along with his own work, shocked a few people, who wrote to the press to complain and the newspapers printed the angry letters. As a consequence, the drawings sold incredibly well. Not bad for a first show in the States.

"I'm proud to have been the one to introduce those drawings to America," he says. "It's quite an accomplishment."

"Yes, that's nice. But what about your work?" Clara asks. "Did it make any money?" He is taken aback at the directness of her question. He feels that he has been beaten to the punch; that his good news has been somehow deflated by her demanding it. Of course, money is not without its importance, but there is more to it than that, he almost says. There is the progress of art. There is . . . But he reminds himself that she should not be excited in her present condition. Her temper should not be agitated.

"I'm getting to that," he says. "Patience. Let me take the baby. You can rest." He stands up and takes Mary into his arms. By now she is tired of crying, and after a couple of turns about the room, her sobs diminish, become hiccups and then a yawn. She snuffles and curls herself into the hollow between his arms and chin, and closes her eyes.

"There, there," he says softly, and passes her back to Clara on the couch. He sits down beside her, takes her one free hand in his.

"I did make money from this exhibition. Actually, it was quite a lot, more than I've ever made before from a single show. Almost all the work I took with me sold. And I have orders to fill for additional prints—enough to keep me, to keep us, going for a long time. Clara, this really was a breakthrough for me. We can certainly take a house for the rest of the year, and probably next as well. And we can hire some help for you, a proper *femme-de-ménage*, maybe a cook, too."

She looks at him, her face displaying disbelief.

"Is that true? Really?"

"Clara, remember how much you loved the little towns out along the Marne when we went driving there last summer?" She nods. "I'm going to go and look for a house we can rent there. A place with a garden, fresh air, peace and quiet, lots of light. Not too far from the river. You can rest. Mary can have space to play, and we'll have lots of room for the new baby when it is born in the spring . . ."

"Do you mean it?" she asks.

"Absolutely."

"Our own garden, and more space . . ."

"Well, there will be four of us very soon. We couldn't have stayed in a tiny apartment in the middle of the city. Growing children need space and freedom."

"How wonderful." She leans back heavily against the arm of the couch. "I don't know if I could have made it through another winter in this place, always worrying about Mary getting sick again and then with the new baby . . . But, oh, just think, a house and a garden . . ."

"And I will put a chaise lounge under the trees for you, so you can sit outside and read."

"We'll have a garden with trees, then."

"We'll have whatever kind of garden you want!"

"Oh, it's too marvelous. When will you go to look for it?"

"Next week. Tomorrow. As soon as you want me to. Send me away tonight if you like," he says. "I'm at my lady's service." Clara laughs and he sees, inside her weary face, the beauty, the brightness he loved there first and that he sometimes forgets in the normal run of their life together. In her arms, Mary stirs and wakes and looks up at her mother with huge, solemn eyes, wise and fathomless.

How beautiful they look together and how extraordinary this moment is, balanced between the struggle of the past and the mystery of the future; hope makes it radiant, he thinks. Clara looking down at the lovely face of their daughter, who has after all come though that frightening bout of fever this winter and is healthy and strong and growing just as she should to become as beautiful as her mother, as clever as her father. All this is his, and he thanks whatever powers there are in the universe for it. For during his time in New York, he reached another decision, which is to come back fully to his wife and child, and to cut off the other entanglements of his time and affection.

His affair with Isadora had gone on, albeit irregularly, for almost three years when he saw her this past month in New York and ended things definitively. They had not been together often, and since their lives had always been outwardly committed to other people, neither of them had ever expected more than this occasional intimacy. Though he continued to be captivated by her, entranced by her vivid energy, he never came to love her. Nor does she love him, not in the sense in which the word ought to be used. They fed off each other, that was all, and when the break came, there were a few tears, but on the whole it was kindly and amicable, something they both felt was overdue.

And then there was the ebb and flow of the correspondence he had kept up, in secret, with Kathleen Bruce; though the links seemed tenuous, that, somehow, was more difficult to sever. More wrenching. But he has done it. And he is glad.

Now his heart can be at home with Clara and his child, and soon with his children! This is where he does not entirely agree with Rodin on the subject of love—which reminds him: he must go up to Meudon later this evening to give him the news about the show. But this is what the older man, for all his great wisdom, does not perhaps understand: that there could be a freedom in this decision to be faithful. There can be depth to it, revelation. He will be able to think, and so work, more clearly. Now that he has no other lover, he can live without the fear of discovery and disaster. And then there are moments like this, whose beauty cannot be equaled, his wife and his daughter gazing at one another, seeing who knows what in each other's eyes.

"Clara," he says, "don't move. Let me get my camera."

"Oh, no, Edward, not now. I'm such a mess," she protests.

"You are beautiful," he says. "Stay there."

—

IT HAS BEEN a long time since he has taken her photograph, so why must he choose this moment, when her hair is disheveled and she is wearing only this old black smock, looking for all the world like a farmer's wife from Brittany? Still, she is so pleased right now that she doesn't care. Let him photograph her wearing a sack! She sits straight on the chair, Mary on her knee, and arranges her comfortably while he fusses with his camera, setting up.

"Beautiful, exhausting girl," she says. "Your father wants to photograph us, so you must behave for at least five minutes."

When Mary fell ill in January, it was hard for Clara. She was all alone, in a small, drafty apartment with her baby and that horrible sticky-sounding cough for company; that cough, which wouldn't go away for weeks on end no matter what powders the doctor gave her. And then Mary had developed shivers at night, which Clara was told must not go unwatched. She must sit up and make sure that the child did not get too warm or too cold. She must not leave her unattended.

It was during those vigils that she came closest to despairing. She would think of Edward, far away, attending to other things; she imagined him dining out, enjoying himself with Alfred and their other friends in New York. He wrote to her often, his letters came every few days, but they were not the same as his presence, not really reassuring or comforting, and because of the delay, they gave her advice about Mary that was out of date by the time it arrived. During the worst of it she would start letters asking him to abandon the show and come back to her on the next boat, but she felt she could not send these—he was there to work; he needed to work, she told herself, as much for her as for himself. So she tore up the letters and told herself to be patient, and stayed up at night watching her child sleep fretfully and wake herself shaking. Then one night something inside her turned over. One night she looked down at the small sleeping form and thought: I hate you. Simply that. She shocked herself, scared herself a little, but nevertheless, she had thought it, quite clearly, and it couldn't be denied. Her brain moved on from there to her husband: I hate you. For being away, for leaving me to this life where I hardly see the sun or leave the apartment, where I have no time to play or sing, or do any of those things that give me joy.

Mary's fever had receded as the weather warmed a little, and Mildred had come to her aid, visiting and keeping her company, looking after Mary for the few hours at a time that she could manage. Clara's emotions calmed. She felt she had been wrong, wicked, to blame her husband for a distress that was not, after all, his fault, and as for hating her daughter—that had been the fatigue and anxiety, the sleepless nights. She was ashamed even to have thought it. It was best forgotten about.

And now! It was as if he had heard her, read her thoughts. A garden and a *femme-de-ménage*. How glad she was that she had not sent those demanding letters; how worthwhile in the end his absence had been. He was fiddling with the flashbulb now, and he glanced up at her and grinned, and she couldn't help smiling back because she loved him and because she felt he had understood what she needed without her having to ask for it. There had been a while, last spring, when she felt he was absent even when he was there, and she had wondered: What was drawing him away from her? Was there another woman? But now she feels he is here, with her, in mind as well as body.

"In the new house," she said, "will we have room for a piano?"

"Of course," he said. "If that is what you want."

"Oh yes, and I'll be able to play without worrying about neighbors and noise, and if I have some help with the house, and with the child—"

"Children," he puts in, smiling.

"—maybe I can get enough finger strength back to begin to think about auditioning for some public performances. I could come up to Paris and work with a teacher here . . ."

"Well, perhaps. But you wouldn't want to leave the children for long periods of time, would you?"

"No. Well, of course. I suppose not."

"I certainly wouldn't allow it: it isn't a good idea for small children to be without their mother. But we can get some help for you and you will have more time for your music." Clara nods and looks at him solemnly. And then quite suddenly, surprising both of them, she begins to cry.

HE HAS BEEN looking at her through the viewfinder of his camera, almost ready to frame his shot, but now he stops what he is doing and stands up.

"Oh, don't cry now, darling. Why are you crying? I thought you said you were happy." He comes and offers her his handkerchief. "Now, what is the matter?"

"Nothing. Nothing. I am fine; and I'm very happy. It's just that it was so hard, this winter . . ."

"Well, it isn't going to be hard anymore, not like that. Now smile for me. I want your lovely smile. There."

He goes back to the camera and takes three pictures of them, Clara and Mary seated on the couch; then standing beside the window where the light is beginning to fade now, early: it is still winter. He is pleased, although already the perfect moment of their happiness is slipping away, disturbed first by her tears, and now he realizes that he must leave soon if he is to make it up to see Rodin this evening as he promised. He puts the camera away, in its case, while Clara lays Mary down to sleep in her crib.

"I will make us some supper," Clara says. "What would you like?"

"I'm sorry, my love," Edward says, pulling her into an embrace, for the first time only her without Mary. "I remembered that I told Rodin that I would go and give him the news and the receipts from the show as soon as I got back. I hate to go when I've just arrived . . ."

"Yes; do you have to?"

"I promised; it is too bad, but it is work, you know. I can't put it off."

"Well, if you must," Clara says, "you must, I suppose. Will you be late, do you think?"

"That depends on him, I guess. I can't just run out right after getting there. I have to stay and talk and—"

"Drink wine and make merry."

"Darling, don't be like that."

"I'm sorry; I only wish you didn't have to go this evening. But you are right, it is work . . . one has to do it . . ."

"I'll be back as soon as I can be."

"All right."

"And then next week I'll go and start looking for our new house. There, that has made you smile at least. Kiss me."

She leans up to kiss him, but he feels the resentment still lingering in the perfunctory motion, the way her eyes flit away from him as soon as she steps back. What can he do? He doesn't have a choice; he cannot afford to offend Rodin, and frankly, he doesn't want to. He would like to see his friend now. He wants to talk over the events of the last month with someone who cares fully for what it means in artistic terms that these drawings have arrived in America, been seen there, reviled, celebrated and accepted. He is looking forward to their conversation. That is not such a terrible thing.

He catches Clara's hand, and pulls her to him again and kisses her, then goes to get his coat.

"As soon as I can," he says. "I promise." She smiles, a watery smile, halfway convinced. He opens the door and goes out onto the landing. While he is waiting there for the clanking elevator to slide up the metal shaft, he thinks he hears from inside the apartment the sound of something heavy falling, shattering on the floor. It is a strangely clean noise, as though an object were lifted and dropped onto the floor, not the clattering fall of something knocked from its perch by accident. He listens again, but he can hear nothing, and the sounds from within are obscured by the hiss of the elevator as it comes to a stop in front of him. He thinks probably it was nothing, and anyway, he is just annoyed enough at her resentfulness that he doesn't feel like opening the door again now.

Surely it was nothing. He opens the elevator and steps inside.

SEVEN

July 1, 1918

WHEN THE OBSERVERS collected at the edge of the airfield the morning after Clark's death, Edward saw that they were quieter than usual, and for the first time they reminded him of the men he'd known at St-Omer. Only Lutz asked, "We are going back there, aren't we?" and Edward nodded yes in reply. They were all thinking, he knew, of the dead boy, how he had looked fallen forward like that, his body already stiffening, still in the harness.

Today, things done routinely for weeks had a new weight to them. The way McIntyre scowled up at the sky as he buttoned his jacket, then climbed into the front seat; how the plane rose, then banked sharply so the ground tilted up beside them like the face of a cliff. Edward, too, was thinking of Clark, and how his hair had been soaked with sweat when they peeled his leather hat away. They circled the airfield once and then set out, northwest, follow-

ing the river. The weather was ambivalent. Big clouds wandered
across the sky, looking lost.

When he saw the front approaching in the distance, Edward felt
a new tension rise inside him, and he scanned ahead looking for
enemy planes. The first bursts of antiaircraft fire made clouds of
black smoke in their wake. They pushed through, gaining altitude,
and soon they were in clear air on the far side. Below them, the
curve of the Aisne salient—German territory.

They turned north near the town of Mézy, where the lines
were almost at the river's edge, and flew back over the terrain they
had crossed the previous day. Looking down, Edward could begin
to make out familiar landmarks: the destroyed town he had seen,
the crossroads beyond it. The army was gone now, but he could see
impressions they had left, the trampled grass and the distressed surface of the road.

Which direction had they gone? From this height he couldn't
tell. They would have to go down to find the clues, the hoof marks
and boot prints in the mud at the roadside. He could perhaps get
a photograph that would give him the information he needed. But
he wanted to fly down and see it for himself. He found he was
yearning for the sensation of speed that came from the ground
rushing past underneath; the beauty of the ruins, and the army
asleep in their shadows. He wanted to feel that they were outrun-
ning the hollow, heavy feeling inside him.

He leaned forward, tapped McIntyre on the shoulder and yelled
to him to take them down. McIntyre nodded and put the plane
into a dive. The ground rose toward them, its intricacies becoming
clearer, and soon Edward could see black and gray circles where
fires had been. He picked up his camera and trained it downward,
and then, out of the corner of his eye, he saw something dark and
fast flash out of a cloud bank a quarter of a mile away to their left.

He turned toward the movement in time to see three mono-
planes of a type he didn't recognize flying straight toward
them. They were black with yellow bands around the fuselage.
Single-seaters. Close enough now that Edward could see the men
inside them.

Quickly, McIntyre pulled the plane's nose up, and Edward was
pressed into his seat as they rose sharply. He could hear the engines
of those other planes, a high growl above the wind. They came on,
boring a hole through the sky, filling it with their ragged sound.
Behind McIntyre the rest of the squadron rose together as though
borne up by the same sea-swell. And then the German planes were
in among them.

The sound of bullets: something insect about it, something
electric in the way it cut the air to shreds, and Edward ducked as
the three planes sped through the middle of the squadron, sending
an arc of tracers out in front of them. The air around him was filled
with that hard, fiery noise, and he felt, rather than saw, the volley
knife past above him.

As soon as they had passed, Edward lunged toward his gun.
He swung it up, aiming at where the enemy planes were preparing to dive. He squinted into the gun sights, following the progress
of the first plane, but then he saw the second German plane
branch off and begin to swing around toward them. He turned
his gun on it. He waited until it was clear of the others. Then he
opened fire.

The gun rattled out its stream of bullets, and he held on, guid-
ing it as well as he could. He saw the plane still coming toward
them and fired again. Then he heard McIntyre shouting something
and the plane begin to tilt beneath him. His stomach leapt sickeningly, and he held on to the edge of the cockpit with both hands
as they banked, then straightened out. When they were level again,

he could see that the first German plane had dropped down and come up on their other side; McIntyre had pulled them out of the way just in time.

Around them, the DH-4's were scattering and turning back toward the lines, flying as fast as they could for home. As they began to pull away, Edward could see that one of them was trailing pale smoke in a steady stream. It lagged behind, the distance that separated it from the others growing greater by the second. The German planes wheeled around it, firing and then breaking away, their lightness a taunt. Edward couldn't tell whose plane it was, couldn't make out the men inside it through the smoke that enveloped the machine.

"Should we go back?" he shouted. McIntyre didn't reply.

Behind them, the damaged plane began to tilt and fall, sliding into a head-first dive and then spinning nose over tail down toward the earth. It plummeted past them, smoke paying out behind it in a slender white ribbon. Edward heard himself cry out, a wordless shout, and then the plane hit the ground and became a fire, the smoke turning black around the flames as its fuel tanks went up.

THE GERMAN PLANES didn't follow them across the lines. After the crash they took off in the other direction, flying in procession back the way they had come. The squadron arrived at the airfield and landed. The damage to the planes was worse than the previous day, but everyone who landed was alive. There were injuries: Kelsey had been nicked by a bullet in the arm. He was bleeding a lot, but he was conscious and swearing when the stretcher-bearers pulled him from the plane.

"Goddamn it, goddamn it, goddamn it," he said as they lowered him over the side. Then he caught sight of Edward coming toward him. "Who was it?" he asked. "Whose plane?"

"I don't know," Edward said. And over his shoulder he heard Dawson say:

"It was Sergeant Daniels, sir." Kelsey let his head drop back against the stretcher, and they carried him toward the ambulance.

Lutz came and stood beside Edward, watching them carry the stretcher away. After a minute he asked, "Do you think there's any chance that Daniels could have got out?" Edward turned to look at him: Lutz was gripping his flying hat in his hands nervously, but his face was full of a luminous, unwarranted hope. Suddenly, the responsibility of providing reassurance was just too much for Edward.

"No, I don't," he said, and began to walk away.

At the door of the pavilion he met van Horn.

"You lost a plane out there," he said.

"Yes, sir. We were attacked."

"Which of your men was it?"

"Sergeant Daniels.

"Well." The colonel paused, as though waiting for Edward to say something to allay his disappointment. Then he said: "Sergeant Daniels was assistant to Lieutenant Lutz, wasn't he?" Edward nodded. "You'll need a replacement for him to help oversee the work of the interpreters. Have a recommendation to me by the end of the day. All right, Captain?"

"Yes, sir." It was that simple: replace the old parts with spares and go on. Edward watched van Horn start toward the hangars.

"Sir . . ."

"Yes?"

"Is there any possibility that we could get that escort of scouts we requested? Since we're losing so many men . . ."

"Two is not so many, Captain," van Horn said, and walked away across the field.

VISIBILITY: FAIR; PATCHY cloud cover. Troops: nil. Enemy planes: Three, unidentified type, with distinguishing yellow stripes around rear of fuselage. Encountered at 2,000 feet, coordinates . . . Edward stopped typing. He would finish the report later, he thought. Instead, he started to go through an inventory of supplies, something he'd been meaning to do for days. *Cameras, 24 K-2s. Plates, glass, 4x5 inches. Developer, potassium oxalate.* Beyond the window, the wandering clouds of the morning had joined to become a wall of white, sealing the world in like a lid. The wind had picked up; he could hear its low sound around the building. He couldn't concentrate. He put down the inventory. He put his head on the desk and folded his arms over it. If he stayed like this, he could blot out his desk with its stacks of papers, his office, the view of the airfield, everything.

Daniels was gone, vanished. Edward had hardly had time to know the man, and now he had simply disappeared. It was the randomness that felt so shocking: with slightly different luck, he might have been over in the smoking lounge right now, playing cards. Someone else, or no one, might have been killed in his place.

Edward went over and locked his office door. He cleared a space on his desk and took out a pen and a sheet of paper: he felt that he must try to tell someone what had happened, but he stared at the paper and no words came. He did not know how he could describe this to people who were not part of the war, who had not experienced it themselves. Angrily, he crumpled the paper up and threw it away. Outside, the rain began. He heard it drumming like impatient fingers on the window glass. He thought about that crossroads twenty miles away on the other side of the lines where it would wash away the footprints of departed soldiers, the tracks of their trucks and guns, slurring and dimming the evidence that they had been there, the marks that might have told him where they had gone. And then a little further on, in the middle of a field, there was the remains of an American plane that looked like it might have been a two-seater but was hard to identify by its wreckage, twisted by fire and the impact when it hit the ground.

On a new piece of paper he wrote: *Dear Marion.* He paused, looking down at her name written in his slanting hand, then he continued: *Today one of our observers was shot down and killed. His plane fell on the far side of the lines. This morning he was here and now he is gone, and I am in the process of choosing someone to take his job. I look at the men who are left and they begin to seem transparent. Tomorrow, they might vanish, too. This war has begun erasing us, one by one.* He knew even as he wrote that he would not send the letter. But he felt certain that if he did, she would understand what he meant; and somehow that was sufficient.

THAT EVENING, AFTER supper, Edward went into the officers' lounge and found Lutz and one of the pilots at the piano there. Lutz was singing something he didn't recognize. He sat down and flipped through a copy of the newspaper left over from the morning.

After a little while he heard a familiar progression of notes from the far corner, and then the opening refrain of *Non più andrai, farfallone amoroso* from *The Marriage of Figaro*, in Lutz's rich round tones.

"What's that?" asked someone sitting near him.

"It's Mozart," Edward said.

"Hey, isn't that Hun music? Should he be singing that?"

Edward looked around. He didn't know the man who had spoken.

"Oh, no," he said. "Listen: it's in Italian."

"Oh, well in that case . . ."

"He's singing to his friend who is going off to war for the first time."

From the corner, Lutz glanced over at Edward and mimed tipping his hat. *Here's an end to your days in the sun, lad / Here's an end to your games with the girls,* he sang. *Among great warriors, holding your pack / a gun on your shoulder, a saber at your right / in place of dancing, a march through the mud.*

THE RAIN CONTINUED all night, but by morning it was another mottled day, with lines of high cloud like furrows in a plowed field. They flew up the river course. Below them, already, the guns were awake, sending shells over the lines in a sleepy, disinterested way. For a while they didn't see anything else in the air.

They flew past Mézy on their own side of the lines, then they cut north and east into the salient. It had been McIntyre's idea to go by a new route, one that took them away from the major towns and roads near the front. It might give them the chance to cover more ground before they ran into any enemy.

We'll have to be our own escort, McIntyre had said when Edward had conveyed the news that there were still no scouts to come with them. We'll go the long way round, and we'll keep our altitude. No barnstorming at two hundred feet. High and safe, he told the pilots before they went out that morning. Let the interpreters find the answers later: that is their job, but they can only do it if we all come home in one piece. Boring! Edward heard someone say, and he looked around to see Tom Cundall half-grin, half-grimace at him. McIntyre heard him: Yes, he said. It's work. It's boring. You want to go joyriding, wait until the war is over.

In the middle of the run, Edward saw something on the ground that he couldn't identify. It was rectangular, the dimensions of a medium-sized building, but there was something strange about it. Around it there was grass, but inside it there was only a dark space without distinguishing features. It was at the edge of a field, some distance away from a small farmhouse. A little further on, he saw another one: rectangular, dark and blurred. He kept taking pictures, hoping that they would show enough detail to tell him what it was.

From the east a group of four Albatroses came climbing toward them. McIntyre put out blue flags on his wings to signal the others. Two of the observation planes hung back to deliver covering fire while the rest turned directly for home. The Albatroses scattered and looped, then came back shooting. When Edward looked back, the fight seemed to be taking place underwater, all the elements slowed down, so he could see with hypnotic clarity the movements of the planes as they circled each other. Then one of the observation planes was losing altitude. Edward watched it descend over No Man's Land until it dipped behind a hill on the safe side of the lines. He just had time to remember its number before it vanished from view.

When he arrived back at the airfield, he realized it was Dawson's plane that had been downed.

FIRE IN THE corner of a field: a diagonal of dark gray thinned as it rose to become translucent. What was it from? What was burning? He looked again, and through the eyepieces of the stereoscope, the landscape resolved into its three dimensions, depth coming from frozen consecutive seconds superimposed one on another. Here was the road, the field that they had seen from the air, the fire. How big was the blaze? It was in the corner of a field, so it was probably a barn, nothing more, though would a barn really burn that fiercely? What had been inside it? Could it have been an ammunition dump? That was certainly possible. He made notes on the tablet of paper at his elbow.

Standing beside Edward, Lutz asked, "Do you see it, sir? In the bottom left-hand corner."

They were in the developing laboratory at the airfield. Behind them men moved around the large central table, putting together the photographs from that morning into a mosaic map of the landscape. Edward refocused the stereoscope so now the bottom of the picture sprang into clarity. The curve of the road. An outcropping of trees along a slight rise in the shape of a laughing mouth. And there: another of the strange imprints he had seen during the morning's flight, square and dark, a little way back from the road.

"Got it," he said.

"What do you think it is?" Lutz asked. Edward looked up.

"I don't know. I thought that the stereoscope would give us a sense of its height. But it doesn't seem to have any."

"Right, sir. It's just a mark on the ground." Edward looked again. Lutz was right: it was no more than a discoloration, a darkening, and the contrast to its surroundings made it seem real, gave it the illusion of solidity.

"It looks like there was a building there, and now it's gone," Edward said. "Nothing left but an outline. I don't know. I've never seen anything like it. We'll just have to report it and keep watching." Lutz nodded. "Let me have a look at the rest of the prints."

More fires, one in Bois de Brulit, one in Etrepilly. Soldiers in the streets of Vaux, forming up into companies in the town square. Vaux had been shelled by the French at dawn that day: the troops might be evacuating for someplace new. Also, a work party on the outskirts of the town, about fifteen men, clustered around an old wooden outbuilding, maybe a dairy. They had two wagons with them, two teams of horses. He made a note of their coordinates, then went back to scanning through the photographs.

A downed plane, French, just outside Bussiares. Some activity in a woods just north of the same town: men entering and leaving the cover of the trees; something big had been dragged up the rise toward it; that was all he could tell. Along the road from Château-Thierry, a line of ambulances, six of them, made their way toward the town. Piles of leaves and branches covered their canvas backs: camouflage. But they were all the same shape, and it gave them away.

Behind him, someone called out: "Dawson just telephoned from a communications post near Mézy. They had a bumpy landing in the middle of a cow pasture, but he is all right. The pilot, too."

A cheer went up from the men around the table. For a moment it didn't matter that they had to go out again that evening, only that for now, one of their number was safe.

LATER THAT DAY he took prints of it to the colonel. Van Horn was sitting at his desk, looking over a newly arrived memo when Edward entered his office.

"Steichen, good. Take a look at this." He pushed the memo across his desk. It was from Barnes in Chaumont. *De Ram Automatic Magazine Camera, four. To be sent to Observation Group 1, Épernay.*

"Are you familiar with how the De Ram works?" van Horn

asked. Edward shook his head. "It has a magazine like the one on a machine gun. Loads the plates automatically. All the observer has to do is point the camera downward and start it going. It will do the rest by itself. They have only just been released for use. These were all that I could get for us. Your men will have to learn how to use them quickly."

"When will they arrive?"

"They're here, and we'll have them fitted tomorrow. You can practice and then start using them to shoot in the evening. These should solve the problem of plates getting damaged when one of your men is killed." He cleared his throat. "I'll also arrange for a couple of scouts to go out with you, too."

"If you think that is prudent, sir," Edward said.

"I do. We've can't afford to lose any more planes, especially not the ones fitted with the new cameras."

So this, Edward thought, is the truth of it: men are inexpensive and replaceable; machines are expensive and rare and must be protected. The escort isn't for us. It's for our cameras.

"Well, sir. I'm pleased that you've unexpectedly found you have the planes to spare." He said it slowly, trying to keep his voice steady. But if van Horn caught the tone of his words, he chose to ignore it.

"Since we only have four automatics," he said, "I thought you should decide which of the men gets to try them out."

"Well," Edward said slowly, "Lieutenants Lutz, Deveraux and Dawson should get them; and then, why don't we give the last one to Gilles Marchand? He's slated to fly with Tom Cundall tomorrow. His work has been perfectly reliable, but it would be good to give him a break."

Van Horn nodded. "Fine," he said. "That's settled. Do you have the prints from today?"

Edward brought up the folder of photographs and set it on the desk. "We saw something new in these," he said, opening the file and searching through it until he found a picture that showed the imprints they had seen. "Here, and here," he pointed. "These depressions. I haven't seen them before. They are like the ghosts of houses. Something was there before. Now it's gone."

Van Horn peered at the pictures Edward handed him. He leafed through them, comparing.

"Interesting," he said. "They aren't shelled buildings. There is no rubble, no debris from explosions or signs of anything burning." He continued to peer at them for some minutes. "I don't know what they are," he said at last. "We'd better get you back up there to find out."

ON THE EVENING reconnaissance flight they began photographing just over the lines, making their way north. They had two Spad scouts flying with them, one on either end of their line. They were half the size of the other planes, and when they rose off the ground, they seemed to Edward weightless, slipping into the sky as if they were returning to their element.

He had been taking pictures for some minutes when suddenly, by the river, he saw them: a cluster of ghosts, those same rectangular imprints in the soil. And then, a little further on, a group of men. They had horses and wagons; there might have been twenty of them, a work detail from the trenches nearby. They were loading something into the wagons, that much he could make out. Ammunition? They were working in teams, three or four of them at a time carrying something large between them.

He looked again. From this height they appeared to be taking apart the walls of the building itself.

"We could lose a little height; get a clearer look at them,"

Edward shouted to McIntyre. Then he heard the dropping note of a plane diving. He looked toward the sound and saw one of the observation planes break from the others and swoop toward the soldiers on the ground.

Later it would seem that he had seen, quite clearly, the expressions on the faces of the soldiers on the ground as they looked up and realized that the descending plane was not their own: the shock of terror that held them frozen where they stood, then the burst of frantic energy as they ran for cover. The way they threw themselves facedown on the earth as the plane slid through the lowest point of its parabola, passing close above them, its forward guns going. These memories weren't real, of course; they came from seeing the photographs afterward, but they persisted, nonetheless, vivid and insistent. He recalled that he had stood up and reached out his hand, as though the plane was as small as it appeared and he could scoop it up and pull it away from the even tinier men below. They looked so helpless that for a minute he didn't care that they were the enemy. He only wanted them not to be afraid.

Then, as though in answer to this thought, there was a burst of fire from the closest outcropping of trees. There must be a machine gun hidden beneath the canopy: the men down there were not helpless, after all. The wings of Cundall's plane shuddered from the impact of bullets, but it held steady and began to climb. Edward felt a flood of relief. It reached the altitude of the rest of the squadron and caught up with them. Edward peered to see if the men inside were all right but couldn't make them out.

They flew on, still following the course of the river and then, quite suddenly, there was a group of German planes behind them. There were several different models, one of them a triplane, something Edward had never seen before. Coming toward them, it seemed to rise vertically like a firefly, its triple wings resolved into a single plane by the steep angle of its ascent. The Germans accelerated quickly toward them, and there were five, no six—he couldn't be sure because they were approaching from the west and the sun blinded him. The Spads swung around and accelerated toward the oncoming enemy, becoming silhouettes against the light. The paths of the planes looped until he couldn't distinguish which were American and which were German. Then one of the Spads was burning and falling. The Germans turned and began to follow the main squadron again, gaining rapidly.

He was quicker this time, on his gun the minute he saw them coming, no hesitation, and he was momentarily elated that he had developed these reflexes as he fired a stream of bullets up toward one of the enemy. They passed overhead, and he began to feel like he'd seen this before, his mind dropping into an alertness that focused only on watching for where the next round of fire would come from, a kind of tunnel vision that at once dulled and thrilled him. The noise of the plane climbed on their left, passed overhead and then came down on their right. Looking up, he saw the pilot suspended upside down over the void, for a moment nothing but momentum preventing him from plummeting to earth. Then the plane arched over and came down on them, firing. Edward swung the machine gun around and crouched to brace himself. He could see the pilot's face, his eyes covered by goggles, but his features clearly distinguishable—nose, mouth, jaw. A human face. He let loose a round of bullets into it.

Under him he felt the plane begin to fall away. He scrambled to get a foothold, a handhold, something, but he slipped and fell backward against the rim of the cockpit and then forward, his head striking hard against the support of the machine gun. The plane was still descending so rapidly he felt weightless inside it, diving steeply, or falling out of control, he couldn't tell which. He levered himself back into the seat and managed to get one of the belts around his shoulder. He gripped the rim of the cockpit with both hands. He saw the ground surge up, filling his vision as they plunged toward it. Then he blacked out.

Incoming Tide. Brittany, 1914. Platinum print.

FIRST SHE EMPTIES the silverware drawer. Knives, forks, spoons—she pulls from where they are stored, bundled in cloths and newly polished and, with the flourish of a juggler, releases them into empty air. They rise from her hands, sinews of light sliding down their surfaces. For a moment, they seem to hang suspended, a bright, hard, chaos. Then they fall. They crash onto the flagstones and scatter, and the noise rings out, calamitous.

She does this again and again, watching him all the time, until the drawer lies empty and the floor at her feet glimmers with complicated silver hieroglyphs. Then, since there is no more silverware, she balls up the tablecloth and hurls it at him. He sees it arc through the air toward his head and instinctively puts his arm up to shield himself. The white mass explodes softly against his elbow. It floats down, silently settling into a heap of crumpled linen, and Edward thinks how oblivious the tablecloth remains to its present use as a weapon. Meanwhile, Clara is searching in the dresser behind her for something else to throw, and, looking up, he sees her pause, then open one of the top cupboards and reach inside. She begins to pull something out of it, something heavy that requires her to use both hands to lift it. That cupboard is where they keep the china.

In a moment he is across the room. He encircles her wrists with his hands—his thumb and forefinger are enough to stretch all the way around—and pulls them away from the cupboard so he is holding her arms in front of her, above her head. This close he can hear her breath coming in bursts. She struggles against him, but he keeps her there, immobile, at arm's length. His anger rises in his chest, a heavy solid mass that makes it difficult to breathe or speak, so when he opens his mouth, all that comes out is a hiss: "How dare you?" he whispers. She stares back at him, her eyes a defiant blank.

From behind him comes the sound of the back door creaking open, footsteps of someone entering the kitchen from the garden. Edward turns toward the noise, loosening his grasp on Clara as he does so. She twists away from him, lets out a high, frustrated sound that is somewhere between a scream and a grunt, and runs from the dining room, shoving the door so it slams closed behind her. There is a crash of dissonance from the front parlor as she drops the lid of the piano, then a sound like wings flapping: she's throwing sheets of music. Her footsteps bite into each stair as she climbs to the second floor. The door of their bedroom opens, then slams shut. Sobbing follows, ragged, just audible.

Edward stands alone in the dining room, which is suddenly, thickly quiet. He puts both hands on the big wooden table in front of him, leans forward onto them. He wants the table to absorb his anger, to drain it away so that he can face the owner of the footsteps, which are getting steadily louder, coming along the corridor toward him. He breathes. The door creaks open. François, the gardener, peers into the room. He looks at the chaos on the floor, then at Edward.

"I heard noises," he says. He waits on the threshold, his arms braced against the doorframe. At that moment, he is the most solid object in the room.

"It's nothing," Edward says.

The old man nods slowly. "An accident maybe," he suggests.

"Yes," says Edward, gratefully. "That's it." François shrugs and goes out. His footsteps recede back down the corridor, as unhurried as before.

An accident, Edward thinks. Yes. He stoops down and picks up the tablecloth, folds it, puts it away. He begins to gather up the silver. From above him the sound of crying continues to slip between the floorboards, under the doors, surreptitiously filling up the house. After a few minutes he isn't sure if he hears it at all, or if some other more tactile sense attunes him to her. He can feel her storm in his solar plexus. His nerves are sympathetic strings, he thinks; his skin knows things.

An accident. It isn't exactly a lie to describe their fights that way, because that is how they always feel to him: like a collision he could not possibly have anticipated or avoided, a disaster that comes out of nowhere. He quite literally has no idea what he said or did to make her flare up so suddenly, but then there are times when she is like this, when she is volatile. An offhand comment or a casual action will open a trapdoor in her and she will fall through it pulling him after her. At these times there is no talking to her. He could go upstairs and sit down on the bed beside her, touch her hair, he could use the softest words he knows, but all this will do is reignite her. Nothing he says will be any good. She will turn it back on him, twisting it into something he never intended. She will hear only insults, disregard, and selfishness. And in any case he is too angry himself to speak to her now.

Usually, when she gets this way, he will simply walk out of the house, taking nothing with him but his keys and jacket. He'll go down to the station in Esbly and get on the next train to Paris. He'll spend a few days in his studio there, not answering the door, absorbed in the process of developing and printing his photographs, and work will dissolve the argument so he can return to her with his anger gone. This has become a rhythm for him. He withdraws to the city after a fight, and each of them has time to become calm. When they first moved to Voulangis, he planned to get rid of his studio in Montparnasse and take all his equipment up to the house on the Marne, where he was building a darkroom against one wall of the garden. The dark room has been finished for years, and Clara has pointed out more than once the expense of keeping two studios. She even once hinted that he kept his rooms in the city for other, more nefarious reasons, and after that he thought seriously about giving them up just to allay her fears.

But each time he is about to relinquish his apartment in Paris, he stops. He knows somewhere that he cannot get by without it. He has found he needs this valve in his life.

He would like to go there now, soothe himself with the sound of the train rocking over the rails, then with work and solitude, perhaps a visit to Meudon to see Rodin. But today that will not be possible. Marion Beckett is driving up from Paris to stay with them for the month of July. She is due to arrive after lunch, and then Arthur and Mercedes will come later in the evening. That Clara should choose this day to relinquish her hold on propriety, when she knows they are expecting visitors—damn her, damn her—it only adds to his annoyance and anger. What on earth is she thinking? It is already half past eleven.

He stands up. If he cannot have the complete freedom of Paris, at least he can get some work done before the guests arrive. He leaves the rest of the silverware on the floor and goes out into the kitchen yard. Louisa is there, hanging sheets on the line. He comes up beside her and touches her gently on the shoulder.

"I'm afraid Madame isn't feeling very well. She dropped some things in the kitchen. When you have a minute, would you pick them up and put them away?"

Louisa frowns and nods. "Yes," she says. "Since Madame is indisposed. Again."

He lets himself through the gate into the back garden. It is a stunningly clear day. There is a loveliness to the summers here that almost defies belief, each blade of grass seems to be lit from within. Later, he will remember that these days seemed fragile in their beauty, but he will not be able to distinguish whether this is the manufacture of memory because of what came after. On this day, he notices the delphiniums are folded, their stored brightness nearly bloomed; François kneels nearby, transplanting larkspur and irises to the bed under the fruit trees. He glances up as Edward makes his way across the bright lawn but doesn't pause from his work. Edward raises his hand in greeting, then goes quickly and unlocks his studio door. He feels embarrassed in front of the old man, even though he knows this is foolish. Clara's temper is not his fault. But still, he wants right now to have walls enclosing him, to vanish into the controlled stillness of his negatives. Their safety.

His studio smells of the unvarnished timber out of which he built the walls, a dusty, sweet odor that calms him instantly. He stands in the vestibule and inhales the smell of wood, turpentine, paint, then comes in and closes the door behind him. The structure is divided into two rooms, a studio for painting and a darkroom for developing and printing at the far end. He put a skylight into the roof on this side to give himself natural light. He crosses the room, laying his hands on the physical objects it contains as he goes, the workbench, the easel, the shelves where he stores his paints and brushes, reassuring himself that they are really there. He loves their solidity, the way they take up space. He loves the balanced weight of the brush or the camera in his hands.

He goes to the door that leads to the darkroom and ducks inside, latching it behind him. He has hung black curtains about two feet behind the door, and he parts these and steps inside, turning on the overhead safelight so that the room appears around him in scarlet. A month ago he took some pictures on a trip to the

Brittany coast and he hasn't yet had time to print them. The negatives are on a shelf over the sink, boxed and labeled. He brings them down and carries them carefully out to his workbench.

Against the white surface, he examines them, one by one. They offer him their miniature worlds with the light and darkness reversed. In this first one, taken on the beach, the low tide is just beginning to turn. The sea has gone out, leaving the rocky shore exposed. His daughters have clambered out to find anemones among the tidal pools, crabs in their slow armor, whiskery fish with transparent skins. Mary is lying stretched out on a ledge of rock on her belly peering down into the water. Her black fingers trace its surface, while Kate stands knee deep in it, looking up at him out of white eyes set in her shadow-colored face. The girls' white mouths smile, their white hair is tangled up with the wind coming off the sea. Above them, a dark sun has blown out of the clouds and is turning the sea's surface to ribbons of slate.

This one he will print, he decides. He'll put it on platinum paper so that he can get the full spectrum of tones. Then maybe he will try gum bichromate, though the picture seems to demand clarity. It is not soft enough for him to bring his brushes to it: the moment should be just as it is, undisturbed.

That day, he remembers, he'd followed the children out over the rocks, chasing this photograph. He had found himself out of breath as he tried his footing on each new ledge, and his shoes slipped on the barnacles and soft green seaweeds that grew up to the high-water line. When he looked up, the girls were already far ahead of him, waving and beckoning, and he laughed and started after them again. Clara, standing on the shore, called: For God's sake, be careful! and he had waved to show her that he was fine, that she shouldn't worry so much. The girls had eluded him for a while before they grew tired from running and climbing, and he could finally catch them. He found them wading and absorbed in the contents of a single pool, as though it were the whole world. He'd lain down on the rock opposite so he could photograph them from their own height.

When they made it, at last, back to the beach, all three of them were exhausted, their clothes covered in green and brown smudges and their hair full of salt. Clara had been angry. Look at the state of you, she said to Mary. Look at your dress. It's filthy.

We were having an adventure, Edward said, and he came up and kissed her on the cheek despite her glowering expression. Isn't that right, girls? Yes, yes, said Mary. That's right. Kate grinned and nod-ded. You can't worry about your clothes, he told her, when you are on an adventure. He was determined not to let her spoil the beauty of the afternoon; he wanted to have peace, he didn't want to deal with her sudden peevishness, her dissatisfaction that seemed to take in the whole world: her husband, her daughters, herself. He took the girls both by the hand and kept walking down the beach away from her.

What if the tide had come in while you were out there? she called after him. I couldn't even see you from here. How could I have known to call for help? Edward? Why aren't you listening to me? Her words followed them over the sand until the wind blew them out to sea.

He carries the plate back to the darkroom and inserts it into the enlarger, focuses the light onto the printing frame, then flicks it off again. He opens the drawer where he keeps platinum paper and fills a developing tray with potassium oxalate. He's irritated to find his mind occupied again with Clara: he had come in here to escape her. Never mind, he thinks as he fits the paper into the frame. What had he said this morning that upset her so much? He goes over the scene in his head. She had been playing the piano in the front parlor. The children were at school until noon, and he'd just come in to tell her that he'd invited a couple of additional guests to stay at the house, Mercedes de Cordoba and Arthur Carles. They would be coming up that very afternoon from the city. They probably wouldn't be staying long, and they were such close friends; it wasn't necessary to make a big fuss for them, or any elaborate preparations. He thought she'd be pleased. She likes both Mercy and Arthur a lot; she's declared it loudly, in that way she has at the end of an evening, when she is tired and a little drunk: I really do love Arthur. He is such a dear man. It didn't occur to him that the news of the impending arrival would be a cause for anger.

But when he told her about it, Clara had stopped playing and looked at him with an expression of disbelief. Then she put her head down on the keys of the piano, so that a chromatic mass of notes rose out of the instrument and engulfed her, filling the room with dissonance.

IF SHE OPENS her fingers just a little bit, she can see the corner of the room where the walls join the ceiling, each making a triangle of gray. Isn't it peculiar how, even though they are covered in the same paint, each surface looks like it is a different color? She has never noticed this effect before; she has never had time to notice. Of course, on the other hand, if she closes up her fingers again, the whole world goes dark. Bruise-colored, black and red, the room vanishes, and takes the rest of the house with it. No more beds to make. No more silverware to polish. If she just stays here, like this, with her hands over her face. That, she thinks, is really a good trick.

She starts to shake again. Is she giggling or weeping? She isn't sure until she feels tears start to slide across her face, dripping sideways over her nose and down onto the pillow beneath her head. How ugly she must look with her nose pouring and her eyes all red, with her blotchy cheeks and the skin around her eyes puffed out, bulging and discolored, her face practically falling off her bones—each time she looks in the mirror, it has collapsed a little further, until she can hardly recognize herself. Never mind—it will match her ruined figure, won't it? It has been ruined really since her second pregnancy six years ago, and no amount of medicinal strengthening compound has given her back the pretty waist that was so admired when she was younger. Stocky, she has become stocky; that is the word. Hasn't she grown stocky since her marriage, people might say, and they would be quite correct. She has become a fat frump, a woman of middle years with her charm fading out of her. With each passing year she is becoming more hideous. And as she does, *his* regard for her is dwindling, she knows; she feels it in his carelessness toward her. Eventually, when he cannot even bear to look at her, then he will at last find someone else. Oh, maybe he won't leave her and their children. He has promised many times that he would never do such a thing, but what difference would that make? As she knows only too well, it isn't necessary that a man should leave home entirely for him to begin keeping his heart elsewhere.

Her throat constricts and she lets out a sharp involuntary sob. She knows that her weeping can be heard all through the house. The interior walls are thin and sound carries. Edward has chided her about this before: You know Louisa can hear the racket you are making all the way down in the kitchen. What if the girls hear you? How will they feel, to hear their mother so upset? Always thinking of someone else's feelings, never hers.

She doesn't care. Let them all crowd around the door and listen with their ears pressed up against it if they like. She has decided never to leave this room again. She will become a recluse, starting today, so what does it matter what people out there think of her, Edward or that silly girl Louisa or old François. She is going to stay right here and to hell with them! She imagines staying in this bed for the rest of her life. They will try to get her to come downstairs. Edward will coax her, plead with her; perhaps he will get angry and shout and storm around like he does when he is upset. Still, she will just smile and look at him sadly, as though he could never really understand, and turn away from him.

Her daughters might be confused at first, but eventually they will get used to it. Mary won't miss her all that much anyway—that girl has never really appreciated her; she has always been her father's favorite, with eyes only for him. She thinks of Clara as mean-spirited and conventional, always wanting her daughters to keep their clothes clean and behave themselves, and wasn't Edward forever undermining her attempts to bring up her daughters with a bit of decency and decorum, always dragging them through swamps and across rivers on his confounded adventures, never thinking that the ruined clothes would have to be washed, and the cuts cleaned with iodine and dressed, and the children calmed and put to bed so they wouldn't be too tired for school the next day—oh, she could just shriek with frustration when she thought about it.

And what about little Kate? Well, she can come and see Mama upstairs if she wants to. Clara decides she will receive visitors; she'll greet them all with the same even temper, never showing so much as an ounce of impatience or sadness. She just won't come downstairs, won't cook another dinner for them, won't clean the kitchen or churn another load of laundry that Louisa has not had time to finish and hang up to dry. She won't make up another bed for a guest invited unexpectedly at the last minute without consulting her. The endless extra chores that the running of a big house demanded from her—those she is done with.

Gradually, she thinks, the mattress will begin to bow around her, as though it's cradling her in a deepening embrace. Through the window she'll see the seasons change, watch the sun trace its path across the sky. She'll become wise with watching. She will no longer be concerned with making a good impression on their friends and acquaintances; not worried about reading the latest books on art and politics and psychoanalysis. It won't matter that Alfred never speaks to her directly if he can help it, or that Arthur is forever interrupting her in his enthusiasm to talk to Edward. She won't care about that tinge of condescension she feels from so many of the women in their social circle: Gertrude Stein, Katharine Rhoades, even Mercy, recently. She doesn't know why, but she suspects it is because she is not an artist. She is just a wife. Only Mildred, and of their Paris set, Marion Beckett, are truly her friends as much as they are Edward's. Only Marion, she knows, comes to the Marne to visit her first and foremost, not just to bask in the glow of her gregarious husband, a man whose charm means he can get away with almost anything.

He'd come in when she was beginning the third movement of a Franck composition for solo piano, the fugue, and stood beside her with one elbow leaned on the top of the unraised lid. That was her stolen hour, the first she'd had to play all week, and she'd been congratulating herself on having salvaged it by getting up early and finishing the silver before the first of their summer guests arrived. One hour was not much, but somehow it would have to be enough, and she had begun with scales, running her fingers lightly up and down the keys, then moving up a semitone. She imagined the notes like water in an ocean wave, caught and held aloft, then gently dropped back down to be picked up again by a different current, another key. C, C-sharp, D, E-flat—her fingers worked unconsciously, and she felt energy begin to flow through them. She started the piece, sightreading as she went, but pleased to be beginning something new. And then there he was, standing too close for her to ignore, flipping through the scores stacked on top of the piano, glancing idly at the titles and waiting for the chance to speak to her.

This appeared to be the nature of the day, then, that everything she tried to do would be interrupted. Earlier, after getting the girls breakfasted and off to school, she had been seated at the kitchen table polishing the last of the silverware, watching her reflection come up clear and upside down in the faces of the spoons, when she heard voices in the kitchen yard. Louisa, and then a deeper voice, male, that she couldn't identify. She went to the window and looked out. Louisa was leaning on the fence talking with a man dressed in the dark rough coveralls of a farmhand. Clara didn't know his name, but his face was familiar: he must work on one of the farms nearby. The two of them were standing very close together. Then the man leaned back and swung lazily on the fence, his arms making the radius of an arc traced by his long body. He said something she couldn't hear and then burst out laughing, the sound harsh in the quiet. Louisa laughed too, high and nervous. Behind her, the laundry Clara needed for tomorrow lay half-finished, shirts and underwear floating in a tub of soapy water, the plunger beside it on the ground, discarded.

Clara had gone to the door, opened it and closed it again hard. The sound of it slamming shut was enough: Louisa started up and looked around, and the man took off hurriedly toward the road. Clara watched him go off across the fields, headed away from the town. He must have come, she thought, from the farm belonging to Claude Perrine, the man who also served as the local *garde cham-*

pêtre. They were on good terms with Claude. If she saw him, she would speak to him about the man. But Louisa, she was another matter.

Clara stopped playing and looked up at Edward.

"I found Louisa chatting to one of Claude Perrine's men this morning," she said. "Could you speak to her about it?"

"Why?" he asked, turning the pages of some Chopin piano pieces. "Is she not allowed to speak to men now?"

"Of course she is. But not while she should be doing the washing."

"You're too hard on her," Edward said. "What harm can it do for her to talk? Will you play this nocturne for us this evening? Arthur loves Chopin when you play it."

"Please, Edward. If I say anything about it, she'll just glare at me."

"I'll speak to her," he said. "I promise." He promises things when he doesn't want to talk about them anymore, she knows; it is his way of ending the conversation and moving on to something that he thinks is more important.

"Darling, I've asked a couple of extra people to come up from the city this weekend. Arthur wrote and said he so wanted to come and paint here again this month, so I told him he could if he liked. He and Mercy are going to come up by train this evening. You can put her in the bed next to Marion and Arthur can sleep in the study. Could you make up the bed in there for him?"

So there it was, her precious hour, gone.

"How long will he be staying?" she asked.

"For the rest of the month, I should think; not too long. I didn't really ask him." He opened the book to a polonaise and held it up for her to see. "Or you could play this one."

Clara put her head down on the keys of the piano. Around her she felt the notes coming up and covering her, as though they wanted to drown her. She wished they could. Above her she saw her husband gazing down with a perplexed look on his face.

"What on earth is the matter?" he asked.

"Nothing." She felt tears rising in her face, her throat tightened. "I just sat down to play. It's been my first chance to practice for days."

Edward nodded. "Well, maybe you should try to practice a little earlier in the day," he said, "when there is less going on. What have you been doing this morning while I've been out?"

He doesn't understand anything. He doesn't even know what she does with her time, and no wonder really, since, in the last year, he has spent so much time traveling.

If she is honest, she knows that her greatest fear is that she will decide to stay in bed forever and he won't notice that she is gone. After all, Louisa can cook and do the chores; he'll have his friends for company; and she is absolutely sure that more than one of the women they know would happily provide the other thing for him. She knows, of course, about Isadora Duncan; that news had reached her about a year after the affair ended. Quite casually, one of their acquaintances, Judith Cladel, who wrote for the newspapers, mentioned that she had seen Edward with that woman at a party in Paris the summer before Clara had become pregnant with Kate. Oh, she had said, I didn't know that she was in France then. Judith had turned bright red and stuttered, well, I'm sure he simply forgot to mention it—but the embarrassment had already told her everything she needed to know. Other bits and pieces of evidence had assembled into a story in her head: other meetings he had "forgotten." Letters he'd gone to his studio to read. The worst of it, she sometimes felt, was how little he had tried to hide it: prancing around with that woman just as though it was the most innocent thing in the world, as though it was absolutely right for him to act that way.

She thinks that the affair had ended by the time she put its pieces together, and she is also fairly certain it hasn't resumed since, if only because Isadora (amazing, shocking woman) has moved on to other liaisons far more notorious. At the time of her discovery she had tried to talk to their friends about it, to find out more of what had gone on; she had written to Alfred Stieglitz, whom she'd been told had seen Edward and that Duncan woman together in New York some years before. He had written back, telling her to dismiss such thoughts from her, as he put it, *silly head*. He did not deny that the affair had taken place: *You married him, knowing all his faults,* he wrote instead. *He loves you as well as he knows how, and works hard to support you. What more can you ask?*

And in the end, she supposes, he is right, for what was there to say, or to do? She had two small children and nowhere to go, and anyway, for a while around the time of Kate's birth he had seemed much more present, had almost loved her the way she had always imagined. But the world encroached: he became distracted again by travel and work. And for all she knows, there may be other women; she no longer feels that she can entirely dismiss that possibility. Women love him, dote on him. If she were to seclude herself she would merely be getting out of their way, making it a little bit easier for them.

From downstairs she hears the sound of the girls arriving home for their midday meal. Louisa would give it to them in the kitchen, and then they would go back to school for their afternoon lessons. She rises quickly and locks the door: she doesn't want to see her children now. Then she flops back down onto the bed and puts her hands back over her face so the world goes dark again.

THE NOISE OF an automobile reaches across the quiet of the valley. Edward hears it approach from where he is standing over a developing bath watching an image rise out of the paper: hard verticals and scattered chevrons coalesce until he can recognize cliffs, wheeling seabirds, the ocean. The rough sound of the engine gets closer.

He waits until the picture has reached its point of greatest clarity, then plucks it from the developer with his tongs, immerses it in fixer, then in water. He clips it on the line above the sink, rinses his hands, dries them on the front of his trousers, and slips out of the darkroom. The brightness of the day makes him blink. He puts up a hand to shield his eyes from the glare just as the car turns into the end of the drive.

Edward still finds automobiles wonderful. He has never owned one himself, but once at a state fair in Milwaukee, he and Lilian climbed into the driver's seat of a Model T when the owner wasn't looking and rode very slowly around the fairgrounds in it (neither of them knew how to shift out of first gear), until the owner and a local policeman caught up with them and showed them, insistently, which one was the brake pedal. This car is black and red, with a raised front seat; it looks like a crossbreed of an insect and a cow. It sputters to a stop in front of the house, emitting one last fierce bang as Marion cuts the engine. The silence that surges up in its wake feels peculiarly empty, as though the world had made room in itself for the sound and wasn't sure how to close it up again.

Marion stands, pulls driving goggles from her face and waves to him across the lawn. She shucks leather gloves from her hands and folds them into a traveling bag beside her on the seat. Her movements are precise, and she has about her a sense of calm order. He remembers all at once how much he likes this quality of hers.

"Hello," he calls, and he comes toward the car intending to help her down. But when he gets there, she has already climbed from the running board and is walking toward him, smiling, holding out her hand.

"Welcome," he says. He takes her hand between both of his.

"Hello, Mr. Steichen," she says.

"I am so glad you've come," he says. "We've all been looking forward to your visit a great deal."

"Well, you *should* be honored," she says, smiling. "My parents are traveling in Russia this summer and invited me to accompany them."

"Russia! That would be novel and exciting."

"Yes, it would, but instead I decided to come here so I could paint and visit with you. Where is Clara?" Behind her the car purrs, creaking as it cools.

"She is upstairs. She was feeling . . . she was feeling a little unwell this morning." Marion looks at him and he feels he's being seen straight through.

"I love the new motorcar," he says.

"It isn't mine, I'm afraid. It is only borrowed for the month. Arthur and Mercy have said they will drive it back to Paris for me when they leave, and so I'll have to take the boring old train back to the city."

"Well, you must let me try driving it sometime while you are here. Hold on and I'll get François to bring your bags inside."

"Oh, not necessary," she says. "I'm sure I can manage them just fine."

"Well, I will help at least."

She has her hair pulled up under a straw hat that ties beneath her chin, and a few strands have come loose and fall across her face. She pushes them aside, impatiently, as they walk around to get her bags from the back of the car, and he thinks how she has changed since he first met her as the awkward, precocious girl sent to Paris for the summer to learn painting. She has grown into her self-possession, and grown into her looks, too. Her body has become more graceful, and her hair has darkened from carrot-orange to auburn; the strands that keep falling out of her hat now, despite her attempts to tuck them back under it, are the color of maple syrup. She pulls two carpetbags from the trunk of the car, and he stops her and tries to take one from her.

"I can't let you carry both of these," he says. "Allow me to keep some of my dignity as a host."

"Well, all right," she says. "You may have the privilege of taking this one," and she hands him the heavier and larger of the two. "Unless you want François to do it." Her eyes, which are laughing as she passes him the case, are green, but in the sunlight he can see that their centers are flecked with gold. She starts toward the house, carrying the smaller carpetbag.

"Do you think Clara is well enough to see me?" Marion calls back to him.

At some point in the last few years she has become beautiful. Not in the fine, delicate way that Clara is, though. It comes from how she moves and smiles, the intersection of her voice, her bear-ing—even her conversation is part of it. He realizes this as he watches her stride toward the house with confident, even steps, push open the door and step inside, calling "Hello?" up into the darkness of the house. The ingredients of this beauty have been with her all along, but somehow they have never suited her until now, as if she wasn't ready to assume them, to admit that they belonged to her. But here she is, and Edward, who for his whole life has prided himself on being able to find that which is digni-fied, lovely and aligned in people—it is after all what he does for a living—has not noticed until this very moment. This surprises him so much that he half-lowers, half-drops the case he has gripped in his right hand onto the ground.

It is her colors: he must capture them, he decides. He has

wanted for some time to do more work with the Lumière autochrome plates, to refine the clumsy color prints he had produced with Alfred the previous summer. But he hasn't had the right subject, until now. He will take her portrait. He will use her as his experiment in color. With this resolved, he feels suddenly happy, lighter; the grimness of the morning lifts off him a little. He picks up the case and follows her up to the house.

MARION PUTS HER bags down in the hall and peers up the stairs. The house looks just as she remembers it; it smells of the rose petals that Clara puts in a bowl on the front hall table. Recollections from her visit here last summer come into her mind as vividly as though she'd never left. She loves this place, and she is delighted to be here, to see her friends. But she is also recalling already those divided feelings she experiences whenever she is around the Steichens: Clara is unwell and she knows that this is Edward's evasive way of saying that she is upset because they have argued.

When he comes in the front door carrying her suitcase, she asks: "Is she sleeping?"

"I don't know," Edward says. He also looks up toward the darkened second story, and in his face she sees an expression of sad bewilderment. He really does not understand his wife and it causes him pain time and again. Marion knows that he will have been surprised by Clara's anger, that he will not have seen it coming, will have been oblivious to his part in causing it. This is how their pattern unfolds; she has watched them repeat it now for a little over ten years. She reaches out and touches his shoulder.

"I'll go up and see."

"Yes, please do. I know she will be happy to see you," he says, and she hears, as clearly as though he had actually spoken it, the ending he has omitted from the sentence: even if she would not be happy to see me.

Marion climbs the stairs and knocks at the door to Clara and Edward's bedroom. She hears a stirring inside, and Clara's voice: "Who is it?"

"Clara, dear. It's me, Marion."

There are footsteps and the sound of the bolt sliding back, and then Clara's face at the door. She's smiling, although it is clear that she has been crying just a little while before. She opens the door and embraces Marion on the threshold of the room. She begins to cry again silently; Marion can feel her sobs, one rising out of another as she holds her in her arms.

They sit down on the bed and Clara wipes her eyes.

"What a welcome!" she says. "I'm so sorry. I wouldn't blame you if you turned around and headed right back to Paris."

"Well of course I'm not going to do that. What happened?"

"Oh, God. It's so stupid," Clara says, "but it was just the last little straw." And she tells Marion about her interrupted hour, Louisa, the unexpected visitors, Edward's suggestion that she should practice earlier in the morning. "I know it sounds like nothing. I don't know why it upset me so much."

"No," Marion says slowly, "no, it does not sound like nothing." But she has no idea what else to say, because she does not know how things might be made better. Being a married woman has responsibilities that come with it; the household must be organized; the children must be cared for; and then there is the constant coming and going of visitors from the house, and Edward traveling so much for his work, leaving her to manage on her own. Over the years Marion has seen Clara drawn ever further from the passions that animated her when she was young. This relinquishment was never an explicit choice, only an ebbing away as time and energy were, little by little, siphoned off for other things. It has left Clara with a restlessness, a dissatisfaction, that cannot be assuaged, perhaps because its source has never been faced, never been named.

And Edward does not help. There were his affairs, of course, which did their damage. But that is not all. There is, she thinks, a discord between these two that is more subtle and dispersed. For although he is in principle sympathetic to his wife's love for music, he does not see how her attention is scattered by the demands placed on it, by the arithmetic lessons and scraped knees and quarrels of children, by the lighting of the stove, the cleaning of linen and dishes which, even with the help that Clara has, cut her day into so many scraps that she herself does not even know why she feels so ragged at the end of it.

This is the bind they are caught in: for all the occasions Marion has felt lonely for the love of a husband or the beauty of children, for those things that Clara has, she knows that she has in their place a single invaluable possession, time, which can be devoted to her painting. And it seems that, unlike Edward, they must choose: they cannot, apparently, have both love and time.

What can be done about it? Marion sighs, and looks at her friend's face and says the only thing that she can think of that will make any difference: "Well, I will help you get ready for the extra guests. The girls and I will go for a walk when they get home from school, and you will be able to play for a while then."

"Oh, thank you. But really, you just got here. You shouldn't . . ."

"Nonsense. With two of us the chores won't take so long." Clara smiles, and Marion thinks, sadly, how little difference this will actually make for Clara and how much it means, this two hours she can now have to herself.

"Come along," she says, coaxing Clara to her feet. She takes her hand and together they descend the stairs.

A LITTLE LATER in the afternoon, Edward, who had gone back to hiding in his studio, is coming across the kitchen yard when he hears the sound of voices in the kitchen and then laughter. Then silence and the sound of splashing. Then more laughter. What on earth is going on, he wonders. He quickens his pace, eager to see what the source of the mirth is. Through the window he sees Clara standing beside the sink, holding what looks like a ladle upside down but then suddenly she disappears from view and he hears again shrieks of giggles. He opens the door and sees his wife doubled over, her dress and hair and face covered in streaks of sparkling soap bubbles. Marion is standing on the opposite side of the room, holding herself upright against the larder door. She is also covered in bubbles. By her feet is a bucket of soapy water and she has a fistful of foam grasped in one hand as though it was a snowball. Both of them are laughing so hard that they can't speak.

Marion finally catches sight of him standing at the door looking at them in amazement. She hesitates for a minute, sizing him up, then raises her arm, winds up and flings a great clump of foam so that it hits him in the chest.

"Hey!" he shouts, wiping it off his shirt. "What is this?"

"We are calling it 'soap tennis,' " Marion says. "It is great fun, but there isn't a lot of back-and-forth. Each game only lasts for one volley. Like this," and she scoops up another fistful of soap and raises her arm again.

"Wait, wait," Clara protests, putting herself into the line of fire. "That isn't fair. He is unarmed."

Marion lowers her arm. "Yes," she concedes. "I suppose you are right."

"Well . . ." Edward says. "That situation is easily rectified." And he leaps across to the sink and, grabbing two handfuls of soap, hurls one at each of the women, marveling as he does so at how different everything seems from just a few hours ago.

EIGHT

July 3, 1918

THE OTHER NURSE on her shift was assisting the surgeons when three new cases arrived that evening, so Marion said she would go down to the ward, make up their charts and report back to the ward sister. She was just sitting down to eat supper, that grayish potato soup that seemed to be a particular favorite of the cooks, but this wasn't the first meal she had missed for an emergency and it wouldn't be the last. Everything was provisional: lunch and holidays and leave and anything else that gave form and order to life beyond the demands of the next instant. A few more gulps of coffee, just a few more, she thought; she got a mouthful of grounds and grimaced at the bitterness, swallowed, stood and brushed the crumbs from her skirt, made her way upstairs.

When the men first arrived, that was the worst part, the hardest part. The motor ambulances brought them up from the casualty clearing stations in batches of six or eight or a dozen, stacked along the sides of the cabins, like bread in an oven. Stretcher-bearers carried them into the ward, calling to her, Where do you want this one, ma'am, got another for you here, banged up pretty bad this fellow, and then the nurses got to see, unadulterated, what the war had done. That was the time that Marion most wanted to be somewhere else, anywhere else just so long as she was away from this, what was left over, the mess of flesh and bone and metal that she came to think of, almost against her will, as *the evidence*. The evidence of contusions where shrapnel had struck bone and left a delicate spiderweb of fissures running across the exposed surface of the femur. The evidence of gas gangrene in the lower leg, the blackening of the flesh, the stench that meant it would have to come off, the whole thing from the hip down. All this was evidence, because surely, someone must be collecting all these sights and sounds and smells together, so that later, when it was all over, the survivors could figure out who was responsible and call them to account. Because this war couldn't all be happening for no reason; it must be someone's fault and they must discover who, and why, and how it was allowed to go on so long, because how else could something like this be prevented from happening again?

At one end of the hospital a room had been set aside for the newly injured. When Marion entered, two orderlies were putting the first casualty into a bed at the far end. The boy on the stretcher shouted out when they tried to lift him, the pain rising to the surface and bursting from him, sudden and unrestrained.

"Go on, son. Clench your teeth and bear up; it'll be over in a minute," said the man standing by his head. Then with a nod to his partner they began to lift him again. This time the boy was quiet, only letting a slight groan escape as they laid him on the mattress. From across the room, the orderlies greeted her with a brief, mumbled "Afternoon, Miss Beckett."

"Is this where you want them?" one of them asked, indicating the beds with a nod.

"Yes, those are free."

They went back outside to bring in the others, and Marion was left alone with the injured boy. Something wasn't right about him, she thought, different from the other men who arrived in this same manner every day in a steady stream; something was strange, but she couldn't tell immediately what it was. She came quickly toward him; he was dressed in a khaki uniform. American, then; he must be American. The dressing on his left side was dark with blood. As she got closer she could see that he was young, in his early twenties at most. His eyes were squeezed shut and his teeth clamped together against the pain. She had that flash of terror that went through her each time she approached a newly filled bed, that prayer to be transported. It lasted only for a moment; she smothered it as soon as it arose. She must be sensible and she must present, for these men who had seen so much worse than this, a countenance of calm. *Maintain a cheerful and orderly demeanor at all times,* the nurses' handbook instructed. She'd made fun of its prim, obvious advice, until she was faced with her first room full of gas casualties and understood the need for such admonitions.

She went to the foot of his bed and lifted his chart from the rail. *Cundall,* she read. *Thomas N. Puncture wound from type D ammunition. Possible concussion.* He groaned again and she realized why she'd thought there was something wrong when she saw him from across the room. Of course, how silly of her not to understand at once what was different about him and also about the skinny boy they were carrying in now, muttering and cursing under his breath in French while the orderlies rolled their eyes.

She knew what it was now. These men were clean.

—

WHEN SHE FIRST got the news of Clara's lawsuit, Marion was already in France. She considered returning to New York immediately; perhaps it would be better to go home and face this disaster, rather than postponing it, living in its ghastly shadow. It seemed like the right thing to do; to get the ordeal over and then perhaps be able to move on.

On the other hand, she didn't want to leave the hospital. It was not that she liked the work she did there; no one could. It was that she never doubted its importance. She had never been completely certain that her painting mattered very much. And since the end of her friendship with Clara Steichen, and the beginning of this terrible war, she had felt adrift, her notions of what was worthwhile, what it meant to be a good person, no longer seeming to tell her much about how to live in this lonely new world. When she began work as a volunteer, serving meals to the troops, she felt the comfort of a clear, straightforward purpose for the first time. She volunteered to train as a nurse, then began work in a hospital for amputees near Arras as soon as she was able.

She thought and thought about whether to stay, trying to reach a final decision, and while she thought, days passed and she was reassigned to the Marne and she realized that she had made a choice by default. She would stay until her term of service was complete. It was a weight off her heart. She came to the Marne and took up her new assignment.

Since arriving there, she had learned how to tell from the shape and angle of a puncture wound whether the projectile had struck point-blank, so that it would be clean and easy to remove, or whether it had ricocheted, and brought dirt and cloth with it. She knew how to administer ether, remove shrapnel from a wound, clean the space where it had been with Carrel–Dakin solution, and finally sew up its torn edges. In peacetime, no nurse would have been given so much authority, but no one worried about such distinctions now. Only if she saw from the swelling that the bullet had struck bone, or if an amputation was necessary, would she alert the physicians. It was a constant balancing act. Of those that needed major surgery, many of them were too far gone by the time they reached the hospital for it to do them any good. She saw men with limbs ripped away, men holding their stomachs to keep them from falling out, men who had lost so much blood that no doctor in the world could help them. Then her job was to administer the morphine, keep the pain away so they could dream that their mothers were beside them, dream that they were home again, call her by the name of their sweetheart, and she would answer, telling them she was whoever would bring them the greatest consolation. Her task was to help them slide quietly from the world without suffering more than they had to and without wasting anyone's time.

Then there were the men who came in not wounded, but sick. Fevers spread quickly down the line because in the trenches they lived so close together, used each other's bodies for warmth in the winter. Pyrexia of Unknown Origin: the men would be sweating and sneezing, shrieking about shooting pains in their legs. There were bouts of cholera, dysentery; she had seen malaria in a few troops that had come north from the fronts in Greece and Italy. And then in the spring they began to see cases of something they had never encountered before. It looked like trench fever at first, the same symptoms, pain and fever, but all the patients suffered from a hacking, persistent cough, which deepened as the disease progressed. After a few days they began to have trouble breathing, their lungs and throats were so full of catarrh. Some of them found blood in their mouths when they coughed. By the end of the week, the nurse who had tended the cases, and the doctors who had made the initial diagnosis, were all sick. One of the nurses on the ward where Marion was working had dropped the tray of medicine she was carrying and reached for a wall to steady herself. I'm sorry, she said. I'm so dizzy. Then she collapsed onto the floor. Two days later, Marion woke herself up with coughing. She went and knocked on the matron's bedroom door and asked to be quarantined with the others.

It became known up and down the front as "the Spanish disease" because it was supposed to have come from Spanish soldiers who'd been fighting in Morocco. It gave you a couple of days of fever, and then it broke or it killed you. Marion had survived it; but often people in the prime of life did not recover. It took them, along with the old and the very young, those weakened by injuries or fatigue, and it sucked them down so rapidly that for almost a month after the outbreak she still looked for Nora, the nurse who'd dropped the medicine tray, expecting to find her in the cafeteria at mealtimes, or reading a novel out under the trees in the hospital grounds between shifts. For the hospital as a whole, though, they seemed to have caught it in time. Once the first cases were quarantined, they saw only a handful after that. Then it died away almost as suddenly as it had appeared, and when it was gone, no one spoke of it much, as if they didn't want to summon it back by uttering its name. They all hoped they had seen the last of it.

But the wounds and the sickness, these would have been less appalling if the men themselves hadn't been so filthy. Amid all this suffering and sickness, what revolted her most was the other creatures that were living on the bodies of the men. She and the other nurses undressed the new arrivals, cutting away the torn material of their uniforms and pealing back the layers of fabric, shirts and undergarments so stained with months of sweat and dirt that it was impossible to tell that they had once been white. Underneath, they found the men's skin alive with infestations, gray bulbous creatures, some the size of a the pad of her thumb that bustled away into the armpits and groins to hide from the light. The amputees she had tended, for all the alien horror of their half-gone bodies, never made her recoil and break her required calm—always be polite and obliging, the nurses' handbook told them; *always be patient and ready to help*—as she had when she first arrived in Châlons and found her first patient's stomach bristling with lice.

BUT THESE MEN were not like that. Their uniforms had been recently laundered; they didn't stink. She looked down again at the chart. Air Service. These were airmen. And something jumped in her mind, name recognition, the bolt of fear echoing through her, this time immediate, belonging to her in particular.

"Where are they from?" she asked the orderlies, her voice sounding abrupt and panicked to her own ears. "Where did they arrive from, these men?"

"Airfield near Épernay," one of them called over his shoulder as he went out to bring the last stretcher in from the ambulance.

WHAT SHE HAD felt when she met Edward on the night of the fire wasn't simple. Through the haze of lost sleep, a weariness that seemed to have seeped into her bones, she had thought for a moment that she was dreaming him. In the hospital, the concoctions of the mind intermingled so freely with the solid objects of waking life that she was never sure how real anything was until she touched it, tested it, to see if her hand could pass through. Among the rows of beds, the charts, syringes and bandages, men would talk at length to people they imagined to be in the room. They would try to use limbs that they no longer possessed. In the midst of all this, how could she be sure he wasn't a figment of her imagination?

He'd walked out of the shadow of the corridor and into the ward, looking as he had four years earlier, perhaps he was a little thinner, a little aged, but there, walking toward her as if his coming had been inevitable, only a matter of time, and that final summer, the very last summer of the world it seemed now, came back to her in a rush that was so fierce that she had to put her hand over her mouth to prevent herself from crying out. She had turned away from him to tend her patients because she needed to collect herself. She could not come unraveled here, and not in front of him. She felt at once a tremendous rush of gladness and also anger and perplexity: all the things she had felt when she was last with him. *An orderly demeanor,* she thought, reflexively. When she spoke, she held her voice steady. She told him to go because she had work to do, which was, at least, not an outright lie.

Now she watched him carried in covered by the gray army-issue blankets, and laid on one of the empty beds. She walked slowly toward him, the complications tumbling away from her, so she thought that she might well turn and find the floor cluttered with a trail of them. She took his chart from the orderly and began to read: *Steichen, Edward J. Head injury, concussion. Fever, probable result of aspiration while unconscious.*

VOICES AND THE clack of footsteps, too loud and somehow solid so each sound dug into him like the toe of a boot kicking, making the sick feeling in his stomach swell and flood through his body until the sickness shaded into an ache that ran through his joints when he tried to move, so he cried out and that made the voices come back louder, they came and went, came and went from beside him. He felt a hand on his forehead, cool and steady, but then quickly too warm and dry, it was a hand with skin made of paper.

If he lay quite still, the moiling inside him settled and he could think a little more clearly. They had been falling through the sky, and then he remembered someone shining a light into his face, feeling his pulse. He remembered he had felt all right apart from pain in his head, and he had slept, but then he had woken up retching with this terrible sick feeling crouched inside him. They were being driven somewhere. There were others with him, he could remember that much but not who they were.

Now there was a face to go with one of the voices and the cool paper hand, a woman's face, fringed with dark hair and for a minute he thought it was Clara, and he felt a rush of gratitude that overcame everything else, that after all this time she was here. This was all I wanted, he thought, for there to be peace between us, forgiveness. But then he realized that the jaw was too square, and Clara never had freckles like that; it was only a nurse, a stranger who happened to have the same colors as his wife. Again he felt the sickness well up from inside him, and he closed his eyes to make the whole complicated business go away.

Later someone was sitting beside him. There was a light, and then it dimmed, and there was someone in the chair near his head, not speaking or moving, just watching over him while he slept. Later still, someone had fallen asleep with their head drooped onto the blankets of his bed and was being woken by one of the nurses. They were speaking together in low tones and he couldn't hear their words, but he could see their figures, clad in white so they were visible against the darkness. He watched as they slipped quietly away. He was in a room full of beds. It was night. He lay breathing. The world beyond his eyelids had ceased to buzz, and when he looked at it, the room stayed in place. The sickness, he realized, was draining away.

"YOU ASKED ME to come and get you when he started to wake up."

"Yes. Thank you. How's his temperature this morning?"

"It's better."

The voices were down by his feet. Edward blinked and opened his eyes. Daylight. He looked around him and found he was still in the same room—a hospital ward. There were men in the beds on either side of him. He could hear coughing, some voices speaking low and further off across the room, and then these two people together at the foot of his bed. He tried to raise himself up to a sitting position, but the world tilted sickeningly away from him. He lay back down. The light hurt so he closed his eyes again.

"Lie still," said one of the voices. "Your fever has broken, but it still isn't entirely gone. You'll feel dizzy if you try to sit up too fast."

"Where are the others who came in with me?"

"Thomas Cundall is here." The voice was a woman's and suddenly, brilliantly familiar.

"Marion?"

"Yes, it's me." She came to the side of the bed where he could see her. He twisted around, this time without lifting his head from the pillow. And there she was.

"You hit your head," she said. "You will feel weak for a while."

"You were here," he said. "At night. You were sitting here."

"Yes."

She looked as she had the night the storeroom had been shelled, weary but composed, but now she remained standing where she was, close beside him, without averting her eyes or turning away as she had then. Instead, she gazed at him, not smiling, just taking in his presence, quietly, steadily.

"I wrote to you," he said. "But I never sent any of the letters. I thought you wouldn't want to hear from me."

"I didn't," she said. "I probably would have torn the letter up and thrown it away without reading it and been annoyed at you for ignoring my request not to write. Or at least, that is what I would have intended to do." Now she did blink and look away.

"It's all right. You had good reasons to tell me to go."

"Not good enough. You might have . . . I might never have seen you again. This"—she gestured to the ward, its rows of occupied beds—"should put things into perspective, and remind you to cherish your friends whenever you find them."

She pulled forward the chair and sat down. He stared at her, taking her presence in, her face that was so familiar and so strange in the context of the place.

"I don't know what to say."

"Me neither. I think I have too many things to say, and they all want to come out at once."

"Well, I'll start with something immediate, then. How long have I been here?"

"This is your fourth day. You were barely conscious when you were brought in. What do you remember?"

"I think I was being looked at by the doctor—that must have been at the infirmary at Épernay. I was being carried into an ambulance, we were driving. I don't remember very much else."

"You had developed a bad fever. It peaked and it's dying down now. You will be fine, but you must rest. I know resting has never been something you were very good at."

"How nice it is to be recognized, even for my faults. But there were others, too? Brought in with me."

"Yes," she said slowly. "There were two others. Thomas Cundall is in the next ward."

"Cundall is here?" She nodded. "Is he going to be all right?"

"It will be a while before he can fly again, but he is recovering."

"And what about the other one?" She was silent just long enough for him to understand. "He's not all right, is he? Who was it?"

"He was French. And his legs . . ."

"Gilles Marchand."

"He was taken up to surgery as soon as he came in, but he'd lost a lot of blood already."

Edward turned and buried his face in his pillow.

Her hand on his arm. "I'm sorry."

"He was very young," he said. "He couldn't walk. He wanted to fly. I had them bend the rules so he could be in one of our sections." Damn Cundall with his lip and his bravado. Got himself injured and someone else killed to no purpose whatsoever.

"Edward," Marion said. "I have to go."

"Please. Sit here a little longer."

"I can't. I'm in the middle of a shift. There are men who need their medicine. But I'll come back as soon as I'm done."

"All right."

"You had a visitor, too," she said. "A man from the airfield."

"What's his name?"

"Lutz. He said when you were awake to send for him." She stood up, then quickly leaned forward and put her face next to his so they were touching. Even though it was tucked away under her cap, he could smell her hair. It smelled like chamomile. Quietly, in a rush, she said, "I am so glad you are all right."

—

THE DUTY NURSE, a woman named Helen (it was she he had mistaken in his fever for Clara) showed Lutz in and directed him to Edward's bed.

"Hello, sir. You look . . ."

"Be honest," Edward warned.

"OK. You look terrible. That greenish-gray complexion: it's not your most flattering color." Edward laughed. Lutz sat down on a chair next to his bed, and Edward saw that he had brought with him a file of photographs.

"I was sorry," Lutz said, "to hear about Marchand." He looked down at his knees. He opened his mouth and then shut it again, as though he wanted to speak but didn't know what to say. Edward thought, It is the same as when Daniels died, this having no words, this overwhelming silence. What could be said, after all, that would be adequate? They sat facing each other trapped by things they did not know how to express.

Eventually, Lutz put the file of photographs he was holding down on the mattress beside Edward. "These are Marchand's," he said. "Or more accurately, these are the photographs his camera took. That De Ram thing kept going. We got a full set of exposures. Even though he probably stopped taking pictures midway through the run. Have a look."

Edward picked up the file, opened it and began to look through the prints inside. There were the initial exposures, taken from 10,000 feet, showing the southern part of the Aisne salient. In them, he could see the river, houses, some troops, nothing unusual. But then he reached the obliques taken when Cundall swooped in on the work detail, the dive that had gotten both he and Marchand shot. And from these he could see, at last, what those men had been doing.

Their reaction unfolded for him in a series of discrete instants. First, they were working, oblivious to the eyes watching them from above. Then one of the officers was pointing upward, straight toward the camera. Then the men were running, scattering. Some hurled themselves toward the nearby trees; some fell down where they were and covered their heads with their arms while around them the ground spit dust as the bullets went into it. Then finally more running figures, fire shooting upward from the trees, some of the men who had fallen still lying facedown on the ground.

After that the perspective began to pull away, and Edward realized that this was the point when the camera must have begun operating on its own. The rest of the sequence showed a broadening view of the scene. He could see the building the men had been working on. It was an old barn, with wooden walls and roof. Half the roof and one wall of the barn had been removed, leaving nothing but a line of bare ground. Next to it there were wagons filled almost to capacity with the long bundles of wood. On the road he could see wheel tracks: these were not the first carts the men had filled.

"This is where those imprints come from," Lutz said. "They are taking apart wooden buildings near the front. We checked on some older photographs of the area: these were all barns, dairies, storehouses, things like that. Why are they doing it? What are they going to use all that lumber for?"

Edward shook his head. "I don't know."

He peered again at the first shot in the series. Here was an instant excised from time, and already where this had been taken, things had changed; time had moved on. He thought quite suddenly of something Rodin had said to him, on the very first occasion he had gone to visit Meudon alone, about photographs not telling the truth because they stop time; the answer to Lutz's question was not in this photograph, but in the hours and days before and after it was taken. He flipped to the last picture. In this, taken from a greater altitude, the river wound through low hills, little towns hugging its banks. The front was visible to the north. Beyond that was the Aisne River, and he could make out the places where it had been forded . . .

"They are going to use the wood to build pontoon bridges," he said. "They don't have the railway junction at Reims that they tried to get in May. So they are scavenging for the material rather than bringing it up from the rear."

"That would mean," Lutz said, "that they are going to come across a river. They are going to come south, over the Marne."

"Yes. They are going to try to take Paris." Edward handed the photographs back to Lutz. "Go and tell the colonel what this looks like. See what he says."

"Yes. Right." Lutz was looking through the photographs again, nodding to himself. He closed the file and stood up, ready to leave. "It's good to see you, sir," he said. "I'm glad you're recovering. Do you know yet when you will be released from here?"

"They haven't given me a day yet, but it shouldn't be too long now."

"Well, the fellows all send their best," Lutz said. "They all said to tell you to get well soon."

"That's good of them. But you are coping all right without me, right?"

"Oh yes, sir," Lutz said. "We're doing just fine."

"Well, that is good to hear. Goodbye, Lutz."

"Goodbye, sir."

It wasn't until he had watched Lutz maneuver his stout figure through the rows of beds, lift his palm to say goodbye again and vanish into the hall, that Edward realized he'd been hoping that they were not managing all right without him.

He'd hoped to learn that he was needed.

He lay back, tired from the conversation. It struck him anew how strange it was to see Marion Beckett in this place. He was still not used to the idea that she was here, close by. A memory came to him from the summer before the war. Sunlight, a river. He closed his eyes.

Woman in a Field of Grass. Voulangis, July 1914.
Autochrome process.

THEY'RE DRIVING ALONG the road that skirts the edge of the valley, running from Crécy-en-Brie through the railway village of Esbly and then dropping down toward the river. Coming over a rise, they see a field that slopes away in billows of sun-parched grass and ends in a hunch of brambles at the water's edge.

"There, there," Marion cries, pointing to where the hedge breaks and they can see through to the meadow beyond. "That one. Stop." Edward shifts down and looks for a place where he can park the car.

They have been driving out every morning for several days now; it is part of the pact that they've made. It originated on the fourth or maybe fifth day of Marion's visit. Edward had been working in his studio that afternoon, looking for the right way to crop some of his Brittany pictures. It was the photograph of his daughters that was giving him the most trouble. What were the right proportions for it? How much sky and how much sea? Nothing he tried seemed quite right, and he was standing over his workbench staring down at it in frustration when there was a tentative knock at the door. It was Marion.

"I am sorry to interrupt you," she said. "I'm all out of linseed oil. I am here to commandeer some of yours. Don't argue: your wife gave permission."

"Well, in that case," he said, "you'd better come in."

She stepped inside, looking around her at the shelves and stacks of canvases against the far wall. She handed him an empty glass bottle, and he went to his supply cupboard and began to fill it with oil. While he was doing this, she drifted over toward the bench, scanning the negatives and prints he had laid out there.

"Do you mind me looking at these?" she asked.

"No, go ahead." He finished filling the bottle, replaced the stopper and handed it back to her. He stood next to her, both of them looking down at the photography on his workbench. "This one," he said, tapping one corner of it with his forefinger. "I can't find the right way to frame it. It seems like there is too much blank space above or below the girls."

Marion took the blotting paper frame he was using and moved it horizontally over to one side. When she did this, the division between the sky and the sea was cut by the long, dark blade of the cliffs further down the coast. The figures in the foreground were moved off-center. Suddenly, it looked right; it looked balanced.

"How about this?" she said.

"Yes," he said. "That is much better. Thank you."

"You are welcome." She picked up the bottle of oil and started toward the door.

"Wait," he said. "I get to interrupt you now. What are you working on?"

"Oh, my goodness. I'm working on a landscape; the view from the end of your field. I am not happy with it at all. I think maybe I need to take a break, make some new sketches, come back to it."

"Well, maybe you do; sometimes you need to see your work with fresh eyes. Anyway, I'd like to look at it, if you will show me."

"Yes, I will. When you are done with your work this evening."

When she was gone, he felt, suddenly, how much he would like to work alongside her. Her calm air would help him concentrate. And he began to hatch a plan, which simmered away in the back of his mind as he cut and mounted and framed photographs that day.

After dinner he outlined his idea to her.

"Here are the rules," he said. "Each morning for a week we go out and drive until we find a new location, one that neither of us has sketched before. We both sketch it and swap, so you hold on to my drawings and I hold on to yours. At the end of the week I choose one of your sketches for you to turn into a painting. You choose one of mine. Do we have a deal?"

"How do I know I'll like the one you pick?" Marion said.

"That's just the point. You have to trust me."

"Don't listen to him," Clara said, linking her arm through Marion's and leaning toward her conspiratorially. "He just wants an excuse to drive your car." Edward looked at her, nervous that she disapproved.

But Clara's smile was unfeigned when Marion said, "You think I'll let him drive? After he almost put it into that ditch last time?"

"All right, all right. I'm outnumbered here," Edward said. He thought how much happier Clara had been since Marion's arrival. How much more at ease and good-humored. She was like a different person.

"Really," Clara said, "I think it's a terrific idea. As long as the paintings that result are dedicated to me."

"Of course they will be," says Marion.

"Yes, of course they will, my darling," Edward followed.

"What about Arthur?" Marion asked. "Should we ask him to come with us?"

"Oh, Arthur never gets up until one," Clara said.

"True. We'll most likely be back before he's even out of bed."

So it was settled. This is the fifth morning, and Edward (who is driving after all) steers the car to the side of the road and stops.

They get down from their seats and, carrying their sketching materials, make their way around to the stile. Edward climbs it first, then helps Marion over, and they walk through knee-high waves of grass, so pale they're almost silver, toward the riverbank.

"Look," Marion says, pointing to the hem of her skirt. It is covered with tiny dashes, grass seeds that cling to the cloth. "You've got them, too." She pulls at one on the sleeve of his jacket.

They find a place where they can get to the water through the trees and underbrush. Along the watercourse in either direction, reeds wave in the shallows, pulled by the slow strength of the current. A kingfisher flashes down to the water's surface. A pair of mallards glide by.

"This is the place," Marion says. "This is just what I wanted." She sits down on the grass of the bank, tucking her skirt under her. She begins getting out her charcoal, her sketchbook. Edward sits a little above her on the slope, his back propped against the trunk of a tree, his feet against the protrusion of one of its roots.

He doesn't get out his sketching materials right away. Instead, he sits watching Marion begin work and thinking that he has not been as happy as this in a very long time. He feels this in spite of the turmoil that they are reading about in the newspapers each day: the Serbians and the Austrians trading threats over the assassination of Archduke Ferdinand; the Russians and the Germans taking sides. He feels very far away from all that.

If only this summer could go on forever, if only he could keep this morning to draw on whenever he needed. This: the marbled green of the river swirling and changing under its own strange forces; the slope of pale grass to its edge; the girl with her fiery hair. This serious girl, biting her lip in concentration, and peering intensely at the water, while her hands work its replica on the page in front of her. This girl whom he realizes he wants to reach out and touch . . . She has turned and is looking at him, smiling and blinking against the light.

"Go on, Mr. Steichen," she says. "Hurry up. I'll be done with mine before you've even opened your book."

"You know, I think I would rather photograph today," he says.

"That wasn't part of the pact."

"I know. I'm breaking the pact."

"Unfair!"

But he is already standing up and walking back to the car to get his camera. He will keep this afternoon, and he will keep its colors, too. When he returns to the river, Marion is still sitting where she was, finishing the sketch, shading carefully along the edges of the water. She is a good artist; sometimes, he thinks, there is a lightness of touch, an assurance to her work, that is almost magical. This happens most often in her painting of faces. When she makes a portrait, you can tell what the subject is thinking. But at other times she is too restrained, as though she were telling herself all the while how the image ought to be, not allowing it to come out of her naturally. He waits until she is finished drawing and then comes to sit beside her.

"It's good," he says. "I like this particularly, the way you get the movement through those reeds over there."

"Thank you. I'm not happy with how the birds look."

"You thought too much, and stopped seeing. You were thinking as you were drawing them, right?"

"Yes, I suppose I was."

"Over here, you looked but didn't judge. You didn't hesitate. You let your eyes carry you."

She is silent for a minute looking at her sketch. He stands and retreats a distance up the hill.

"Turn around, will you?" She turns and looks at him, her face full of sunlight. Her hair curls over her shoulders, and against the green of the river, it's scarlet. He takes the picture.

"Wonderful. I'm going to develop it using autochrome. I've been waiting for another chance to try it." He changes the plate. "Can I take another one? Just come up here." He beckons to her.

"Not only are you breaking our deal, but now you are making demands," Marion says.

"Please. I promise it will only take a minute."

"All right. Though I'm sure it isn't entirely proper behavior for a married man . . ." She trails off and both of them are suddenly aware that the joke, intended to put them at ease, has only called attention to the tension that has come between them. "Making demands on women in isolated fields . . ." She tries again and only makes it worse.

"Could you come up a little way?" he asks, turning his attention to his camera. "Just here." He points to a spot on the ground. "Would you sit?"

"All right." She comes to the place he indicates and sits down.

"Lie on your side."

"What?"

"I want to get your hair against the background of the grass."

"Oh." She lies down. "Like this?"

"Yes." He puts the camera down and comes to kneel next to her. He reaches down and takes a handful of her hair and curls it in front of her so that it seems to grow from the earth like the grass, as though the woman lying there is also part of the growing things in this place. Marion's hair is soft in his hands.

"Perfect," he says.

He retreats to where he was before and raises the viewfinder to his eyes. When he looks through it, the picture is wonderful, the contrast of the pale grass, the dark trees, the woman caught between the two. He takes the photograph, and it is not until he brings the camera down from his face that he sees something isn't right. It is her face. She looks terribly unhappy. This was not what he wanted.

"What on earth is the matter?" he asks her.

"I don't know. I don't really like having my photograph taken. I think I'm not used to it."

"Well, I don't mean to upset you. But I've been wanting to take your picture all summer."

"All summer? You mean for the whole past week?"

"Well, all right, yes. But how wonderful these are going to be. I'm almost mad at myself for not having done this when you visited last year. Look at this line here; it's beautiful." He reaches up and runs his forefinger along the line of her jaw, which curves down from her ear, a perfect half-heart shape to her chin. A second later he realizes that this was the wrong thing to do, absolutely wrong.

She flinches, and pulls her face away. Not looking at him, she says: "You know, we'd better go. Clara will be wanting us back soon. It is almost lunchtime and she invited Mildred today."

She starts to walk off across the field in the direction of the car. He gathers up his equipment and runs after her.

"Wait!" he says. She doesn't stop. He raises the camera to his eye and takes a picture of her walking away through the grass.

Back at the car she says, "I will drive."

"I'm sorry," he says, "I just meant . . ." Marion has put her hands over her face, as if she needs to generate the courage to come out from behind them and face the world again. He falls silent.

"It's all right," she says. "We've had such a nice week, haven't we? Let's not spoil it." She sounds as if she is addressing herself as much as him.

"Yes," he says. "You are right, of course."

On the drive home they are quiet, sitting far apart on the seat.

"Have you heard from your parents?" he asks, the question sounding stilted even before he's finished asking it. "Have they reached Petersburg all right, I mean?"

"Yes," she says. "Only the other day I got a letter from them. I showed it to you."

"Right. Of course you did. I should have remembered." They lapse into silence again. Edward stares at the passing fields, feeling glum and wondering what exactly has been broken.

Just as they reach the last rise before they come in sight of the house, Edward feels Marion reach across the seat and take his hand in her gloved one. He is surprised. She doesn't look over at him; her eyes are fixed on the road, but there is her hand, squeezing his, offering a truce. A wave of relief washes over him, unexpectedly powerful. With this single gesture she has restored the lost balance to the world. He presses her fingers between both his palms, and when she withdraws her hand, it is only to shift gears and slow the car, so they can pull off into his own driveway, and there is Clara waiting for them in the doorway.

"Honestly, my dears, I was beginning to worry you'd gotten lost," she chides mockingly.

"No need," Edward calls. "Here we are." Marion climbs down from the driver's seat.

"Did you find a good location?" Clara asks.

"Yes, yes, we did. A lovely one. Right by the river," Marion says. To Edward she sounds almost like her usual composed self, but not quite. She is speaking a little too fast. Her words tumble out in a hurry as though she is short of breath. Clara looks at her and furrows her brow.

"Are you all right?" she asks. "You look flustered; you have quite a high color in your face."

"Oh, I'm fine. We just had a long walk uphill to get back to the car."

"Well, come in and have a drink of water. I'll tell Louisa to bring it to you upstairs if you'd like. You can lie down a little before lunch."

"Thank you," Marion says, and goes inside. Edward comes to the door after her and kisses Clara.

"Marion seems out of sorts," she says. "Is something wrong?"

"Not that I know of. The long walk, I assure you, was her choice, not mine." He shrugs. "I'm sure she'll be OK." He goes inside, puts down his sketching materials and camera on the hall table, and begins to take off his jacket. When he looks up, Clara is still standing in the door, watching him with an expression he knows he hasn't seen on her face when they returned from their expeditions the previous four days.

"You probably need Louisa in the kitchen right now, don't you?" he says. "I'll take that glass of water upstairs to Marion."

"That is thoughtful of you," Clara says.

"Well, it seems like the least I can do, after dragging her all over the countryside these last few days."

"Were you taking pictures, too?" She is picking up his camera from the side and turning it over, as though looking for something hidden underneath it.

"I took some pictures of Marion by the river. I got inspired."

"Well, one never knows when inspiration will strike . . ."

"Quite so. Go on, darling. I'll be there in just a minute."

THEY ARE HAVING lunch outside today, under the trees. They are talking about whether or not there will be war. It is two weeks since the heir to the Austrian throne was shot and killed when his procession took a wrong turn into a back street in a mountain-ringed town called Sarajevo. The man holding the gun was a Serb nationalist whom no one had ever heard of, even in his own country. He just stepped out of the crowd and pulled the trigger. And now, this morning, the Russians have announced that they will not tolerate an Austrian invasion of Serbia; they will fight, if necessary, to defend it.

Edward and Arthur move the big kitchen table out to the lawn, just under the outstretched boughs of the crab apple tree. Because it is such a perfect day it seems a pity to spend any of it cooped up inside. Louisa brings out the place settings. Kate and Mary pick some flowers, and these droop picturesquely from a vase in the middle of the table's flat white expanse.

"Why are they hanging over like that?" Kate asks, trying to prop up the shriveled head of a bluebell.

"Because they are sad," Mary says authoritatively. "About the war that is going to come."

"No war is going to come," Clara says. She and Marion are carrying the dishes to the table. "At least it isn't coming to our garden."

And now here they all are: Edward and Arthur, Mercedes and Marion and Clara, Mary and Kate and Mildred Aldrich, who has driven up the hill from Huiry to join them for the day. Mildred is still holding her copy of this morning's newspaper, and every so often she uses it like a gavel to emphasize a point she is trying to make.

"Have you read the list of demands they've given the Serbian government? Entirely unrealistic," she says, the pages of newsprint thumping onto the table in time with her speech. The bread crumbs on the cloth jump with each blow. "Pass the salt, please, dear."

"Certainly. Would you like some of the brioche?" Clara asks her, passing the shaker. "It's very good. Louisa made it this morning."

"Thank you very much," Mildred says. "The demands are ridiculous and, furthermore, the Austrians know it. They don't want the Serbs to comply. They want vengeance for their precious archduke, so they will set goals that can't be met, and then when, surprise, surprise, they aren't, they will invade."

"Well, that doesn't mean that there is going to be war here, though, does it?" Edward says. "This is an issue between Austria and Serbia and maybe Russia. I mean, war is always terrible, don't get me wrong, but this one needn't involve France."

"Papa, what is Serbia?"

"It's a country all the way over on the other side of Germany, Catkin. It's very far away from us. Besides," he says, turning toward Mildred, "what about *The Great Illusion*? Didn't you find his argument convincing? Why on earth would France—"

"It isn't France one needs to worry about. It is Germany."

"Why would either of them get involved in a local conflict that has nothing to do with them when it would be bad for both?"

"Yes," Clara says. "I read Mr. Angell's book. I think he's right: why would countries that trade with each other so much want to go to war? They will sort this problem out through diplomacy, I'm sure."

"Oh yes, yes." Mildred waved her newspaper dismissively. "Norman Angell is very convincing if you believe that people always act in their own best interests."

"Well, people might not, but what about whole countries?" Mercedes asks.

"I don't think," Marion says, "that whole countries are any more enlightened than individual human beings. They get swept up by emotion, too, and behave very foolishly indeed."

"What is it, Catkin?" Edward says.

"What does 'enlightened' mean?"

"It means that you have special wisdom and insight. It means seeing things clearly when other people might not."

"Ahh, here are the goose liver and the cheeses. At last. Thank you, Louisa. Would you put some water on for tea when you go back inside?" Louisa nods. "Would anyone like some of this?"

Clara lifts the plates that Louisa has just set at her elbow, heavy with the solid wedges and squares of cream and yellow and white. They begin to circle the table, passed from hand to hand among the guests. People sit forward a little, waiting to receive the platters as they come around, and for a moment the conversation is set aside, supplanted by the immediate task of eating, murmurs of approval and thanks, the clinking of forks on plates. In the hush, Edward looks at his wife where she sits at the opposite end of the table.

She has turned to say something to Marion, who is seated beside her. They are speaking quietly so he cannot hear what it is. She seems to be in good spirits. There: she is smiling as she replies; now she laughs, throwing her head back softly, putting her palm to her chest as though to restrain her heart, to keep it tucked inside her.

And yet he can't shake the feeling that something has upset her. Perhaps it is this worrying talk of war that is fraying her nerves. It is as though she has withdrawn some portion of herself from the world; pulled it back inside for safekeeping.

Today should be the last of his outings with Marion, he thinks; it is time to move on from sketching and begin working in earnest. In a sense, he feels they have already silently agreed to this with that last touch of their hands before they returned to the house. He is taken with the idea of working on autochromes all summer, with the pictures of her forming only the first in an extended series. He will see what he can do with color. As the world shifts through its modulations of deepening green toward gold and orange and finally gray, he can take it all in through his camera.

He will miss his morning drives with her, and this thought strikes him with a pang he had not anticipated. This week he has found himself stopping by in the afternoons to see what she is working on, has wanted to solicit her help and criticism. He looks forward to talking to her, to comparing notes, more than he does with Arthur now, though Arthur and he have critiqued each other's paintings for years. It is Marion's second opinion that he seeks out; it is she he goes looking for with his new batch of prints at the end of the day.

He is not inured to the underlying reasons for this. But he feels content, virtuous even, to divert his affection for her toward the platonic, and if there was an unmarked boundary that they approached today, they drew back from it just as quickly. He is pleased with his self-restraint and hers, the way that they have kept their attention on their work and not succumbed to the obvious temptation of each other. The time in his life when he felt compelled to turn everything into romance is over; to his great relief, he finds he has outgrown it. Though sometimes, especially on a day like this, when she is bathed in the gold and green summer light, he is caught off guard by a gesture of hers, an angle, and finds himself holding his breath, thinking involuntarily: exquisite, exquisite . . .

"You are too young to remember the last American war," Mildred is saying. "But I was a little girl in Boston when the boys went marching off to save the union. Everyone turned out in the streets to cheer them on to victory. We had no idea how horrible it would be."

"But this war won't be like that," Arthur puts in, his mouth still full of Brie and bread. "Not with all the new technology—the railroads and airplanes and motorcars—that the armies have now. That's what all the newspapers are saying. This war will be different. Victory will happen in a matter of months."

"That's what people were saying in 1861, my dear," Mildred says. "That's what people always say at times like this."

"Well, if it does come to war, the French will be ready to fight. They won't let 1870 happen all over again."

"I will fight for France," Edward says, "if it is attacked."

Louisa comes back with cups on a tray.

"Who wants tea?" Clara asks. Her voice sounds to Edward strangely light and aerial. An acrobat trying to create the illusion that the laws of gravity do not apply. "Who wants coffee?"

"Oh, me please, coffee," says Arthur. "And the Russians—they'll fight, too. They won't let the Austrians just roll over the Serbs, so in return they'll be invaded . . . Milk, please, no sugar."

"Who else for coffee?"

"Yes, they'll likely raze Petersburg and carry on to Moscow." Arthur nods and frowns, reassuring everyone that this is not idle chatter; he means what he says.

"I think I'll just go inside and help Louisa," says Marion, standing up abruptly.

"No need to do that," says Edward. "She can manage all right."

"Really, I don't mind at all." And she sets off toward the house before anyone can try to dissuade her. Edward looks at Clara, inquisitively, who shrugs: she doesn't understand this either. She finishes serving the tea and then quickly excuses herself, following in Marion's path across the grass to the kitchen door.

MARION FINDS HERSELF confronted with Louisa's badtempered manner of doing the dishes, picking each one off the pile and not so much washing it as spanking it with dish jelly and cloth, and then slamming it into the draining board on the other side. She feels suddenly sheepish, as though she will only get in the way. She stands for some moments with her back resting against the kitchen door. Even with Louisa boiling away at its center, the cool and relative quiet of the kitchen seem welcoming.

Eventually, she summons up the courage to interrupt.

"Can I help you?" she asks. "I'll finish those if you like." Louisa looks up, surprised, but not displeased.

"If you like," she says. "It is necessary to rinse them in the very hot water, though."

"I don't mind. I'd like something mechanical to do right now." Louisa shrugs and moves out of her way. Marion stands at the sink, scrubbing, rinsing, stacking, watching the balance shift steadily from one side of her to the other. She likes the simplicity of this task: it's easy to measure cause and effect. Just now, it is the only thing in the world that seems to have this characteristic. Everything else has been thrown into confusion. There are so many forces pushing and pulling at her that she can't separate them, one from another. Why had she stood up so suddenly and left the table in the middle of the meal? She isn't sure she even knows why herself.

All this talk of war upsets her; she isn't the kind of person who can continue happily immune to things like this. She is worried about her parents, who are still in Russia. And even if they are all right and she only reads about it in the paper, she will still feel the odd, blank upset of strangers suffering, her inability to feel what they are feeling, to truly understand what they are going through. And as if Mildred and her doomsaying wasn't enough, Arthur seems to treat the prospect of a European war with something close to gleeful relish.

Yes, the idea of war, hovering over everything. Or is it, in fact, not that at all that has upset her? Is it instead the way that he had been looking at her from the far end of the table? With an expression that ran right through her like electricity, so intense she was convinced that everyone around them must see it suspended between her and him, a thread of light, though when she looked around, they seemed all to be stunningly oblivious. For after all, what is a look? It is not illegal; it is not forbidden by marriage vows. And he has always had that consuming way of examining the things around him—he is an artist, after all. What would one expect? Perhaps no one noticed because the way he looked at her was nothing out of the ordinary. That would be so much worse, because it would mean that she is making up all the strangeness between them, the way that they have become acutely aware of each other's bodies in space, how her skin lit up when their fingers touched accidentally as he bent down to look at a new painting she had begun. That would mean she wants it to be this way . . .

And then as she was sitting there, trying to concentrate on her food, on the conversation at the table, Arthur had to start talking cavalierly about the Russians and the coming invasion as though it was a sure thing. She had felt a tightness come over her chest, and before she knew it she was on her feet, stuttering what she hoped were polite excuses and heading back to the house.

The kitchen door opens and Clara steps inside.

"He is awful, I know. So tactless. I'm sorry," she says, and for a second Marion isn't sure whom she is referring to. "He doesn't think before he runs his mouth, just says whatever is on his mind without pause. He knows perfectly well that your parents are in Russia."

"Oh, that's all right," Marion says. "I should know Arthur well enough to expect that from him. He doesn't mean any harm by it."

"Yes, but still, you'd think he could show a little sympathy."

Marion sighs and puts down the dish she is in the middle of washing.

"You know, there is probably nothing to worry about. Probably nothing will happen: all this will be forgotten in six months."

"I'm sure you are right."

"And even if it does come to war, there will be plenty of warning. Foreigners traveling in Russia will have lots of time to leave before any fighting starts. It is a big country. Where are they now?"

"Petersburg. You are right; I'm sure they are quite safe. I'm silly to worry about them. I shouldn't be anxious about something that probably won't even occur."

"That's right." Clara touches her shoulder and says: "There now; don't worry about Arthur. What does he know about international diplomacy? Did someone make him ambassador to the czar of all the Russias when he woke up this morning? Remember last week he didn't know the name of the Russian prince, Alexei, the poor little thing with the weak blood."

Marion smiles, grateful for these ministrations. But when she looks over at her friend, whose eyes are wide with sympathy, she feels a sickening flare of guilt erupt in the pit of her stomach, a jagged shock that sizzles through her body and down into her limbs. How can she bear to stay here another minute with the thoughts she's been having in these last few days? They aren't even thoughts, really; they aren't definite or clear enough for thoughts and yet they are too active and compelling for feelings. She read Dr. Freud's book about dreams last year, and he has a word that seems apt but which she hates: drives. Like a machine. Involuntarily, she turns away from Clara, disgusted with herself.

Clara, mistaking it for a retreat into her former sadness, squeezes her hand harder: "There, there, dear. Don't be upset. Come back outside when you are ready," and Marion nods slowly.

"Thank you," she manages. Clara goes out, and Marion looks around her at the room, which seems to have grown larger without either the table or Louisa's palpable disapproval to occupy it. The two wooden benches look bereft and abandoned. She goes and sits down on one of them. Dr. Freud also says that in order to become civilized, we repress our drives or divert them, learn to delay their fulfillment, bury them. It is only when things go wrong that they rise up and make things awkward for us. Well, she could bury this; she would bury it. She can make herself forget about this day by the river, the strange feeling of him arranging her hair, an act of caring that seemed almost maternal, feminine in its carefulness. Most of the time she is doing fine, and all she needs is to put in a little more effort to stop it breaking through to the surface. Cut off a little more air and light. And eventually, she is sure, the feelings will die away.

WALKING ACROSS THE GRASS, Clara sees the tableau of guests at the table before she can hear their words clearly. There they are, all rushing to fill in whenever there is an opening in the conversation, all trying to talk at once, Mildred using her newspaper now to brandish like a sword. She catches words: Viviani, Jaurès, the socialists. They are talking about France. She alternately loves and hates their vitality, their willfulness and self-assurance. Sometimes she feels buoyed up by it, sometimes smothered.

At the head of the table, she sees that Edward is following her progress with his eyes. His face is anxious and questioning, waiting to see what hers will reveal. She feels suddenly a stab of jealousy: He is so concerned about her friend. Was he that concerned last month when she took to her bed for the day? Was he even that concerned when Kate hurt her ankle during a long walk just the previous week? He had said, Don't fret: she'll be all right. She's a strong, growing girl, she'll recover, and then he had gone back to work. Why is he always more interested in the troubles of others than in those of his own family? Why is he so especially concerned about Marion all the time now, so gentle and solicitous of her?

She stops herself. She will not let this go any further. She will not allow these doubts to surge up and overwhelm her. She has decided, simply, that she will shut them out, the chorus of voices that tell her how, underneath her, there are currents moving that she cannot control. She made this decision before they returned, this morning, later than usual from their drive. She will make it as many times as she has to. She trusts Marion. She is not like so many of the other women they know, who will allow themselves to be carried away by their romantic ideas, who are selfish and do not think of others. Marion is principled, thoughtful, and the trust of her that Clara feels is such a pleasure, such an amazing relief from her usual wariness. She needs that trust; she cannot imagine doing without it.

But then . . . she flinches, because she cannot bear to think about it. She cannot bring herself to name the possibilities that sprang into focus, sickeningly sudden, when she saw the looks on their faces as they pulled up to the house earlier. They had seemed tired, yes, but that wasn't unusual: often they had to walk some distance to find the place they wanted to sketch. They had told her about climbing over fences, skirting around muddy meadows, picking their way along the paths through densely brambled woods. Today, though, they had no description for her. Edward said something vague about sitting beside a river, but both of them seemed distracted, flustered. Marion in particular was upset.

She is not a fool. She knows her husband's capacities, his magnetic attachment to beauty. But she does not believe even he would bring this into their home. She will not think so little of him.

And so she makes this decision: It is better to act as though there is nothing wrong, no doubt in her mind or in her heart. It is better to be merry, to continue the motions and conventions of life, the waking, eating, dressing, the entertaining of guests, the raising of children. This goes for the rumbling about war as well. It is better to swim with the current and hope to be carried through to more placid waters. She will not worry. She will not linger over things, or rehearse the past. She will simply carry on, and if she has a moment of doubt, she will remind herself that this is what she has chosen.

She approaches the table. She does not meet Edward's searching gaze right away. First she takes her seat at the opposite end from him, settles herself and looks around at her guests. Is anyone lacking anything that they might want?

"Mercy, have you had enough to eat? Arthur, some more coffee?"

"Yes, please. I'd love another cup." Arthur holds out his empty cup toward her, and she takes it and pours it full, a rope of black liquid descending gracefully from the swan-neck spout.

"Everyone else all right?"

"Yes, thank you, dear. You must sit and finish your meal," Mildred says. "In your absence, we have moved on from expressing our baseless opinions about the international situation to expressing our baseless opinions on matters domestic."

Only after all this has been accomplished does Clara look up and meet her husband's eyes. For a minute they try to read each other's faces and find such an alloy of emotion that neither of them can say for certain what the other one is thinking or feeling.

NINE

July 9, 1918

EACH NIGHT HE was in the hospital Marion would come to sit beside him. He'd see her walking along the line of beds as a swaying circle of light, momentarily illuminating pieces of the room: an arm drooping to the ground like a vine, a restless body twisting the blankets around it in its search for sleep. She'd put the lamp down on the small table beside his bed, where it threw caramel-colored light, cut by blue shadows, over their faces. Her hair was down: she'd removed her cap and unpinned it so that it fell over her shoulders. It was her gift to him, he realized; to be beautiful even in this place.

On the third night after his fever broke, she came as usual and sat in the chair next to the head of his bed.

"They are saying you'll be ready to go soon," she said, "if you continue to improve." She was speaking in whispers so as not to wake the men in the beds around them. "You'll be able to go back to Épernay. Maybe by the end of the week. Isn't that good news?"

"Yes," he said. "I guess it is." She pulled her feet onto the chair, so she was sitting with her knees crooked in front of her. He remembered: she used to sit like that to draw. He savored the familiarity of the posture, felt grateful to her for this small way of being as she had always been.

"You don't sound very certain about that," she said. Then, looking him directly in the eye: "Are you afraid?"

"Of what?"

"When you are flying, are you frightened?"

"Oh no," he said without hesitation. "Once we're off the ground, I'm not afraid, because it doesn't seem real. I mean, you are flying, so it feels like a dream." As he spoke, the image of that last German plane diving down toward them formed in his mind. How he had watched it loop around and begin its descent, gathering speed as it came toward them.

"But you aren't afraid of falling? Even in dreams I remember that I might fall."

"I only think of that during takeoff. Once you feel the force of the air, how strong it is, you can't feel afraid anymore."

"Well, *you* can't," she said. He saw her smile. "I am quite certain most people could find it well within their ability to be stricken with terror."

"Maybe," he said. He was thinking about the German pilot; how, as the plane got closer, he could see the features of his face; all except the eyes, blanked out by goggles.

"It is not like that for most of the men," Marion said. "They are afraid all the time in the trenches. They don't say it, because they don't want to sound like cowards. But you can tell. It's the way they clench their teeth when they talk about it. They've seen so many people die right in front of them. If the pain isn't too bad, they can hardly hide how pleased they are to be injured."

"If you fly," Edward said, "people just disappear. They are there and then they are gone the next day. You never see them again. It is almost as if they have just walked away and decided not to tell you where they are going." He was thinking of the moment when he had opened fire into the face of the German pilot. He saw the propeller shattering, the windscreen shattering, the face shattering. *I have no hatred for Germans as individual men,* he'd written to his sister, months ago before he left America. *All I want to do is record this war, so that people will know what it is really like.* He shut his eyes, but the image of the pilot's face did not go away.

When he opened them again, Marion was watching him, her expression full of curious sadness. He reached up and twisted his fingers into her hair and through it until he could hold her face cupped in his hand.

"If you were afraid," she said, "I wouldn't tell anyone. I wouldn't think less of you for it."

TWO DAYS LATER, Edward was told he was well enough to leave. He stopped to see Tom Cundall before he did. When Edward opened the door of his room, Cundall was propped up in bed, and at first glance it seemed as if he weren't badly hurt. In greeting, he made what was meant to be a nod, but really was just a flick of the eyes.

"I don't move much at the moment," he explained. "Everything hurts."

"Well, don't try." Edward walked over to the side of the bed. The room was small, reserved for serious injuries—it contained only one other bed and that was empty and stripped. Cundall saw Edward look at it.

"Had two fellows through there already," he said. "One of 'em left yesterday afternoon. Only here for a night. Boche shell took his nose off. Made me quit my complaining pretty damn quick, that's for sure."

From up close, Cundall's face was framed by bruising that spread up his back and neck like an ink blot. At the edges it was turning violet and eerie yellow. He grimaced as he shifted his weight a little so he could look directly at Edward.

"I know about Marchand," he said.

"Our orders said to go and investigate anything unusual on the ground," Edward said. He didn't feel it was his place to mete out blame, or to dispense forgiveness. "The photographs he took may turn out to be useful."

Cundall suddenly gritted his teeth and closed his eyes as the shadow of pain passed through him. "It comes and goes in waves," he said. He opened them again. "You're getting out of here, sir?"

"Just got my release papers. I'm going to get a train back to Épernay today."

"Well, good for you. They say I'll be here for a while, and then they'll send me away to convalesce somewhere further from the front. In any case, I won't be flying again for a long time, if at all."

"I'm sorry to hear it," Edward said.

"Oh no," Cundall said. In his voice was a trace of his old cockiness. "Don't be sorry, sir. I'm not."

EDWARD TURNED DOWN the offer of a car, and instead he and Marion walked into town to the station. As they went, he tried to take her hand, but she withdrew it and said: "We aren't allowed to do that. Nurses, I mean. They have rules. If one of the matrons saw us holding hands, there would be trouble for me."

As his condition had improved, she had pulled away from him again. Her initial relief at finding him alive had been supplanted by wariness, as though she'd remembered the difficult history they shared, the reasons why she should keep distance between them. He wanted to shake her and say, not here, not now, after all that we have been through, surely those things can be set aside. But he did not dare for fear that she would shut him out completely.

They were early for the train, so they decided to get a cup of coffee while they waited. When they entered the station café, she chose a table where they sat opposite one another, not side by side. And so sitting there, with his hands by his sides, and her not quite close enough to touch, he decided he might as well question her about Clara. It was partly revenge for her coldness. But she responded so calmly, he realized she'd been waiting all along for him to ask.

"In the autumn last year, when I first arrived in France, I went to see Clara in Voulangis. The thought of working in a hospital, of caring for the wounded, made it seem important to go and try to talk to her one more time.

"She wouldn't see me."

"What do you mean, she wouldn't see you?"

"I had written to tell her I wanted to visit, and I'd heard nothing back. I should have left it at that, but I didn't. I went to your house anyway. It was Kate who let me in. When I asked if Clara was there, she told me her mother wasn't feeling well." She hesitated and looked at him questioningly. "Should I tell you this?" she asked.

"I asked you about it."

"Kate remembered who I was but not very well—to children that young, three years is like a lifetime. I asked if she would tell Clara that I was there, and she said her mother was sleeping and didn't like to be woken up, but that I could come in and wait if I wanted. There was a fire going; the room seemed well kept. We sat beside it and I asked her about how things were for them. She said she was going to school and she liked it, but she didn't like all the soldiers in the town or the noise that they could hear from the guns. She missed Mary, she said. I asked her if she got letters from you. She said no."

"I wrote to her every week."

"Then she changed her mind and said yes, but that her mother didn't like it when letters came from you, so she often threw them away without reading them.

"We talked for a while and then Clara came down. She told me to leave. She would not listen to anything I had to say. Rather than make a scene in front of Kate, I did as she said."

"Kate—how did she seem to you?"

"Well, she looked to be in good health, energetic and talkative. She seemed grown-up for her age. It was like talking to an adult, someone who was used to taking care of things for others. I wanted to help her. I asked her if she needed anything, if I should return and visit them again. She shook her head and said no, that there was nothing they needed and I definitely shouldn't come back. A few months later I heard that they had returned to America. Then in May, I received the letter from the lawyer."

Her hands fidgeted with the napkin beneath her cup of coffee.

"In retrospect, it was a foolish thing to do, going there, disturbing them like that, an unwelcome face from the past. But I wanted to try. I wanted to see Clara, to find out if there was anything left of our friendship that could be salvaged. I didn't do it to make life more difficult for anyone. You understand, don't you?"

"Of course." He reached over and took her hand. She let him.

She said: "It seems to be my usual trick: good intentions paving the road to somewhere unpleasant. Perhaps I should stop having such good intentions all the time."

Outside, there was the sound of pistons and the shrill whistle of an approaching train.

"There it is," Marion said. "You'd better take your bags out."

"When can I see you again?" Edward asked.

"I have leave due at the end of the month. But if there is a big push, it will be canceled. I'll write to you."

She offered him her hand and he took it. They stood looking at each other. Then, unexpectedly, she leaned forward and kissed him quickly, hesitantly, on the lips. He caught her face in his hands and kissed her again, this time for longer and more deeply. Outside, the whistle blew.

"You'd better go," she said. "They don't stop for long at each station. Go on."

"Will you come with me to the platform?"

"No. I don't think I can manage that. I'll stay here."

"OK." He picked up his kit bag from the floor beside him and made his way to the train.

He was settled by the window of the carriage when he saw her come out of the café and go to the edge of the platform. Almost at a run she made her way down the cars until she found him. She put her fingertips on the glass and he put his on the other side, so that their hands were mirror images of each other. Then the train began to move.

AT THE ÉPERNAY airfield, the men were getting ready for a new German offensive. They did not know when it would come, only that it would happen soon. There were more American troops than before in this part of the front. They had taken over some sectors from the French: the 26th Division had replaced the 2nd Division between Vaux and Torcy; the 3rd Division was still deployed near Courthiézy; and the 369th Infantry was to the east of Reims. Other smaller units of Americans were mixed in among the French up and down the line. As soon as Edward arrived back, van Horn called him into his office.

"We drew up a report based on those photographs Marchand took and sent it to Major Barnes at Chaumont," the colonel said. "He passed it on to General Mitchell, who found it extremely impressive. His office telephoned several days ago and recommended you and Lieutenant Lutz for promotions. Major Barnes is being transferred back to the States to oversee training operations there. You will replace him as head of the Photography Division; Lutz will go with you as your assistant. You'll also be attached to General Mitchell's staff at Colombey-les-Belles and promoted to the rank of major. Congratulations."

"Thank you, sir."

"Mitchell asked that you report to his office as soon as you are ready."

"Who will run things here during this next push?"

"Lieutenant Dawson was covering your duties while you were incapacitated. He'll just continue to do so on a more permanent footing."

"Well," Edward said, "this is good news."

"Yes, isn't it just?" van Horn said. "A nice, safe desk job, just at the right time . . . When can you be ready to leave?"

"By tomorrow if necessary," Edward said, trying to sound unfazed. He would not allow van Horn to goad him.

"Good," the colonel said. "I'll arrange a car to take you over there, first thing."

So this was how it worked, Edward reflected as he left the

meeting and walked across the field toward the developing lab. The accumulated deaths of men added up to one useful (apparently, as van Horn said) piece of information, and the man in charge received a promotion. He had done nothing to deserve any special acclaim, nothing that Gilles Marchand and Daniels hadn't done, nothing that Deveraux and Dawson didn't do everyday. He was just the name on the top of the report. He hadn't even written it. Lutz had.

But he had to admit that van Horn was right about one thing: he was relieved at the thought of not having to go out there again, not having to see the men around him disappearing, and maybe one day himself being one of those who just didn't come back. *A nice, safe desk job.* Van Horn had known what he was feeling, had seen in his face the longing to be out of danger—because of course the colonel must have felt it too when he was offered *his* promotion, *his* nice, safe desk job.

Edward went into the lab. It was almost empty at this hour, when most of the men were at breakfast. He sat down and began looking through the stacks of photographs from the days he had been away. There was the countryside of the Marne, miniaturized and far below him. He felt suddenly, strongly, that he wasn't ready to leave yet. He wanted to stay at Épernay until this next battle was over. He knew that this attitude made no particular sense. He didn't doubt Dawson's ability to run things when his turn came. There was no reason his particular help was needed here by the men or by the army. Somebody else would do just as well, or as badly, as he would, because everyone in this war, including him, was replaceable.

It was only that this place, for him, was not interchangeable with other places. Now he thought about this landscape as contours, obstacles and cover, places to hide and targets to destroy. But in that other life, the one that Marion recalled to him each time he saw her, he had loved this country for its beauty. The cover had been woods, the contours, hills, the obstacles had been rivers, shining in the summer sunlight of those last days of peace. If the attack was going to come south, toward his house, where all his memories were stored up in the photographs that he had left there, he wanted to stay until it was safe or until it was beyond saving.

He went back to van Horn's office, knocked and was admitted.

"What is it, Steichen?"

"I'd like to remain stationed at Épernay. Until this next offensive is over."

Van Horn stopped what he was doing. "What?"

"I want to stay, even if it means passing up the transfer and promotion. For this next offensive. If it is possible."

"Well, I guess it can probably be arranged. You can stay here for a few weeks more and then go. But why would you want to do that? You've never seen a serious offensive before have you, Steichen? You don't actually know what that is like. Don't you want to think it over a little more, before you turn down this offer?"

"No. Sir, I want to stay here."

"Why?"

"Because it was my home."

Harvest. Voulangis, August 1914. Gum print.

ON THE FRONT page of the morning paper is a photograph of men and women crowded around a station ticket office. They are well dressed, the sort of people whom you would see climbing out of taxis in front of a theater or strolling in the public gardens on Sunday afternoon, but in their eyes is a common look of mounting panic. Many of them have their mouths open, shouting. Some are waving tickets or other kinds of papers, hoping that these will be seen and recognized, that they will be enough to buy passage out of this city, and out of this country that is on its way to war. Above the picture is the headline, all in capitals: "RUSSIA TO MOBILIZE."

Edward has spread the paper out on the kitchen table and he is standing hunched over it, his hands planted on either side of its pages when Marion comes downstairs. Clara has gone out riding early in the morning, taking Mary with her. Arthur and Mercy have driven back to Paris two days previously, taking Marion's car to the city with them. Kate is outside in the garden. So it is only the two of them awake in the house. He turns toward the sound of her footsteps and beckons to her. She comes and peers over his shoulder to the newspaper headline and the photograph below it.

Her eyes click back and forth along the lines of print. Soldiers moving to the border with Austria. Railways and roads commandeered for military use in a time of national emergency. In Moscow, Czar Nicholas reviews rows of saluting troops. Foreigners flock to the stations and ports looking for passage out by rail or by sea. As she reads, the color drains from her face; he sees it go, sees fear take root in its place, as though it were an infection, caught from the faces in the photograph.

"My poor mother . . ." she says, without moving her eyes off the page.

"I'm sure that they are all right," he says. "They are in the capital, far away from the border." He tries to keep his voice steady. Marion looks at him. She nods.

"Yes, I know. They are far away from it all." She doesn't sound convinced.

"If you know their hotel, you can cable them from the *mairie*. I'll drive you into town." He sits on the table, facing her. She is on the verge of tears.

"I . . ." she says. "I . . ." But she cannot seem to find anything to complete the sentence. Instead, she looks back at the newspaper, squints at it as though this will allow her to see through the lines of newsprint to what is not written, to the future. Her eyes flutter over the page like trapped birds. He wants to do something to comfort her, embrace her, but he is hesitant to touch her.

"Yes," she says more definitely. "Yes. Take me into town. I'll send them a telegram. If I send it now, they may be able to reply today. That is, if the wires aren't too busy . . . I'll get my coat."

When he pulls the dogcart around to the front of the house, she is waiting outside.

"I told Louisa to keep an eye on Kate," she says as she climbs up. "I told her we wouldn't be long." Her self-possession has returned. Only a slight hesitation before each sentence gives away that anything is out of the ordinary. And this: When she climbs onto the seat beside him, she reaches out and takes his hand. She doesn't look at him as she does it, but she takes it and holds it, and they ride to town like this.

—

THEY DO NOT hear from Marion's parents that day or the following one. She puts a brave face on it.

"After all," she says to Clara, "there are all sorts of reasons why they might not be able to send word right now," though she doesn't enumerate what these might be.

"Yes," Clara agrees. "I'm sure they will cable as soon as they can. I'm sure they are fine." They are both willing it to be so. By saying it, they will make it true.

Marion keeps busy. She helps Louisa and Clara around the house. She reads to Kate, sitting out under the trees in the back garden. From Edward, she retreats. He watches her but doesn't have any sense of what is taking place beneath her implacable reserve. What can he do? The single, simple touch of their hands as they drove to town that day has brought to the surface again feelings he thought he had successfully dismissed. He feels confused and divided, wanting to touch her, to be close to her, and guilty for even thinking it at such a time as this. There she is, reading to his daughter; conversing with his wife. She is so close. She is a million miles out of reach. His frustration makes him short-tempered. The following morning he is sitting at the table thumbing through the newspaper for the third time when Kate wriggles under his arm and up onto his knee.

"What is it, Catkin?" he asks. She is blocking his view.

"Daddy, what is going to happen in Russia?"

"I don't know, sweetheart. Nobody does. The soldiers are going to go and fight."

"Why?"

"To defend their country. Now go on and find your mother. I'm in the middle of something." He lifts her off his knee and sets her down on the ground. "Go on."

"Daddy, what's a . . ."

"Kate, did you hear what I said?" It is only when he sees her shrink back away from him that he realizes his voice has risen and he is almost shouting. He is shocked at the ferocity of his own reaction, instantly sorry, standing there with his arm raised pointing toward the door. Kate runs out, and he sits back down and pretends to go on reading.

That night as they are going to bed, Clara asks, "Why were you angry at Kate this morning? What's wrong with you?"

"Nothing's wrong with me," he says, feeling that same irritation from earlier well up in him again. "She has to learn not to interrupt people."

"Well, yes. But you've always encouraged her to ask questions." She looks at him, searchingly. "Is that all that is the matter?"

"No, that isn't all," he says, turning over, turning away from her. "In case you haven't noticed, it seems like there is about to be a war."

"Fine," Clara says. "Never mind." And she puts out the light and turns away, too, so they are lying in the dark without touching—tense and unable to sleep. I don't know, Edward thinks silently. Clara, I'm sorry, I don't know what is making me act like this, so quick to anger, so changeable. Or perhaps, I do know, but I can hardly bear even to admit it to myself, much less tell you the truth to your face. Maybe I'm just not fit for human company right now.

So the next day he tries to go back to work in his studio. At least this will take him out of the bell jar of the house. But he finds, once he gets there and closes the door behind him, that he can't really concentrate on printing and developing and cropping photographs. Each day the papers are bringing more terrible news; fighting has begun in the east. In Paris, Jaurès is shot dead at an antiwar rally by a man who escapes into the crowd; the police claim they have no leads. In Berlin, Viviani meets with von Moltke. Edward pores over these stories for hours, sitting with his feet up, near the table in the front room, smoking cigarette after cigarette down to the nub. Outside, the weather, heedless of human affairs, continues to be beautiful.

THEN ON THE third morning they are sitting at breakfast when they hear faintly the sound of a drum. It is coming from the road. Edward goes to the door and opens it. The others gather around him, peering out, blinking a little in the sunlight. In the doorways of houses up and down the street other families appear. The women send their children out to the fields to call the men, who come in, singly or in small groups, still wiping the earth from their hands. The drum continues, three taps and then a pause, growing closer, accompanied by the dry sound of boots on stones.

Over the rise comes the *garde champêtre* for the commune of Voulangis. He has the cylinder of a drum strapped to his body, and it precedes his ample belly down the road. He is breathing hard from the climb; beads of sweat stand out on his broad forehead. As he approaches, Edward can see that he is beating the drum with the side of a long wooden spoon.

It makes a preposterous picture, this fat man, wheezing his way up the road. Edward has known him for years—not well, but to greet in passing; Claude Perrine owns a small farm out beyond his own house, along the road to Crécy-en-Brie. Perrine can usually be found in the café in town, drinking a glass of beer and putting off commune business until tomorrow. But now no one snickers behind their hand, or looks at each other smiling. There is only a hush over everything, the kind usually reserved for the interior of churches. Even the children are still, sensing something in the behavior of the adults that they have not known before. When Perrine reaches the crossroads just beyond the house, he stops.

"Come and hear; come and hear; come and hear." His shouts

fall through the strange quiet. "Come and hear; come and hear." People file from the shadows of their houses and drift toward him, gathering around but not coming too close, as though this would make them responsible for the news they know he is bringing.

"We are going to war." François has come in from the field and is standing by Edward's elbow. The old man slips past him to join his wife and son, the other villagers, as they move in concert toward the crossroads. Edward leaves the porch and follows them. He stands a little way back, but within earshot. When the crowd has grown sufficiently large—men in front and women hovering at a distance behind, leaning over walls and fences—Perrine pulls a long scroll from his satchel and begins to read.

"France is in danger. In accordance with the Three Years Law of 1913 and other provisions of the law of the Republic ..." A young woman begins to cry and an older woman puts a hand on her shoulder and whispers to her to be quiet. "All able-bodied men between the ages of eighteen and forty-four must report to the town square of their commune for orders. Tomorrow morning." People begin to turn away, back to their houses. "Anyone found in dereliction of his duty," Perrine continues, "will be ..." But the end of his pronouncement is drowned under the shuffling, shifting noises of the crowd as it begins to disintegrate back into individual men and women. Children run ahead of the heavy, slow steps of the grown-ups, calling out to each other with shrill voices, using words they do not yet understand: War! We are going to war! Long live France! Long live our army!

Behind them Perrine rolls up his proclamation and puts it back in his bag. He wipes his forehead with a handkerchief and tips his hat to Edward. Then he continues on down the road, the sound of his drum following him until both disappear. Edward walks back to his house, feeling more like a foreigner among these people than he has for a long time. He will not have to register, and he will not have to fight.

STANDING UNDER THE eaves, Clara cannot hear the exact words of the proclamation that is being read out, but she doesn't need to. She can see what it says from the faces of the listeners as they turn toward home: bewildered, surprised; their eyes big with worry. The women are walking close together, some with arms around each other's waists.

"Did you think," one of them says as she passes by, "that it would come so soon?"

"I didn't think it would come at all."

"I'll have to get his clothes washed. So they will be ready by tomorrow. I'll have to finish lining that coat."

"What will he need a coat for. It is summer. Besides, they'll be given uniforms."

"How will we get the harvest in without the men?"

"Shhh. We'll find a way."

They do not look at Clara as they pass by, these women whom she has known by sight for years now. They are too consumed with their own cares, their own immediate future, which is something she is not a part of. Foreigners have special dispensation: her husband does not have to report tomorrow. The women hurry by and disappear into their own houses. There is nothing for her to share with them.

Kate comes out of the house and nuzzles up to her skirt.

"Why are all the people so serious?" she asks.

"Nothing you need to worry about sweetheart," Clara says. Edward comes through the front gate, pulling it shut behind him.

"But why are they sad? François is sad. Everyone is sad!" Kate's voice quavers, and she stamps her foot insistently, demanding that the sadness disperse and that things go back to being as they were before. Edward sits down on the stoop beside her. With her standing, his face is almost level with hers.

"Yes, my love. Everyone is sad," he says. "Because there is going to be a war. But you are going to be safe because it will happen a long way away from here. We don't need to worry." He takes Kate into his arms. Against his shoulder her head of tangled brown curls looks terribly small.

The next morning the papers say the Germans have invaded Belgium. The men leave early to report to their units in the town. They are quiet as they go. Edward is awake in time to see them depart: he takes pictures of the women watching from the doorways until the men are out of sight.

THERE IS A ring at the door. Edward goes to open it. Standing outside is Claude Perrine and another man, a deputy constable with a weasel face and wire-rimmed spectacles perched on his large nose, whose name Edward has never learned. Perrine's forehead is damp with perspiration.

"Claude," Edward says. "Won't you come in and have a glass of water or some beer."

Claude inhales noisily.

"I cannot," he says. The deputy hovers beside him.

"Well, what can I do for you?" Edward asks. There is something odd and aloof in Perrine's manner. He has never known the man to refuse a drink of beer before. Perrine clears his throat.

"You are Mr. Edward Steichen?" he asks. Edward blinks at him, confused.

"Yes. You know I am. Claude, what is this about?"

"This is official business. It must be done officially. Did you write last week to a Mr. Alfred Stieglitz of 291 Fifth Avenue?" Perrine draws an envelope from his pocket and presents it to Edward.

"Yes, I did. What are you doing with my letter? What is this about?"

"Your friend Mr. Stieglitz, is he a German?"

"No, he's an American." The deputy is taking notes on a small pad.

"And to your knowledge, has he ever resided in Germany?"

"What? Yes. He was an art student in Berlin. But I fail to see—"

"And you, you are what nationality?"

"I'm also American."

"And your wife?"

"Look, Claude, what is the point of this? You know where we are from. Clara is from Missouri. My parents live in Milwaukee, Wisconsin—"

"I would suggest," said the deputy, speaking for the first time, "that you simply answer our questions. Where is your family from originally?" There is an air of immense satisfaction in the way he delivers these lines, and Edward realizes that the man is enjoying himself.

"My family is from Luxembourg," he says, managing to keep the irritation out of his voice.

"Are you sure?" says the deputy.

"Of course I'm sure. Who would forget a thing like that?"

"It may not be a question of forgetting."

"What on earth are you suggesting?"

"It would also be advisable," the deputy says, pushing his glasses up his nose officiously, "for a foreigner, especially one with a name like yours, to be as cooperative as he can with the authorities."

"With a name like what?"

"A German name." The man is putting his notebook and pen

away in his jacket. "Good day, sir," he says. Beside him, Perrine, unhappily, tips his hat and follows him down the path from the garden. Edward watches them go, then closes the door and turns back inside.

Clara has been listening from the stairs.

"We shouldn't stay here," she says. "We should take the children and go."

"Go where? This is where we live."

"They are going to start making things difficult for foreigners, even for Americans."

"I won't be intimidated."

"It's all very well to be principled, but what about the children?"

"What would they learn if we left now? To run away at the first sign of trouble?"

"That man was practically accusing us of being spies. Do you think that for once you could make things less difficult, not more? Why does it always have to be . . ." But he doesn't wait for her to finish. He goes upstairs past her and into his study. She lets him.

BY THE NEXT morning the Germans have crossed into Luxembourg. Clara cries; Marion stares at the news dry-eyed, then puts her arms around Clara. The two women stand in the salon, embracing, Marion saying "Hush, hush" into Clara's dark head.

"We aren't safe here," Clara says to Edward, who is sitting on the other side of the room. She comes and takes his hand in both of hers. "I told you. We have to leave. I don't understand what we are waiting for."

He doesn't reply. He ignores her eyes, looking past her to where Marion is standing. Her face is half-turned away, so he cannot see her expression, only that her head is drooped forward as though she is very tired. Clara follows his eyes, then stands and goes purposefully toward the door.

"Where are you going?" Edward asks.

"What do you care?" she shoots back.

"Clara, please. Where?"

"To get Mildred. She's all alone in her house up there."

"No she isn't. She has Amélie."

"We will be safer if we are all together," Clara says with a finality that silences him.

"Shall I go with you?" Marion asks.

"No, no. No need. I'll be just fine on my own," Clara says with forced lightness. She pulls on her boots and goes out. He hears her drive away.

Marion looks over at him, where he has remained sitting throughout Clara's preparations to leave.

"You should be gentler with her," she says. "You shouldn't be so—"

"So what?" She is looking at him with her head on one side, as though she were admonishing a child. He wants to be angry with her: how dare she tell him how to speak? But he finds he cannot. Under her gaze, he feels like he is coming unraveled. How can she stand there so calmly like that? He can hardly bear to look at her.

"I'll be upstairs with Kate if you need me," she says.

A WHILE LATER there is the sound of wheels outside, and Edward looks out expecting to see Clara drive up with Mildred. But it is Louisa instead who has been into town and caught a ride back in the baker's cart. She is running up the driveway with a piece of paper in her hand. It is a telegram.

"Go and tell Mademoiselle Beckett. It is for her. From Russia."

Edward bounds up the stairs two at a time to the third floor and knocks on the door of Kate's room, then opens it. Marion looks up from the book she is reading and sees his face, then the folded paper in his hand.

"Oh, God," she says. She comes out into the hallway. She takes the paper from him.

"I'd better go to my room to look at it. No, I'll open it here. Oh, I can't do it. You read it." She pushes it back into his fingers. He tears through the seal and reads.

"They are safe," he says. "Your parents are on a boat to England. They are both fine. They will cable you as soon as they arrive."

Marion takes the telegram from him, as though she needs to see it herself to believe it. Her hands are shaking as she reads.

"Look at me," she says. "How ridiculous I am. Now that every-thing is all right, I'm going to pieces." She starts laughing and puts a hand up to cover her mouth, only to discover that she is crying, too. "How silly I am," she says, and reaches out for his arm to steady herself. "I think I'd better sit down."

He guides her down the stairs and along the short hallway to the room where she is staying. She is still crying, and he lays her down on the bed and sits beside her, clearing the stray hairs from her forehead. She puts an arm over her face, so the crook of her elbow covers her eyes, and continues to sob, and then he knows that this is not only about the telegram but also about the whole of the summer, about the things that have passed between them, and about Clara, and about Mary and Kate, and about the war that is closing in on them. Through all of it, she has never lost her self-control until this very moment. He peels her arm gently away from her face. Then he leans down and kisses her on the forehead. When he pulls away, they look at each other for a long time. He kisses her again, this time on her cheek, and she moves closer to him so that their faces are resting against each other. They stay like that, perfectly still. He can hear the sound of her breathing close to his ear. He doesn't know how long this lasts. But then there is the noise of the door downstairs opening, and voices. They spring apart, guilty and suddenly alone in their own skins again. There are footsteps on the stairs. The door opens, and Clara comes in saying, "Well, you were right. She claims she is fine . . ." And then she sees them. She stops speaking and stares, her gaze going from one to the other, her mouth a little open, as though she has temporarily forgotten its existence.

"Clara . . ." Marion's voice is plaintive. Clara continues staring, and then slowly she begins to nod, yes, she nods, yes, this is how it is, I see, I knew it all along. She turns and walks away down the hall. The door slams shut behind her.

"Clara, wait," Edward says. He is still seated beside Marion on the bed.

"Go after her," Marion says, pushing him away, so he staggers to his feet. He hesitates, looking at her. "For God's sake," she insists, "go on!"

He leaves without a word and follows his wife down the hall to their bedroom. She has locked the door, and he pounds on it with his fist.

"Clara, let me in. Please." He listens but he can hear nothing from within. "Clara. Open the door." Still there is only silence in reply. He leans against the locked door, listening. He tries one more time: "Whatever you think," he says, "you are wrong. Nothing happened. I promise."

He hears the bolt slide back and the door opens. There is his wife, her eyes hard with anger and her mouth set. She stands in the doorway barring his way. In a low voice, filled with derision, she says, "You promise, do you? What exactly is it that you promise?"

"Clara, let me come in. Do you want everyone in the house to hear this? Do you want the girls to know?"

"I would have imagined you could have thought of that before you decided to have your tryst," she spits the word into his face, "in the house while your daughter is right upstairs."

He steps forward, takes hold of her arm and moves it by force so that he can push past her into the room. She spins around and stares after him, outraged.

"Don't you touch me," she says.

"I'm not going to. Close the door," he says. "Right now, Clara."

After a moment's hesitation, she shoves the door closed.

"Now sit down." She remains standing. He shrugs. "Fine. Stand, if you'd prefer." She is waiting to hear what he has to say.

"Clara, I know what you are thinking. But you are wrong. Marion got her telegram from Russia and she felt faint, so I took her inside."

"And nothing happened?" she asks, mimicking his words. She is trying to meet his eyes, but he finds himself staring hard at the floorboards. "Nothing at all?" He is silent. "You can't even look at me, can you?"

"It isn't what you think."

"What do I think?" she says, advancing toward him. "Tell me: What do I think? That all summer you have watched her and watched her and watched her? That you've looked through me ever since she arrived here? Tell me all of that isn't true. Say it with a straight face."

"Clara, Marion is your friend. She came here for you."

"Yes, she was. She was my friend. Now you've managed to take even that."

"Don't shout," he says. "Please. You're being dramatic. I don't know how to say this more clearly. Marion and I are not having an affair. How could we be? Clara: you are my wife."

Clara sits down on their bed. The animating anger drains from her. She looks lost suddenly, sitting there with her shoulders drooped forward, lost and afraid and small. She says, "It is always women who are artists, isn't it?"

"What do you mean always?"

"The others, they were artists, too. Kathleen Bruce. And that Isadora Duncan."

"What?"

"Always," Clara continued, "the ones who had the freedom to do as they wanted. I was never enough for you. You were never contented with me."

"Clara, those things happened years ago. I can't undo them."

"Oh, shut up, shut up," she says, covering her ears with her hands. "I have become a convenience to you. I always was one." And in a single movement she unlocks the door and goes out before he has a chance to stop her.

SHE IS FALLING past the surface of the earth. As she runs across the garden and into the field beyond, it is as though the world has been stood on end and she is plummeting across its sheer face, helpless to catch herself. She sees the familiar things of her life, the house, the kitchen yard, the garden with its ordered flower beds and trees, the broken wooden gate that leads to their one field, all flash past her, and, one by one, they are carried away, leaving her. She runs out into the open field, and all of them dwindle and shrink behind her.

In the center of her mind as she runs, there is a small calm room, like she imagines the eye of a tornado must be. From this place comes a voice that observes the tumbling world with detachment. Well, says the voice, what did you expect? Let them go. It is better to know the truth, the worst of it, the limits of what is possible. That way, you will have no false hopes or expectations and no one will have the power to hurt you anymore.

The field is planted with sweet peas this year. The snarled green plants catch at her feet as she runs. She keeps going until her lungs are ragged and sore, and then she decides, simply, that she will not run any further. Why don't you just lie down and rest? suggests the voice in her head. Yes, that is what she will do. She flops onto the ground between the rows of plants, exhausted and dizzy.

The soil is sun-warm and soft, but when she is still, her mind lurches abruptly back toward the house, to what she'd seen when she pushed open the bedroom door and found them there, leaning together on the bed. Their postures gave them away, but more than that, their eyes: looking at her with a mixture of shame and fear. What else, really, did she need to know? And that he could, even after that, stand in front of her, denying everything, pushing her aside. As though she couldn't tell the behavior of a guilty man when she saw it. As though she could be taken for a complete fool.

Everything is gone. The thought rises, wailing, from the middle of her body. I had a friend, and now she is gone. I thought I had a husband, too, but I do not, and now I see I never did. He never loved me as I loved him. I wanted him to look at me and see a reflection but for him love never meant that. He loves women the way that one loves a beautiful landscape or a vase, the way one loves a painting or a photograph.

Don't think about it, says the voice from the quiet room inside her. What good will that do? Just lie here and breathe. Above her the sky is an astounding blue. The earth smells dark and metallic, and over it, she inhales the green aroma of the pea plants. Her chest strains, hollowed out, as though things have been removed from its cavity, the heart, and perhaps the lungs as well, to make space for planting. Could she become part of the field, soil filling her in, consuming her? Through the place where her breastbone used to be the spiral tendrils of plants will emerge and twist toward the light.

Quite suddenly, there is the sound of the gate that leads from the garden creaking open and someone comes through it. Whoever it is walks through the rows of plants, skirts making rasping noises with each step. A woman is coming. Oh, God, she thinks, please let it not be Marion. Then again, she does not want Louisa to see her like this either, does not want to face that girl's sulky insolence (and wouldn't she enjoy immensely the spectacle of the mistress of the house collapsed on the bare ground, her garments covered in dirt). Doubtless Edward has sent her out here because he is too much of a coward to come himself. That would be typical of him, would it not?

"Louisa, you may go back inside," she calls out. "I am not in need of your help right now."

"Well," says a voice that is neither Louisa's nor Marion's, "I would like to help you anyhow, even if there is no need."

"Mildred!" Clara sits up, and when she turns around, there is Mildred striding toward her, now only a few yards off.

"After you left, I thought that you were probably right that we would be better off all together, and so I drove down from Huiry. But it seems that I've arrived to find your house in quite a state of confusion. Louisa told me what happened." Clara begins to cry. "Oh, my dear." Mildred's face is full of pity. "I am so sorry."

For a few minutes they stay as they are, not speaking, Mildred standing just a few feet from her while Clara cries quietly, tears sliding out of her, rising and subsiding, then rising again.

"I don't know what to do," she says, between waves. "What should I do?"

Mildred sighs. "You must try to think of what is left," she says.

"What is left?" Clara asks.

"Your children."

Think of what is left. Think of your children. What about them? Well, Mary, even though she appears so grown up, will need help to get through this trying time. And what about Kate? Yes, little Kate. She is the reason to find from somewhere the ability to go on. There is a war coming. This is not the time to go to pieces. Later, when the children are safe, you can decide what to do. For now, there are other, more pressing concerns.

Clara wipes her eyes with her thumbs. "Yes," she says. "You are right." But when she thinks about the prospect of standing up and walking back into that house, of resuming the life that goes on there, the effort seems overwhelming, impossible. She looks up at Mildred, wincing as though burned by the thought. I would rather die right here, she thinks. I would rather disappear. "I can't," she says. "I can't do it."

"Yes, you can!" Mildred says. The force of her voice is almost physical, and it catches Clara by surprise. When she looks up, Mildred's eyes are hard and determined. "You can," she says. "You must." She puts her hands on her hips, fists clenched. "Get up, child." She has never addressed Clara this way before, and not until now could either of them have realized the truth contained in the name, its alloy of love and fierceness. Mildred comes forward and offers Clara her arm, and Clara grasps it and begins to get to her feet. When she is standing, Mildred helps her to shake the dirt from her clothing.

"All right," Clara says when she has dusted herself off and taken a deep, steady breath. "I'm ready." Mildred nods. Very slowly, they make their way back toward the house.

In the next field, Clara sees, they are bringing in the harvest. A steam thresher, its pistons strumming, moves over the hunched back of the hill and, following it, old men and women reach for the fallen stems, binding them into bales. The children run among them gleaning what the machine leaves. Some of the women have babies bound to their chests. The old people stop every few minutes to rest, and then keep going. The thresher pants along with its blades spinning and its wheels biting into the earth.

Yes, Clara thinks, it is necessary to go on. One has no alternative. It is necessary to complete the task at hand: that is what war demands, even of those who do not want it.

TEN

July 15, 1918

IN THE EARLY morning the Germans began to shell the French and American lines on the east side of the Aisne salient well before dawn. Edward was woken when McIntyre pushed open the door of his room.

"It's started," he said.

"I'll be right there." And then he was out of bed and on his feet, pulling on his uniform and running with the others to the lab. He passed out the cameras to each of them.

"We're looking for the coordinates of their field artillery and mortars," he told them. "Keep your eyes open. Good luck." They saluted, and then they were gone.

As soon as they were in the air, he could see the intensity of the barrage. Fires had broken out up and down the line, and groups of men were struggling to put them out, while around them more shells came down. On a main route out of Épernay, a convoy of motor ambulances had been hit and the scattered remains filled the road, making it impassable. People were clearing the debris out of the way. They moved tires and the twisted metal of the chassis. They carried the wounded and the dead as far from the wreckage as they could.

Further on, the early morning shelling had crept forward in a solid wall across No Man's Land and over the Allied lines. The walls of trenches had collapsed inward where shells fell near them, and he saw men shoveling mountains of dislodged earth. He saw them digging, and then stopping to pull things from the pile: there, the body of a man, hauled out arms first, legs dragging under him useless and shattered. Or there, a man threw down his shovel, bent down and came away with something long and mangled, a part of a body. It might have been an arm or a leg, Edward couldn't tell. The man who found it threw it to one side and kept digging.

Then the gas attacks began. Edward saw the first gas shells fall, the high-pitched scream of their flight, then the mustard color billowing silently outward from the point of impact as the wind carried it. Where the shells landed close to a trench, the gas poured over the sides, like slow water, until the trench and the men inside it disappeared. One minute they were there, pulling on masks, struggling to get away, and then they were gone. And after it came the German troops, small knots of them, running, diving for cover at the sound of Allied fire, then inching forward again to seize the trenches as the haze cleared.

In photographs, attacking soldiers are a mottle of darkness, and it isn't clear whether they are winning or losing the battle. From the air an attack and a retreat look roughly the same. This is what Edward learned watching the Germans climb from their positions north of the Marne and push forward after the retreating French and Americans. In the trenches there were men who hung on bravely until they were cut off and couldn't escape. Perhaps they didn't realize that it was too late, or perhaps they did. He couldn't know that. He could only see them rally and charge forward even after all the units around them had fallen back, and then he glimpsed them only for a second before the speed of the plane snatched them out of view.

THE FOLLOWING MORNING there were two fewer planes to go out. One had made it back to the airfield with the pilot and observer alive but was so badly shot up that it wouldn't fly for several days. The other had gone down over No Man's Land and crashed nose-first into the side of a shell crater. Edward had been too far away to see it go. Apparently, the pilot, Shapiro, had struggled free and had been seen running away from the wreck. No one knew what happened to him after that.

The Germans had come south from Château-Thierry, where they had shelled the Allies from the steep ridge to the north and then managed to cross the river below the town where it was shallow. From the sky above these new lines, Edward could see Voulangis and the rise where his house stood. He could see the descent down toward Huiry, where Mildred had lived. He thought, too, that he could make out the station at Esbly.

Along the eastern side of the salient and to the north and west near Soissons, the Germans had managed to push the Allies back several miles. If this continued, it would not take them long to capture the railhead at Reims and then press on to Paris.

On the second morning, the barrage moved forward and some of the towns south of the river were destroyed. Soldiers had taken up positions in the rubble, and in the small ellipses of trees that crowned the low hills. They could be seen, now, only indirectly by the smoke of their gunfire, or when they had to scatter to escape an incoming mortar. He couldn't tell which direction the fighting was moving. He put his camera up and gathered as much into it as he possibly could.

Then, during their second run of the day, he saw khaki-uniformed soldiers advancing out of a wood very close to the river. They were pursuing a group of men dressed in slate-gray. The men in brown, he realized, were Americans. One of them threw a grenade toward the retreating Germans: it exploded in their midst, downing all but one, who dove toward the water just in time and lay with his face to the ground while showers of earth fell around him. Then he crawled into the river and began to swim. From the plumes of red that rose behind him, Edward could see he was badly hurt. Midway across he slipped under and didn't resurface.

The Americans made their way to the water's edge. He watched them as they began to dig in where they were, burrowing into the soft soil of the riverbank to wait for night.

WHEN HE RETURNED to quarters, Edward found McIntyre waiting for him in the officers' lounge. He was sitting with a book open in front of him, staring past its pages at the wall. He started when Edward came in, then shook his head as though to clear it.

"Almost drifted off," he said. He rubbed his eyes and temples with one hand. "Listen," he said, "some bad news came in. I thought you'd want to know."

"What is it?"

"Knightly. There was an accident at St-Omer. Engine malfunction. Not his fault.

"Jesus. That's terrible," Edward said. "I can't believe it." St-Omer was supposed to be safe, he thought. It was not supposed to be a place from which bad news came.

"Even training flights," McIntyre said, echoing his thoughts, "you just never know." He stood up. "I should turn in." He put a hand on Edward's shoulder as he made his way toward the door. "I'm sorry," he said. "It's a hell of a way to say good night."

IN THE DAYS that followed, Edward watched as the battle moved back and forth below him. At Château-Thierry, the Germans were pushed back across the river. They came on toward Épernay, though, pushing the line forward on either side of the river where its course turned south and east. The lines move steadily up toward the airfield and toward the village of Voulangis beyond it. They were shelling this country now. He could see the damage to the roads that lead to his house as the fighting made its ragged progress along them.

At Vaux men from the 26th Division fought in the dense bramble thicket between the trees, inching forward on their bellies until the Germans were within rifle range. The Germans threw grenades in among the trees, blasting away the green canopy, splintering branches, hurling up leaves and dirt, and afterward, there was an emptiness cut from the middle of the woods, where the earth could be seen black and bare. Slowly, the 26th retreated, and the Germans came after them until they reached high, clear ground on the other side. Now there was nothing but open fields ahead of them. They slumped exhausted against an outcropping of rock, with the woods finally at their backs, one of them binding up the bloody fingers of his friend, who had his other sleeve clenched between his teeth to prevent himself from crying out.

—

THEN ON THE morning of July 17, the Germans stopped forcing their way forward and began digging in. The turned earth could be seen from above as soon as it was light, the crooked fissures appearing out of nowhere and the men crouching inside them. The trenches were shallow and narrow: there were no fortifications yet surrounding them. They were just thin black lines, spreading and connecting with each other, as though the surface of the earth were cracking open.

Edward had prints ready by midmorning and ran them up to show van Horn.

"They've halted the attack," he said. "At least in this part of the line."

Van Horn flipped through the series, his lips pursed and frowning.

"Send these to Chaumont right away," he said. "If they've stopped here, it doesn't mean they have stopped everywhere."

But they had. Edward could see from the photographs taken by other observers that all along the length of the salient, wherever they had made advances, there were the same marks of digging, stringing barbed wire, the same signs that meant tired men had collapsed with their backs to the wall of newly excavated dirt, huddling down and getting ready to defend themselves: their turn now to prepare for an attack.

MARION DID WRITE to him as she had promised she would. Her letter came toward the end of the first week of the battle.

Dear Steichen,
I have never seen anything like this. Since the beginning of

this attack we have been overcrowded and every day they bring in the wounded, so many that I think at the end of each shift it isn't possible for us to absorb even one more. And yet the next day they come and we find space for them, on the floor, or in one of the tents that has been put up outside on the grounds. We do our best for them, but everything is in short supply. This above all makes the work difficult. At first I tried to hold on to each of the faces, keep them pictured clearly in my mind, as though to lose them was a form of surrender. But after the first few days, they began to blur, and now I have trouble recalling any of them at all.

But I am holding together. I sleep for a few hours each night, and it is surprising how little rest one really needs. I have some time to myself each day, and because I am too tired to read, I find my mind calling up memories from before the war. Do you remember you took my photograph by the river, that last summer? It made me simultaneously happy and unhappy. I knew I had changed into something new for you. It scared me and I was angry with you, and at the same time, I wanted you to keep watching me as you did that day. I knew also that I was losing something of myself with each passing second.

When things are calmer on the front, I will have my long overdue leave. It will begin in two weeks, most likely, if our side continues to advance. I'll write to you again when I know more. I will probably go to Paris.

I think of you.
Marion

SEEING THE COUNTERATTACK was like watching time move backward, the massive barrage flung back across the lines, the motions of the opposing armies crawling toward their old abandoned positions. In the space of a day the Germans gave up all the ground they'd taken south of the Marne.

At Soissons, General Mangin led the French 1st Moroccan and the American 1st and 2nd divisions in a surprise attack at dawn. They took the high ground south of the town and the railway station that supplied all the German troops in the Aisne salient. Now the troops there were cut off and could be reached only by the unreliable roads. The American divisions tried to advanced north of Château-Thierry to surround the town. They got close to it; Edward saw only a quarter of a mile of ground between the men fighting their way forward and what was left of the main highway that lead out of town to the north. But toward the end of the day they were beaten back.

Looking at the photographs at the end of the second day, one of the sergeants, Reece, the skinny one with no chin, said: "It's almost as if the German offensive never happened."

He held up two prints for Edward to see. Both showed a bend in the river and the front stretching along its northern bank. Reece pointed to the dates in the corner of each: one was from late June. The other had been taken that morning. A farm in the corner of the first picture was standing. In the later picture it was a wreck of timbers and stone. Otherwise, they were identical.

"We should really send these to Berlin as well as Chaumont," Edward said, "and suggest to them that we just pretend to have the next battle. We might as well."

There was a knock on the door of the lab. Dawson entered. His mouth was twisted up in an odd grimace.

"Sir," he said. "It's Lutz." His eyes shifted from object to object in the room.

"What happened?" Edward asked. His stomach turned over. Dawson's expression told him everything but the details.

"Over the country north of Courthiézy, his plane . . ." He stopped speaking and twisted his mouth back up into that misshapen knot. He leaned onto one of the tables and stared at its empty surface intensely, fighting to compose himself. When he spoke again, the words came slowly, each one a great effort. Lutz's plane had crashed. It had gone down near the front. It had been trying to land and then tilted too far forward and plummeted straight into the ground.

"It was just an accident. Not an enemy plane in sight. They dived too steeply and crashed. Like they told us at Tours. It just went straight down. I saw it . . ." His voice ran dry. Edward put down the prints he was holding and walked quickly from the room. In his office he locked the door and then crumpled against the wall, his head in his hands: I could have saved him, he thought. If I'd left when I had the chance.

That night he dreamt of falling. He was plummeting downward, not toward the valley of the Marne, but toward the cornfields near Milwaukee, and then the ranks of buildings that cover the island of Manhattan. In the dream he didn't feel fear, only curiosity at seeing these old familiar places in this new way, and he realized it was the first time in weeks he had not been afraid. He woke with a clear, new thought in his head: Even bravery is no good; in this war, even that is obsolete.

Slowly over the next week, the lines shifted northward, away from Paris and, less conspicuously, from Voulangis. The Allies crossed first the Marne and then the Vesle and finally the Aisne. Then on August 5 the orders came to halt.

A FEW DAYS later, a letter arrived from Mildred Aldrich. *Dear Steichen,* she began.

The Paris papers all carry reports of fierce fighting in the Marne and of the Germans in retreat, but as usual there are no details given. I hope that you are safe and well. I'm certain that you have done more than your duty.

I wanted you to know that I have written to Clara of the matter we discussed when you were here. We have exchanged several letters on the subject during the last month. At first she seemed determined to proceed. It is vindication that she seeks as much as revenge; she wants her point of view to be accepted by the world, for people to know that she has suffered, too.

But after I implored her to reconsider, she seems now to be softening. I will write to her again and see whether she will relinquish the suit and settle. I am hopeful that she may be prevailed upon to withdraw it. I will of course tell you the outcome of our discussion.

Meanwhile, the reports of victory hearten us. Amélie has secured a travel permit to go to the Zone of Armies to see some of her family who remained in Huiry. I remembered the case that Kate gave me for you. I will ask her to collect it from my house while she is there. The next time you come to Paris, if I am well enough (to my immense annoyance, my illness of last winter has returned), I can bring it to you. Though I know it does not depend on such inducements, I hope that we will see you soon.

Mildred

Edward sat down the same evening and drafted a response.

Dear Mildred,
I cannot tell you the pleasure and relief it gives me to read that you may yet change Clara's mind. My greatest thanks to you

for interceding in this matter. You have already done more than I could ever have asked.

The worst of the fighting in this area seems to be dying down, and I am scheduled to get some overdue leave. I will come to Paris and will probably stay near Bastille; there is a pension off Rue du Faubourg that is quiet, and calm is what I want above all. I would delight to see you when I arrive. If Amélie has the case that Kate left me, all the better.

I plan to arrive in Paris in a week's time. But I have something I have to do first. When I get leave, I'm going to go, at long last, back to my house in Voulangis.

Refugees. France, September 1914. Gum print.

FIRST THERE ARE men in uniform moving along the roads, heading north and east. Companies of infantry in ill-fitting blue coats and red trousers, their silhouettes deformed by the heavy packs they carry. They trudge past at a steady rate, and their marching seems to Clara to be an involuntary movement, like the tremor that passes along a pinched nerve. They don't want to go to war, or rather their desires have become suddenly irrelevant. Whatever their feelings, they proceed and stop when they are told to. Sometimes they halt at the crossroads beyond the house or in one of the nearby fields. She brings them tea or water, bread if there are not too many of them. Mary helps her. Seated under the trees, the men play cards, betting for matches. They are grateful for the tea and the officers are very polite.

As well as the foot soldiers, there are cavalry and companies of gunners. Their horses pull the heavy carriages of the .75s and machine guns, the wagons full of ammunition. There are auxiliaries bringing the canteens and the ambulances. The roads are full of them, sometimes too crowded for any other traffic to pass.

She doesn't want her children to see the guns, which are so strange yet so uncannily familiar. They look just the way she imagined they would, the smooth metal barrels tilted skyward, descending to the complex apparatus of bolts and screws that is used to fire them, the hinged door where the shell goes in. Kate, in any case, hides from the soldiers, refusing to come out of the house when they are around, or ducking behind a chair, a wall, a tree, if a group of them come suddenly into view. She has been staying in her room a lot in the past weeks. Under normal circumstances this would worry Clara. She'd coax her daughter downstairs, try to bring her out of that shy dreaminess into which she's disappeared. But nothing is normal at the moment. If Kate wants to stay in her room reading all day, then let her. At least it keeps her out of the way of the grown-ups, and away from the tense atmosphere in the rest of the house.

Soon, on the roads, there are civilians as well, fleeing the fighting. They are heading in the opposite direction from the soldiers, an undertow sliding quietly south and west against the war's prevailing current. There are only a few to begin with and then each day there are more—old men, women, small children—riding in farm carts or pushing wheelbarrows filled to capacity with all that they could salvage of their lives: clothing, pots and pans, furniture, lamps, piles of books tied into bundles. Some of them are bringing animals with them, a crate full of chickens or a single cow yoked to their wagon with a rope. She sees a family who have balanced an armoire across the handlebars and saddle of a bicycle: they are taking turns pushing it and walking behind, keeping it balanced. They make slow but determined progress, stopping often to rest. She wonders why on earth anyone would put themselves through such an ordeal for an old wardrobe. She sends Mary after them with water and sandwiches. She watches them until they pass the crest of the next hill.

Edward carries his camera out and takes photographs of people, their baggage, sometimes of the soldiers as well, although he is cautious about this after their visit from Perrine. He talks to the refugees, falling into step beside them for a while. Clara watches him, his long stride easily keeping pace. Then he leaves them and comes back toward the house, until he meets someone else along the road. Sometimes he will stay outside for hours, talking and taking pictures, returning only as it gets dark.

Since the day when Clara found him and Marion together, a frosty truce has crystallized between them. She and Edward avoid each other as much as possible in private, though they are civil in front of their children. On one or two occasions, or perhaps it is more than that (she does not care enough to recall), he has come to her when she is alone and he has tried, again, to apologize. He has repeated his claim that there was nothing going on behind her back, asked her to forgive him. But if there was really nothing going on, why all this begging forgiveness? She is not stupid; she has known him for too long, lived through too many of his infidelities. Now when he comes to her looking as though he wants to say something, she turns and walks out without giving him a chance to start.

For her part, Marion keeps out of the way, although this hasn't been easy. In the immediate aftermath of Clara's discovery, Marion, too, had come and solicited her, tried to explain that she was making a mistake. For a minute, seeing her friend's distress, Clara thought that perhaps she was telling the truth. How she wanted to believe it! But then she remembered their stricken expressions when she entered the room that day. The angle of their bodies leaning together. The way he could not afterward look her in the face. How disgusting it was. She has nothing to say to either of them.

But because of the mobilization, Marion cannot leave; none of them can. There are no passenger trains—there haven't been since war was declared. Edward has driven to the station several times and they have told him repeatedly that the railroads are being used only for war purposes. The stationmaster could not or would not say more than this. Nor are the newspapers any help in getting accurate information. They say that the French are fighting valiantly and will be victorious over the German aggressors. They are filled with stories of noble sacrifice, the confidence of the High Command in a swift victory. They talk of atrocities committed against Belgian civilians by the Boches. They do not explain the people on the road; they do not say whether Edward and Clara and their children should stay or leave.

So they wait, all of them, for a sign, something that will tell them what to do next. Inside, the house feels like it has grown thorns up and down its corridors, every room prickling and uncomfortable to inhabit. Mary, of course, could tell at once that something had happened between her mother and father. As might be expected, she asked her Papa about it—Clara came upon them in the salon one day talking with serious faces, and when they saw her, they both stopped, alarmed, and looked at her. Since then Mary has not mentioned it; none of them have. They are all acting as though nothing has happened. It has gone under the surface, but all of them feel it, seeping, poisonous, into everything.

Clara keeps busy: the women in town have all begun baking their own bread because the bakeries are short of men to work in them, and so she buys provisions and joins them. She helps François bring the last of the summer vegetables in from the garden. They begin planting the corgettes and squash for autumn, even though she has no notion of where they will be when this crop is ripe and ready for eating. When this is finished, she drives to Mildred's house and helps with her planting. She feels better when she is doing something with her hands, and this is why she brings provisions to the soldiers and the other travelers. She is creating a hard shell for herself, and it keeps her from collapsing, or flying to pieces right there in the middle of her own house. In a sense, the war has been a great boon to her. It has given her a reason to maintain her composure.

ONE MAN TALKS about a town to the east of them that burned.

"We saw the light of it from miles away, and that's when we began to make preparations to go away. One house must have caught alight after a bomb exploded and it spread: you know how the buildings are in those small towns, so close together. There will be nothing left of the place by now. It was on a hill, so we could see it behind us as we were leaving, orange and the black smoke hanging above it in a cloud. Must have burned for three days."

"Don't exaggerate," his wife puts in. "Two days, it only burned for two days."

They all have stories, these people, of what the war looks like or sounds like. For some of them it was enough to hear the guns in the distance and they were ready to pack their belongings and leave.

"It sounds like thunder when it's far away," one of them tells him. "But fast, close together."

"It sounds like a gigantic drum," another says.

Edward takes their photographs as they pass by, capturing tired faces and bent backs, the strange piles of belongings that they have made of their lives. He asks them where they are from, and at first the names of the towns are unknown to him. He asks them where they are going, and some of them say that they are going to their relatives in the south, or to friends in Toulouse, Orléans, Marseilles. But many of them shrug and say they do not know for certain. They are only going away from the war.

Gradually, the names of the places these people have come from start to sound more familiar. They are towns near the Aisne, only a few miles to the north. He checks on his maps at home, and indeed, if the stories that he's hearing are right, then the war is now no more than a day's walk away. But still there is no definite news; no information from the government. Nothing to tell him for certain what to do.

He decides to wire Alfred in New York. They may be getting a more accurate picture of what is going on precisely because they are further away. He drives to town and sends the telegram: WHAT SHOULD WE DO? The words go out into the world in clicked points and dashes, racing down thousands of miles of cables to their destination across the ocean. He watches the operator send them behind the desk of the *mairie*. Then he comes home to wait for an answer.

He has been spending as much time as possible out of the house. Even these photographs are in part a reason for him to be outside, away from the cauldron that his own home has become. When Clara left him on the day of their fight, he had gone immediately to his study and closed the door. He'd stretched out on the bare floor and closed his eyes and felt himself tossing on the waves of anger that surged through him. He felt cheated, but he wasn't sure by whom. By Clara, he supposed, by her accusations, her unwillingness to listen to reason. But was it only by her? Look me in the face, she had said, and he couldn't make himself do it.

But as the week passed and Clara refused to soften toward him or even speak to him, his feelings hardened into anger at her intransigence. He has not been unfaithful to her. He has not had an affair. He is sorry for what happened, but damn it, it isn't the worst thing that anyone has ever done, and it is not as if she is the easiest person in the world to be married to, with her temper tantrums and her suspicions.

It is spirals of thoughts like this that send him out with his camera first thing in the morning. He walks along the roads to discover what miseries the war has unearthed. These uprooted people have been driven from their homes by something so much more tangible than his own ridiculous difficulties. He hears their stories, and when he goes home each night for their stiffly awkward evening meal, he retells them, hoping that Clara will realize that there are bigger forces at work in the world than her own misconstrued jealousies. Hoping she will see her resentment in the proper perspective. But she will not turn toward him even briefly. And after a while he stops trying to reach her.

Marion is a different matter altogether. That same afternoon she had found him in his study. She knocked, then slipped inside and stood with her back to the door, and he remembers how sad she looked then.

"I'm sorry."

"No, I'm sorry. It was my fault."

"I should leave. Tomorrow if possible. I just want enough time to try to talk to Clara and tell her . . ." She trailed off. "Actually, I don't know what I'll tell her."

"Well," he said, "I suppose that's best. I suppose it's best if you go."

"Will you go to town and find out when there will be a train?"

"Yes." He stood up and moved toward the door, and she moved away, skittish even to be in the same room with him now.

"She won't forgive us, you know," Marion said, not looking at him.

"What is there to forgive exactly? We didn't do anything. She'll see that in a while, just let her calm down and she'll see reason. She'll understand."

"No," Marion said, "I don't think she will." Her voice was low and he fought an overwhelming sense that the right thing to do was to go over to where she stood and put his arms around her.

"I'll go and see when you can get a train to Paris," he said, and went out.

THE DAY AFTER he sends the telegram, a reply comes from New York. ADVISE STRATEGIC RETREAT, it says, and Edward feels a momentary pang of annoyance that Alfred has taken this as an opportunity to display his wit. He supposes that is a luxury one has, being so far away. COME TO NY, the telegram continues. They do not only have to leave their house, but they must leave France: nowhere here is safe now.

He drives to town one more time and asks about trains. The stationmaster repeats that he doesn't know, so Edward tells him he won't leave the office without some idea of whether and when a westbound train might stop there. The man shrugs. If they want to leave, he says, they can wait to get on one of the trains that are heading back toward the coast after taking soldiers to the front, but it could be a day or more before one stopped at Esbly. They would have to come to the station and be ready to get on it when it arrived. He couldn't say when that would be, but it was usually later, in the evening.

Edward drives home. When he arrives, it is just beginning to get dark, and the house is illuminated, the windows letting an orange glow out into the dusk. He can look in and see Mary and Kate sitting by a fire in the salon. Clara is across the room from them, seated at the piano. She is singing softly, and after a minute he recognizes the song. It's one of the countess's arias from *Figaro: Dove sono i bei momenti,* she sings. *Where are the golden moments of tranquility? Why can't I forget the joys that used to be?* Upstairs there is a light in the bedroom that is Marion's. Looking in at them like this, he feels that he is seeing a scene that is now inexorably part of the past and that will never exist in the present again, not even if the war were to end tomorrow. There is so much to leave behind here, in this house, in France. They will not even have time to stop and see Rose and Rodin before they leave. He has tried to think of a way to do this, to break up their journey, but he is worried that if they stop in Paris they will not make it to Marseilles and the boat that he hopes will take them from there back to America.

For a minute he stands outside in the dark, watching them, listening. Then he opens the door and goes in.

THEY CAN ONLY take with them what they can carry, so each of them must choose carefully what to put in their suitcases. Clara tells the girls that they can each take one thing from the house besides their clothing and personal belongings. Kate immediately chooses the piano.

"You can't take the piano, Catkin," Edward tells her. "It's too big. Choose something else."

"But what will Mama play if we leave it behind?"

"I promise there will be pianos where we are going, and Mama can play on those."

"Where are we going?"

"To New York."

"Have I ever been there before?"

"No, my darling, but you'll like it. It is a big city with very tall buildings and lots of people, like Paris."

"I don't want to go," Kate says. "You go and I'll stay here and look after things until you get back."

"You can't stay here on your own. Your mama and papa would

miss you too much, and besides, it won't be safe here. We have to leave to make sure that we keep safe. Now go on upstairs to your room and start to get packed. And choose something else to bring with you." Kate nods her head and begins to climb the stairs, but midway up she stops.

"Papa?" She is looking down at him through the banisters.

"Yes, Catkin?"

"If it isn't safe, why aren't we taking François and Louisa with us when we go away?"

THE NEXT DAY is consumed with packing and readying the house for their departure. Edward ferries his paintings inside from his studio and locks them up in the attic, along with the silver, and Clara's dresses and jewelry that they won't be able to take with them. His photographs and negatives are already stored inside a big closet in the study. He looks through them and decides that he can probably manage to take only one small case. He leaves the task of choosing which ones will go into it until after he has finished the other things he needs to do.

Marion has only a little to pack for herself. She offers her help tentatively to Clara, and it is accepted tentatively. On his trips to and from his studio, Edward sees the two women sorting through the food in the pantry, seeing what can be taken to neighbors and what must simply be thrown away. They seem to be speaking only a little, when it is necessary to the work they are doing. He watches the kitchen emptied of its life.

Clara rides over to Huiry to tell Mildred that they are leaving and ask her to come with them, but again, Mildred refuses. She will stay and wait it out, she says. Without children, she doesn't see any reason why she should remove herself.

"I just arrived last year," she tells Clara. "I intended to retire here, and I don't see that the war is necessarily a reason to change all my plans." Clara tries to persuade her but eventually gives up and comes home. Edward cannot believe it when she first relates this to him, but then he thinks that this stoicism is just what he would have expected.

By the evening they are ready to leave. Clara brings the girls' bags downstairs and sets them near the front door. Mary has chosen some books to bring with her; Kate has decided on her favorite blue teddy bear instead of the piano, and this now perches on top of the luggage, a wall-eyed lookout, its lumpy limbs straddling the top of a suitcase. Edward and Clara put Kate to bed when she starts to yawn. He stands in the doorway of her room, watching Clara pull the sheets up to Kate's chin; this is the first moment of peace they have had together in weeks. Clara stands up and rubs her eyes.

"I'm going to go to bed," she says and makes her way down the hall to their room.

"I'll be in soon," he says, but she has already gone.

Edward isn't sleepy, and anyway, he still has one last thing to pack: his photographs. He has left them until now because he doesn't want to have to make this choice. It is too daunting to go through the files upon files of prints and plates and choose a handful to save. The others, the ones he leaves behind, might be fine when he comes back, whenever that turns out to be. But he is thinking of the stories of burning towns and houses reduced to rubble that he has been hearing all week, and he knows this is not something he should count on.

What, then, is it necessary to save? He takes the first few files from his closet—they are all ordered by date and series. He sits on the floor of his study and begins to spread them out in front of him, spaced like Tarot cards. These are pictures of a wood in winter, near his parents' house in Wisconsin. Some of them have been sold, but not all. They are several years old, silver chloride, the blacks soft as charcoal. He absolutely must save this file for certain. He puts it into the case.

But it turns out that he feels the same way about the next file, too, and the one after that and the one after that. In fact, he can't bear to leave a single one of them behind. He makes choices and then changes his mind. He is paralyzed, unable to even begin to sort them out.

Just when he is about to give up completely, the door creaks and then opens a little. Clara steps into the room.

"I couldn't sleep," she says. She looks at the uneven stacks of photographs around him on the floor. "What are you doing?"

"I'm trying to choose which ones to bring with me. I can only take a few. Just enough to fill this." He holds up the small, square-edged case for her to see.

"That is not very many." She comes and sits beside him on the floor and starts to sift through the piles of photographs. He is about to object, but then he feels too tired to bother. She begins to pull individual prints from among the hundreds that are there.

"This one," she says. "And this one." She holds them up for him to see. He nods, and puts her choices into the case. She picks up another sheaf of photographs. "This, this and this." She is going through and pulling out what seem to him to be not necessarily his best work, but rather the most important moments from his life, from their life together. He wonders for a moment how she is able to know this so automatically; but, then, this strange insight of hers seems wonderful after the absurd nightmare of the past weeks, and he does not want to question it too much. He is grateful for any evidence of human understanding. Before long they have filled the case with photographs and plates. Clara puts the rest of the pictures away in the closet and locks it.

"What should I do with the key?" she asks. "Should we bring it with us?"

"No," he says. "I don't think we need to do that." She opens the top drawer of the desk and puts the key inside, where he always keeps it. She pauses before she slides it closed. "Just as though we weren't leaving," she says.

When Edward wakes up the next morning, it is not yet fully light, and he stares around the dim room, unsure of what has woken him. Clara is asleep beside him, her dark hair visible against the white pillow beneath. Then he hears it: low and distant, booming, repeated in uneven staccato. Like a drum, he thinks. Like thunder. He lies in the dark, listening, until dawn.

FRANÇOIS DRIVES THEM to the station in the afternoon. From the top of the hill that leads down to the railway line through Esbly, they can see that they are not alone: the street outside the station is crowded with carts and people waiting with their luggage. They look like the things that wash up on a beach, gathered around the entrance to the station house with an air of not quite knowing how they got there. They are all hoping for a train that will stop and carry them west.

They wait. François sits up front and smokes his pipe. All of the trains that pass are going east and none of them stop. The sun begins to sink and the light turns golden. They are quiet mostly; none of them have slept well. Edward sees the effects of weariness on the faces around him, the drawn mouths and sunken eyes, and knows his own must look much the same. Only Kate is restless.

"When will the train come?"

"Kate, Papa doesn't know," Mary says.

"Why not?"

"Because nobody knows, Catkin. We just have to be patient and wait."

"OK. But can Mary and I walk into town, just while we are waiting? We can buy some licorice for the journey."

"No."

"Why not?"

"Because we have to be ready when the train does come, because it might not stop for very long and we don't know when there will be another one."

"I see." She settles down and begins explaining this to her blue bear. Edward sees her wagging her finger at it, her face serious. "We have to be ready because there might not ever be another train. Not ever."

"That's not right, is it, Papa?" Mary asks. "There will be another train eventually."

"Yes, I promise. This will not be the last train. They just aren't coming very often at the moment."

"Katie, come here and I'll read to you," says Clara. She lets the little girl snuggle up beside her. She opens the copy of *The Adventures of Huckleberry Finn* that she has been reading to Kate.

Edward listens to Clara's voice, not really hearing the words, only the gentle up-and-down of its cadences. Kate puts her head down in her mother's lap and is soon dozing, and Clara closes the book and begins to put it away in her portmanteau.

"Wait," Edward says. "Keep going. Would you?"

Clara nods and opens the book again. When she gets tired, she passes it to Marion, seated opposite, and she takes over. They hear about Huck and Jim on the raft, about the cruelty and vicissitudes of Huck's father, the freedom of the river. Around them the light is going.

Then, from far away comes a high, sustained whistle. Edward stands up on the front seat, trying to see down the tracks. Gradually, the noise of the locomotive detaches from the gloom; the rails shake; they can see its single headlight. Around them, people are standing up and stretching or clambering to the pavement. They pass trunks and cases down, carry or drag them toward the platform. As the train approaches, an urgency catches among them and spreads quickly. They shout instructions to each other. The platform is soon filled with people; they jostle to get up the steps.

"Let's go," François says, and Edward jumps down to take the bags he hands over the side of the cart. Marion and Clara each pick up a suitcase and join the stream of people. Edward takes another and follows them. To their left there is a crash and swearing. Two women bend over a trunk that has come open, throwing something white onto the damp cobbles: when he gets a little closer, he sees it is a wedding dress. The women scoop it up and stuff it back inside the trunk, leaning on the lid to get it closed. Then they set off again, half-lifting, half-dragging, the trunk between them.

It takes three trips to get all the bags to the platform. By now the train has pulled in, hissing steam. It is a cattle train, and the wooden carriages are windowless except for a long slit about two thirds of the way up their sides. People have already flung open the heavy doors, and they are loading children and belongings inside, helping the elderly climb aboard. A company of Territorials have come out of the first carriage and are stretching their legs and helping people put their baggage into the cars. Edward tells Mary to wait by the bags and goes back to get the last things he has left: a small box of Clara's, and his case of photographs.

When he reaches the cart, he finds François standing beside it looking distressed.

"I didn't notice," he says. "I didn't see that she was gone."

Kate is nowhere to be found. Edward looks toward the station, but the crowd is now so dense that he couldn't see Kate even if she were there. Marion and Clara appear out of the throng.

"Where is Kate?" Clara asks.

"I don't know," says François miserably. Clara shrieks and turns to Edward.

"I thought you had her. I thought you were keeping an eye on her." She starts across the yard and then goes out into the street, calling Kate's name. Edward stands there as though frozen to the spot. He has no idea what to do now. Marion steps forward and puts a hand on his arm.

"I'll take Clara up and we'll put the luggage onto the train." Her voice is calm and steady. "You and François go and look for Kate. Clara will never find her when she is this upset."

Edward nods, and before he has time to say anything Marion has set off after Clara. He sees her guide Clara back toward the station. The two women climb the steps and disappear into the crowd.

Edward and François split up and make their way around the periphery of the station yard. They shout for Kate, but there is no reply, no sign of her anywhere. Edward stops the few stragglers still making their way to the train.

"Have you seen a little girl?" he asks them. "About six. Dark hair. Carrying a blue bear . . ." But they shake their heads: no one has seen her. François goes out into the street and begins searching the gardens of the houses that line the road. But how far can she have gone in so little time? Edward takes one more turn around the station yard. He is just about to give up and follow François when he sees something move beside the station house. Peering into the dark, he can make out the form of a small child, crouched in the building's shadow. He bounds over and scoops her up into his arms.

"I hid," she says. "From the soldiers."

"I can see that. Never, never do that again. Do you hear me?" He is too relieved to be angry. He carries her across the yard. They move through the confusion of the platform until they find Clara and Marion handing the last of their bags up to Mary, who is already on board the train. He passes Kate into her mother's arms.

"You'd better get on board," François says. "It will be leaving soon. Here." He offers Clara his arm so that she can climb up. She puts Kate inside next to Mary.

"Smells bad," says Kate. "I don't want to go in there."

"You have to," says Clara. "Now sit down and be good, for God's sake."

"My photographs," Edward says. "They're still in the cart. I have to go and get them."

"Is there time?" Marion asks, as she follows Clara inside the car.

"I'll be as quick as I can," he says. He sprints down the platform and back to the cart where his case is right up on the front seat. He hears the sound of the train whistle signal its departure. He grabs the case and heads back toward the platform. It is heavy, because of the glass negatives, and he doesn't want to jostle it too much for fear that some of them will break. As he is climbing the steps to the train, he hears the whistle sound again, and with a clunk of pistons, the train begins to move. He sees the door to the carriage where his family is beginning to slide away from him.

"Papa!" Mary is leaning from the open door and waving frantically. Edward picks up his pace, but the train is moving now faster than he can walk. When he reaches François, the old man says, "You won't make it on there with those." He taps the case, which Edward has clutched to his chest. "Leave them. I'll make sure that they get back to the house safely." Edward hesitates for an instant. François says: "Go on. Put them down and run!"

Edward pushes the case into his hands and takes off down the platform. He catches up with the carriage door and jumps inside, just as the train begins to gather steam. He lands in straw and topples forward onto his knees. When he looks up, he sees Clara and Marion seated near each other opposite him; there are Kate and Mary. They fling their arms around him from either side. Beyond them there are other faces, curious and frightened. He can just make them out in the swaying light of the single lamp that hangs from the roof of the car.

WHEN THE TRAIN reaches Paris, she will leave them. She will disembark and attempt to catch another train going north so that she can get a boat to England to meet her parents there. After that Marion does not know what she will do.

Thinking about what it will be like to depart from Edward and Clara at last, Marion anticipates tremendous relief. She can hardly wait to get away from them. Oh, to be free from the constant anxiety of the last few weeks, from the waiting and watching and measuring her words before she speaks. To be among people who do not blame her, who do not want anything from her. She will stay in London for a while and rest, she thinks, before attempting the voyage home. She will be with her mother. She starts to cry quietly, thinking about it, but that is all right. In the darkness of the car, no one can see her well enough to know.

However, it is not only relief at this ordeal ending that she feels, but also something that pulls against it. She wants to stop time, go back to the beginning; to make different choices that don't lead here, to Clara's cold silence, to the memory, which in spite of everything she cannot shake, of how it felt to touch his hands and feel his face against hers. She wants things to be as they were before this terrible summer. But where was the beginning? Was it this June when she drove out of the city full of high spirits to spend the summer with her friends? Was it one of the many evenings that they spent together in Paris, at Leo's or at Judith Cladel's? She can't tell. She doesn't know thinking back when her feelings for him started, only that after a certain point they were evident to her, undeniable.

When they reach Paris, she will climb down from the train and he will help her take her bags from the floor here. They will stand on the platform and they will say goodbye, and after that she will probably never see him again. She will not see either of them, not as friends, not as they have been until now. For her own sake as much as theirs, she realizes that they cannot write and they cannot see each other. They cannot keep up the pretence of polite acquaintance. The train lurches as it starts across a trestle. She puts a hand out to steady herself against the wall.

How much is being lost right now. She feels very small compared with the terrible changes that are taking place around her, so much light is vanishing from the world, and what can she do to stop it? She is only a single tiny person sitting with her knees pulled up under her chin on the floor of a windowless carriage going west. All she can do is try to remember what she has loved so that it does not entirely disappear. She closes her eyes and feels the motion of the wheels beneath her as the train goes on, rocking across the face of the darkened land.

ELEVEN

August 10, 1918

IT WAS THE first heavy rain in weeks when Edward arrived, alone, in Esbly. Early in the afternoon he stepped off the train onto the nearly deserted station platform. There was the small station office, its wooden walls, its sloping roof, just as it had been the last time he'd seen it. There were the narrow houses with their walled gardens lining the road that climbed away from the railway line until it disappeared over the crest of the hill.

He had written to François to tell him when he would arrive, but he'd received no reply and didn't know what kind of reception to expect. He had been in touch with the old man periodically since leaving Voulangis, a few letters in a few years, in which François had given him news of the house and the town.

So he was relieved, almost delighted, to see the familiar figure seated on the box of his trap waiting for him when he came down the station steps. François raised his hat and his face cracked into a broad grin.

"Your journey was comfortable?" he asked.

"Yes. Much better than when I left here last time," Edward said.

"Climb up. We'll go to your house. You'll see that not much has changed. Thank God."

They drove up the hill and along the road that curved around the valley's western side. When they turned off the main highway, the dirt road was uneven and its hollows had filled with rain; their wheels flung up sheets of water behind them. The country here was so lush—tree trunks black, leaves bowed and dripping. It was this that had first drawn him here to paint, the feeling of every-thing wanting to grow and be alive. Soon they were coming over the hill, passing through the crossroads where four years before Claude Perrine had announced that war was beginning. They rounded the last bend and there, looking more worn than when he last saw it, was his house.

The steep angle of its roof cut dark out of the white sky, a sil-houette, gaunt and imposing, surrounded by the swaying arms of the fruit trees he had planted years ago. How overgrown they were, unkempt and untended, and then as they drew closer he could make out slurs of damp down the walls, cracked paint on the woodwork of window frames, shutters and doors. The front gate was beginning to bloom with rust; all the plants had overtaken their beds. The smell of green damp. One of the windows on the ground floor was broken and patched.

François stopped opposite the front entrance, and Edward jumped down. When he reached the gate, he paused. He had been here so many times in his imagination. The way he pictured this return had evolved over the years with the changing circumstances of his life, so that at first he'd pictured coming back with Clara and the children, resuming their life as though they had never left at all. The girls would go back to school; he could return to work in his studio; they would have guests in the summer and visit Paris for parties and theater. At dinner they would tell stories about the time they'd had to leave because of the war of 1914. Then, when Clara left him and returned to France, he'd imagined following her and finding her here, penitent, sobered by her experience, ready to mend the breach between them. In other moods, when he had been too angry to desire reconciliation, he pictured showing up unannounced and taking Kate away with him, back to New York to her sister, to the greater part of her family, to safety.

He had not thought of coming here alone, to be greeted by an empty house, unused for many months and wearing the soft signs of its disintegration. But he found, standing there in the doorway, that he did not mind it. He had let go of those other hopes. By himself he could feel the place, its effect on him, undisturbed. It was something like vertigo, he thought, the experience of coming at last to a place one has longed for, so that the arrival was like stepping into a dream, not in the sense of a wish fulfilled, but because the objects in the place seemed to be carrying a message for him that he could not quite read, that disappeared just at the moment he was about to decipher it. The sounds of the place were nearly solid, the wind dissected by the buildings, the protesting shriek of the gate as he pushed it open. His footsteps, muted by the grass that had overgrown the path. The door in front of him: he turned the handle and pushed. It swung slowly back.

Inside, the smell of damp was even stronger. The things of his old life crowded in on him: there was the wooden breakfast table in front of the window to the left and before him the fireplace flanked by bookshelves, the books still in them, the chairs arranged before it, and against the far wall, Clara's piano, her scores still stacked on top. He crossed the room with automatic steps and began to leaf through them. François came to the door, and Edward stopped, feeling as though he'd been caught stealing something.

"It is not too bad," François said. "The condition of things. Since Madame left, I have come to check on it maybe once in a few weeks. There were some English staying here. Officers. But other than that, it is quiet."

"Thank you," Edward said. François shrugged.

"The keys are behind the door," he said. He started to go. "I'll bring you some supper over later."

Edward found the keys hanging on the same hook where he'd always kept them, the back and front doors, the study, attic and cellar. And with them a second set: keys to his studio in Paris. He moved through the house, room to room, opening each and letting in the light, taking stock of what was left and what was gone. In the cellar he found his wine rack empty; the kitchen, too, held nothing perishable. In one corner of its ceiling, by the pantry, there were brown and purple blotches spreading from the corner like bruises. He brought a stepladder and looked at the marks more closely. Wet rot. It was spreading across the room from its outer wall. Well, if that was all the structural damage to the place, then he should be grateful. It would not take much to fix it. It was in the kitchen that the window had been broken, the one he'd seen from the road; François must have patched it with boards. Again, nothing that couldn't be repaired.

He climbed the stairs and found the bedrooms tidy. There was no sign of the damp in the floors in any of these rooms. It crossed his mind that this was odd, since the damage in the kitchen had clearly come through the ceiling. Which room was directly above the kitchen? Mentally, he sketched a map of the two stories and realized that over the kitchen was the study. Of course. The study, which he hadn't looked at yet, because he would have to spend some time sorting through the photographs that were stored there, in the wardrobe that stood across from the window . . .

With rapid steps he crossed the hall and fumbled at the study door for the right key, his fingers suddenly clumsy from hurrying. He found it, slid it into the lock, turned, pushed open the door. A cool cross draft hit him even before he entered the room. Across from him the window stood open, and the curtains, discolored and bedraggled, waved listlessly back and forth. A huge damp stain spread in the shape of a smile beneath the sill, reaching all the way to the skirting board. Against the right-hand wall the door to the storage closet stood open. And on the floor in front of it, torn and crumpled and heaped chaotically on top of each other, lay hundreds of photographs.

They covered the floor in the far corner so thickly in places that he couldn't see the boards underneath. Some of the edges flickered in the breeze. He started forward, thinking he ought to close the window, then stopped: to get to it he would have to climb over the pile of photographs and he didn't want to step on them. But then again, what did that matter? Close the window, don't close the window, stomp on them or not, it made absolutely no difference now. So instead, he remained rooted where he was, taking in the room as he found it, trying to etch it into his brain so that he would be sure to remember it. Look, he told himself; keep looking and don't turn away. It was all he could do.

Eventually, he went over to the open closet and looked inside. One of the upper shelves had collapsed. From what he could tell, the rain had come in and waterlogged the wood until it could no longer support the weight of the boxes it held. And when it gave way, it took the shelves below down, too, so the contents of all of them spilled out onto the floor. There were a few boxes of negatives still in the bottom of the closet, but these too were rain-damaged.

He knelt down and started to go through the photographs that were strewn furthest out. He pulled them one by one from the mass of papers and turned them face up, so that he could see what was left.

Pieces of Fifth Avenue at night. Almost fifteen years before, when he and Alfred had begun taking pictures of New York after dark, testing what was possible to capture without daylight. Street-lamps surrounded by haloes; their light sliding across the forms of cabs and late-night walkers, the façades of buildings, with their ranks of shadowy windows; all the different qualities of darkness. Or on nights after it had rained, light ribboning the streets silver. Or here: woods in New Hampshire, midwinter, the trees black characters written against the snow. The Brooklyn Bridge on a hazy day and the angle looking up so the bridge flew out into the sky until it disappeared. There were portraits he'd done on commission, and portraits of friends, of Lilian and Carl, of his parents Mary and Jean-Patrick, of Clara and Kate and Mary, of all of them together, each image torn or buckled, their illusions cracked by white fissures of paper, or their dimensions warped out of proportion. Edward took each one and gently smoothed it against the floorboards. Then he stacked them up, laying them carefully down, one on top of another.

As he moved through the mass of papers, he found the condition of the prints became worse nearer to the open window. Here, many were water-damaged, their subjects so blurred that only he could have known what they had been: a series of nudes, the figures of the models pitted with raindrops, or smeared so all that could be distinguished of them was a limb here, a torso, the arch of a back. Gardens that seemed to evaporate, pieces of houses, faces, and streets suspended in gray mist. Nothing left whole. A portrait of Clara. He remembered taking it one day in his Paris studio nearly seven years ago. She had been quiet that day, pensive, had watched people passing in the street below the window, and he'd found her solemn expression intriguing, like the look of a person watching a boat pull away from a quay. Look up, he'd said, look at me, love, as he took the photograph. Now all that could be distinguished was her left eye, staring at him out of the disintegration around it.

He worked his way toward the open door of the cupboard, stacking and sorting, feeling at once the necessity and fruitlessness of this labor; that he had to do it; that it would do no good. He did not notice the time that was passing until he heard the door open downstairs and François's footsteps, and looking up, he realized it was evening.

"THERE IS BREAD and beer." François put the basket down on the kitchen table. "Some lamb and potatoes."

"You didn't have to do this."

"My wife insisted," François said. "She thought you would be tired after your journey. And there is nothing to eat here."

"Well, thank you. It is nice to have food cooked for one instead of for one hundred." Edward sat down at the table and began to unwrap the parcel. He pulled the stopper from the bottle of beer. "Will you stay and have some?" The old man nodded. He took two glasses from a shelf and sat opposite, straddling the bench. Edward poured the honey-colored liquid and pushed one of the glasses toward François. Then he set out the food. Although he'd gone all day without eating, he was not very hungry. He felt sick, almost dizzied by his discoveries of that afternoon, too restless to think of food.

When he had eaten a little, he asked: "Have you seen upstairs in the study? Did you know what happened to my photographs?"

François shook his head. "I never unlocked any of the rooms—I only came to make sure nothing had been disturbed."

"The window was left open. It ruined all the prints I left behind."

François looked confused. "They are destroyed?"

Edward nodded.

"I didn't know," François said. Abruptly, he stood up. "Let me see?"

"All right." They went upstairs and Edward opened the door of the study. He had managed to clear about half of the photographs from the floor.

"They were all over," he told the old man. François looked aghast.

"I did not know. I would not have left them like that."

"I know you wouldn't. I don't know why Madame didn't write to tell me that she'd found them like this. She was angry with me, but that would not have been too much to ask."

François was silent for a minute. Then he said, "Madame didn't find them like this."

"What do you mean?"

"When she arrived, the photographs, were fine. They were locked away, just as you left them. I remember, she told me she was relieved to find they had not been damaged. Also, I saw the study once or twice while Madame and the little mademoiselle were living here. Madame used the desk for writing letters."

"Then the English soldiers who were staying here after Madame left, could they have left the window up when they were here?"

"That is possible," said François. "Yes, that is likely." He rubbed his hand over his forehead. "It's terrible."

"Yes, it is. But there is nothing to be done about it now."

"I suppose that is right."

"Let's go down and you can finish eating."

"All right. I can help you drink the rest of the beer."

They went back downstairs.

"The English officers," François said. "They must have gone in and opened the window and then left it. Maybe they didn't know to close it." He helped himself to what was left of the bread.

"Yes," Edward said. "Probably they didn't."

"And then the rain comes in and does the damage."

"When did you say the English were here?"

"In May," said François, chewing. "But my memory is not so good. Maybe it was April."

"I see."

It was not enough time for that kind of damage to have occurred. He knew it and François knew it, too. The question that neither of them wished to ask aloud or even acknowledge loomed over them as they sat finishing the meal. Edward changed the subject; he asked François about the people they had known in town; about his family. And François replied: His wife was fine. His son had been wounded at St-Mihiel in March, but thank God, was alive.

But then, after the old man left and Edward was once again alone in the house, he could no longer push it out of his mind. He tried to make himself go on thinking that it was the English officers who had accidentally left both closet door and window open, as he readied himself for bed. He decided to sleep in his old bedroom. He'd contemplated taking the spare room instead, but no, damn it, the place wasn't haunted. Why should he act as though it was? He lay down on the bed that he and Clara had shared and closed his eyes.

English officers were billeted in this house. They took the keys from behind the door and opened all the rooms because they needed to use all the beds. One of them opened the window in the study to let in some air and then wondered what was inside the closet. Though it wasn't strictly speaking permitted for him to do so, he somehow found the key in the top drawer of the desk, or maybe Clara had left it lying out somewhere. So he, this unknown officer, opened the closet and saw that it contained boxes of photographs. He started looking through them. And then he was called away for some reason, and in his hurry he left the door and the window ajar, and never came back to close them. It was not implausible.

But something about it troubled him. He lit a lamp and went back into the study. There were the photographs, the ones he had not had time to clear up, still on the floor. There was the window, still open. He had not closed it. And the closet door, too—he had left everything as he found it. It could have been an accident, a mistake. But then something occurred to him. Why on earth would someone leaving in a hurry have bothered to lock the study door?

He went to the desk and slid open the top drawer. There was the key to the storage cupboard, carefully put back, where only he and Clara knew that it had always been kept.

HE STARED FOR several minutes at the key, as if he needed to be sure it was really there. Then, numbly, he slid the drawer closed. The sound of it clicking back into place seemed final, set against the quiet of the house. He picked up the lamp from the desk. It flung up slanted shadows from the photographs where they lay piled on the far side of the room. There they were. All his years of work, all the love and care that had gone into the creation of those prints, had come to nothing, wiped away by a single, casual act of malice. They were gone, and he was stranded here, in the present, alone with all the loss that he had been keeping at bay, all the dead, Daniels and Lutz and Marchand, Clark, Cundall wounded, the men whose names he didn't even know, whom he had only seen from the air, getting shot, blown to pieces, deafened, buried in earth. And the other losses, too, quieter but no less painful, his daughters, his friends, his marriage, even his idea of what his marriage had been—came pouring on him in a rush. The room was swept away, the walls and the floor, all that he'd taken for solid, and he was sinking, vanishing beneath the flood. He thought: I'm going to drown.

Then, through the darkness, he saw something descend, a long gold filament, very thin but strong. He reached out and grasped it. It began to pull him to his feet. It was a thought, obscure at first but then gradually becoming clear, urgent. Go, it said, to the one person who could understand what this means.

HE FOUND HER as she was getting off duty, leaving the hospital building for the dormitories just across from it. She was walking beside Helen and two of the other nurses, and when she saw him, she broke away and came to where he was standing, waiting to one side of the steps up to the main entrance.

"What are you doing here?" she looked alarmed. "You look like you haven't slept."

"I went to my house in Voulangis. I found . . ." He stopped. She waited for him to go on, but the words stuck in his throat. He thought, I shouldn't be here. But coming to find her had been his only clear thought since leaving Voulangis. And looking at her face lit with concern, he did not think that he could bear it if she told him to leave.

"Can I be here? Is it all right for me to be seen talking to you? I'll go if you think it is best."

She took both of his hands in hers. His body flooded with relief.

"Go into town," she said. "There is an inn just off the main square, the Vieux Palais. Wait for me there and I'll come as soon as I can. As soon as it gets dark."

"I thought there were rules."

"There are, but there are also ways around them." She turned and ran after the women she had been walking with before. He saw them talking and saw the other nurses squint back at him. He watched until they went inside.

The inn Marion had mentioned was easy to find. He got a room and told the concierge that his wife would be meeting him later. Then he sat in the nearly empty café downstairs, scanning the pages of a newspaper, trying to read it. It was after nine when she appeared at last.

From the front hallway, he heard the concierge say, "Mrs. Steichen?" and Marion's faltering reply: "Er, yes. My . . . husband, is he here?"

"He's in the café."

She was wearing her own clothes. She came and sat down opposite him. For a few moments they sat in silence and studied each other's faces. Then Marion asked, "What was it that you found?"

"My photographs. They are ruined. Someone took them and . . ." He made a gesture with his hands as though he were flinging something into the air, his fingers exploding outward. Marion stared at him, horrified.

"They were left out to rot. I think that Clara—"

"Oh, God."

"Everything is gone," he said. "I don't know what to do." He covered his face with his hands. He heard her chair scrape back and felt her come and sit beside him, felt her arms around his shoulders. She pulled his fingers away from his face and kissed his closed eyes, then his forehead, then his lips. She took his arm at the elbow and got him to his feet.

"Come on," she said, and she led him out of the bar and up the stairs to his room. She undressed him, removing first his shoes and then his jacket, then his shirt, putting him to bed the way you would a child. Then she lay down beside him and held him so his head was against her chest, and her voice close to his ear saying "Hush, hush, hush" over and over, until at last he found himself falling piece by piece into sleep.

THEY WOKE UP inside each other's warmth, Edward first swimming to the surface of sleep and knowing right away where he was. Marion lay in his arms with her back to him, and he pulled her closer so he could kiss the space on her neck just below her ear, that tiny corner that was almost always hidden by her hair. She stirred when he did this and turned over so she was looking into his face. She put her arms around his neck and began to kiss him.

They were tentative at first, and then he moved, sliding his arms all the way around her body so he could fold it into the hollow of his own, and they could kiss more deeply. He found his way through the clothes she was still wearing to her body, the smoothness of her skin astonishing him because it had been such a long time since he had touched another person like this. She helped him to pull the last garments off both of them until they were finally naked. Edward drew away from her and took her in with his eyes, her surprising beauty, her skin freckled so that it was golden against his own.

They made love slowly, and he thought that inside them they were gathering up all the strands of his sadness and hers, the sadness of the world, and transmuting them into something else, something like joy. Her force moving against him, the feeling of her arms around his torso, of her mouth and breasts: all of it felt precious to him, almost too precious and marvelous to bear.

Later she kissed the skin between his shoulder blades.

"How astonishing," he said. He turned over to look at her. "I have a week of leave. I'm going to stay somewhere in Paris. Somewhere quiet, private. Will you come and meet me there?"

"I think I can," she stretched, folded her body into his. "I don't know if I'm terribly happy or terribly sad," she said.

"Me neither. No, no, I am happy. What else is there left to be?"

THEY WENT ON to Paris, Edward first, Marion following a few days later. They stayed in a small hotel near Bastille. When they were alone together, they could elude, temporarily at least, the shadows that fell across their peace. They could forget the threat of Clara's court case. They could push away the war and its losses. They could almost, it seemed, slow the passing of time, bring the minutes and hours gradually to a stop. When they were alone this was possible: to balance in the present tense.

"I don't want to share you, not even with the strangers who look at you in the street."

"Well, you can't keep me prisoner," Marion said.

"All right. But let's see if we can spend the entire week without letting go of one another's hands. It will be an experiment."

They could turn their banishment into a game.

In the afternoons they walked until they found themselves in places they'd never seen before. They let the city wash over them and through them, the sunlight, the tiny dusty shops of the back streets.

Edward became absorbed in the process of discovering this woman he had known for so many years and taken so long to notice. He learned things about her now that only a lover could know: what position she slept in, one knee crooked up to the side of her body and her hands tucked under her chest, fists clenched as though for protection. How she liked to press her forehead into his neck when they made love, or how she would glance down at her body and frown slightly whenever she was newly naked. And other more ordinary things, details of her past. She liked to drink tea in bed. She always read the first page of any book twice. She liked Rilke and Blake; disliked Tennyson; loved *Jane Eyre*.

"Clara always preferred *Wuthering Heights*," she said. "We used to argue about it, but I don't remember who won."

She had wanted to paint ever since she was a little girl and discovered a book showing art from Italy on a shelf in her father's library.

"When was the first time you fell in love?" he asked.

"I was sixteen. That was why my parents sent me to Paris that summer I first met you. They wanted to get me away from New York, away from him."

"Who was he?"

"The son of our housekeeper."

"How romantic."

"They didn't think so. He was not what they had in mind for

me: penniless and a socialist. They thought it was a disaster. So much so that they found a new position for his mother with a family upstate while I was out of the country. By the time I came back that September, she was gone and he was gone. I never saw him again."

"Were you heartbroken?"

"Of course I was. I told them I'd never speak to them again and that I was going to leave to go after him. But I couldn't find him."

"And did you make love?"

"Now you are prying."

"So you did, then."

She stretched and yawned. "What about you? The first time you were in love."

"I was sixteen, too. She lived in Milwaukee, near my family's house. Rosa. After that, Clara. And after that . . ."

He picked her up and carried her to bed. Sometimes it seemed that talking was an unnecessary intercession and instead they could just touch and that would be sufficient. How astonishing, Edward thought, after all this time. He spent a long time undoing the buttons at the back of her dress, and watching the pale V of skin emerge at the seam. How miraculous the bones of her back were, especially the shoulder blades, which moved like wings when she shrugged her way out of her sleeves so that her dress slid to her waist. And when she twisted to face him: her clavicle like an ancient musical instrument; her breasts and the soft skin of her belly.

HE WAS GENTLER than she had imagined he'd be, more patient.

"What is this from?" He was examining a scar on the inside of her arm, just above the elbow.

"That's where I fell when I was a child and cut myself. I was running down the stairs, even though I had been told a million times not to. I tripped and went forward into the parlor door, which was paneled with glass. I put out my arms to stop myself. My mother was so upset when she saw the blood."

"And this?"

"That is where my brother bit me when we were having a fight. I was five and he was three. It's so faint, I'm surprised you can even see it."

"What were you fighting about?"

"I can't remember. It must have been important, though, because we didn't usually hurt each other."

"And this?"

"That is just a birthmark."

It was only now, of course, that she could admit to herself she had imagined these things at all: what he looked like without his shirt on, or how he would touch her. In the moments before she slid into sleep, she had thought of him, at certain seasons, although she had always told herself that this was impossible, told herself this for years while he had been Clara's husband and her friend.

He was so beautiful that it made her laugh. No one should look like that; it seemed ludicrous to her that someone should appear as he did, not perfectly formed, but with a magnetic immediacy to his movements. Whatever he was doing absorbed him. When they were together, he was curious about her in the way a child is curious, fascinated by the idiosyncracies of her body as the few other men she had known never were. He was delighted by discovering, for example, this small birthmark on her stomach just above her left hip. He ran his fingers over it, watching how it shifted shape when she moved. She had never been looked at with such intensity before. It dismantled her. She would come apart, her body gathering itself up and then falling sweetly to pieces each time they made love, still amazed that he was really there beside her.

Because it was so difficult to describe or understand, his beauty made her want to paint again for the first time in years. What would it be like to try to fix that quality of intensity? She found her mind tracing his lines and wondered, Could she capture them? Some part of her that had been dormant began to stir.

And yet she was aware of how this same quality translated into the possibility of carelessness. Most of the time they were together, she tried not to think about the complications of their shared past. But inevitably sometimes she would remember when she had seen this other dimension of him. She would recall Clara trying in vain to get his attention to ask him something simple while he was talking about painting with Arthur or photography with Alfred. He just doesn't *think*, Clara would say in frustration, and this was, Marion now realized, half-true. He did think, but with his eyes. He became consumed and lost sight of other things and other people. When she lay by him those nights, kept awake by her own restless mind and body or by the sounds from the street, she understood that the other side of his vitality was a potential for neglect.

A GROUP OF little girls, all sisters, came out of mass in Le Sacré-Coeur. It was Sunday morning, and Edward and Marion had climbed Montmartre for the view and arrived just as the services were ending. The girls, five of them, were ushered out ahead of their mother, and the younger ones ran down the white steps in front of the church and up to the railings nearby. They were laughing and describing to one another the landmarks that they recognized: There's Eiffel. There's Arc de Triomphe. Can you find our house? asked one of the older ones. I can, I can! The three youngest all pointed, with absolute conviction, in entirely different directions.

After their mother called them back, Edward said: "Because of the war, I got used to never seeing children. I am a little surprised to discover they still exist." He looked after the family as they were walking away. "I miss my daughters," he said. "I wish, at least, I still had my photographs of them."

He took Marion's hand and began to walk down the stone steps that wound across the face of the hill.

"It could have been the English soldiers who destroyed the photographs," he said. "The ones who were in the house after Clara and Kate left."

"Yes," Marion said. "It could have been them. Or there could be another explanation entirely, one you haven't even thought of."

"Promise me something." His voice was quietly fierce as though he were trying to harden his words into something solid.

"What?"

"Never to tell anyone else what I thought happened to the photographs. As far as the rest of the world is concerned, they were destroyed by accident, by damp. That is what I'm going to tell people. Promise you will keep this secret for me."

"I promise," Marion said.

IT WAS THEIR sixth day in Paris and they were coming down to breakfast late again, almost late enough to be lunchtime. Marion was ahead of Edward on the stairs. No one was around, the other guests all out at this hour, and he caught her by the waist on the first landing, drew her back and kissed her on the neck. She pushed him away, smiling, and ran down the stairs ahead of him.

He saw her go as far as the top of the last flight of stairs, and stopped. She was staring across the foyer toward the front door of the hotel, and though he couldn't read her expression from where he stood, he saw her look around her as though searching for a route of escape. He came down toward her, wanting to know what she had seen, and she turned, putting a palm up as though to push him back, away from her. Her mouth formed the word "Don't." But by the time he understood, it was too late.

Mildred Aldrich sat on a chair just to one side of the front entrance; at her feet was a small brown valise. She stood when she saw him. My goodness, he saw her mouth silently. Of all the . . . For a moment, he pictured the scene as it might have appeared from above, the three of them frozen in place with startled expressions on their faces, watching, waiting to see what the others would do. How strange it would look! The meaning of the encounter wholly invisible unless you knew its past, the future it implied. If you were to see a photograph of this, everything that mattered would be hidden.

What happened was that Mildred turned and, without a word to either of them, went out the front doors into the street. Edward started to follow her, but he felt Marion's hand on his shoulder restraining him.

"Let her go. What would you say to her anyway?" she asked. Her voice was calm, and when he looked around, her face wore a resignation that was almost relief. He understood. The worst had happened: they had been discovered. There was nothing more that they could do to prevent it.

"I can't," he said. "I have to try to talk to her, to explain." He took the stairs two at a time and ran out into the street through the still-swinging door. He scanned the street and found her. She was at the corner about to climb into a taxi. As he reached her, the driver put a square brown case inside the trunk of the car for her and then came around to help Mildred inside.

When she saw him, the expression on her face was one of acute annoyance.

"Why," she said, "did you tell me that Clara was wrong? Being lied to does not number among my preferred pastimes, Steichen."

"I didn't lie. I . . ."

She cut him off.

"I was rather pleased with myself for finding the place you were staying from the brief description in your letter. I wondered why you hadn't gotten in touch when you came to town. Amélie brought the case that Kate left for you. I came down here to give it to you, feeling like a real Good Samaritan. Now I feel like a fool. What am I supposed to say to Clara when I write to her?"

The cabdriver coughed impatiently where he waited beside the car. Mildred sighed and climbed into the backseat. Edward came forward and stood in the way of the open door, so she could not pull it closed behind her.

"Monsieur . . ." the driver objected.

"It's all right." Mildred said. "We'll only be speaking briefly." The driver relented and stood back. Mildred looked up at Edward. Her stern face broke into sympathetic sadness.

"None of us know where our feelings are going to take us," she said. "Of all people, I should know that. If you think I condemn you, you are wrong. But you can't expect me to say nothing to Clara about this. Now let me go."

He stood back and pushed the door closed beside her. Inside, she leaned forward to direct the driver and he watched the car pull out into traffic and drive away. It was only after it was already out of sight that he remembered that the case she had been carrying must have been the one that Kate had set aside for him when she left Voulangis. He had missed getting it from her. Now he might never get it.

He walked to the hotel and climbed the steps, feeling heavy and defeated. Marion was waiting for him in their room. She was seated on the bed, holding her head in her hands. He stood in the doorway and watched her despairingly.

"Oh, God. I did not want this to happen."

"Come in and close the door," she said without looking up.

"What should we do?" he said.

"Nothing," she said. "There is nothing we can do now." She tossed her head back and held out her hands to him. He came and took them and sat down beside her. "We have one more week together," she said. "I think, if we can, we should not waste it with worrying."

"Yes," he said. "You are right. Of course, you are right."

He put his arms around her. She bent her head down so it was next to his chest.

"I can hear your heart," she said.

The Little Galleries. New York, October 1914.
Palladium print.

"STAY HERE AS long as you like. I mean it. Don't worry about the rent until you get on your feet." Alfred is in one of his expansive moods as he opens the street door, ushers them through and shepherds them up the stairs into the small second-story apartment. He shows them through the rooms pointing out this and that detail or amenity—electric light everywhere! an icebox!—while Clara and Edward follow like sheep, numb and silent with exhaustion. They pass through the parlor, the dining room, the kitchen, and the tour ends in the large bedroom at the back where they can finally drop their bags and then collapse, Clara into an upholstered chair by the window and Edward on the edge of the bed.

Their ship arrived at the piers on the west side of Manhattan around noon, and they stood on deck and watched the city come toward them across the water. The railings were crowded with people who, like them, had fled from the war in Europe, who all had about them an air of mute shock as though they still couldn't quite believe what had happened. When the boat docked, they crowded down the gangway, blocking it as they struggled with trunks and cases and salvaged furnishings. The quay was packed with waiting friends and relatives. Clara scanned it and found Alfred, standing a little back. She waved when she saw him.

They caught a cab across town to this building just a few blocks above Madison Square where Alfred has his Little Galleries of the

Photo-Secession. There is an apartment over the gallery that Alfred also owns, and he has offered it to them, a wonderful act of generosity considering that they have almost no money and no immediate prospects for getting any. He has saved us, Edward said to her when the offer reached them by telegram in Marseilles. Alfred has saved us. Alfred and Emmy, she almost said, but decided that it was too much effort to correct him.

At the moment, it turns out, Alfred and Emmy are having a certain amount of trouble in their marriage. It appears that Alfred has met a young woman named Georgia or Virginia O'Keeffe, something like that, a painter, and that she has quite taken over all his attention. He met her at a show in the gallery right downstairs from where they are now, and, immediately, she got in an argument with him about the relative merits of the drawings on display. That did it. He was instantly smitten.

"You should see her works on paper! So powerful, so primal! You know, she came to that exhibition of Rodin's drawings that you brought over from Paris, how many years ago is it now?"

"Six," Edward says. He raises a hand to massage his temples; Clara can see from his face that he is absolutely worn-out.

"Yes, right. Six years," Alfred says. "Has it really been that long? Anyway, we narrowly missed meeting on that occasion." Mary and Kate are running through the apartment opening all the cupboards and closets and closing their doors again with a bang. Clara can hear their progress through the rooms, front to back, in a series of sharp, hard sounds: Bang! Bang-bang!

"Girls! Please," she calls. "Calm down. That's enough noise."

They come in meekly and sit down on the side of the bed.

"Thank you, girls," Edward says. "Mama and Papa are very tired now and we need you to be quiet, all right?"

Alfred is hovering beside the door, his excess of energy a jarring contrast to the room's grown-up occupants. Edward turns to him and opens his hands in a gesture of supplication.

"How can I ever thank you?" he says. "For this apartment, for all your help, everything."

"Oh, my goodness! Please. What do you think we would do? Let you starve on the streets while this place stood empty? No, that would have been unkind in the extreme."

"Well, still, we are all very grateful," Clara puts in.

"Yes," says Edward, "very." He reaches into his jacket for his cigarette case and offers it to Alfred, who takes a long white cylinder from it and says, "I suppose you'll be looking for work when you get unpacked."

"Yes, of course. Do you know of any commissions going right now? Anyone who needs a portrait taken of themselves? Or their niece? Or their lapdog? Really, I will photograph anything that will sit still long enough—I'm not going to be picky."

Alfred purses his lips. "To be honest, there isn't much right now," he says. "People have gotten tightfisted because of the war. Even the rich are feeling the strain of all this uncertainty. Commissions have almost dried up and no one is buying art photographs." He pauses to light his cigarette and inhale. He looks down at the skirting board, thinking, and then suddenly he brightens up: "You know what? I do need someone to take a series of pictures of the galleries downstairs for our records. I've been meaning to do it myself, but I've been so busy with the magazine and other things that I haven't gotten around to it. You could do it, though, and I could pay you a commission. I mean, it would be completely dull work, no art to it whatsoever . . ."

"My God, I couldn't care less about that," Edward says. "Right now, I just need work. Are you sure you don't want to do it yourself and save the expense?"

"No, no. As I said, I'm far too busy right now. And the money doesn't matter in the slightest."

Clara feels a pang as her feelings are cut neatly in half by this generous offer. For on the one hand, it is so thoughtful and kind of Alfred to pay Edward for a service he could very well perform himself; he doesn't really need these photographs very badly or he would have found the time to take them. He is, again, going out of his way to help them. This is the gruff manner in which he cares for the people whom he values: under his brusqueness, he is also kind.

But on the other hand, when he says that the money doesn't matter, Clara knows that the money in question does not come from him. Alfred has no wealth of his own. His money belongs to his wife, the woman whom he is openly flouting with a younger mistress, and whose company he has never cared for, as long as she can remember. He can spend her money on whatever he chooses: as her husband, her fortune is his. For years, Emmeline has effectively covered the running costs of *Camera Work* and has funded the exhibitions at 291 Fifth Avenue. Alfred has used what they have for worthy ends, certainly. But now he is facing a dilemma: leave his wife for a woman he loves who is as poor as he is and try to do without the generous support his projects have always had; or stay in his marriage and enjoy this ability to be casually magnanimous to people whom he deems deserving, like Edward and Clara.

Edward takes only a moment to think through the offer before he says: "Well, if you are sure the pictures will help you, then of course I accept. When do you need me to start?"

"When you are rested. You obviously need to have some time to recover from your journey, and when you are done with that, you must come and have some supper with me and O'Keeffe. I'm sure you will love her and she has so wanted to meet you. You'll have so much to discuss—she studied with Chase before his death, you know, and you can see it in her work. Strong, American lines. A boldness which marks her out from other painters immediately."

Clara takes this as her cue.

"Come along, girls. Let's go and see about making up the beds so that you can take a nap." She gestures for Mary and Kate to come with her as she goes to the door and, good girls, they stand up and follow her out. Edward and Alfred, Clara can tell, are about to get into one of their long discussions, and she has no energy to fight her way into it right now. She is not sure she would want to even if she were awake and well rested. She feels a weight land on her heart and press it down: nothing has changed. They have come through the fire of escaping from the war, the stark events that might have transformed them, and yet here, back in New York, the men are talking in the front room, just as they always did, and the invitation to dine with this woman who has so captivated Alfred was not issued to her, only to Edward.

Through the journey, she kept herself inside herself. She kept herself suspended, held back, as she followed through the motions of life to which she was committed. She found that she and her husband had habits of caring that had built up through their years of marriage, and that she could fall back on these through the crisis. They had managed well together: changing trains in the chaos of war-scarred Paris, getting themselves and their daughters onto the boat at Marseilles, coping with the cramped quarters of a sea voyage in which every room was full to twice its capacity and people were sleeping in the dining rooms and on the decks. She had seen Edward's relief to find that she was still as he had always depended on her to be: supporting him, supporting their children. But inside, she was withdrawn, waiting. She watched all that went on as though this life no longer belonged to her. She was weighing it up, deciding whether to reenter it or not. When they reached New York, she had still not made up her mind. Nothing he had done or said, no moment of clarity, had pushed her heart forward into certainty.

She finds the airing closet next to the small side bedroom that the girls will be sharing and looks inside. There are sheets and blankets, and she takes some of these down to put on the bed inside. She remembers once declaring she would never do this again, and she almost smiles thinking of it. She can just make out snatches of the conversation from the bedroom:

" . . . Marion was with us until almost the end."

"Ah, the lovely Miss Beckett. She got out of France, I assume?"

"Yes. She went to England."

"And will she be coming back to New York from there?"

"I don't know. I don't think that I will be hearing from her very soon."

"Why not?"

"There was an incident before we left Voulangis . . . Clara did not cope very well with the pressures of our last month there. She became very emotional, very distraught. Anyway, I think that she would not look kindly on my receiving correspondence from Miss Beckett."

"But I thought they were great friends."

"So did I."

There is a pause in the conversation. Clara leans against a shelf in the cupboard. She feels the wood in a hard band across her forehead. So he does not think she coped well. He has no idea how well she has managed.

"Well, I will find out where she is," Alfred is saying. "Mercy and Arthur Carles—they will probably know."

"If you do . . ." Edward hesitates. "If you do get news of her, please, would you let me know what it is? I would like to be certain that she is well."

Listen to the yearning in his voice. He cannot disguise it. He is not trying to. Listen to his version of the events of the past few months. It is as though they have been living on different sides of the planet, not in the same house. In his story she was simply unbalanced and burdensome to deal with, and all the things that she had done to keep their family from falling apart he does not mention, he does not even seem to have noticed. Even now, he is longing for news of Marion.

She stands and reaches for a set of sheets from the shelf in front of her, but even as she does so she finds that the apartment has shifted: it has become suddenly cramped and the air is so thin that it is hard to breathe. She hears laughter from the room where Alfred and Edward are. She feels her heart coming forward, beginning to decide.

TWELVE

August 1918

THE LAST DAY before Edward left for Colombey-les-Belles, he and Marion decided to walk along the river. They were quieter than usual, not wanting to dwell on their impending separation, but also unable to ignore it.

When they reached the place where the Boulevard du Palais crossed to the the Ile de la Cité, they stopped and leaned against the embankment wall, looking down at the water.

"Will you get more leave before the winter?" Edward asked.

"It depends on how the war goes," she said. "If it continues to move east, then there will be less to do at the hospital."

"Will you come and see me?"

"I will try. But I can't come to Colombey. Too many people will know about it." She stood up. "Shall we walk across the bridge?" He nodded, and they strolled across to the island, past St-Chapelle and the Palais de Justice.

"Well, maybe we could travel somewhere together. When the war is over."

"Maybe," she said.

He knew from her tone that she didn't believe it, and when he thought about it, he didn't either. But he went on anyway: "Where would you like to go? If we could . . ."

"Greece," she said quickly, joining in the make-believe. "I've never seen Athens or the islands."

"Well, we'll go. As soon as there is an armistice. We'll see the Acropolis, the Parthenon. We'll take a ferry to the islands. Isadora Duncan has a house there that she could lend us."

"It sounds wonderful."

"Yes, it will be wonderful. Then we can come back to France and stay at Voulangis. I'll hire François to replant the garden just the way it was before, and you can paint there. I can arrange for Mary to come over from New York when the school year is finished."

"Please." Marion had shut her eyes and the expression on her face was pained. He had gone too far.

"I'm sorry," he said. They stood miserably looking at each other, feeling already a distance growing between them. He reached out for her hand, but she drew back and he felt a flare of anger at her: why make it worse than it had to be by pulling away now? He looked down at the pavement, disappointment seeping through him.

"Just come and see me the next time you can," he said.

Marion nodded, biting her lip.

THE NEXT DAY he went back to the war. With Barnes gone he was in charge of the deployment of the ever-growing number of observers and photo interpreters working near the front. They would come from the States, and he would see them when they first arrived, tired from the sea voyage but eager, sitting through the instruction that he knew could never be enough to make them ready. Many of the men who had flown reconnaissance in the Marne were reassigned to the training centers, so he saw them in his frequent travels through the Zone of Advance. Dawson had been promoted to captain. In September, he got news that Deveraux had been killed during a flight over Amiens. From time to time he heard of other deaths and promotions. He thought of the ones who had died often; they would come to him suddenly and vividly, appearing before his mind's eye: Lutz singing Mozart; Marchand's uneven walk. He knew that this was because, somewhere inside, he still did not really understand that they were dead.

At Colombey he was also in charge of the photographers who worked on the ground, documenting the life in the trenches. Now his work took him regularly to the front.

He saw where the men lived for weeks on end on the muddy floor of a trench, how when the autumn rains came these trenches flooded so that even the duck boards the men put down vanished under water. The rains dislodged soil from the walls, and the dugouts filled in and there was no shelter, so soldiers got lost among the dead-ends of collapsed earthworks. He saw how when they dug a new sap or a communication trench they would unearth the remains of men who had been there before and who had died there. Sometimes they would find whole bodies, but more often they would find parts, hands or legs, sometimes just a finger. Sometimes bones, already stripped clean by the rats. And the smell of the living and the dead was suffocating.

He took his camera with him, but he found that he couldn't bring himself to photograph these scenes. In mid-September, on a tour through the trenches near Verdun, he saw a young lieutenant with the top of his head blown off, still not aware that he had been killed. The man's brains showed through his broken skull. The photographer who was with him, a man named Ball, snapped a picture, and Edward raised his own camera halfway to his eyes, but in the end he couldn't do it. He was accustomed to looking for beauty. Something in him, below the level of thinking, simply didn't want to record what he was seeing, didn't want the world to remember it. He put the camera down and walked away and was sick on the ground. His temples throbbed, and for some minutes he was too dizzy to stand. He felt a hand on his shoulder.

"You all right, sir?" It was the photographer.

"Yes," Edward managed to say. "I'll be fine in a minute." He was ashamed to have been ill in front of men who had to live with things like this everyday.

"I did the same thing the first time I saw a man die like that," Ball said. "I'd be lying if I said you ever get used to it. You just numb up after a while."

He had failed, in that moment, in his first ambition, his reason for wanting to come to war. He had wanted to record this war so that the world could see it as it really was but he had not been able to do that. He straightened up and made himself go on with the tour. Only much later, when he described to Marion the man's bewildered face as he reached up to feel where his hair used to be, did he find himself sobbing, tearing angry lungfuls from the air.

"How can they stand it?" he asked. "The men in the trenches—how can they go on?"

"They can't. They stay because they have to. Because they don't have a choice."

"My sister was right," he said, "when she told me not to come to France. She knew, somehow. It is wrong to be any part of this."

"People were already fighting and dying," Marion said. "You came here to protect your home."

"Nothing is worth that," Edward said. "No country. No home. And if everyone just refused to fight anymore, if everyone just stopped . . ." She held him until he was quieter.

"You are helping to gather the evidence," Marion said. "Even if you can't take the pictures yourself. You must keep working. It is all that you can do."

It was November, and she had been able, at last, to come and see him. She had left the hospital and was on her way to Paris and from there back to New York. The war was almost over by then; everyone knew that it was only a matter of time.

"And yet more wounded were coming in everyday," Marion said. "It all seemed more pointless than ever." She was standing with her back to the open window, smoking a cigarette, the sheet from the bed gathered around her like a robe.

"What will you do when you get back to New York?" he asked.

"I'll find a studio and try to paint. That is what I want, above all. To be able to work."

"I wish . . ." He stopped. There was no point in continuing, he knew, because it did not matter what he wished. In the oblong frame of windowsill and sash, her bare shoulders were outlined against the dark. She had the white sheet bunched up in her right arm, which was drawn across her body like she was holding a shield. Her left hand was flung out, the wrist tilted back so that the cigarette in it pointed toward the ground. Her beautiful angles, he thought. Her lines.

"Will you stay there for a minute?" He stood up and went to the chest of drawers that stood near the door.

"What are you going to do?"

"Wait." He pulled open the drawers and brought out his camera, the one he had brought with him, again, when he left Épernay. He removed the camera from the box and went back to sitting on the bed directly across from her. He took out a rag from the case and wiped the dust from the lens.

When he looked up, she had come out of the window and across the room to him. The photograph he'd imagined was completely gone. She put her palm up so it blocked light from the lens.

"No," she said.

"Why not?"

"No record of this. For heaven's sake, Edward. Don't forget what I'm facing. What you are facing."

He said, "You were such a beautiful photograph, there in the window, just a moment ago."

"Remember it," she said. "Remember that I love you."

The next day she left for Paris and then for America.

THE ARMISTICE CAME and the war was over. Edward found he couldn't join in with the celebrations, the music and the crowds dancing in the streets. He remained at Colombey-les-Belles and began a project documenting American installations on the Western Front. He felt lonely and exhausted; he went through the motions of his work because he did not know what else to do. The world seemed full of ruins, and then as winter wore on, there was the Spanish influenza, which spread from the soldiers coming back from war to the civilians. It moved through the population, laying low young and old so quickly that those who were well one morning might be dead the next. Everything seemed to be disintegrating around him.

In January, he received a letter from a lawyer in New York who said he repesented Miss Marion Beckett in the action Steichen vs. Beckett. Clara was going forward with the suit. He would be called to give evidence by lawyers for both the plaintiff and the defendant. He obtained the necessary leave and made preparations for the journey. He wrote to Alfred, asking him to arrange for a lawyer.

The *New York Times* ran an article on the case: "Artist's Wife Sues for Loss of His Love," the headline said. Well, he thought, now everyone knows.

Before he left Paris, he went to see Mildred Aldrich. She received him with equanimity, though not warmth, and he sat in the same chair by the fire as when he'd visited her in June. He felt hesitant to ask her what he wanted to know, but fortunately he was dealing with Mildred: she did not have to be asked.

"I did not tell her," she said. "I didn't say anything about seeing you and Miss Beckett in the summer."

"You didn't?" He was surprised.

"No," she said. "In the end, I decided that it would only encourage her to pursue this dreadful suit if I told her. She did not ask me about it specifically; so it was not exactly lying." She paused, drew a handkerchief from her sleeve and coughed into it. The sound was hoarse and wheezing. "However," she continued, "now that she is going ahead, I will testify for her. I am going to Boston to see my sister, and after that I will come to New York. I will tell them what I saw."

Edward took this news in; he felt as though someone had filled his body with icy water.

"I am sorry," Mildred said. "I have to go and tell the truth, or my part of it. What else can I do?"

"But the truth is so much more complicated than this," Edward burst out. "Clara's accusations are wrong. She claims I did things I didn't do. She claims I was unfaithful when I was not. There was nothing wrong with my conduct toward Miss Beckett before the war."

"But you *loved* each other; Clara could see that. She is charging that your affections were alienated. Well, weren't they?"

"God knows I never intended Clara any harm. How will it help any of us if you testify? Clara can have money without resorting to this, if that is what she wants; the Becketts have offered her as much as she will get if she wins and more, if she will only settle out of court."

Mildred coughed again, and Edward thought that she looked frailer than when he'd last seen her; the big chair cradled her like a cupped hand. Her voice was clear, though, when she spoke: "If we don't tell the truth when it is difficult," she said, "then we really have descended into chaos; then there is nothing left of the old world. The war has taken everything, even our sense of honor."

"What would you know about it?" Edward said. "What would you know about what the war took away?" His anger rose out of him as if from nowhere. He stood up. "I apologize. I should not have come," he said. "I'll show myself out." He started toward the door. Out of the corner of his eye, he saw Mildred pull herself to her feet, preparing to come after him, but as she did so, she was seized by a fit of coughing more serious than any that had preceded it. She shook so severely that she almost lost her balance. For all her defiance, he thought, she really is very ill. He came to her, and reached out and put a hand gently on her shoulder to steady her as the door opened and Amélie came bustling in. She shooed him away, and helped Mildred back into her chair.

"What are you doing?" she said angrily to him. "She mustn't be excited. The doctor told us, no strain, no excitement."

"I'm sorry. I didn't intend to upset her." He stood back and watched Amélie kneel down beside Mildred, stroking her head and talking to her softly in words he couldn't hear. The gentleness between them struck him. As he watched Amélie spread a blanket on

Mildred's lap, tucking it carefully over her legs, he thought that this gentleness was all he had ever wanted, and that he might in another world have had it with Marion, or even with Clara perhaps. In this world, he was simply alone, watching the tenderness of others.

"Lying under oath is not a small thing, Steichen," Mildred said. "Why don't you go to New York, tell the truth and take the consequences?"

"Because they are not just consequences for me. Because of Miss Beckett."

"Because you love her. I understand that. She seems a person worthy to be loved. But then, you see, Clara has a point." She put her head back so it rested against the antimacassar. She spoke without looking at him.

"Clara is more like you than you think," she said. "The bad things she has done, they aren't excusable, but they make more sense if you understand that you two have always been the same kind of creatures, wanting the same things. She wanted to be loved completely, just as she loved you. She wanted to play music and to write it; not just to entertain her friends but as her life. To her, this was as serious a desire as anything that you have ever felt about photography. How would it have felt to give up taking photographs when your children were born? To give up painting?"

Through the net of his anger, Edward saw the years of his life stretching backward empty of his work, without the endeavor and excitement of it. At present, it had been more than a year since he had taken a photograph because he thought it was beautiful. And how did it feel? Like sleepwalking. Like a part of him was missing. Like there were rooms of himself he couldn't find the way into anymore.

"It would have made me miserable," he said to Mildred. "It would have made me crazy."

Clara Smith Steichen and Kate Rodina Steichen.
Voulangis, September 1917. Gum print.

THEY HAVE NOT had many visitors since they came back to this house after the war began. Most of the Americans they know have left the country, and the few who remained are restricted from traveling because they are foreigners. Occasionally, one of the women from town will stop by to deliver some news, to sit in the salon, drink tea, exchange pleasantries. But Clara always feels when this happens that she is being harvested, the subject of gossip for later that evening, speculations on where the rest of the family is, the father, some kind of artist, and the older girl, who used to live in the tall house outside of town. Well, she will not give them more grist for the mill. She deflects prying questions with a tense smile and talks instead about the weather; needless to say, this has not proved especially conducive to intimacy. Besides, these people here, they are not educated enough to discuss politics or art. She cannot make friends with them just because they happen to be in her front parlor.

So most of the time they are alone, she and Kate. Old François comes by sometimes, but he will let himself in by the kitchen door. He does not need to ring the doorbell like this. She is upstairs, lying down, when she hears it. It is still afternoon, still light outside, but she is feeling indisposed today. Lately, she has often come over like this, so heavy and listless during the day and then sleepless at night. And when she does, she has less and less inclination to fight against it. Why should she remain up and dressed? For whom? She has finished her chores for the day, and what reason in the world requires that she be upright?

She hears Kate open the front door, and a woman's voice begins speaking, a voice that she knows terribly well but cannot believe that she is actually hearing. Because it is not thinkable that its owner should come here; it is not possible. And it continues to seem impossible and unreal even when Kate climbs the stairs, knocks on her door and comes into her room, saying, "Aunt Marion is here. She asked if she could please come up and see you."

Well, so she has come back. How extraordinary. How genuinely bizarre that after all this time she should have the nerve to show up in this place and expect to be invited in, to be received as a guest. What does she want? What could she possibly be trying to do, apart from stirring the muck from the bottom that had only just begun to settle?

"What shall I say to her?" Kate asks. "She is downstairs now."

"Tell her I am not well enough to see her."

"She says she has come all the way from Paris."

"I do not care where she has come from. If she wanted to visit this house, she might have done the commonly courteous thing and written in advance of her arrival."

"She says she did write, but she never heard back."

Ah, yes, that is right. There had been a letter, Clara remembers, some weeks before. It was not the first time that Marion had written to her since the war began. Early on, when Clara was still in New York, there had been a steady stream of letters, but she had declined to respond to them or even, after a while, to read them, and when she returned to France, she had certainly not forwarded her address. So it was two years since she had seen the handwriting on that envelope. They used to write to each other every week. She looked at the sealed letter for about ten seconds. Then she threw it away.

For she has no desire to reopen the past, all its ugliness. In this house, of course, she lives with its ghosts all the time, but they are ghosts: they remain trapped in their orbits; they do not change or falter. It is possible to learn to live with them, to allow them their space in exchange for a little independence. Indeed, they are far easier to accommodate than the living, who cannot be relied on, who betray a lifetime's friendship or ten years of marriage for a whim of the senses, who show up unexpectedly on your doorstep demanding to be seen and heard anew.

"Go downstairs and tell her I will not see her!" she says, and Kate flinches, taken aback at the anger in her voice.

"Yes, Mama." She goes out without another word, and instantly Clara is sorry, sorry, poor child, none of this is her fault. It is the selfishness of her father that has caused all this pain and trouble; and the duplicity of that woman who is now waiting in the salon. And in this place how serious Kate has grown. She acts far too old for her ten years. She watches the world in that solemn, silent way she has; she is not surprised by anything. She hardly smiles, and Clara cannot think of the last time she saw her daughter laugh. It has been hard for them; it has been cold and lonely. The war, which they can hear at dawn and evening, the sound of the guns audible from just beyond the horizon, has made everything feel like it is made of glass, fragile. Kate moves and speaks with the caution of an old woman, as though she is always afraid that something inside her will shatter without warning.

Clara can hear their voices from below, Marion's rising questions and Kate's replies. It is not fair that Kate should have to confront this visitor on her own, Clara thinks. I can look this woman in the eyes and tell her to leave. That, at least, I can do. She stands up and begins slowly to dress herself.

When she is ready, presentable, she slips quietly onto the landing and goes across to the stairs, trying not to make any noise. She wants to appear as though from nowhere, just as Marion herself has done; but more than this, she wants to know what is being said. From the direction of their voices they must be sitting near the fireplace. She can hear them clearly now, and her heart jumps into her throat, her stomach leaps because the sound is so familiar; it sends her mind spinning back in time, three years, to memories she'd buried, things she had not thought since she last heard that voice. Measured and low, how she used to trust it, to depend on it for solace and counsel. It is too horrible, this being reminded. She cannot go down. She cannot face her yet. She sits on the top stair, where she is still out of sight from below, and listens.

"I go to school in the village," Kate is saying. "Mama sometimes volunteers at the local ambulance with the wounded soldiers. Or she used to, when she didn't feel bad so much."

"Is your mother frequently unwell?"

"She has been feeling poorly for these past few months. When we first arrived, she never was. But now she goes to bed often when it is still light out."

"I am sorry to hear it. Has she seen a doctor about it?"

"She has not. It is not easy to see a doctor. Most of them have gone away to the war."

"And what about you, Kate? Are you in good health?"

"Yes. Mama says I am too sad all the time, but it is hard to be merry here. I miss Mary and . . . I miss Mary very much. I write to her two times a week and she writes to me almost as much."

"And what about your papa? Do you write to him?"

"Oh, no. I do not want to write to him. I do not like him anymore."

"But do you get letters from him?"

"No. Well . . ."

"Catkin, it is all right. You can tell me."

"Well, I do, but Mama doesn't like it when I read them. So I throw them away instead."

"Kate, I know your papa loves you very much. I know he misses you."

"How do you know?"

"I just do."

"Have you seen Papa and Mary? How are they?"

"No, I have not seen them. But I am told by friends that they are well."

"That's good. I'm glad about that."

Clara thinks she feels her chest cracking in two, a fissure opening behind her sternum and racing through her body until she's sure it will fall to pieces right there on the stairs. There is so much light in the voice, so much hope. Kate wants her father and her sister; she wants her family to be as it was before. And how can she explain so her daughter will understand that she could not stay with him a day longer, that she had to leave? For when they arrived safe in New York, and the immediate demands of escape were gone, she discovered that underneath her enforced calm something in her had turned over. She saw him begin to adjust to life in the city; she saw him in the company of friends; she saw him reunited with his mother and sister, witnessed their joy and relief at finding him well. It surprised her that he could walk around, talk, smile, concentrate on work just as though he had done nothing wrong. She would watch him, amazed at his resilience, his imperviousness, and she hated him for it. She realized that she no longer wanted him to be happy. Instead, she wanted him to suffer as she had; she wanted him to lose the things that mattered to him.

So she left. She had taken her daughter with her, and come here, to this place, where she did not have to see him anymore.

And the act was part revenge and part salvation because she knew if she stayed in that apartment with him she would go mad. To keep any part of herself in tact, she had to leave. This house was the only place she knew to go.

And who is this woman to come here and raise her child's hopes, confusing her with false reassurances? Who is she to come and praise him and talk about how he loves his daughter? He had not loved her enough to be faithful; he had not cared about her enough for that.

With her heart racing, she gets to her feet and goes downstairs, into the salon. Kate is sitting on the rug by the fireplace, and Marion is perched on the front of the big overstuffed armchair. She looks ill at ease, and when she sees Clara, she rises as if she is being drawn up to standing by a string. Her face dances with nervous energy, something close to fear. She opens her mouth, about to speak, but before she has a chance to start, Clara cuts her off.

"I think," she says, "you had better leave this house now."

LATER, SHE HEARS a soft knock on her bedroom door.

"It's me, Mama," Kate says from outside.

"Come in, sweetheart." Kate sits on the end of the bed, cross-legged. "I am sorry that you had to see her. If only I hadn't had this dreadful headache . . ."

"It's all right, Mama. She was kind."

"Sometimes the people who seem the most kind can be the most wicked. Did you get some supper?" Kate nods. "Well, kiss me good night then and go off to bed."

Kate leans over and kisses her, then gets up to leave. In the doorway, she pauses and says, "When the war is over, will we see Papa and Mary?"

"Katie, don't ask me that. You know I cannot tell you. "

"I am sorry, Mama. Good night."

But though she feels enervated from the day's events, she cannot sleep. For hours, she turns in her bed, rest just out of reach. Each time she feels herself slipping toward it, something calls her back into the waking world, a noise in the house, or out among the trees. The dull rumble from the guns of the front. At last she opens her eyes and climbs out of bed. She goes across the landing to his study and lets herself in.

When she can't sleep, she comes here, raises the sash and sits on the sill looking out. Tonight the fields are silver. The moon is risen and almost full, and there is the river in the distance, and stars in the lower regions of the sky. She can watch as the light changes and brings back another day, gray and ragged, there to be endured. Her mind will be threadbare from lack of sleep; great dark circles have appeared under her eyes making her even uglier, she thinks, than she was before. When day comes, she will send her daughter off to school, and then she will settle into her chores, the running of the household, which, when they first arrived, made her feel solid and whole. She had her own clear, hard edges; her days were dictated by necessity: she must do certain things or her daughter would go hungry, they would be cold, there would be no light. At first she had loved this urgency, this simplification of life, and she had felt it as a kind of independence. In the spring, she'd had a photographer come from town to take their picture: she and Kate, sitting in the garden she had tidied and planted, to show she did not need him even for that. She had made copies of the picture and sent them to friends and relatives. *We are getting along really quite well here*, she had written. *We are doing fine.*

But this isn't the case anymore. She is tired of living in this house with the past all around her, the good memories in their way more terrible than the bad ones. It was never independence; it was only distance; she still waits each month for him to send her money, so the food she buys, the coal that they keep warm with: it is still his. The house is his. So is the furniture inside it.

And then, too, some nights she will come in here and unlock the closet where all of his photographs are stored. She will light a lamp and lift down one of the boxes from the shelves and open it. Inside, there are the scenes of their life together, the landscapes they had traveled through, their children as they grew from babies. The emotion she has when she does this is a combination of long-ing and disgust. Here is his vision, elaborated in hundreds of dis-crete moments, plucked from time and fixed on paper; here are the things that he chooses to tell the world about itself. It is a beauti-ful vision, one in which nothing is ugly and broken, nothing dull and repetitive; the pictures he makes are of a world that can be understood and can be loved therefore without reservation.

But she knows that there is another version; that there are things his vision omits to show. The real world is far messier and more confusing than these photographs betray. As many dreams are denied as fulfilled; as many loves fail as endure. Wars begin for fool-ish, petty reasons, and continue inexplicably for years. Husbands leave their wives in spirit and in fact; women who tell of such betrayals are dismissed or disbelieved. She understands that she did not come here to leave him; quite the opposite. It was by coming here that she could try to hold on to him, to both of them, as she used to believe they were.

But now, perhaps, she can let go of the old story. When she told Marion to leave that afternoon, she felt something in her revive. Some willfulness, some ownership of the present and the future. From her sister's letters, she knows that, at home in the States, the Liberty Loan campaign is hiring staff, and that they will consider applications from women. Perhaps she should take her child and go back to America, where she can work, where her independence can become real. If only she could walk into a new life without the weight of the past, clean.

What she longs for, more even than she longs to have her family back whole, or for her husband to have been the man she hoped he'd be, is to be understood. To be believed. It is a terrible thing that he had been unfaithful, but it was far worse that the world accepted it as at most a minor foible of his character; or even as his natural right as a man. As though her feelings were evidently of less import than his; if she was hurt, well, she was wrong to be so sensitive. She was being dramatic. She was making a fuss. *You married him, knowing his faults*, Stieglitz had said, as though this fact absolved Edward from responsibility for his actions.

She is not certain yet how she will do it, but she knows that she will have no peace until she can show the world that she knows its secret mechanisms. That she is onto its schemes. She wants her vision of things to be expressed, accepted. In a different life, it might have been expressed through music, but in this one she must find another means to tell about what she sees. And she knows that to do this she must first relinquish his way of seeing. She must rid herself of his perspective. She is trapped under water, tangled in the weeds at the bottom of a lake, and above her she can see the light of the surface but she can't quite swim up to it yet, she is still caught and held down. But she is ready, now, to try. She will find out what it takes for her to be free.

She will not have to do much to begin it. The records that we keep of the past are delicate things, in fact, susceptible to sun and to damp. All she must do is leave this window up, just as it is right now and leave the closet door ajar. The weather will do the rest. It will be an act of neglect, and this feels right to her, the appropriate reaction to all the things that she has lost because they were not important enough to save: her music, her husband and her dearest friend. Such a small thing, to leave a window open like this in a room on the second floor. No more than a minor oversight.

She takes the key from where it is kept in the top drawer of the desk and unlocks the closet so the door swings open . . .

THIRTEEN

February 1919

EDWARD SAILED FOR America a few days after he saw Mildred. After a week at sea, he watched the Manhattan skyline rise out of the harbor, the city still daunting in its grandeur, oblivious to his small struggles. Mary met him at the quay. She waved to him as the boat docked, standing with Lee and Lizzie Stieglitz, his old friends and Alfred's brother and sister-in-law, on the end of the pier. Her dark hair tangled in the wind off the water.

He ran down the gangway to embrace her.

"How beautiful you look! So grown-up . . ."

"Papa, it's only been a year. I haven't changed that much."

"A year is much too long." Lee Steiglitz took one of his bags and they caught a cab across town to their house in the East 40s. They spent the evening talking. Mary was doing well at school, especially in science; Lee, who was a doctor, helped her with her work. That was why she had done so well, she said. Lee waved her away: Not at all. She showed a natural affinity for biology and chemistry. She was top of her class in those subjects. Mary shrugged shyly. It isn't that I don't like painting and drawing, too, she said, and Edward realized she was worried he would be disappointed that she didn't want to pursue art.

"Well," he said, "I couldn't be more delighted. You have found something you love to do, so you must follow your inclination. My daughter, the scientist. How marvelous." Mary smiled and began to talk enthusiastically about her classes, her teachers, her plans. The Brearley School had been closed because of the influenza, but if it opened again in time for her to finish her classes, she would begin a course in medicine at Vassar in the fall, a year before her Brearley classmates would be eligible to enter college.

Edward thought how remarkable she was; with all that had happened to her family, she was not crushed by it. He wanted to tell her he was sorry; that he would have given anything to prevent this. Before she went up to bed that night, he said, "I wish I were here for some other reason . . ."

"Hush, Papa. It is not your fault. There was nothing you could have done." She said it with such confidence that for a moment he almost believed it was that simple.

The next day he went to meet with his lawyer.

"Miss Beckett's attorney has asked you to give testimony on the final day of the trial. You will be questioned by him and by Mrs. Steichen's attorney. During the interim you should make no attempt to contact either Mrs. Steichen or Miss Beckett."

"What will happen," Edward asked, "if the verdict goes for Mrs. Steichen?"

"I assume," the lawyer said, "that you will subsequently be seeking a divorce from Mrs. Steichen. You can do so on grounds of abandonment."

Edward realized he had not clearly formed this determination; there had been so much else to think about. He had grown accustomed to living without Clara, to being alone. Then there had been the moment in Voulangis when, confronted by the destruction of his photographs, the dwindling hope that his family might be reunited had flickered and gone out. Now he was presented with the end of his marriage as an all-but-accomplished fact. It seemed both chilling and inevitable.

"Yes," he said. "I don't see any reasonable alternative. After this we could never live together again."

"So then you will be settling the question of whether you or Mrs. Steichen will have custody of your two daughters."

"Yes, I guess we will."

"Well, if the jury finds for Mrs. Steichen in this suit, it could go hard for you in the divorce proceedings. The courts do not tend to look favorably on fathers who philander, or rather, fathers who philander and don't hide it well enough. If you would like to have access to your children in the future, you must hope that the verdict goes against your wife."

"I see."

"Your interests are best served if Miss Beckett is found to have a reputation beyond reproach. Miss Beckett has informed us of the possibility of damaging testimony from a Miss Mildred Aldrich. Is that correct?"

Edward nodded.

"Our strategy will be to discredit her. Any meetings between yourself and Miss Beckett that occurred in France were purely accidental and the result of your mutual service in our valiant Expeditionary Force. Miss Aldrich is an elderly woman, and we will attempt to convince the jury that she is confused about what she saw, just as Mrs. Steichen was. Beyond that, much will depend on you and Miss Beckett appearing to be honorable people wrongly accused. Your war record will help." He drew out a cigarette from a gold case on the desk. He lit it and inhaled meditatively.

"I would say," he continued, "that our chances of prevailing are really quite fair. Yes, indeed. You have cause for much optimism."

THE PRESS WAS there; not in large numbers but in sufficient force to ensure everyone's discomfort. On his way into the court-room, Edward was waylaid by a man from the *New York Post*.

"Does your wife's suit have any merit?" the man asked, his pen quivering over his notebook.

"No, of course it does not," Edward's lawyer cut in. "Mrs. Steichen's accusations are unfounded and we will prove this. They are a slander on the name of a hero of the Great War." He took Edward by the elbow and walked him toward the courtroom. The man came after them, still talking.

"Major Steichen. Is it true that Miss Beckett posed nude for you in your studio as your wife alleges?"

Edward rounded on the man, his outrage boiling up. In his ear his lawyer hissed, "Don't rise to it, damn it."

They entered the courtroom.

THE PROCEEDINGS WERE as unbearable as he'd imagined they'd be. Clara gave testimony and then Marion. He watched as old friends were called to the stand to vouch for his character, or his wife's. Was Mrs. Steichen jealous of her husband? Marion's lawyer asked. Was she prone to outbursts of anger?

Was Mr. Steichen often away from his wife for long periods of time? The sort of spans that would have afforded opportunity to meet a paramour? Clara's lawyer asked. He saw their lives being sifted and put on display. It was excruciating.

Marion did not look at him during her testimony. She spoke with her head down, her face flushed with embarrassment throughout. No, she said, she had not done any of the things that Clara's suit accused her of; she had been properly attired on the sole occasion she posed for Major Steichen, which was a photograph taken out of doors; she had never encouraged any romantic advances from him; she had encountered him by chance during her time in France, when they were both serving in the American war effort, she as a nurse.

Edward was struck by the fact that everything she said was true. Of course, there was a huge sin of omission. But Clara's lawyer had not asked them about the summer of 1918, only about the one four years before it. He watched Marion up on the stand, bright red with shame and almost in tears, and he thought, I'm the only person who knows why she is so upset. She is doing something she knows is wrong. But there isn't any right thing to do, under these circumstances, only bad and worse. He had to look away then, for fear that he would start to cry himself.

He was called to testify toward the end of the third day. As he was being sworn in, he looked out across the sea of faces in the courtroom. Among them were friends and strangers, some reporters. People were wearing the white masks over their nose and mouths that were supposed to ensure against the influenza that had come from Europe with the returning troops. To one side Clara sat with her lawyers; Marion with hers to the other. He saw Alfred seated near the back. When he looked, however, he could not see Mildred anywhere.

The whole proceedings struck him as so absurd that for a

moment he actually felt like laughing. What a colossal waste of time this is, he thought. It is obscene for us to spend a single day on it. Here we are, *alive*, possessed of that extraordinary gift of remaining *still alive*. So many people, he thought, are no longer in that fortunate position, Lutz and Knightly, Gilles Marchand. Rodin. And yet we who are so lucky are exerting our energy making each other suffer. What an insult this is to the dead in all their millions.

He gave his testimony in as steady a voice as he could maintain, then midway through he found that he was crying. He was unearthing things that should never have come to light. He spoke of Clara throwing cutlery and breaking plates; of her sudden flaring anger that would catch him without warning. He told of her jealousy of Marion and how it had been wholly unfounded. There had been nothing improper in his conduct toward Miss Beckett in the summer of 1914. There had been no affair between them. He had not seen her after that, until he encountered her by chance at a hospital in Châlons. He had been in town to get supplies when a bomb struck a medical storeroom. He was helping to evacuate the patients from the building when they met, he said. He heard an approving murmur pass through the crowd.

And had he seen her since that time in Châlons? the lawyer asked. Edward saw the line in front of him between obfuscation and untruth. He stepped over it. In Paris he had met with her, in a public dining establishment, he said. They had met to discuss this impending legal action, and had parted civilly after about an hour. They had not seen each other since.

When he was finished speaking, he returned to his seat in the back of the court. He felt the stares of the audience follow him as he walked through the room, and when he glanced up, he found they were sympathetic. They had seen an honorable man falsely accused. That was what they wanted to see.

From the bench the judge was asking whether there were any more witnesses that the plaintiff's counsel wished to call. The two men seated next to Clara put their heads together and spoke quietly. The elder of the two stood up.

"Your Honor, just this afternoon, we have received word," he said, "that the witness we intended to call, Miss Mildred Aldrich, is unable to appear in court at this time. We move to have the proceedings adjourned until such time as she may be present."

The judge considered this for a moment.

"Why is Miss Aldrich unable to be in attendance today?"

"She has been taken severely ill and has been confined to bed on her doctor's orders. She has been forced to remain in Boston with her family."

"Can you produce evidence of Miss Aldrich's unfitness for travel?" he asked.

"We have written notification from her physician," said the lawyer. He held up a single sheet of typescript.

"Approach the bench so I may examine it."

The proceedings were adjourned. As the courtroom began to clear, Edward saw Clara talking intently with her lawyers; she was clearly upset. After a minute she turned away from them and left the room, while they continued to gather their papers together. He approached them tentatively.

"Excuse me."

The elder of the two looked around, surprised.

"Major Steichen . . ."

"Miss Aldrich, can you just tell me, what does she have?"

The man went through his papers and found the doctor's letter he had just presented to the judge. He got it out and reread it.

"Acute bronchitis," he said.

"And where is she at present? I should like to go and see her."

"She's at her sister's house," the lawyer said, "but I shouldn't think that traveling there would be a good idea. I believe Mrs. Steichen intends to go and see Miss Aldrich as soon as practicable. You might find it a little awkward to visit her just now."

BOSTON—DREADFUL, GRAY place that it was, still full of dull late-winter snow; the streets that turned by the windows of her cab lined with pockmarked drifts: the dreary end of the season, the time when nothing has been promised yet and nothing renewed. Clara watched the cold city slide past, far, far too slowly, the minutes endless, the traffic signals all against them. How could it be taking so long? She checked her pocket watch. It had only been a few minutes. When they arrived at the address, she jumped from the cab and flung money at the driver, approximately the right amount, she hoped, and then ran up the stairs and hammered on the door. The housekeeper answered.

"I'm here to see Miss Aldrich," Clara said quickly. "How is she?"

"Who is it, Agnes?" A woman came out the back drawing room and peered down the corridor. Mildred's sister, unmistakably, for she looked just like Mildred only a little shorter, or so Clara thought until she approached and it became clear that this woman's spirit had worn her face into quite a different shape from that of Clara's friend. Her cheeks were drawn in sourly and her eyes bore a look of steady disapproval.

"Lady for Miss Mildred."

"I'm Mrs. Steichen." Clara came in past the maid without waiting to be formally invited. "You must be Mrs. Burke." She held out her hand to the woman, who physically drew back from it as though it might sting her.

"Oh. You're the one . . . Well." The look on her face said, I know who you are, the cause of all the trouble. It said, I should have thought you'd be ashamed to come here, after all that you have done. It said, Don't you think it would be better for everyone if you excused yourself and departed? What she actually said was much more delicately vicious: "I don't really know that you should come in."

For a moment Clara considered it. She had not expected such a prickly welcome, but, on reflection, it did not surprise her. She felt that in one way or another, she had always been greeted in this way, with disapproval, with voices telling her to restrain herself, to accept the world as it came, to stop being so noisy, so frivolous, so emotional. With the exception of a few people, the world had been mostly agreed that she should sit down and be quiet. One of those exceptions was, at present, upstairs in this very house. She would not leave without seeing her. She stood where she was. She kept her hand stretched out, insistently, in front of her.

Gingerly, Mrs. Burke took it in her own.

"Where is she?" Clara asked. "Is she well enough for me to see her?"

"She is upstairs. But she's asleep, and I don't think she ought to be woken."

"Well, let me just look in on her, and if she's sleeping, I'll leave. I promise." She started to climb the stairs without waiting to be given permission. "Which room is it?"

Mrs. Burke hesitated. That woman would dearly love to throw me out, Clara thought. Heavens, she would like to turn me out into the street when I have traveled all this way, and wasn't that typical of the cold of these New Englanders, so high and mighty, so proud that they have been here, freezing, for more than three hundred consecutive winters. Fine, I'll find it myself. She went down the corridor opening doors as quietly as she could, until at last she found one that opened into to a darkened bedroom. Inside, she could see the outline of a large bed pushed against one wall and, as her eyes accustomed to the dark, a figure propped up on the pillows. She paused, holding the door open, and stared through the gloom. The metallic odor of fever, of the body fighting itself.

Mildred seemed to be still, sleeping, so she started to withdraw.

"How rude. You just got here." Her voice was rasping and weak, but it was unmistakable, and Clara thought how Mildred and her sister Mrs. Burke shared the same sternness, but with the difference that in Mildred it was animated by affection, by love of the world and the people around her, while in Mrs. Burke it was underlaid with fear.

She came to the bedside and stood looking down at the old woman where she lay.

"I am not leaving," she said. "Shall I light a lamp?"

Mildred nodded. Clara felt on the wall and found the light switch. In the gold, electric light Mildred looked paler than Clara had ever seen her. Her skin was covered in a sheen of fever-damp and her breathing was audible. She did not sit up, or even lift her head. She just looked up from the pillow, her eyes steady and puzzled. Perhaps she is trying to figure out what has happened to her; perhaps she is confounded that she should be so sick. She could imagine Mildred talking to the disease, scolding it: An outrage! A woman can't cross the ocean in peace? But in fact, she said nothing; she did not seem to have the strength for it.

"I came up from New York. I don't even mind anymore if the case does not go in my favor. I only wish that you were well."

Mildred took her hand and patted it. She coughed, a wet, strained sound, then took a slow breath with her eyes closed. Clara thought she might be going back to sleep after all. But then her eyes opened and she said, "But you were right."

"What do you mean?"

"In Paris. I saw . . . together." She was interrupted by another spasm of coughs, and when she finished, she lay quiet, absorbed in the work of breathing.

Clara leaned forward and said, "You saw them? Please, don't try to speak. Just nod." Very slowly, Mildred nodded. Clara sat up and looked away.

"Oh, God," she said. "Oh, God. But how can it be proved without you? It must come out, how terrible he has been, how little he has cared. And you are so sick from your journey. You came all this way for me, to testify in the case, and now look what has happened. And all because of him! I am so sorry . . ."

"Stop," Mildred said. She spoke with effort, but her voice was nevertheless firm and insistent. "You can't undo it." She turned onto her side underneath the covers, and looked at Clara.

"You can't undo any of it. But you can decide what comes next. It's only this you can't choose," and she raised her hand and tapped the covers as though to indicate . . . what? The comforter? The bed? Clara wasn't sure what she meant by the gesture. She waited for Mildred to go on, but the old woman just lay breathing, recovering from the exertion of speech. Her words had been sharp, almost angry; they were a refusal to accept Clara's apology of a moment before. She did not understand what they implied.

"What is? Mildred, darling, I don't understand. Please help me to know what you mean!" Mildred had her eyes closed again. Clara thought, Please don't go to sleep now. Mildred's lips moved and she was speaking but so quietly now that Clara had to lean toward her just to hear.

"This part of life, the last part, you must do, but the rest is yours," she said. "The past is set. For heaven's sake, let it go."

MILDRED DID NOT recover. Edward learned from her sister, after he sent several letters inquiring after her, that she had suffered a resurgence of her bronchitis from the previous winter during the boat trip from France, and deteriorated quickly after her arrival. She was laid to rest in Boston, without ceremony. The city was struggling to cope with influenza deaths and speed was of the essence.

The trial resumed, and the jury went into deliberations. They did not take long to return. They found the defendant Miss Beckett not guilty and fined Mrs. Steichen for court costs. After the foreman read the verdict, Edward saw Marion across the room, embracing her parents. Her family surrounded her, so he couldn't even see her as they all but carried her out of the room.

On the other side of the aisle, Clara put her head down on the table in front of her and began to sob. Edward sat and watched her, her body bent and shaking, while all the people filed past him. He felt disgusting; he had lied and he could not undo it. The version of events that Clara gave was wrong, certainly; but in the end it was no more wrong than the one that he'd presented. At this moment they were, as Mildred had said to him, the same kind of creature, or if anything he was worse, for Clara at least believed her own side of the story. He wanted to go up and speak to her. Here they were, both left terribly alone to struggle with the devastation. They did not love each other anymore; but they had done so once. In this cold, clear space, their anger at each other might be rendered null by sheer exhaustion. They might find some small peace from looking each other in the face, from acknowledging one another to be there, to be real.

He walked toward the front of the courtroom and her hunched form. With her face pressed against her crossed arms, she had not seen him. A few feet from her, he stopped, intimidated to go on.

"Would you care to comment on the verdict, Major Steichen?" A notebook was thrust into his face and the man from the *Post* stepped around from behind him. "You must feel some satisfaction at seeing your accuser vanquished like this? Your innocence established? Your good name restored?"

Edward backed away from the man, but he pursued him down the main aisle. "Do you intend to remain in New York following the trial? How do your children feel about their parents fighting in the public eye?"

"Go away!" Edward shouted at him. "Can't you leave me alone?"

"Hmmm," the man said. "Irritable. Combative. Not really the behavior of someone whose conscience is fully clear."

Edward turned and fled. The last thing he saw was Clara lift her head and, bleary-eyed, look after him, her expression one of immense and bewildering loss.

AFTER THE TRIAL Edward returned almost immediately to France to complete his tour of duty. He did not, anyway, want to stay in New York. It was not just the publicity, though that was unpleasant enough. Mary was back at school; Kate was still with Clara and hence, for the moment, out of reach. There was no one in the city whose company he really wanted right now apart from that of his children, and Marion.

Marion, of course, he could not see: his lawyer was clear on that point. If he intended to divorce, if he wanted a chance for custody of his children, he must avoid scandal or an appearance of scandal. Even though she was only blocks away from him at her parents' house near Central Park, he must stay away from her. It made him absolutely furious, but he was caught. There was nothing he could do. He wrote to her explaining that he was leaving and that he could not come to her; he gave the reasons. *Do you think*, he asked, *that when this is all concluded that we might meet again under other circumstances? In my mind's eye I see you at your easel in my garden, and some days that vision is the sole thing that sustains me. Please, consider it. Please.*

In Chaumont he finished his documentary work and then began the process of dismantling the Photography Division that he and Barnes had built. It was arduous work and boring, the logistics of sending men and equipment back across the ocean, but he did not mind that. It gave form and structure to his life where, left to his own devices, he would not have been able to keep going. Most of the time he felt a kind of dry, weary rage that spread out and covered the world like dust. He resented everything, strangers in the streets, houses with closed doors, the sounds of cars, people laughing. Then, in midspring, he received a letter from Marion. It was short and it told him what he already had come to expect:

> *Sometimes I can almost see it, the future that you imagine for us, but then my vision is obscured by the memories of those horrible days. I think that the trial has poisoned us for each other. When you look at me, you will always feel its presence, a heaviness weighing on us both; it has changed who we are for good.*
>
> *Don't forget what I said in France. I mean it no less now.*

This was the final kick, the severing of his last link to the world of the living. He moved through the aftermath of the war automatically, performing his duties because there was no alternative. It has happened, he thought to himself on more than one occasion. I've become a machine.

In the fall, he was honorably discharged from the army, flung back out into civilian life, with a couple of suits of clothes and keys to his old house in his luggage. He went to Paris first, stayed in his old studio in Montparnasse, but the city was immediately abrasive to him now, too noisy. People were celebrating the coming of peace but it was with a desperation that rang false and hollow. It made him nauseous. He decided to leave and go back to Voulangis. But before departing, he would go finally to Rodin's house in Meudon.

The last time he'd been there, it was August 1914, a lifetime ago. He'd arrived to find Rodin sitting out on the patio drinking white wine. They had talked about whether there was going to be a war. It was all anyone talked about during those last months. Edward remembered saying that he didn't believe it was going to happen. Neither side had anything to gain from it.

Rodin hadn't replied. He'd poured another glass of wine for them both, and offered Edward a sandwich.

Now a ticket booth had been installed at the front gate. Inside, a bored-looking girl with short-cropped hair glanced up at him from a magazine she was reading. The house was a museum now, and that was good, Edward thought; that was what Rodin had wanted.

"Good morning," Edward said to the girl.

"Good day, monsieur." He smiled at her and walked through the gates.

"Monsieur?" the girl called after him. "Monsieur!" she was leaning out of the booth, her boredom transformed into irrita-tion. "Entrance to the museum is twenty centimes." She pointed to a sign below her window that stated the price in clear yellow lettering.

"I'm sorry," he said, pulling the money from his pocket and putting the coins on the counter. "I was a good friend of Monsieur Rodin. I visited here so many times, it didn't occur to me I'd have to pay."

"Monsieur the Artist seems to have had a lot of good friends. None of them wish to pay the entrance fee." Her mouth, a thin, sour line, hung on her face. Another patron trying to evade the fee. She scooped up the money and handed him a ticket.

"The grave is around to the back of the house, at the bottom of the property," she said. "Follow the signs."

Here it was: the house, still ugly; stout trees either side of the drive, their branches joined overhead; the white exhibition hall behind the house, the garden with its steps and levels. Rose's greenhouses by the western wall. Everything was as he'd last seen it. The way the path crumpled unevenly underfoot, pushed upward by the roots of the trees. The view of the city from the garden steps.

He would turn the corner, and Rodin would be there, he was sure of it. He'd be sitting out on the sunken patio under the trees, reading the newspaper and surveying the morning. He would look up, shift his reading glasses down his nose and peer at Edward over their rim. And I'll have to tell him, Edward thought, that I've forgotten those prints I promised to bring. Why didn't I remember them? What excuse can I make this time? He felt irritated with himself. How could he have left them behind again?

From around the corner, he heard voices, a man's and a woman's, the woman asking a question and the man answering, and he thought that Rose must be there, too. He pictured her sitting in that formal way that she had, her hands folded in her lap and her back held very straight. She would smile a little when she saw him, as if the smile were a small self-indulgence that she allowed herself, like a chocolate. She would nod at him and then rise and get him a cup from inside in the kitchen, pour him some coffee from the pot that sat on the table between them. He hurried forward toward the voices.

It was not Rodin, of course, and the table and chairs were gone. A boy stood in the middle of the patio where they'd been, and a girl stood next to him. He was dressed in the uniform of a British gunnery officer and he had a book open in his right hand, which Edward saw, as he approached them, was a Baedeker. He was speaking, explaining something to the girl. They looked up as Edward approached, smiled in greeting and began to drift away down that path.

He let them wander on and then followed after, down the slope to the place where, six years ago, Rodin had erected the façade of a château at the end of his land, just because he liked it and he could. Those were the days of abundance for him. He had it packed in crates, brought from the country and put back together section by section on his lawn.

It was under this that he and Rose were now buried, side by side. Edward went down the slope toward the white outline of the mausoleum. The couple who had gone before him were standing looking up at the cast of *The Thinker* that sat sentinel over the graves.

There they were: the names inscribed on the stones, the dates of their lives, beginning and ending. He made himself stand there and read the names out loud, saying them softly so only he could hear. He knelt down and traced the inscriptions with his fingers. After so many deaths, he thought somehow he would be better able to understand this one, but instead, he was aware of something resistant inside him: a great stone or a vacuum, a refusal, so that he was left staring, dry-eyed and scraped out. Why is there nothing else, only this feeling of being at once heavy and empty? He thought reflexively of the person of whom he would want to ask this, the person whom he could ask a question so large, which was, of course, Rodin himself. In his head, he began to compose the letter he would now never write to his friend: *Why can't one get hold of it? It seems so impossible to get the mind around permanent absence. How long does it take to understand? All I can do is stay here and listen to the sound of the wind, while strangers blow around your grave like ghosts.*

Everything is lost in the end, he thought. It is inexorable, the process by which the world strips away what you think belongs to you. The only thing you can do is to give what you can, when you can, as Rodin had done for him. The only small power that you have is the power of generosity, the power to choose to whom you give away what is precious.

He went back to his rooms in Montparnasse and began to write a letter to Marion.

AT THE END of the court case Marion felt all the good drain from the world. The universe was crooked and broken, without the possibility of justice or clarity. Impulses to do good were confounded. Impulses to love turned to poison.

She found a studio uptown and tried to paint again, but she felt so sick at heart that she could not begin. She would stand in front of a blank canvas for hours, sifting through preliminary sketches trying to find something that moved her sufficiently to try to paint. Nothing held her attention because nothing held her feelings. After weeks on end of this she took the canvas down from her easel and put her paints away; she did not want to look at them sitting idle.

She would go to her studio anyway during the days and just sit, silently, and watch the people in the street below, going about their business oblivious to her. Then she began sleeping there. She secluded herself, seeing as few people as she could. She preferred to be alone. It was easier than enduring the forced conviviality of the world trying to return to what it had been before.

The Spanish influenza that she had seen in France in May swept through New York, stronger and more rapidly contagious than before. She read about its onset in the papers; saw the first cases begin to fall ill but now here, among civilians. When the trial was over and the publicity surrounding it died down, she volunteered to nurse those in the temporary infirmaries that had sprung up all over the city to deal with the burgeoning caseload. Because she had been a nurse and had recovered from the disease already, she was sent to a hospital on the Lower East Side where crowded tenements were filled with the worst cases she had yet seen.

There was no cure and no remedy; nothing to do but make the sick comfortable and wait. Nurses and doctors wore protective masks throughout the hospital wards, so it was a world of people without mouths, the bottom halves of their faces blank. When they spoke, their voices were muffled and echoing, as though all their conversations were recordings.

Each day that winter and into the spring, she distributed medicine and food, took temperatures, gave injections. The patients weakened; their skin turned waxy and slick; they breathed, in the end, only with tremendous difficulty, and she saw their bodies grasping for air, their chests heaving with the effort. They did not want to let go; and sometimes, she watched them struggle up from it and come back to themselves. But more often, she watched them slip away, subsiding into death, or kicking against it, but going under in the end all the same. A kind of iron calm descended on her, different from the frantic work the war had demanded or the listlessness she'd felt following the trial. She moved steadily; she listened to all the sounds around her, the sound of her own breath. She absorbed each death not as an individual event, but as part of a great tide. She did not designate each one its own specific grief. In this way, she kept going.

She thought of Edward when her mind was not busy, saw him in the faces and movements of other people. When she returned uptown to her studio, exhausted at the end of the day, he was so strongly etched in her mind that she was almost convinced she would open the door and find him, though she knew that she would not. Sometimes she would try to imagine it: What if she said yes? If she went to live with him? But she could never quite picture it. She could not see how they would emerge from under the weight of the past, not together.

Then unexpectedly she received a letter from him. It came by the second post, in the middle of the day, so she did not get it until she returned from the hospital that evening. It surprised her. She did not know what it would say; it would not, she thought as she tore across the top of the envelope, be another request that she live with him as his mistress. She knew him and something about his limits; he had his pride; he would not ask her again. When she felt the weight of the envelope, she realized there was something inside it besides paper. She found it and withdrew it. It was a set of keys. She unfolded the letter. It was short, one side of a single sheet.

Dear M—

A few weeks ago, I was discharged from the Air Service, and now I am going back to Voulangis. I will rebuild my studio and darkroom there, and that is where I intend to live and work from now on.

The keys I've enclosed are for the apartment on Montpar-nasse, my old Paris studio, which I will not be using anymore. They are the only set.

The place is quiet, and spacious enough for one person to paint in. Sometimes the sink leaks and in winter, you should keep the fire in the stove going all day because it gets drafty. But the light there is good, especially in the mornings. It is yours if you want it. Accepting it entails no obligation to me. You said you wanted to go back to painting so I offer you this.

That was all. She looked at the keys, then closed her fingers around them; they were solid, the metal cold on her skin. There were two on the ring. One must be for the front door to the building and the other for the apartment. She had not been there in years, but she remembered the place quite clearly. The front apartment on the third floor, with a big window, which looked out onto the boulevard, where people would be coming and going all day, beginning to rebuild their lives after the conflagration, to look however they could for hope. She should go there and be among those who had seen what she had seen, who knew those terrible things, too. Perhaps there she could begin the process of making sense of this sore, skinned world. Perhaps she could find something she loved or hated enough to want to paint it.

He had given her this chance, this possibility. She did not know if she would take what he had offered, but she felt inside her the smallest stirring of something alive, something capable of growth and perhaps renewal. She understood that she was loved and that she was free.

She slipped the keys into the pocket of her skirt along with the letter so she could feel that it was there as she walked through the rest of the day.

Wheelbarrow and Flowerpots. Voulangis, 1920.
Palladium and ferroprussiate print.

FRANÇOIS SAYS, YES, he will help. He thinks that Monsieur Steichen is crazy. He indicates this with a shrug and a sucking sound drawn through his remaining teeth. Crazy. But not so crazy that François won't do what he asks.

They have a little kerosene to spare. That will help. François retrieves it from the shed near Edward's studio while Edward goes upstairs to the attic to begin bringing the canvases down to the garden. There are nearly a hundred stacked against the sloping walls. He lifts two by their frames and carries them down the stairs.

With François's help he soon has a waist-high pile of frames and pictures built into a ramshackle pyramid on the lawn. Isolated away from the trees and the flower beds, it looks lonely.

"Go ahead and light it," he says to François. "We don't want to make it any bigger than that."

"Some of us don't want to make it at all," François mutters. "If I'd known you didn't want these, I would have burned the frames for firewood three years ago when we had the coal shortage." He douses the pile in solvent. "You light it," he says. "I don't want to be responsible."

Edward fishes in his pocket for a match. He strikes it and watches the fire swarm over its head. He throws the match in among his paintings. Flames begin to lick across their exposed faces.

François curses quietly in Breton and slouches into the house.

Edward had considered facing all the paintings inward, so that he wouldn't see them as they burned. He started to make the pile with all the blank reverses showing, just pale canvas and wooden frames. But he changed his mind and turned the paintings to face him as he made their funeral pyre.

So now he sees them vanish one by one. First, fire consumes the portrait of a small boy who stands chewing his thumb and staring as the flames stroke upward toward his white collar. The son of one of the farmers from Voulangis. He would have been twenty-two this year if he had not died at Soissons. Beside that, a vase of sunflowers starts to blacken and crumple. A view of the river from the hill behind this house. Bowls of fruit, women leaning on the railings of a bridge, people in a rowboat on a sunny day. All of them disintegrate before his eyes and their rags move in the fire's currents as though they were alive.

François emerges from the back door carrying three more paintings. He lays them carefully on top of the rest. Edward nods with satisfaction and then goes to retrieve more. He feels a sudden surge of elation: He's done it. He hasn't lost his nerve at the last moment. By nightfall all his paintings will be ashes on the lawn.

THE THOUGHT THAT the paintings must go had tugged at him ever since he'd returned to Voulangis. It was spring and he was living alone, undisturbed except by François, who came in to work in the garden. He went to work repairing the damage to the house: the damp in the walls and the floor, the broken kitchen window. He sanded and painted the woodwork outside. He replaced one of the walls of his studio and put new shingles on part of the roof where they had fallen away. When the studio was ready for use, he started to bring the paintings downstairs from the attic; but he found he didn't like them anymore. They felt stilted, romantic in a way that rang false. He left the paintings where they were, locked the attic up again and retreated downstairs.

These days he was lonely as he had never allowed himself to be before, when he had filled his days up with war work. He initiated proceedings for a divorce from Clara early in the spring; she was contesting some of his claims and it seemed likely that the negotiations would go on for some months yet. He received regular letters from Mary. She would come to France when the school year ended in summer to stay with him—he counted the days until her arrival anxiously. Through Clara's sister Charlotte, he was also trying to arrange for Kate to accompany her, but he knew that this was a delicate process that could not be rushed. He must be patient and persistent if he wanted to see her.

Other friends were slowly returning to Europe now that it was at peace, or at least too exhausted to fight anymore. He would go up to Paris to visit occasionally; he was pleased to see people, and pleased to get away when he left at the end of the evening. He heard from François that Amélie had returned to Mildred's old house in Huiry: it belonged to her now. It had been left to her in Mildred's will.

"She still has some things belonging to you," François said. "She said she wished to return them."

"Well," Edward replied, "I'll go and get them from her when I have a chance." But somehow the courage to face the woman's loss, and his part in causing it, eluded him. He put off going to Huiry, then put it off again. Weeks passed and it faded from the front of his mind.

So mostly he was alone. He had begun taking photographs again, but he was dissatisfied with what he produced. As with his paintings, he felt that the old subjects, the old ways of depicting them, were no longer right, or real; they were too delicate to survive on the barren side of the war. He looked at the way he'd obscured his subjects with soft focuses, with retouching, and he couldn't imagine why he'd ever thought it was necessary. But he did not know what else he could do.

One afternoon he was taking a walk along the edge of his back field. The path followed the boundary line between his land and the neighboring farm and then dropped into a small wood on the far side. He thought that if his daughters had been there they would have liked this walk on this afternoon. He thought that they would have gone into the wood and strayed immediately from the marked path, their boots stirring up last year's dry leaves. He followed where he imagined them leading, up a slight rise and clambering over the barrier of a fallen tree trunk. On the other side, he could see something gray and bulbous lying on the ground. He went toward it until he could make it out clearly. It was a soldier's helmet, French, its edges rusted so that it was eaten away at the brim. It was half-covered by leaves—it must have been lying there through at least one change of the seasons. He stood up from it and formed a quadrangle with his fingers framing where it emerged from the forest floor. Then he went back to the house to get his camera and returned to the same spot.

When he looked at the helmet through his viewfinder, he was again confronted by how uncanny it was. A hat, half-buried in leaves; the mind did not immediately have a place for such a thing; it was simultaneously familiar and strange, and this was why it had captured his interest. It caught the viewer up short; you had to look at it twice to figure out what it was, and what it meant.

This is what I want, he thought. The techniques he used to use to mystify and obscure the world, the platinum paper that made it look like a dream, none of that seemed necessary now. He did not need to look far afield for appropriate subjects, or wait for a scene of beauty to align itself for his lens. He could just cut the world up into its component shapes, as he had done from the air; what would make them interesting was not painting over what was there, but showing it simply in all its inherent peculiarity. He took the picture, and after that, he began to use his camera again, everyday.

His work now was very different from what it had been. He wanted to show each thing as part of its context. He wanted to show only the hinges, and let people imagine the door, and the room it led to. Because, he reasoned, when you photograph a woman sitting in a chair reading, in a house during a summer of peace, you are only showing a small sliver of the story. If the woman is smiling or crying, that is only one of her multitude of feelings. The rest you must always guess at. He wanted to take pictures that emphasized this partiality of vision.

He no longer wandered for miles looking for the perfect scenery, or the ideal light. Instead, he focused in closely on the ordinary things around him, the face of an insect, the stamens of flowers and the mottle around them. A pair of eyeglasses and their shadow. Terra-cotta flowerpots that François had piled inside a wheelbarrow and left there. Edward cut the print so that it showed only the round mouths of the pots, and the long cylinders they formed stacked one inside another.

"They look like artillery," François said when he showed the picture to him. "Like the barrels of the .75s that the Territorials set up on the hill."

People saw things differently now, Edward realized. They didn't just see flowerpots, they saw guns. But when he looked at his paintings, he felt pulled back into a time he could no longer understand. He thought that it would be better to get rid of them, start again in this new, bare world.

He told François he was thinking about destroying his paintings.

"Why?" the old man asked.

"Because I don't like them much anymore."

"All that work for nothing. What a waste!" He shook his head.

"Well, I think next Thursday, I'm going to get rid of the paintings. In the afternoon. Will you come and help me?"

François hesitated, then finally said: "Yes. If you are determined, I will help."

HE IS JUST adding the last canvas to the pyre when Amélie arrives. She climbs stiffly from the cart she has driven in and comes to lean over the garden wall, watching him. Her dark hair has gray in it now that he had not seen before, but perhaps it is just that the bright sunlight shows it more clearly.

"Amélie," Edward says. He is unprepared for her visit. "I have been meaning to come down for weeks to see you." She shrugs.

"François said that you would be home this afternoon," she says. "I thought I would come to you. What are you doing?"

"I'm burning my paintings."

"Why?"

"To be free of them."

"Well, you know best."

"Look, I don't know how to say it. I miss Mildred very much; she was a dear friend, a brave spirit. I am sorry for everything that happened, and if I could do anything to change it—"

"You can't," Amélie says, flatly. "It was no more your fault than mine. I should have stopped her going to America when she was ill. I'm here to bring you some belongings of yours that she was keeping; your daughter left them with us. Madame, I know, wanted to make sure that you got them."

"Well, let me offer you something to eat while you are here. Why don't you go inside and make yourself at home? I'll be there in a minute."

"Thank you, I will." She starts off toward the front of the house, then calls back to him: "They are in the back of the cart."

"I'll get them on my way," Edward calls. He watches her go.

He pushes the outlying edges of the fire together with a stick. It is getting lower now, so he leaves it to burn down. He can come back to douse it in a while. He goes around to look at what is in the back of the cart Amélie drove here; under a tarpaulin in the back he finds a single brown leather case.

His heart jumps when he sees it. It takes a minute for him to summon the courage to pick it up because it might not be what he hopes. It's heavy for something that size, and he catches his breath, because, yes, that is just about what it should weigh if it is full of paper and glass. He picks it up and carries it inside. Amélie is seated in a chair by the fireplace in the salon.

"This," he says, "is not clothing."

"What is it?"

"I don't know yet." He lays it out on its side on the floor and kneels in front of it. Then with his thumbs he slides both the catches out until they pop and the lid lifts slightly. Inside, he can see that there are photographs.

He opens the lid of the case all the way. His photographs, and below them some of his negatives. These are ones that he had tried to bring with him when they left in 1914 and then, in those last minutes, had to leave behind. They are set out in the same neat rows that he had stacked them into trying to fit as many as possible into this small space.

His whole life in discrete moments, stretching back to those first years when he'd hardly known what to do with a camera. The self-portrait he'd sent to the Philadelphia Salon, which Stieglitz had chosen to exhibit, the first time anyone had ever praised him for his efforts. Then, underneath that, the first series of photographs he'd taken of Rodin, and the first of Clara, playing the piano, her hands arched over the keys, her back to him. Then on, up through the years: Clara holding Mary when she was a baby; Marion and Clara standing at a distance from each other on the plaza outside Notre Dame; Rodin and Isadora at Meudon; harvesttime in the fields around Voulangis; all of their old friends seated around the table, eating lunch in the garden; Mary and Kate by the seashore in Brittany; an autochrome of Marion lying in a field of long grass. And then, at last, the war: refugees making their slow way along the roads away from the fighting, and the soldiers going in the opposite direction, their faces blank, or afraid or set with determination. With each new print that he turns up, the memories explode inside his head, painfully vivid but wonderful as well. He wants to spend a long time lingering over each one, letting the stories it carries with it seep into him and carry him along as far as they will take him.

"Look," he says to Amélie, "what my daughter has given back to me."

Amélie stands up and comes so she can peer over his shoulder. "Well," she says. "Well."

"And look: here is one more. She must have added this to the case before she drove it to Huiry." He holds up one of the prints. It is a picture of Kate and Clara. They are seated outside in the garden, here, at Voulangis on the lawn. It looks, from the flowers behind them, like late spring. Both of them are dressed up in their nicest clothes and they look uncomfortable. Clara's eyes are ringed with dark circles and Kate has a lost, anxious expression in her eyes. But, still, there they are. Clara has her arm extended so her hand is cupped over her daughter's smaller one, protecting it. She is sitting up straight, proudly. Kate has smoothed her pinafore down and tucked it under her bent knees. They are looking back into the camera, their eyes saying, We are here.

HISTORICAL NOTE

The Last Summer of the World is a work of fiction. While many of the people and events in the novel have bases in reality, I have taken significant poetic license with the details of the characters' lives and motivations. In the interests of creating a coherent and integrated story, I have invented incidents that probably or definitely did not take place and in some cases altered the chronology of the real occurrences described.

Between 1906 and 1914, the photographer Edward Steichen did reside in France. He came to Paris first as a student in 1900 and then, after a stint in New York, he returned to Europe with his wife, Clara, and their young daughter, Mary, living first in Montparnasse and then moving, shortly before the birth of their second daughter, Kate, to a house in Voulangis, a village to the east of Paris.

For those years, Steichen and Clara divided their time between their country house and two daughters, and their many friends, a group that included Henri and Amélie Matisse, Leo and Gertrude Stein, the journalist Mildred Aldrich, the painters Arthur Carles and Marion Beckett, and Edward's great mentor and friend, Auguste Rodin. But beneath an idyllic surface, there were tensions stirring between these two headstrong and artistically inclined people. As her later writings indicate, Clara was coming to feel increasingly discontented in her marriage, even as she longed to fulfill the idealized role of self-sacrificing wife and helpmeet. This situation was not helped by Edward's rumored infidelities with, among others, the British sculptor Kathleen Bruce and the dancer Isadora Duncan.

Then, in the summer of 1914, larger events overtook them. The Steichens and their friends watched as Europe descended with disorienting speed into war, and, simultaneously, the stresses inside Edward and Clara's relationship erupted into a bitter fight that tore the family in half. Clara accused Edward of being unfaithful with their mutual friend Marion Beckett, who was staying with them for the summer. Edward denied the affair, and only the urgency of evacuating their children from the path of the war made them temporarily put aside their quarrel. In the end, they left their home and returned to America, taking with them only what they could carry, just three days ahead of advancing German troops.

Once they were all established in the States, relations between Edward and Clara deteriorated still further, and finally in the summer of 1915, Clara took her younger daughter, Kate, and crossed the Atlantic once more. She lived for the next two years in their old house in the Marne, enduring the hardships and privations of wartime.

When America entered the war in April of 1917, Edward

Steichen joined the new Photography Division of the Army Signal Corps and was assigned to help develop aerial reconnaissance photography for the American Expeditionary Force in France. He was responsible for organizing reconnaissance ahead of the critical Second Battle of the Marne; for most of the war his role was administrative, although he did take aerial photographs of the front, which he later exhibited. He returned to his house during this period for the first time since abandoning it in 1914 and found that his photographs and negatives had been severely damaged during the intervening years. According to Steichen's biographer Penelope Niven, he and Marion Beckett did encounter each other at one point during the war. Steichen's sister, Lilian, told her daughter Helga Sandburg that her uncle was having a love affair with a beautiful American woman while he was serving in France, though she did not, apparently, give any further details of the woman's identity. In 1919, Clara Steichen sued Marion Beckett in New York, charging that she had destroyed her marriage by conducting a protracted affair with her husband. Clara was unable to prove her claims and lost the suit.

Of the photographs described in the novel, some but not all of them are genuine Steichen photographs from the early decades of the twentieth century. Notably, *Self-Portrait*, 1898, was the entry that Steichen sent to the Second Philadelphia Salon, and which first brought him to the attention of Alfred Stieglitz. Also, the photograph *Wheelbarrow with Flowerpots*, 1920, was part of a series of experiments Steichen made in photographic abstraction during the years immediately following the war.

In 1923, Steichen, then living in his old house in the Marne, burned his paintings, because he wanted to devote himself henceforth to photography; only those paintings that had already been sold survived. He remained in Europe for several years after the war before returning to America. In the 1920s and '30s he worked for *Vanity Fair*, and took some of the most well-recognized portraits of that era, including pictures of Winston Churchill, Greta Garbo, Paul Robeson and Charlie Chaplin. He was reunited with his children, and eventually married his second wife, the actress and writer Dana Desboro Glover. In World War Two, despite being fifty-six years old at the war's inception, Steichen again volunteered and was sent to the Pacific to document in photographs life on board an aircraft carrier. In 1946 he became the director of the Photography Department of the Museum of Modern Art in New York and orchestrated "The Family of Man" exhibition in 1955, his attempt to show, through photography, the common humanity of all races and cultures in the face of the rising tensions of the Cold War.

After her divorce, Clara Steichen lived in the Azores and later in Vermont. She wrote an autobiographical work entitled *An Ozark Childhood*, which was never published. She did not remarry. Mary Steichen became a physician, and Kate Steichen became an opera and choral singer. Marion Beckett returned to the United States, and in the 1920s adopted two children. She lived and worked in Washington, D.C., sharing an apartment with the painter Katharine Rhoades. In 1925 her paintings were shown at the Montross Gallery in New York.

In 1960, after Dana's death, Steichen married Joanna Taub. He died in 1973.

ACKNOWLEDGMENTS

MY GRATITUDE AND admiration go to my editor, Jill Bialosky, whose acumen improved this book immensely, and also to my agent, Gail Hochman, whose guidance and support were invaluable. Thanks also to Evan Carver and Adele McCarthy Beauvais.

I was lucky to have many insightful readers for this manuscript during the process of its creation, including my sister Joanna Mitchell, J. M. Tyree, Michael Cunningham, Ernesto Mestre, Jenny Offill, Lewis Braham, Cari Luna, Halimah Abdullah, and Philip Kadish. Irini Spanidou, Lauren Acampora, James Helgeson, Joseph Pearson, Stacie Cassarino, Monica King, David Bain, Kate Davis and Christina Wulf all gave much-appreciated encouragement. My parents, Lois and Christopher Mitchell, were amazing in their love, support and provision of air-conditioning at crucial moments. Wendy Brandchaft and Charlie Plotkin gave me my very first writer's grant and believed in me all along. My grandparents Elaine and Bernard Brandchaft gave their whole family a love of reading and thinking.

Certain books were extremely useful in the research for this novel, most especially Penelope Niven's outstanding biography of Edward Steichen, published by Clarkson Potter. I also referred extensively to John Keegan's *The First World War*, John Ellis's *Eye-Deep in Hell*, and many other works from and about the period in which the novel is set.

Thanks to the Julia and David White Artists' Colony in Costa Rica, where I finished an initial draft of the book.

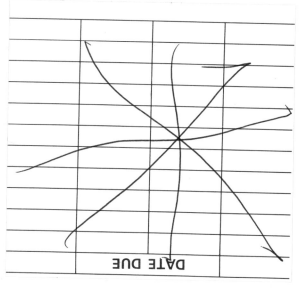

DATE DUE

6-97